It Was You

Adam Baron is an actor and comedian as well as a writer for TV and radio.

It Was You is the fourth novel in his series featuring Billy Rucker, following *Shut Eye*, *Hold Back the Night* and *Superjack* (all available in Pan Books).

Adam Baron

It Was You

MACMILLAN

First published 2004 by Macmillan
an imprint of Pan Macmillan Ltd
Pan Macmillan, 20 New Wharf Road, London N1 9RR
Basingstoke and Oxford
Associated companies throughout the world
www.panmacmillan.com

ISBN 1 4050 2105 5

1 3 5 7 9 8 6 4 2

A CIP catalogue record for this book is available from
the British Library.

Typeset by Intype London Ltd
Printed and bound in Great Britain by
Mackays of Chatham plc, Chatham, Kent

For Janice Franklin Baron

Acknowledgements

The encouragement given to me during the writing of this novel was essential, inspiring and far beyond the call of duty. Heartfelt thanks then to Jane Gregory, Broo Doherty, Anya Serota, Sarah Turner and Liz Cowen.

Thanks to Janet Whitaker for her interest in my writing. I'm so excited! Appreciation also to everyone at Gregory and Company and Pan Macmillan for working so hard to help this story make it from the keyboard to the bookshelf, and beyond.

Finally, Naomi. Without you there would be no words at all. I would follow you to the ends of the earth (again).

My son, my executioner
I take you in my arms
Quiet and small and just astir
And whom my body warms.

Sweet death, small son, our instrument
Of immortality,
Your cries and hungers document
Our bodily decay.

We twenty-five and twenty-two
Who seemed to live for ever
Observe enduring life in you
And start to die together.

Donald Hall

Part One

Chapter One

Josephine Thomas tries to stand. It's the second time she's tried but again she can't make it. Instead she starts to drag herself along the cement floor towards the street end of the alley, the way she'd come. The alley is dark, the stained concrete walls seeming to close in on her. Jo is scared. She calls out but her voice doesn't make it to the top of the alley walls let alone through or over them. No one responds and she begins to feel cold, colder than she ever has. Her fear grows but she knows that if she can get back out to the street she'll be fine. Someone will see her, even though it's after midnight. She thinks about her mother. She has to get out of there, for her. This wouldn't be fair, not after Dad. She pictures her mother, at home, early in the morning. Next morning. She's standing on the step outside, chatting to Blonnie Watkins.

Jo didn't even know she'd been stabbed. Not at first. When the guy grabbed her and wrapped a hand over her mouth all she wondered was why he'd sprayed liquid ice into her side. It was only when her assailant dropped her and fled up towards the mouth of the alley that she realized. She felt: her hand came back warm and sticky. Blood. She didn't even see him. Just a dark shape waiting in the bend. Then a flurry and pain and footsteps running away.

Jo drags herself along, stops, and does it all again. That alley, it usually stank of piss but there's something else now. It's her, her blood. She starts to cry but stops herself. She curls up and pushes forward, like a cater-pillar. Moving hurts more than anything she's ever known but she's close now, only thirty feet from the street. She feels a flood of relief. Not far and actually, if she's still, the pain slackens. In spite of the blood it can't have been anything much after all. Jo feels fine except for the tiredness. Tiredness drags at every cell in her body. She can't help it. She closes her eyes and then wakes, suddenly. It's later, she can tell. No. She shouldn't do that. She has to keep going. She curls her fingers into a drain grille and pulls, groaning at the effort. She gains another foot.

She sees her mother again, on the step, still chatting to Blonnie, shaking her head at the latest mess her boys have got into. Then she sees him. Her mother sees him: PC Evans, cycling along the top lane. Blonnie is in full flow and Gwen has to nudge her.

'Oh, Jesus,' Blonnie says. 'What the hell have they done now? Well they're not here, I can tell him that. I don't know *where* they stayed last night.'

Jo's mother doesn't respond because she's frown-ing. The PC, young Rhodri, his face is deathly pale. She wonders what's up and swallows, before laugh-ing to herself. Poor Rhod, only twenty-two. It's not the boys, it's Blonnie's big Dave he's come for. Blonnie sees it too and braces herself, looking up towards the muffled snoring above their heads. But once the PC has propped up his bike he ignores Blonnie. He asks Mrs Thomas if she will go inside.

Jo wills herself on. She can't let this happen. Rhod Evans, he kissed her once. His dad came, on the same bike, to tell her and Mum what the swing bucket had done. Jo gains another few feet. Her mother had gone mad, wrecking the kitchen before running down the street. Jo tells herself again that she has to get out of there. But she feels a bit dizzy. She just needs a second, only a second, then she'll make it. Right to the end. It's late, that's why she's tired, but she'll be OK when she wakes. She woke last time, didn't she? Her eyes close. She's moving faster now. She can see Blonnie, standing next to the bicycle with its worn, sprung leather seat.

Blonnie's arms are folded. She's thinking no, it can't be, not again the poor woman. Jo sees Blonnie gasp. From inside the cottage comes a sound, like a table being pushed over. It's followed by a scream.

A shrill, loud and horrible scream.

Chapter Two

That autumn London was about as beautiful a place as it can ever be. The country had been spared the weeks of rain that had left whole counties underwater the previous year, and in their place came crisp clear days that were tailor-made for a man whose job mostly entailed walking around the city looking for people. Watching shivering fourteen-year-old girls slouching on street corners near Brick Lane was no less depressing, and neither was checking cardboard constructions behind the Strand for ten-year-old boys. Peering through the smeared windows of runaway kids' lives was never going to be a happy task, whatever the time of year. But with the air tasting cleaner with the cold, and the trees lit with a thousand shades of orange and red, I felt that I was a lucky man to be living in London then, and to be doing what I was doing.

It wasn't just the weather. Things seemed to be going right for me that October. The immediate future looked clear and simple for the first time in years. It may sound strange but I put it down to the fact that the girl I was seeing was working abroad. It wasn't that I was glad she was away, the opposite was true, but the huge hole of her absence had shown me what a presence she had been. It was like gradually emerging from a fog I'd never properly realized I was surrounded by. So while the world was gradually closing down, drawing the sap back into itself, I felt powered by a full and growing energy.

But then, suddenly, London stopped being such a beautiful place to be. Just like those people the autumn before who had thought they were living on dry land, everything I had in the world was underwater. The banks had burst, the torrent had risen, and all I could do was cling onto the wreckage.

It was a cold bright Monday morning and I was driving up through Islington to my office, squinting against a low sun that was squeezing out the last drop of juice from its summer recharge. The traffic was like a giant jigsaw puzzle and when I say I was driving what I really mean is that I was sitting very still for what seemed like lifetimes on end before edging my car forward a couple of feet. Strangely enough, though, it didn't bother me. Sometimes the mere mechanics of moving around the city I live in get me as frustrated as a colour-blind man with high blood pressure trying to do a Rubik's Cube. Wearing mittens. But that morning it was as if I was floating above the traffic, not sitting right inside it.

I was still in a good mood as I turned away from Highbury Fields into the car park of the Lindauer Building. I raised a hand to Ron in his booth and the barrier was raised in front of me. I brought my Louis XIV Mazda to a halt and put the engine out of its misery but didn't bother locking up. I wasn't planning on staying in my office for long. I'd only driven up to check the mail, not having been to my office for two or three

ADAM BARON

days. That and put some photographs in the post to a woman whose son I'd found the day before. The woman's voice had given away how much she cared about the confused young boy who had decided that the delivery bay of a furniture store behind Tottenham Court Road was a better place to live than a three-bedroomed house in the suburbs of Plymouth. I didn't imagine that the pictures I was going to send her would be of any real comfort but I wanted to give the woman what news I could.

I walked across the car park towards the huge, land-bound ocean liner that is the Lindauer Building, filling my lungs with cold air tinged with the scent of leaf mulch from the park. I used the side entrance and stepped into the waiting lift. The Lindauer is a former carpet factory, split up into a maze of design studios and business units. Any later in the day and it would be alive with the distant and close clatter of drills, printing machines, sanders and other unidentifiable machinery, making you feel as though you were rising up through the belly of a giant beast. But as it wasn't yet nine the place was quiet but for my whistle and the deep, slow drawl of the lift. When the plastic number three lit up I yawned, waited for the doors and stepped out.

After walking down the empty, school-grey corridor, I opened up my office. I slid the photographs I'd brought with me into an envelope, which I addressed before putting it on the edge of my table, where I'd probably forget it when I went out again. I then bent down to the three-day accumulation of mail that my letter box had seemed to regurgitate onto my office floor in my absence. The first thing I came across was a catalogue from a mail-order design company offering to

8

rush me some genuine beech light-cord pulls with the urgency of a UN airlift. I went through the rest quickly, and after discarding the very kind offer of a million pounds from the *Reader's Digest* people, I dumped the entire pile in the bin. I then spent five minutes standing, very still, by my window.

In the middle of winter I get quite a good view from my window. Any other time of the year, however, and the high-rises of Hackney and neatly laid-out gardens stretching out towards them are obscured by the leaves of a huge oak tree. The tree is the curse of my textile-designing friends in the studio next door, who yearn for the light it keeps from them, but I have always enjoyed the company it provides, the leaves that sometimes stroke my window like a lover's fingertips. What I have also come to appreciate is that the oak is not just a tree, but a home.

To birds.

OK. I'm going to admit it. Birds. Not just birds, but looking at them. I'm going to say it: watching them. I never meant to be a, oh, Christ, birdwatcher. A year ago and I'd have laughed at you, but ever since someone I once knew pointed out the array of wildlife right outside my office window I've been hooked by my jittery, feathered neighbours. I even bought a little book so I'd know my coal tit from my pied wagtail, another signal that time is beginning to run through me faster than a bag thief through a shopping mall.

Today all I could see was a solitary chaffinch. I was trying to decide whether it was male (pinkish chest) or female (bully crown) when a knock on my door interrupted me. I stuffed the book into my desk drawer, where no prospective client looking for a hard-nosed private investigator would see it, and sat down.

'It's open.'

When I saw the petite figure of Jemma in my doorway I relaxed. Jemma and her friend Cass have rented the studio next door for over a year now. I've always liked both girls but I took to Jemma more, probably because of the bright smile she always seems to find for everyone. Jemma has long hair the colour of butterscotch, round grey eyes and a small nose that wrinkles when she laughs. Her light, friendly disposition usually transforms her from girl-next-door pretty to very nearly beautiful, but right then she looked serious. Her expression confused me for a moment but then I nodded to myself. I knew, of course, what the cause of it was, and the fact that I'd forgotten it, even for a split second, didn't make me feel very good.

Jemma stood in my doorway without moving, her eyes fixed on my table.

'I guess you know why I'm here,' she said after a second or two.

'I think so.' I filled a smile with compassion, hoping she hadn't seen my previous cheeriness. 'I thought you might drop by sometime. Come in.'

Jemma moved forward but stopped.

'You don't mind?'

'Don't be silly.'

'Shall I get us some tea first?'

'Why not? Though can my tea be coffee? Ally knows how.'

'Of course. Yes. And thanks, Billy.' The cloud covering Jemma's face lifted for a second. 'Thanks a lot.

I knew you'd care, even if not many other people seem to.'

Jemma's footsteps disappeared down the hall to the cafe and soon the wolf howl of an espresso machine filled the air. I took a long, deep breath, the light mood that had carried me in that morning having vanished into the air. It had been replaced by a solid lump of guilt. I couldn't believe that I'd managed to forget the event that had snuffed out the usual light behind Jemma's eyes so effectively. A death. A sad, lonely, pointless death. Jemma had said that I cared, but I'd hardly given it any thought at all since it had happened. I'd tossed it out of my mind like an apple core out of a car window. I'd let it bounce off into the past.

Two weeks before I'd driven up to the Lindauer much as I had today, marvelling at the trees in Highbury Fields, the madly coloured leaves rioting at the prospect of being evicted from their branches. I'd turned into the gate only to find three patrol cars sitting outside the building, taking up half of the visitors' spaces. After resisting the impulse to back straight out and head to the nearest airport, I parked up myself. I went round to the side door, where a tired-looking WPC was standing with a clipboard in the crook of her arm. I asked what was up in as casual a voice as I could but, instead of answering me, the WPC asked me a question: did I recognize the following name?

'Josephine Thomas,' she said, looking down at her clipboard.

I shook my head.

'Jo,' she insisted. 'Most people called her Jo.'

'Oh,' I said. I thought about it. 'Yes. Or, at least, I know of a Jo but it might not be her. A Welsh girl?'

'That's right.'

'Then I do know her, or at least who she is. *Three* cars? What did she do, park in a red zone?'

'No. Josephine Thomas is dead I'm afraid, sir.'

'What?'

'She's dead. She was murdered last night. A mugging we think. We're pretty sure. She was stabbed, and she bled to death.'

'Oh,' I said again. 'I'm sorry.'

'What for? It wasn't you who did it was it?'

'No.'

'Well then. You weren't to know, sir, were you?'

I shook my head and I said Christ and the poor girl and I asked the WPC what, exactly, had happened. Apparently Jo had been working late the night before. She'd taken the last bus but never made it home. Instead she was attacked, in an alley leading to the estate she lived on, only yards from her flat. It wasn't known whether she had resisted her assailant but as well as being robbed she was stabbed. The WPC asked me if I was a friend of the girl.

'No,' I said. 'I've only seen her a couple of times. I think we only ever spoke to each other once. On the way out.'

'You didn't see her yesterday?'

'I'm sorry, I wasn't here. Who found her?'

I think I'm supposed to be asking you the questions.'

'I'm sorry.'

'That's OK. I probably shouldn't say much but it'll all be in the paper by this afternoon, so why not? I can't see what difference it'll make.'

I listened quietly as the WPC ran through what else was known at that stage. She told me that the victim's body had been found at four that morning by a young couple who'd been out clubbing. The police had arrived shortly after. Because Jo had been stabbed and robbed, the initial feeling was a smackhead, too long since his last bag. Dalston's the place for them all right, though most settle for burglary and car crime as a means of paying the dream seller. If it was an addict, and he'd shot up immediately after killing Jo, then he'd probably be coming down from it about now.

'That's going to be one hell of a hangover,' the WPC agreed.

I asked if a murder weapon had been found but that was one thing the WPC wouldn't tell me. What she did say was that Jo hadn't died instantly after being stabbed. There were indications that she might have lived for anything up to an hour. I didn't ask what those indications were because I knew what happened to a stab wound when a heart was still beating. And I didn't ask how the WPC knew this detail. There was a look on her face that I hadn't encountered for some time but which I instantly recognized. She'd been at the scene. She'd looked under the tent they would have gotten up and her eyes had fallen on the motionless form lying there. She'd have seen the huge sheet of blood Josephine would have been lying on.

I gave the WPC my name and her eyebrows drew together as if, given a minute, she might remember where she'd heard it before. Instead of giving her that minute I headed off towards the stairs. Walking up I felt strange. As a policeman I'd been told about murders and felt, in that moment, an abstract sympathy. Real feeling only came later, when I got a sense of who the victim was, what effect their death had had on those around them. Hearing about Jo was similar. My stomach clenched at the image I'd created of her last hour but I'd been a DS long enough to understand the simple truth that in London people get murdered. They get murdered almost every single day and in every kind of way. It's a sad fact but you can't let each and every act of horror into you. Self-preservation alone means we filter the things that appal us, we somehow decide whose misery we are prepared to embrace full on. The news of Jo's death sent a wave of depression through me that morning but I wasn't going to pretend that my life had really been changed by it.

Upstairs, in the cafe along from my office, the reaction was similar. Most of the other tenants had never seen Jo, let alone met her. Jo had only been in the building four or five times. The sympathy expressed was genuine if unspecific, the news a little like a door banging open on a stormy night. Everyone shivered at the claw of wind reaching in but it wouldn't take long to slam the door shut again.

For Jemma, however, it was different.

Jemma set a big latte down in front of me and I took a sip. She was drinking herbal tea, a paper tag poking out like a bookmark. As if she'd forgotten what sip she was on. She was wearing a Muji pinafore dress, her hair pulled back by a scrunchy. Jemma's door key hung on a piece of string around her neck and I smiled as I remembered how she'd locked herself out a couple of times. I pushed my cup to one side, trying to imagine what she was feeling. It was Jemma who Jo had been working with the night she'd died. She had seen her only minutes before she'd got her bus, had still been working there when Jo was being attacked. Jemma hadn't found out what had happened until she came in the next morning, ten minutes after me, and met the same WPC at the door. Her grief had shattered the atmosphere of quiet empathy in the building, and on two occasions in the weeks since I'd heard it slicing through the wall that separated our two spaces. Both times I'd wanted to go and see if she was all right but Cass had been with her, as well as some other people I didn't know. I'd done nothing and felt uncomfortable about it, and I was glad that I now had the chance to register my concern.

Jemma lifted the cup to her lips and blew across it. I asked her how she was.

'Fine,' she replied.

'Really?'

'Really. Why shouldn't I be? It didn't happen to me, did it? I didn't get stabbed.'

'No,' I said. 'You didn't. But you and Jo were friends, weren't you? Good friends?'

'We were,' Jemma admitted. 'Yes. Jo was helping me with my scarves. For Harvey Nichols. They ordered two hundred, amazingly, not that I care now. That's why she was here. I met Jo on foundation. She was doing acting. I used to share a flat with her.'

'Well then,' I said. 'It must be hard for you.'

'I don't need sympathy.'

Jemma drew her lips together and then studied her knees. I could see her telling herself to keep it together.

'I'm sorry, Billy. Everyone is being so nice to me

and I can't stand it. You weren't to know. But I don't need anyone to make me feel better. This isn't about my feelings, OK? This is about what happened to Jo.'

'OK.'

'She deserves the sympathy. Not me.'

'I understand that. But losing someone is hard too.'

'Maybe,' Jemma said. 'But even so, what I feel is nothing compared to her really close friends and her family.'

'Do you know them?'

'No, but I'm going to have to meet them next week.'

'Have to?'

'At the funeral. The police are going to release the body soon.'

'But why "have to"? Won't it be good to share your grief with other's who were close to her?'

'They won't want me there.'

'Why ever not?'

Jemma frowned, like I was the dimmest boy in the class.

'Because it was my fault. Because if it weren't for me there wouldn't be a funeral. Jo was helping me.'

'I know, but . . .'

'She wouldn't have been here so late otherwise. I let her stay till nearly midnight. *Midnight*, Billy. She stayed because she knew I needed help but I should have made her go.'

'You weren't to know what would happen.'

'No? But I should have known it *might*. Especially knowing where she lived. An estate in Dalston? I live in a nice square off Upper Street with my boyfriend, it was all right for me going home. I didn't have to walk down an alleyway full of drug addicts, did I?'

'You can't blame yourself for where Jo lived. Or for what happened.'

'Can't I? Aren't friends supposed to look out for each other? I told her to take a cab, you know? I even made her take an extra tenner.'

'Well then.'

'But I didn't check, did I? She said she'd get Ron to phone one from the gate and I just said fine. As soon as she said goodbye it was as if she didn't exist. All I could think about was my deadline, the fact that my scarves were going into a posh shop. She probably saw the bus and thought, why not? I should have called the cab myself. While she was bleeding to death I was probably sewing some bloody tassels on. Oh shit.'

Jemma tried to hold out but her face began to break up, like a sandcastle at high tide. Her body started to shake, almost without moving, and I sighed. The extent of Jemma's sorrow chastised me. She'd never been a DS, she didn't think that some murders were everyday occurrences, to be shrugged aside. I pushed a box of tissues towards her but she didn't take one, gripping the desk instead. I reached forward, prising Jemma's slim, dye-stained fingers from the surface and reattaching them to my own. Jemma held on tight, fighting her grief down until finally it withdrew. When she'd calmed down I relaxed my grip and held her hands gently, until we both felt self-conscious. I let go, setting her wrists back down on the table top.

'You have absolutely nothing to reproach yourself with. You haven't done anything wrong and no one thinks you have.'

Jemma took some more deep breaths and pushed away the last of her tears. She didn't argue with me, simply shoving my words to the side. I could tell she didn't agree with me. She just wanted to move on.

'You know what I'm going to ask, don't you?' Jemma said after a second or two.

'I think so.'

'You must feel like that financial adviser bloke on the top floor. Every time he goes for a coffee people hassle him about their mortgages. You look for kids normally?'

'That's right.'

Jemma nodded to herself. 'It's been two weeks and nothing has happened. The police won't tell me anything, except no one's been charged. I can't believe they can't catch some druggie. Will you see what you can find out?'

I tried not to let the sigh that ran straight through me out into the room.

'I can try. But the police will be doing everything there is to do.'

'That's what they said to me.'

'And they were telling you the truth. Two weeks isn't that long and, anyway, they might already know who did it. They just can't say, maybe because they're after more evidence or the kid's under-age. Anything could be happening, you just don't know. And even if they haven't got anywhere yet, they won't give up. You know that, don't you?'

'I suppose.'

'And it's much more than I could ever do. I usually do things that the police aren't interested in. Where there's a gap for me. But they will be interested in this, Jemma, and I'm not sure there'll be anything for me to do that hasn't already been done.'

'I realize that. But what the police are doing isn't the point. It's what I'm doing. Just carrying on with my life, sitting behind my knitting machines as if nothing has changed. Even if you don't find anything, it doesn't matter. At least I haven't just sat there. So please don't say no. If you do, I'll have to find someone else.'

'I won't,' I said. 'I'll make some calls. I've got a couple of friends still on the police who'll fill me in. They'll at least tell me more than they've told you. I'll let you know what they say. They might just be closing it out.'

'And if they're not.'

'Then I'll see what else I can do. That will come second, though.'

'Whatever you say. I trust you. I'll pay you, of course.'

'That won't be necessary. It'll just be a couple of calls.'

'Even so.'

'Even nothing.'

'Are you sure? Really? If you have any expenses, at least.'

'Make me a scarf sometime,' I said. 'It'll save me going to Harvey Nichols. As far as I'm concerned that's worth a hell of a lot.'

'I will do,' Jemma said. 'I will.'

'One thing, though. And it's very important.'

Jemma looked at me, seriously. 'What?'

'No tassels.'

'No, Billy Rucker, I hadn't got you down as a tassels kind of man.'

Jemma nodded, allowing the ghost of a smile to pass across her lips. It felt good to have put it there. But then her eyes lost focus again and she had to clench her jaw. Her hands still sat on the table top and I thought about holding them again but I didn't quite do it. I just hoped I could help her. A crime with no personal motive was almost impossible for one man to get anywhere near. I prayed that the police came up with something soon to bail me out. If they didn't, Jemma was going to be disappointed by my efforts, maybe even more so than if she'd just sat next door and let the police get on with it.

Chapter Three

It was after nine now but the hall was still empty. Save for the smell of fresh coffee signalling to me like a crooked finger. It drew me on to the cafe, four doors down on the other side of the hall. The Sanctuary is housed in a medium-sized, cosy unit, the back third sectioned off into a small kitchen. Mike and his Italian wife, Ally, who run the place, are my closest friends in the building. They were both working, getting ready for the day ahead. Mike roared out a hearty greeting when I stuck my head round the door and Ally asked me how I was.

'All the better for seeing you, O increasingly round one. But what are you doing on your feet?'

'It's him,' Ally said, casting a barbed glance at her husband as she looked up from the carrot she was grating. Her thick, dark hair was tied back behind two delicate ears. 'First he puts this ball of crazed snakes inside me and then he makes me work like a slave all day.'

'Disgusting. You should sit down right now. The next five weeks should be spent reclining in a comfortable chair being hand-fed Belgian chocolates while having both feet massaged simultaneously.'

'Hey, thanks, Billy. Thanks a lot, mate.'

'Are you listening to this, "Mr Hurry up with Those Sandwiches for Godsake"? Oh, why didn't I marry you, huh, Billy?'

'Because he wouldn't have you. And he's going to marry the lovely Sharon, aren't you, fella?'

'Am I?'

'Are you, Billy? Michael, has he told you something?'

'Hold on, hold on!!' I put my hands up. 'It's a little early for that.'

'So, nothing's going on then, mucker?'

'Yes, all right. We got back together. OK, I admit it.'

'Finally!'

'But our relationship currently stands at a spectacular nine days.'

'This time, Billy, but it was ages before. You have to add that on.'

'Yes, OK, Ally. I will. But we have a long, long way to go and there's no guarantee anyway. Also, as you know, Sharon just happens to be in Afghanistan at the moment, which even in the age of the Internet makes matrimony difficult. Married people – you just can't help trying to get everyone else to join the club too, can you? What is it, you get a percentage from the vicar?'

'No. It's just because it's such a wonderful club to be in.' Ally beamed up at her husband, her eyes full of sarcastic adoration. Mike grimaced back then raised his eyebrows. Ally punched him on the arm with one hand, the other curling beneath the impressive bump that had been steadily growing amongst us like an alien for the last seven and a half months. The irony vanished from her face, replaced by a soft smile.

'And so is this club,' she said.

I shook my head, marvelling once again at the fact that the two people in front of me would, in five weeks' time, be parents. Parents! How the hell did that happen? Actually I knew how it happened, but what I didn't know was how I'd suddenly got to the age where two of my best friends were having a baby. Wasn't it only last week that we were drinking tequila and smoking weed and talking bollocks all night? The idea was wonderful and bizarre at the same time, as was the fact that I was to be the child's godfather. They'd only asked me last week, and as well as feeling deeply moved and honoured, there were shifting sands of pure terror moving in me.

We chatted away a little longer. I asked after little Billy, as I called him, and was told that little Michael was fine. As was little Sophia, as Ally referred to her baby. She showed me the last scan she'd had done, and I looked with slight unease at the black-and-white photo until the features became clear. I suddenly had an image of a bouncy little two-year-old, running through my open office door, Ally following. She was a little girl with curly black hair, achingly lovely, and she'd just learned to call me Uncle Billy.

'She's beautiful,' I said. 'You can tell that already.'

'He's handsome, you mean. Good left foot too, you can feel him practising free kicks. Just what we need down Stamford Bridge.'

'They wouldn't have him. He's only half Italian.'

'And he's not a he either.' Ally looked serious for a second, shooting another, meaning-laden glance at Mike. 'You keep calling her that. My family, we're all girls. You better get used to the idea, my *love*.'

Mike took hold of Ally's shoulders. 'I don't care. You know that. Chelsea's got a women's team too.'

'Oh yes? Well, wait till my papa takes her to the San Siro.' Ally winked at me. 'Then we'll see who she wants to support.'

Mike looked disgusted as he turned back to the rolls he was unpacking. I left Ally and Mike to their prep and walked back down the hall to the lift.

Chapter Four

I spent the rest of the day in that place Islingtonites only speak about in whispers to frighten their children up to bed: South of the River. Land of drive-by shootings and drive-through McDonald's. Precisely, I spent it in the no-man's-land between Camberwell and Brixton, looking for a young girl called Denise, who had disappeared from her home in Birmingham six months before. This, as Jemma had pointed out, is what I usually do. I find kids for parents who have lost them. Parents who have fucked up and failed in the only really important job there is.

I'd been looking for Denise for the last two weeks, on and off, ever since a watchful young dude called Jared had slunk his way into my office one afternoon and handed me a picture of her. I'd taken Jared for the missing girl's younger brother but Jared told me he was actually Denise's husband. I said that I'd keep an eye out for his missing wife, but in the days that followed I hadn't looked too hard, simply showing Denise's picture around while I was out looking for other kids. Denise was perfectly within her rights to skip both her town and her young husband, having reached the elevated seniority of sixteen years. There was also the fact that I didn't know what she was leaving behind. I'd interfered once before in the life of a runaway and even though I wasn't there to see them I was sure that the consequences for her had been pretty terrible. I hadn't meant to hurt the girl but I'd sworn it would never happen again.

Just the day before, however, I'd got a tip-off. It came from a retired bus conductor of my acquaintance, a wise and wizened Barbadian called Joe, who sometimes gets his former colleagues on the network to keep an eye out for the kids I'm looking for. Joe had told me that a young girl with Denise's dyed black spiky hair had been seen hanging around the Brixton area. One driver had spotted her two days in a row and from what he'd said it sounded like she might be hooking for the 22 Crew. The 22 are a posse of enterprising Jamaicans who operate their people-management concern out of a cafe on Brixton's Railton Road. The 22 are the leading employers in their field, always on a recruitment drive, and it didn't seem unlikely to me that a young runaway from Birmingham had been persuaded to follow a career path with them.

Even though finding Denise was just bread-and-butter stuff the tip was fresh, so I decided that Jo Thomas could wait until later. After leaving Mike and Ally, I walked downstairs and the Mazda, given a few slaps, sputtered its way into life. I rejoined the traffic, moving a little faster now, as if a stopper had been pulled out across town somewhere. Even though I'd felt Jemma's pain, Jo's death still hadn't really got to me and I wondered once again why not, when it had had such a profound effect on my neighbour. Other people's problems, other people's lives in variable degrees of storm, while I seemed to be sailing along to the place I most wanted to be in life. Like the traffic that morning I'd shrugged it aside without making any conscious decision to do so. I suppose there was too much weighted on the other side: my own expectant happiness. The image of Sharon, soon to be more than an image.

I got to Brixton just after eleven and cruised slowly past the tube station, where used tickets were already being traded by a thin, ragged sub-species of human. Along the High Street clusters of wary young men leaned back on the store fronts while stout old women heaved striped bags of shopping past the discount shops and pizza restaurants. I drove round the one-way, then checked out the spot Joe had told me about, a leaf-littered stretch of road lined with Portuguese cafes. Denise wasn't there. The only person touting for business of any kind was an enthusiastic evangelist dressed in a pink zoot suit, his cheap PA system translating the jewels of his message into a hissing, unintelligible babble.

My fresh tip was already stale but as I was down there I decided not to give up straight away. The spot may have been free of sin but I doubted that the evangelist had caused that. It was more likely the police, acting on the complaints of local residents. Young mothers who had seen their toddlers bending down to used needles once too often, old ladies fed up with pulling their dogs away from used condoms. I knew that the girls had probably just moved, and gang turf also meant that they wouldn't have moved too far. I headed up towards the thundering interchange that is Loughborough Junction, keeping my eyes open. It didn't take me long to find out that that's where the circus had moved to. But was Denise Denton one of the attractions?

I parked in a bus lane across the highway from the six girls who were working the street and reached for my F1, checking each girl out with the zoom. Two of the girls were shivering outside a snooker hall. Another two stood in the doorway of a DSS. Two more were working the junction itself. Unfortunately for me, but not for her, Denise wasn't one of them. I waited for half an hour, hoping that none of the girls' supervisors had spotted me watching what was going on. The day was still clear but that particular area of London wasn't the finest canvas for autumn's delicate brush: a furry grey mist choked the air, smearing the store fronts and the window sills. The health risks of prostitution are well known but I suddenly thought of another one: asthma. If I'd been them I'd have worn a cycling mask, though that probably wouldn't have endeared me to prospective clients. Or maybe it would have. As it was, the girls didn't do anything to attract trade, simply keeping an eye out so that the park wouldn't have to wait any longer than necessary. A couple of them got lucky even though it was a chilly Friday lunchtime.

If Denise had been with a punter she'd have been back by now, so I couldn't see any point in waiting longer. Instead I locked up and walked down to the snooker hall, where I asked the two girls if they knew the face in the picture I was showing them. They both said no, as did the girls who had been outside the DSS but had walked up to see what I was doing. I gave each of them a copy anyway, in case they changed their minds or ran into Denise. My number was stamped on the back and I assured them all that if they rang me and

I came and found Denise, there would be fifty quid in it for them.

'I'm not the Bill,' I said. 'I won't do anything to her. I won't even tell anyone. I just need to know that she's all right.'

All four girls took copies of the photo and I thanked them before walking up to the junction itself. By now there was only one person standing there, a tall girl of about eighteen. Or forty. It wasn't possible to tell. Her face was ageless, pale as an ice lolly with all the syrup sucked out. A cold sore squatted on her lower lip like a squashed bluebottle. My eyes were drawn down from it to the hipbones pressing like mountain ridges through her beer-stained mini dress.

Beer-stained? I'm staying with beer-stained.

'Business, love?'

The girl was trying to be casual but her voice was fuelled by desperation. I ignored it and told her, politely, that while I was there for business, my business wasn't 'pleasure'. I showed her Denise's photo and studied her face as she looked at it and I thought that I did see recognition there. When I told her about the fifty notes she looked at me.

'What are you?' the girl said. 'Daddy?'

I explained that I wasn't Denise's father, hiding my deeply felt hurt at being thought anywhere near old enough. I could see that the girl wanted the money but I could also see that she wasn't sure about talking to me. I didn't push it. Whether she'd call me or not was one thing but right then, with the other girls watching, she needed to give me the flick off. Like I'd done with the other girls I simply thanked her for her time and turned to go.

'Wait.'

The hand that had taken hold of my left wrist was strong, even though the arm it was attached to was little more than a broom handle with veins. I stopped and looked back, thinking the girl had changed her mind.

'You sure you're not interested? French for twenty. Without, like. You can have me for forty, though, I've got a place close by. Come on, love, I can see you want to.'

The girl's mouth trembled and the dead fly jumped. It took me a second to realize that she was smiling. Once again I said no thanks.

'Come on, love, I'm cold you know? What about a hand job? Down here, come on, darling.'

The girl moved closer, pushing her sunken groin into mine, her grip on my arm closing even tighter. I tried to tell her again that she'd got the wrong man but she ignored me. The bones of her free hand went for my crotch and I couldn't help it; a reflex jerked me backwards. The girl didn't let go of my hand in time and the pull yanked her forwards. Before I could catch her she fell, stumbling over, her elbow joining the pavement with a sharp, loud crack. I put out a hand to her, to help her up, asking if she was OK. I put my other hand on her shoulder but she lashed out at it, clambering to her feet on her own. Once she was up she rushed at me.

'Hey!' I said. 'Come on. It was an accident. Come on.'

I reached for my wallet to give her a tenner, one hand fending the girl off, but it was no use. She'd snapped. Her arms wheeled around me, aiming at my head, her feet jabbing into my shins. I tried to shake her off gently but I couldn't. The girl was raging at me, trying to get at my eyes with her nails. I pivoted and swung her, hoping she'd spin off, but she managed to cling onto the sleeve of my jacket. She was spitting at me, trying to claw my face. When she realized I wasn't going to let her do that she stopped for a second in order to tell me that I was going to die. Then she showed me something to underline her point. A triangle of rusty brown steel arced suddenly towards my eyes. I don't know how she'd managed it but in her free hand she'd produced a Stanley knife. The point was now underlined, italicized and covered in highlighter.

I ducked beneath the blade and kicked the girl's legs from under her. When she was down for the second time, I aimed a foot at her wrist, sending the knife scuttling across the pavement like a frightened roach. I walked towards it and kicked it further up the street.

'My boyfriend, he's gonna kill you,' the girl screamed at me. 'Bastard, he's gonna kill you!'

I crossed back through the stationary traffic to my car and sat for a second, waiting as my heart slowly calmed down five octaves. Oh my. The girl was right: I was getting too old for this. I should have gone bird-watching. To my knowledge no one has ever tried to slash David Attenborough. I edged into the nearest lane, next to a Volvo estate being driven by a well-dressed middle-aged woman, who cut a deep glance at me, her face curdled with disgust. She must have seen what had happened. I could feel my face reddening. I wanted to stop her, to tell her, to explain. I hadn't done anything wrong. Instead I had to endure her contempt, as the same tide carried us back to safety, to north London.

Chapter Five

Three hours later someone else took a swing at me. This time it was a short, stocky man with greying hair and a fading tattoo on his left shoulder. While some people would perhaps have been offended at this I welcomed the man's punches, effective as they were at reducing my life to the simple and immediate business of getting out of the way of them. And throwing some back at him. After three minutes a bell sounded and I waited as a woman called Sally Sullivan ducked into the ring and had a friendly word with my opponent. Then she walked over to me.

'What's the matter?'

Sally's voice hit me harder than any of the punches I'd just been dodging. I shrugged.

'Nothing.'

'Then what are you doing?' Sal folded her arms that way she had, which told you she wasn't going to take anything from you. 'Calista fucking Flockhart could put more weight behind her punches than that.'

'Oh,' I said.

'Well? It's Jeff, isn't it?'

I turned my back on my opponent. 'Sally, it's difficult. He must be forty-five if he's a day.'

'He's fifty-one. And he's been boxing about six times as long as you have. Most of that in the Marines.'

'I know, and he's good, but . . .'

'You want to take it easy on him. I see. Don't be so bloody patronizing. Jeff's tougher than Darcey Bussell's big toe.' I couldn't help smiling. 'How would you feel if one of those teenagers over there thought the same about you?'

'I'd kick his spotty arse.'

'Which is exactly what Jeff wants to do to you. So stop farting around. Anyway, you know what he just said? "I'm taking it easy on the kid, Sal. He's fit and he's quick but he looks a bit raw." '

'Right,' I said. 'The kid.'

'So stop wasting ring time and do some work.'

Jeff and I went another couple of rounds. In spite of what Sal said I could feel the age difference as I dug uppercuts into his softening midriff and made him walk a lot of ring. Added to that was the fact that I was fitter than I've ever been, having increased my two nights a week to three. I wasn't sure why but it might have been in response to a change I'd seen in Mike recently: a slowing down, a slight rounding out that wasn't just physical. I also had a desperate, psychic war to win against my inner twitcher.

Afterwards I stretched. The workout had been great but images from the day soon began to drift back into my mind. Jemma. Then the hooker, the tracks I'd seen running up her arm like death-watch beetles. I wondered if the girl I'd failed to find would end up like that. I didn't know if she would or wouldn't but I wasn't going to get involved. I thought about the promise I'd made to the other girls: that I wouldn't hurt Denise, wouldn't reveal her whereabouts to anyone. I meant it. I wouldn't tell Jared where she was. I'd done that once: eight years ago. One damp night not long after I'd set up on my own I'd taken a guy down to a squat in Streatham, where his fourteen-year-old daughter was staying. The guy had seemed genuinely devastated that his baby girl had run away, had wept at my office table as he told me about the death of the girl's mother and bullying at school. I promised him I'd find her and I did. I thought I was giving both sides a second chance. The father of being a better parent and the girl, Carolyn Oliver, of backing away from a life on the street. Backing away from alleyways and blow jobs, needles passed round in a circle.

It was only when we walked into the miserable hole she'd taken refuge in that I realized what I'd done. The thin, pale girl cowered in a corner at the sight of her father. His face set like concrete. His only word was 'Outside,' spoken in a voice that made my blood run cold. His daughter was terrified, something I could tell even though her face was almost completely hidden behind a curtain of lank, mousy hair. As she rose up from the floor I saw the damp stain spreading between her legs, sticking her skirt to her thighs. The dignity with which she walked past me, and past her father, out to his car, stays in my mind to this day.

So if any of those girls called me I would simply take Denise's picture and maybe tell her that her husband wanted her back. Then I'd tell Jared how she was and what she'd said, showing him the pictorial evidence. For this I'd charge a flat fee inclusive of update reports if I ran into Denise in the near future. It's not ideal. Not for my clients, not for me, and certainly not for the kids I look for. But name me one thing in this world that is.

The bag was free and I thought about a quick session but I felt a pull in my shoulder from a hook I'd tried to extend. I was walking over to the showers when Sal flipped a switch on the beat box, and clapped her hands. There was a girl at her side. By the look of the girl – muscular, tracksuit and trainers, hair in a tight ponytail – she was a kick boxer and had come on the wrong night. But she wasn't. Sal introduced her as Cherie, a masseur. Or rather she was doing a massage course and needed some guinea pigs. Someone asked if the lotion wouldn't get stuck in their fur and everyone laughed. I laughed too. I couldn't believe my luck. When Sal had turned the music back on I approached the girl. I introduced myself, told her about my shoulder, and asked if she could fit me in on Sunday.

'That was easy,' Cherie said, a smile appearing on a pleasant if rather flat face. 'But what's wrong with now?' She opened her hands.

'Now?'

'Why not? After exercise is best and my place is only five minutes' walk.'

'Your place?'

'Where I've got my bench. And my oils and stuff.'

'Oh, right.' I thought about it, glancing up at the clock on the wall. It was certainly tempting and I couldn't, actually, see why not. I hadn't got anything planned for that night although I had left a message with a former colleague of mine, asking him to call me.

I'd go and meet Andy Gold if he was free, to talk about Jo, but I could easily fit the massage in first.

'Great.' I shrugged.

'Right,' Cherie said, suddenly looking a little nervous. I guessed it was the first time she'd done this and, actually, the concept of inviting strange men back to her place was not, when I thought about it, very wise. I'd tell her that – right after the massage.

'Give me ten minutes to shower,' I said.

When I was all clean I towelled off and then dressed, shutting up my locker after me. I was walking back out to Cherie when I heard my phone, ringing from my coat pocket. I reached for it, wondering if it was Andy. I looked at the caller display but the number wasn't familiar. It was probably one of the girls I'd spoken to earlier. I didn't really want to schlep down to Loughborough Junction again that day but I would do, if Denise was there. I hit the green button.

'Billy? Billy, where are you?'

The voice wasn't Andy's, or an informant's, but Mike's. I was surprised. Mike didn't often call me at home, let alone on this thing. I saw him four or five days a week as it was. I asked him how he was and when all I got in reply was silence I thought I'd hit cancel the way I sometimes did, by pressing the phone too hard against my cheekbone.

'Mike?'

'I'm here.'

'Right,' I said. 'Well, this is an honour. What can I do for you? If you're going to ask me about my church attendance record, I'll tell you now it's pretty poor. I'll buy good toys, though.'

'Listen, Billy.' Mike moved straight through the joke.

His voice sounded raw, desperate almost, and I frowned. 'Are you busy? Right now?'

'Not this second,' I said, looking towards the door. 'I've got five minutes.'

'Billy, can you meet me?'

'Yes.' I shrugged. 'Sure. I'd like to. I'm going for some massage and then I'm heading home. I could see you in, say, a couple of hours?'

'Shit.'

'Mike? What is it?' I was alarmed.

'It's me, Billy, that's what.'

'I don't understand.'

'Neither do I, believe me. Can you meet me now?'

'Of course. If you want. But hey, give me a clue. What is it?'

'It's this.' Mike paused, letting a long sigh hiss out through his teeth. 'I'm at home. Ally's out, she's at one of those classes. I begged off, saying I wasn't feeling well. But I'm not ill.'

'Then what *is* the matter?'

'The matter is I've got a bag packed. And I'm about to leave.'

'Leave to go where?'

'I mean, leave Ally.'

'What?'

'I'm going to leave her. I was about to, at least. Billy, I've even got a fucking cab waiting. I was just going out the door but I thought I'd call you first. I don't know why, I just thought you might . . . I mean you know us both. Shit, I can't do this on the phone. Please, can you meet me?'

'Of course. Just don't do anything stupid. Give me twenty minutes. And Mike?'

'What?'

'Cancel the cab. You hear me?'

'I will. I'll pay him off. Thanks, Billy.'

'Don't worry about it.'

Mike tried again to tell me what the hell was going on but I told him he was right, not over the phone. We agreed on a place to meet and I hung up. I'd tried my best to sound calm and understanding, but I was far from being either. I was flat on my back. I looked at my phone, hardly able to believe what Mike had said to me. Leave Ally? Now? I could hear the complaining whine of boots on canvas pushing beneath the door, backed by the echoing whump of the boom box. I walked out towards them and told Cherie I couldn't make it after all. She was disappointed, now that she'd got used to the idea, and I guessed Sal must have OK'd me. I heard her say Sunday then, after all, and I agreed without really listening. Jeff walked over and asked me if everything was OK.

'No,' I told him. 'No, it isn't.'

Chapter Six

Mike was already at Tate Modern when I arrived. I'd dropped my bag off at home and taken a cab down to the other side of Blackfriars Bridge, where I jogged down some stone stairs onto the South Bank. Mike's words rang through my head and I told myself not to get outraged. Not to say anything until Mike had filled me in, told me just exactly what the hell he was talking about.

Mike and Ally have a small flat in the Borough, twenty minutes' walk along the river from Bankside, so we'd agreed to meet outside the members' bar of the huge gallery, up on the fifth floor. Sharon had bought me membership of the Tate just before she'd left for Afghanistan.

'You can walk around not being able to concentrate on the pints of frozen blood in Lucozade bottles because you're missing me so much,' she'd told me.

I showed my card to the security guard, before holding the door for Mike. I followed my friend into a slick, white, L-shaped room, the edges of which were lined with tasteful leather sofas and small, moulded-plastic cocktail tables. We were greeted by soft lighting and the sound of polite people enjoying themselves. The room was busy, mostly full of artsy young professionals drinking wine or well-dressed women of a certain age nibbling on olives.

I told Mike to put his cash away, bought two bottles of beer and looked around for a space. There was nowhere to sit so we walked right through the bar and out onto the balcony. Just last month the balcony had been packed every night but it was now cold enough to have deterred everyone else but us. I didn't get the impression that Mike wanted to be too close to anyone anyway. I don't know if other people spotted it but he seemed to stand out. He was on edge, his eyes flicking around the room. I could tell he was trying his best to keep a lid on whatever it was he was feeling. And he was only just managing it. I was trying to keep a lid on what I was feeling too.

Mike didn't speak for a while and I told myself not to prompt him. I was still stunned by what he'd told me and didn't want the conversation to start badly. We stood side by side on the broad balcony, leaning against the railings and looking out over the Thames towards St Paul's. Wren's masterpiece seemed huge and stately from so high up, the way it must have when it still dominated London's skyline. To its right, two lit City churches were visible amongst the tightly packed mesh of glass and steel. To the left the Eye, all of north London in front. In between it all was the river, high and silent, moving like a black snake through the city. It really was an impressive picture and two French girls had followed us out, braving the cold to see it. They stood at the other end of the balcony, clutching hold of each other, teetering on the kind of platform heels that should have required planning permission.

It was a dry, clear night, just a few dense clouds

moving like airships along the river. Mike and I leaned out over the railing holding onto our bottles to keep them from hurtling down on the people milling below. I still didn't know what to say to him. I thought about the cafe that morning, the tension I'd noticed. The sarcasm an inch over the border from the banter they usually employed to keep sane, working and living together as they did. Mike still didn't speak and I realized he wasn't going to: he was waiting for me to start. In as calm a voice as I could I asked what was going on. Mike turned to me and sighed through his teeth the way I'd heard him on the phone. He set his beer bottle down on the railing top.

'We were supposed to go away,' he said eventually.

I took the thought in, nodding.

'When we got married. It's what we said. We said we'd spend another six months in the cafe saving and then lease it out or else just let it go. We were going to go to Africa. Don't ask me why there but we'd planned it. Two years, maybe more. It was a big secret, something we kept reminding each other of, you know? We said we weren't getting married to settle down but to push each other, get more out of life. We agreed that.'

I pursed my lips and nodded. I was with him so far. 'So what happened?'

'I don't know.' Mike shrugged. 'After the wedding, Ally, she just stopped talking about it. Stopped getting excited when I brought it up. When I talked about actually doing it she said sure, OK, but why don't we put it off, just another six months? She said she liked being married, just living in London together. It didn't really worry me. I said OK, figuring we'd just have more cash when we did take off. I liked the way we were living

41

too, it was a brilliant time, but I didn't want to do it for ever. Ally said she didn't either and I believed her, I did. And she knew how important it was for me. Something I really wanted to do. Then . . .'

I let out a breath. 'Then she got pregnant.'

'That's right. She got pregnant. When she told me I didn't know what to think. It was a fluke, she'd missed a couple of days on the pill when we went away one weekend. But the thing was, she told me like it was supposed to be some happy, great thing. She told me, her face lit up, and she just left a space for me to get really excited in. As if this one thing wiped out everything we'd planned. As if the thing that I'd been dreaming of since I was sixteen was nothing. She was so psyched, so amazed and happy. But I was stunned. My first thoughts – fuck, I'm ashamed – but you know what they were?'

'You didn't know if you wanted it.'

'No. I did know. I knew very well. I didn't. One day maybe, one day definitely, but not *then*. But I couldn't even bring up termination or anything. Ally was just so far down the road, you know? Mentally. Right away I could tell it was unthinkable, so much so that she didn't have a clue that I was considering it, that it was the first thing that came into my head. I should have said something.'

'But you didn't.'

'I couldn't. She was so happy. I felt like a twat. I went along with it. I told myself not to say anything I'd regret. I told myself to take the thought in. Give it a chance, you know, not say something that I'd regret, that would never go away.'

'But nothing changed? You never got round to being happy about it?'

'No, I did! I actually did after a couple of weeks. And properly happy. I thought about it. I saw us in Kampala, or Addis Ababa, yeah?, getting on a bus with the baby in a sling. Cool young parents. People do travel with kids. It would have been great. But when I brought that up Ally said no way. Like I was crazy to even mention it. We have to wait, she said. Do it later. When the kid's at fucking college! Eighteen years and then we'll be old, we won't do it. And even if we do, I can't wait. This is my life. It's my *life.*'

'And you've spoken to her, told her that?'

Mike's laugh was dismissive. 'I've tried. She says we just have to catch the ball that fate has thrown us.'

'She has a point, Mike. I mean, before, when she first told you, when you could have changed it, I guess not. You could have done something. But now? *Now,* Mike?'

'I know. Shit, I know. I love her. And I love the idea of having a kid with her. I told myself it was OK. I've been pretending it's OK for months, pushing the feelings down. But this is just going to cut out a slice of my life. One that I really need to feel like I'm me. It'll be gone. And the closer it comes to Ally having this kid makes me feel like I can't accept that. I just can't accept that I'll never have those two years, have them to live or have them to remember. I'll always resent her. Even more than I do now.'

Mike stopped speaking for a second and looked back across the river, a bitter, taut expression curling his face. I kept my eyes on him. Mike is a tall man, six-one or two, with the long scruffy hair of the Seventies'

Chelsea players he has often expressed his wish to be. He usually has a slightly bumbling, impossible to dislike demeanour, that makes men want to buy him a pint and women take him home to Mother. It wasn't there now, though, and I wondered whether I'd ever actually taken the time to get to know Mike. On his own. Thinking about it, I'd always been friends with Mike and Ally: not with Mike, or with Ally. Mike 'n' Ally, like a sun strip on a Capri. I'd met them both on the same day, at the same time: in their cafe, Mike asking me if I was new to the building or just visiting; Ally chiding her boyfriend to leave me alone, that it was my business why I was there. I'd been part of their lives. I'd got to know their story. How Ally had come to the building looking for a studio to make her jewellery in. How she'd put the jewellery on the back burner and come to work with Mike, turning his cheap and cheerful sarnie joint into a little powerhouse, the heart as well as the stomach of the Lindauer Building.

I knew that Ally was honest and easy to tease, the way people who only think the best of others often are, and I knew that Mike was laconic and very generous with his time and his friendship. But what I was really familiar with was the energy they put out together. The fact of their being together in my mind was probably what made the idea of them breaking up seem so wrong. I'd lose them out of my life. Even if I saw them separately, I'd lose them.

There was also the fact that Ally was pregnant. Whatever Mike thought he couldn't walk out on her now. Could he? If the answer was yes, then, even though I'd met him eight years ago, the day I moved into the Lindauer Building, I definitely didn't know him.

Mike was staring straight ahead, looking right down the barrel of the decision he had to make. I put a hand on his arm.

'Look at it another way,' I told him. 'Christ, I accept what you're saying. You must be terrified, but no one gets to do absolutely everything they want to do in life. And you can't blame Ally. She's going to be missing those things too.'

'But she doesn't care! OK, if she'd said, shit, I'm up the duff, oh no, Africa's out, what a pisser, that would have been different. I never would have made her have an abortion. But she stopped being excited about the trip months before.'

'You think she did it on purpose? Got pregnant?'

'No.' Mike shook his head in frustration. 'Not consciously. But yes, in some way. Some way that women get when they're round about thirty. That made her forget to bring her pills when we went away for the weekend. I don't know. Something else inside her was stronger than the dreams we had. And because of that she gave me no choice, none at all. I'm tied to this.'

'You shouldn't think of it that way. As something that's just going to be restricting. I'm sure . . .'

'You're right. It doesn't have to tie me down. I do have a choice. That's the terrifying thing. That's what's horrifying me, pushing me towards doing something so terrible, something I'd never for a second imagined I could do. That choice, Billy. The fact that if I want to go to Africa I can. I can do it. All I have to do is be a bigger bastard than I ever thought it was possible for me to be. All I have to do is get on a plane.'

'You can't.'

'No? What else do I do? Go to the baby club with Roger and Caroline? Always book a holiday in a place where they've got a kiddies' club and a nice safe beach?'

'No. You only think you have to live like that. I don't know but maybe you can have what you want. Give Ally time. She might agree to go away in a year or so. You don't know. And you don't know what you're going to feel in five weeks' time either. That kid you'll have . . .'

'Will just represent everything I've given up.'

'No,' I said again. 'Just because most people have kids in a certain way doesn't mean you have to. Talk to Ally. Let her know how crucial this is to you. You'll have to modify things but you can still get everything you want. The child will be yours as much as Ally's so you've got just as much say as her. And if you don't get what you want it's your fault for not pushing for it, for not going for it. You can't blame other people for your own life. You can't blame Ally. And you can't blame the child you're going to have together.'

Mike's eyes welled with tears and his jaw trembled. He was being broken apart in a way that I could never understand. I didn't know whether what I'd said had any relevance. I just didn't want him to leave his pregnant wife. For them, for the baby, and also for me. Tears rolled down Mike's cheeks but I couldn't tell whether they were out of love for Ally or of anger at her and the position he was in.

Mike lifted his hands to his face and an odd thing happened. Odd because I can still see it so clearly. Mike's elbow brushed his Budvar bottle, which was standing on the edge of the railing we were leaning on.

The bottle tottered. I watched as it pivoted, in slow-mo, then spun on its base. The bottle straightened and then, just when I thought it was about to right itself, the neck lurched towards the huge space in front of us and the whole thing tipped over. I seemed to watch the bottle for ages but then, in one of those strange, unbidden surges, my arm rushed forward and my knees dropped. My hand darted through the thin, black bars of the railing. Between my little finger and the very bottom of my palm I caught the bottle just before it plummeted to the ground below. I looked down at the tiny figures there, moving like cells in a Petri dish, saw the suds disappearing towards them. I looked up at Mike.

'Christ,' he said, his mouth open, looking over the railing. 'I could have killed someone. I could have killed somebody.'

I drew the bottle back towards me slowly and set it down on the concrete floor.

'Be careful, Mike,' I said.

Chapter Seven

Fifteen minutes later Mike and I were walking alone the river towards London Bridge, a cold east wind making us squint. We strolled past the Globe Theatre, white as a goose in the night air, and then under South-wark Bridge, where a man dressed as an Elizabethan clown was singing an Oasis song, accompanying him-self on a lute. It got a pound coin from me. When we emerged I looked out over the Thames, the dark sur-face spotted with light. It was high tide now and the water was moving in shifting eddies, not knowing which way to turn.

I'd managed to persuade Mike to tell Ally what he was feeling. Give her a chance to respond. I told him that Ally loved him and wouldn't want to stifle him in any way. Mike said he'd try to put a clamp on his feel-ings, for now at least, and hold onto the love he had for his wife. He still looked a mess, though, dread stamped on his features as I wished him goodnight. He said he was going to speak to her that night, as soon as he got in, and I thought about the conversation they were going to have. I really hoped that Ally would be able to reassure him, help him through the doubts he was feeling. Ally and Mike were so right for each other. Anyone who knew them could tell that.

After Mike had gone I thought about a cab but decided to walk home, back towards the Tate, then over the new foot bridge, again wondering why they'd seemingly decided to model it on the interior of an Eighties' wine bar. I carried on past the cathedral and up through Clerkenwell Green to my flat. It only took thirty minutes: London can sometimes be a lot smaller than the traffic in the daytime lets on. I emerged on Clerkenwell's fashionable Exmouth Market and walked along to the side street at the other end and the former photographic studio I've lived in for eight years. All the way I was thinking of Sharon. Having Mike's problems thrust into my face as well as Jemma's really made me want to see her. I couldn't wait for these treacle-slow days to go by, couldn't wait to be standing at the arrivals' gate, scanning the weary faces for two fresh green eyes. The three months she'd been away had gone pretty quickly, I'd even enjoyed the pain of missing her, for the certain knowledge it brought with it. But I couldn't believe these last two weeks were ever, ever going to end. I suddenly realized that, like Mike's, my life was also going to change dramatically. Unlike him, I wanted it to.

I spent most of the next day back at Loughborough Junction looking for Denise Denton. It was the coldest day of the year so far and I saw a few hats, quite a few scarves, people beginning to cover up in inverse relation to the trees. I heard a lot of Eminem, banging out of passing cars, watched a wino drink himself unconscious on White Lightning, and bizarrely, I caught a glimpse of Prince Charles in the back of a sleek black Jag. I didn't see Denise, though. She wasn't around and neither, fortunately, was the hooker I'd tangled with. I passed out more photos and told myself that was about the end of it. I had something more important to look into.

At six-thirty I was standing at the bar of a pub on Islington's Liverpool Road. I was waiting for Detective Inspector Andrew Gold, and he didn't keep me long. When I saw him struggling through the door with his briefcase I ordered him a pint of Stella. By the time he'd made it through the crowd, mostly men watching the football highlights on a wall-mounted TV, the pint was sitting on the bar with lines of white foam running down the sides. Without even looking at me Andy lifted it and sank it down to a couple of inches. He slammed the glass back down on the bar top and let out a long, growling belch, before looking over my shoulder. I turned to see a table of four men getting up to leave.

'Get us a pint in, Billy,' Andy said. 'I'm fucking parched.'

The Rising Sun was packed and it took me a while to get the barmaid's attention again. I spent the time looking round the pub I used to frequent four, five, even six times a week. It hadn't changed. There was no espresso machine, no list of New World wines chalked up above the bar. The clientele wouldn't have stood for it, they wouldn't have countenanced the removal of the chipped, wood-effect Formica tables or the replacement of the booze-encrusted, red-paisley carpet. I wondered why every coppers' local I had ever set foot in was a fleapit. There was a bright, clean boozer round the corner that would have made the safest of havens for any number of rapists and drug pushers because no member of the Queen's constabulary would ever have set foot in it. Entering the Rising Sun was like walking into a diseased lung.

I carried the drinks over to Andy, who was sat at a small round table in the corner where no one would notice us unless they were really looking. Andy had finished his pint and took a long pull of his new one.

'Fuck, that's better,' he said. He pulled open his tie like a condemned man pardoned just before the drop.

'Bad day?'

'Oh, you know.'

'Not any more. Tell me.'

'Usual crap. Middle-aged woman down Lea Valley way tells some kids to stop sitting on her car. Instead of saying yes, miss, sorry, miss, they gang-bang her, chuck her in the canal.'

'Lovely.'

'S' what I thought. Girls as well as boys, you believe? They all helped. We bring in some suspects and she identifies them. She's like positive: posse of black teenagers, you know the type. Haven't spent long enough in school to have learned more than four words each and two of those are mother and fucker. We're happy, of course, but the only problem is they can't have done it. They mumbled something about being in Old Street, which I took to be a crock of shit, but there they are, on CCTV. The woman just shrugs. She thought it was them but she just wants someone to blame, any stroppy black twats. So today we collar some more and she says it again – that's them. And this time it might have been but how the hell do we know? Jesus, Billy, I think you were right to jump ship.'

'I think that too.'

'Yes, well. You certainly look all right on it. You're even thinner than the last time I saw you, you cunt. When was that?'

'A year ago. Maybe more.'

'Was it? Anyway.' Andy ran both hands back through his black, glutinous hair, reminiscent of a cormorant caught in an oil slick. 'I've had a terrible day, so I hope you appreciate the inconvenience of continuing to discuss police business once my shift is over.'

'I do, Andy, I do.' I'd known this was coming. 'Here.'

Detective Inspector Andy Gold was not the first person I'd called in my efforts to find out background on the murder of Josephine Thomas. I had other contacts on the police and I'd tried two of them first, but one was on holiday and the other, a woman named Coombes, was on a course. She was back Monday and I could have waited but I'd tried Andy instead and he'd agreed to meet me. Who knows? Maybe I actually wanted an excuse to see my former partner. Maybe I wanted to see the kind of man I might have become.

Andy stuffed the three twenties I'd palmed him into his back pocket and then stretched, showing me a full Scrabble board of filled teeth. He smiled.

'Thought you might be calling me.'

'Oh?'

'Not my case but I heard about it. Recognized the name of your building. Victim's parents was it, hired you?'

I shook my head. 'A friend of hers. Another girl from the building.'

'Whatever. Nice little earner for you. Fart around a bit, tell 'em you're getting somewhere but you need a bit more cash. Unless you think you can do what twelve murder detectives and thirty odd beat boys can't?'

'No,' I said. 'The friend's just in the dark, feeling powerless. I said I'd try to find more background for her, that's all.'

'Well, I've got that for you. Got some piccies too. And I hope you're not thinking of eating later or getting laid because these are quite likely to put you off doing both for quite some time.'

Andy pulled his case onto his knee and played with the combination. Two young women in office clothes squeezed by us and Andy waited until they were past to hand me a hard-backed A4 envelope. I slid my hand inside and pulled out a selection of photographs, which I looked at as discreetly as I could. The first was of a girl lying naked on her back on a mortuary table. The lighting was bright and uncompromising, showing me one deep stab wound in the girl's side accompanied by five or six shallow, superficial slashes. The stab wound was purple and small, more like a puncture than a fatal wound. The skin surrounding it was a fading, bloodied yellow like raspberry jam stirred into custard. The snap was taken from the side but there were others taken from the top, the other side, the feet and head, the photographer's flash gun finding its way into each and every pore and fold of the girl's flesh.

'Nice, huh?'

'Very. You're not on this, you said?'

'Me? No ta. Carpenter – remember him?'

'Carpenter?'

'Humourless fuck. Pen-pusher, brings the *Guardian* into the station but you never see him look at it.'

'I remember. Just surprised he ever came to head a murder. Personal hygiene issues?'

Andy nodded. 'The only roll-on he's ever used is a car ferry. He's got his lot working like tossers doing stuff that's never going to get them anywhere.'

'Didn't mind you copying the file?'

'Would have if I'd told him. Not much point, though. I can give you everything Carpenter's got in two words.'

'Being?'

'Fuck and his good friend all.'

'Really?'

'Really. No weapon. Found the girl's purse but that's it.'

'Prints?'

'Sure, but no idea whose. He's got nothing else and he's starting to panic, especially as some helmet'll probably crack it when a junkie caught with a bag of H shops one of his mates. You want a Scotch with that?'

'I'm all right.'

'OK, but you don't mind if I get myself one? Looking at PM photos does tend to bring a thirst on. Here.'

'What?'

'Look at the size of her.'

'So?'

'I've got a theory. It's a new terrorist group. They're Muslims, ultra-thin Muslims.'

'What?'

'I reckon they've issued a fatwa. A fatwa! Yeah, geddit? A fucking fatwa!'

While Andy was at the bar I went through the rest of the pictures, all the time filtering them into the kind of thing I could talk to Jemma about. There were reasons why the police didn't tell you things and I was looking at some of them. The next pictures were individual shots of the victim's clothing, laid out on a white background. All of the garments were blood-soaked, a white vest-type undergarment torn where the knife had gone through. Just a little rip, easy to mend. Following these I was faced with the scene photos, the glimpse under the tarp that the WPC outside the Lindauer had taken. There were ten of these in all, close-ups of the body plus wide shots that told the whole story. I remembered the expression on the WPC's face and looking at these pictures I understood it more. Jo hadn't just taken a while to die. She'd tried to drag herself out of the alley, back the way she'd come, onto the road. Smears of blood followed her to her final position. There were small black pools at intervals of five or six feet, where she'd stopped and tried to get her breath. The final one, with Jo's body lying in it, was the biggest one of all.

The last picture in the pile was a headshot of Josephine, smiling into the lens. It was a studio shot, taken for acting purposes, and from what I remembered of her it looked about as much like Jo as the slab shots had. When Andy came back I slid it and the rest of the pictures into the envelope and then skipped quickly through the typed notes that were also in there. They were photocopies and Andy said I could keep them. There was detail, the bus route, time of death, but nothing concrete bar the prints: Josephine's purse had been found in a litter bin half a mile away. I could see why Carpenter was worried and I could also see that, actually, there might be a space for me here. I spoke to kids all the time, kids on the street who heard things. If the perp was a user who'd freaked, it was just possible that I might get a whisper, one that wouldn't blow the way of a desk hugger like Carpenter. You could paint the word on the street in bright yellow letters ten feet high and he still wouldn't see it.

'You sure about this? Just a mugging gone wrong?'

'Me?' Andy laughed. He'd been gazing through the smoke haze at the two office girls. I saw them checking us out. One looked Japanese and she smiled shyly. 'I'm not sure about anything. Not my case.'

'But that's what's being said?'

'At the moment. Anything wrong with that? She didn't have any enemies, except the thin Muslims. Just unlucky walking home. Shouldn't have been alone, not in Dalston at that time of night. Perp sees the girl, sticks her and robs her. Her purse was gone.'

'I know, but why do that to her? Hit her with something maybe, threaten, but stabbing her?'

'Billy! Some cunt three days cold, not enough cash for the candy man! He doesn't think like you.'

'I know. You're right. But there's something. I don't know. Her coat was open. When she was found, in the scene shots.'

'So?'

'Seems odd. In the middle of October?'

'She couldn't be bothered to button it from the bus? It wasn't far.'

'It was pretty cold that night.'

'Doesn't matter, she can't be bothered with the fuss of undoing it again in five minutes. Or – what am I saying? – she was being mugged for God's sake. They were after her money. He stabs her first and then searches her.'

'Yeah, you're right. I'm just picking at the edges.'

'I know. But don't stop, Billy, because I really do hope you beat Carpenter to it. It'd be great to see his face if you did. In fact, if you do get anywhere why don't you give me a call? You pegging it is one thing but me doing it on my spare time's another. If that happened Clay might finally realize what a useless fucker Carpenter is.'

'You'll be the first person I speak to, Andy,' I assured him. 'Aren't you always?'

Andy nodded and then a grin appeared on his face. I thought it was at the idea of unearned glory, something he'd always been a fan of, but his gaze had gone past me.

'Now then,' he said, reaching for his case, 'if that's all, which I assume it is, let's go and see how far those sixty notes you gave me go to impressing those two smart lovelies, shall we? It's been a pretty frustrating day, but you never know, one of us just might get to bang someone up tonight after all.'

Chapter Eight

I didn't stay long with Andy. Or with Lauren, or Jenny. It was already seven-thirty and I had a date to keep. Andy tried to get me to have just one more but instead I went home, showered, and then slid my arms into a deep pink Turnbull & Asser double-cuff without a tie. Over it I pulled on a forty-year-old Gieves & Hawkes four-button I'd found in a shop up the road on Camden Passage, and which fitted me so well I was instantly converted about reincarnation. By eight-thirty I was walking down Exmouth Market again, this time away from my flat.

The evening was warmer than the day had been, something I'll never understand. I buttoned my jacket against the breeze and sank my hands into my trouser pockets. I stopped for a second outside Fred's, a cafe/bar at the top end of Exmouth Market, to sympathize with Max, the owner, who was scrubbing at the graffiti some kind soul had chosen to bless his establishment with the night before. He turned to say hi to some locals walking into the already humming bar and then we both looked down the street at the probable culprits: a group of ten boys and girls from the estate on Margery Street. Mouths open, seemingly invertebrate in fake, over-sized Tommy gear. They were all smiling, one of them buzzing Max with one of those really witty pens that send out a red laser beam. Max held a hand up against it and dirty laughter burst out of them like a squeezed blackhead. I let out a breath, thanking God Mike wasn't there. Fourteen years of self-sacrifice and you end up with that. The comedian with the laser pen turned it off as I moved towards him.

When I got to Moro, Exmouth Market's top, chic eatery, I stopped and looked through the window, pulses of relief running through me. Relief because I wasn't looking at slab shots with Andy Gold or going over Mike's domestic woes. I smiled to myself in anticipation of the night I had planned, the night I'd had planned for two weeks now. The events of eight months ago had put a serious dent in the relationship between myself and the man I consider to be my best friend. I'd started them by going out with his sister and ended them by persuading a Maltese crime lord not to kill him. Things had been strained between us but now that we'd done more talking than Ricki Lake and Oprah stuck in a lift, all we needed to do now was to go out on a big one. To eat well and drink well. To buy over-priced champagne for under-dressed women, one of whom Nicky would probably take home, the other I'd end up boring to death about my distant girlfriend. This was something that would definitely make treacle time go by, as would the hangover that was even then rubbing its hands together in anticipation.

I waited at the smooth, steel bar for my friend and hoped he wouldn't be long. I couldn't shift the grim pictures of Josephine Thomas's last movements from my head; added to that I had Sharon to think about. There had been a message from her when I'd got back from seeing Andy and she'd sounded strange, her voice betraying distance beyond the literal. Maybe it was because of seeing Mike yesterday, but her voice had watered the vague irrational doubts that I hadn't even realized were within me, but which had sprouted up like weeds. Would she come back and tell me, sorry, she'd made a mistake? Would I lose her again, just when I thought I'd got her back? I told myself I was being stupid. I ordered a cold Spanish beer and watched the barman get it with the anticipation of a Tuareg herdsman looking up at a bank of gathering rain clouds.

I downed half the beer and thought about Mike. He hadn't called, which I told myself was a good sign. Then I told myself it was a bad sign. Admitting to myself that I had no idea what kind of sign it was, I turned to see Nicky making his way through the thin crowd lining the bar like David Niven's moustache.

I couldn't believe it. I was dressed as I was because Nicky has the sort of dress sense that would have had Cary Grant fiddling with his tie. Not today. He was wearing a pair of old jeans and a sweatshirt with a rip in the sleeve.

'Fuck me!' Nicky chuckled as he ran expert fingers inside my lapel. 'You could have said.'

'You mean you could have said. You normally get dressed up to go down the chip shop.'

'I know, I know.' Nicky was laughing now. 'But I figured you'd be your usual undercover self.'

'Undercover self. Charming.'

'I didn't want to look like your accountant. I could go home and change.'

'I'm hungry. Sit down. That's if they let you stay.

But don't walk too close to any of the tables. People might think you're the bus boy.'

'Get me a drink and shut up. And don't think that wearing that admittedly fine suit makes you look anything other than an unconvincing extra in one of those shite British gangster movies. Anyway, a beer? I thought we were going out. Excuse me, my love, can we have two vodka martinis please?'

We ate at the bar. The food was good and the red slid down easy as a kid in velvet shorts down a polished oak banister. Over coffee I told Nicky about Jemma and about meeting Andy Gold. He was more interested in what was going on with Sharon and I told him I'd find that out when she got back. Nicky picked up on my doubt and told me to stick at it, and I remembered the troubles that Mike and Ally had got through a couple of years before they were married. How they'd split up, but had to keep working together. How Mike had hooked up with an ex and how Ally had had a brief fling with Andy Gold of all people. They'd got through all this and come out the other side, only to face more stress now. Nicky narrowed his eyes, his look telling me there was something he thought he knew, and had done for a while.

'It pissed you off that, didn't it?' Nicky smiled at me.

'What did?'

'Ally. Her and Andy Gold.'

I couldn't see any point in denying it. 'Too right,' I said. 'And not because of Mike. Something had to give. But I mean her and *Andy*. You've met him?'

'Oh yes. But women don't actually care what men look like. Not really. Something that should be of great comfort to you.'

ADAM BARON

'Why, thank you. It still amazes me that she did it,
though. With him! I really judged her at the time. I
don't know why. I mean, it's not as if you've never slept
with a girl I didn't actually think much of. I don't judge
you, so why should I judge Ally? Because she's a
woman?'

Nicky shook his head. 'Because, Mr Rucker –' he
turned to me with his arms folded – 'you were jealous.'

'What?'

'You were jealous. Because when she slipped it was
with that no-mark, not your good self.'

'Bollocks.'

'I'm right, but don't feel bad about it. You can't help
fancying your mates' girlfriends. Take you and me.'

'You. And me.'

'That Sharon, now she . . .'

'*Alert. Warning. You are entering a highly dangerous
area.*'

'Hey.' Nicky held his hands up, his smile even
bigger. 'It's not my fault I can see she's stunning. If I
didn't know there was something wrong with her I'd be
in like Flynn.'

'Wrong with her?'

'To paraphrase Groucho Marx: I'd never want to join
a club that would have you as a member.'

'I see. Oh, look, the bill. Blimey. Somehow it all got
put on your credit card. How the hell did that happen?'

It was four a.m. and we standing outside a club deciding
what to do next. We were caned. We were 24-carat, full-
fat, Ivy League hammered. Mike was with us. He'd
called just as Nicky and I were walking out onto the

Market. I'd thought straight away that it was another cry for help. One which I would heed, however pissed off I'd be. Instead Mike told me he was embarrassed, really embarrassed, that he just couldn't believe the way he'd acted yesterday.

'I'm calling to apologize, Billy. I feel like such a twat.' I could almost see him shaking his head. 'Things are pretty intense at the moment. I've been working too hard, I think. You really put me straight. Ally and I had a great chat. I'm really beholden to you and I was wondering – can I buy you a few pints to make up for yesterday? Ally said I should go out, won't get many chances soon. How about it?'

The question surprised me. I was relieved Mike was OK, but I didn't want to impose my friend on Nicky. But Nicky could read my thoughts and he put his thumbs up.

'Tell him to stick a suit on, though,' Nicky called out. 'Then you'll look like my minders.'

We'd met Mike in Soho, in a bar that was full of 'well pukka' fellas and trainee IT girls, so we didn't stay long. After that Nicky took us to the Soho House on Dean Street, where most of the British film industry were standing around looking at each other and where Nicky informed us that he had a not inconsiderable amount of cocaine about his person.

'None for Billy, though,' Nicky said. 'He fell into the cauldron when he was a baby.'

After an hour at the House Nicky'd decided that he knew too many people and there was a new place he wanted to try. We walked up Wardour Street to another members' bar and as usual I tried not to be impressed. As a former purveyor of high-class narcotics

and the current owner of a hip Smithfield bar and restaurant, Nicky gets into all the places he ever wants to
go. I have my own network of after-hours booze haunts
but they tend to be below porn shops or up badly lit
stairways over cab offices. Lacking the vases of gar-
denias and the pretty girl to sign you in. In contrast,
Sixty-Two was a smooth, tastefully lit, first-class lounge
with a restaurant attached. We walked up a flight of
stairs and down a long thin corridor before Nicky produced a swipe card, which he used to open the door. I
expected to see a team of hard-working rocket scientists
on the other side of it but I didn't. Instead we were
greeted by a large, busy room with a pale wooden floor,
covered by low leather sofas and even lower smoked-
glass tables.

'What are we drinking?' I asked.

'Champagne,' Nicky said.

'Excellent.'

'And absinthe.'

'Oh dear. By ourselves? Or with even more of your
very, *very* closest friends?'

'That, my smart chum, remains to be seen.'

Mike and I sat at a table while Nicky went to use the
toilet, not for its intended purpose. Or yes, actually, for
its intended purpose.

The celebrity count was lower here, down to Geri
Halliwell and that guy from TV whose job it is to spend
a hundred quid redecorating people's living rooms.

Mike drummed his hands on the top of his thighs
and scanned the room. When we'd met him he'd been
like a wild horse let out of a trailer and he hadn't
calmed down any. I didn't think it was just the Gian-
luca, as he called the coke, and I wondered if his chat

with Ally really had smoothed everything out. I was going to ask him but Nicky came back and then the waitress came over with a champagne bucket and three glasses of green liquid, which Nicky set about cooking up with the professionalism of a hardcore smackhead.

We were having a great time, though it wasn't quite the night I'd expected. In spite of the chemical help it was far more low key and I had the not unpleasant feeling that this might well be one of the last times that I'd ever go out like this. It wasn't just that Mike would have a child soon. In the future I would want Sharon to be here as well. Nicky too was far more mellow than I'd ever known him. We weren't running around, pointing out girls to each other, trying to hook glances from across the bar. Neither of us had any desire to do that. In fact we'd probably have spent the rest of the night on our own if Ruth and Heather hadn't asked if they could share our table. Heather, she told us, was a PR, with the requisite blonde dye job and little black dress. Ruth was an American film exec over on business.

Nicky instantly perked up, sliding the charm on like a silk shirt. He ordered more champagne and was generous with his stash and after an hour or so Heather's curvy, comfortable body was snuggled nicely into his. This left me talking to Ruth. Mike had succumbed to the inevitable and was fast asleep, his head on his chest in the corner.

All of a sudden it was the night I'd expected. We seemed to have gone back at least five years. We drank three bottles of champagne, and made several trips to the toilets in ones or twos, remembering too late that once you start on the stuff you have to keep starting. Nicky was engrossed with Heather and I too was enjoying myself. Ruth was funny and sharp, and it felt good to be able to talk to her, and find her attractive, with the knowledge that I wanted nothing to happen, I wasn't forever thinking about which way it was going to go. I told Ruth about Sharon because I thought it was only fair but she didn't seem bored to death. So much so that when the lights came up she asked me if I knew another bar where we could go. Nicky suggested his: the Old Ludensian. It was the natural place and would have everything we needed, but Ruth had another idea.

'So you really are a PI, that wasn't just bullshit?'

Nicky kissed the side of my face, like a Labrador.

'He is! He left his trenchcoat at home, that's all. He'll call you schweetheart in a minute and slap you around.'

'No, he looks too nice.'

'Don't believe it, he's so tough he uses that tooth-paste that tastes of TCP. I've seen it in his bathroom. Look at him, being strong and silent.'

'That's the absinthe.'

'Well, if you really are a PI we should go to your place. I've never been in a PI's office.'

'And neither have I! I can't believe it! All these years. We can go to my place after.' He turned back to Heather. 'I own a bar. Did I tell you?'

'You told me!'

'A very, very cool bar. I own it. Did I say?'

'My office? You really want to?'

Ruth put her hand on my arm. 'You got anything to drink?'

'Whisky,' I said.

'Great. Anything to sit on?'

'Some chairs, a sofa bed.'

'That'll be like a davenport?'

'What?'

'A couch that turns into a bed. If you want it to?'

'If you want it to.'

'Then let's go,' Ruth said.

The night air hit us like a truck. In the back of the cab Ruth settled in next to me. Earlier I'd noticed a wedding ring on her left hand. Seeing it there, I'd felt invulnerable in a Frodo Baggins kind of way but its power didn't seem to be as strong as it had been. No, I was safe. I knew what I wanted to do. Nicky and Heather clearly did too because they were practically doing it. Mike, meanwhile, had fallen asleep again, facing backwards, impervious to the car horns and the jolts and the corners. His head was knocking gently against the window, stubble rash raw on the jowls that were beginning to blur his jaw line. He wasn't ready. That was the simple truth. I wondered if I ever would be. Again I thought of Sharon and the message she'd left. Here was I, my emotions running towards her like a flood tide, but what was she doing? I had a flash of her in an expat embassy bar, with some floppy-haired Oxbridge foreign correspondent telling her how much he cared about the Afghan people as he filled her wine glass. Shit. The cab swung onto a roundabout and Ruth's hand curled round the top of my knee.

Outside the Lindauer Building we all made to clamber out but Mike said he wanted to take the cab on home. I was the only one who tried to persuade him not to. I wasn't sure why but I wanted him to come in. Your last night, I said. Mike didn't look sure at all but eventually he agreed. Ruth's smile looked a little forced. Again, the air hit me, right in the stomach this time. We all walked towards the gate, the security bar down across the entrance, a low-watt bulb burning in the little booth next to it. I told everyone to keep the noise down but Mike said not to worry.

'He's asleep, the useless sod. Look at him. Ron, half man, half chair.'

We all laughed. Even through the booth we could hear the sound of snoring. Ron sat with his arms folded and his neck right back, his mouth wide open like a goose in the rain.

The Lindauer Building stood in front of us, dark and impassive. It usually gives off an impressive quality of permanence but on that occasion it was moving slightly, from side to side. We set off towards it and Ruth stumbled into me.

'I've got you,' I said, keeping her upright.

'Good,' she replied. 'Have I got you?'

I laughed for an answer, pretending I didn't know what she was talking about. I could feel her hip on mine and the side of her breast against my chest as she held onto me. Mike stumbled ahead of us and I suddenly wished he hadn't come in after all. I didn't mind Nicky knowing, he was still living on the same planet as me. But no, I wasn't going to do this. Was I? No, I wasn't. Pulling my keys out of my pocket was a good excuse for disengaging myself from Ruth. I found the lock somehow and called the lift. From behind me came the voice of Nicky Spade.

'It was 4.21 in the a.m. The building was dark as an empty grave. The two broads wanted to see where I worked and, hell, that was fine by me. I got paid by the day. The brunette was tall, willowy as a young tree and you sure wanted to have a climb. I was with the blonde and she was hot as a stolen Caddy.'

In the lift he carried on. It was rubbish, Dick Van Dyke bad. And very funny. The lift jerked upwards and my stomach lurched like a dishwasher. It was coming in waves now and I tried to stare through it, running a checklist through my arms and legs to make sure they were still part of the team. When the lift stopped it made Ruth stumble, propelling her into my arms again, and for some reason this was the funniest thing that had ever happened, ever. Once more I could feel her, her breasts not quite as full as Sharon's, her legs a little longer. When the lift doors opened our little slip was overtaken in hilariousness by the fact that Heather, who had been leaning against the doors, fell right out into the corridor.

Nicky helped Heather up and we all followed Mike towards the cafe, and my office. Heather's fall had actually had the effect of bringing her round a little and she moved ahead of us, with Nicky.

'I walked 'em along the corridor. The lights were dead as . . . something that had been killed. A long time ago. Through the window at the end of the hall the moon looked like a rock of crack in a velvet glove. Hey, that one's not bad. We were drunk as Shane MacGowan on Dean Martin's stag night. Billy's mate Mike had more booze in him than Al Capone's bathtub. He was up ahead, his keys jangling in his hand like a dead man's bones. The door said Sanctuary Cafe. The blonde wanted mixers but I had all the juice I needed right next to me.

'Big Mike turned the key and gave the door a push. Then he stood in the doorway, not moving. Then he moved. Backwards. "Hey," I said, "quit stalling." Then the big sap dropped to his knees. Helping him up wasn't going to be easy, but then I'm a guy who likes things difficult. When I got to Mike I . . .'

I looked past him into the cafe. There. There was blood, blood covering everything. Everything. Everything. The whole place was covered with blood. And there was a girl. She'd . . . She'd been . . . she'd been cut up, she'd been all cut up. Oh, Jesus. Oh, sweet heaven.

It was Ally—

Part Two

Chapter Nine

The world had changed. It would never be the same. Ever. Nicky's face told me that. The rest of my life would be lived in a different space, a different time. Everything before that second was wiped away.

When I stepped past Nicky and looked into the room, I couldn't see Ally's face because Mike was holding her, drawing her up into his arms. There are six tables in the cafe, all covered by laminated table cloths. The biggest of the tables is circular, about four feet in diameter, and Ally was lying across the centre of it on her back, her legs hanging down towards me. I couldn't see her face to begin with but I didn't rush to her like Mike did, I didn't try to give her the kiss of life. It wasn't that I could barely move. It wasn't that every last ounce of breath had been knocked out of my body, that my throat felt like it was being bound by piano wire. It was because Ally's death was more evident, more certain, more complete than anything I have ever seen. I couldn't do anything but stand, to be flooded by what I was seeing, my mind clicking the reality of what my eyes were telling it into place, slowly, one piece of information at a time. Then it stopped, refusing to accept anything else. Shutting off, blocking out the very last piece of information it was receiving, not able to process what my eyes were sending it.

There should have been noise. The room itself looked like it was screaming. All I could hear was my heart. Mike was saying something, I could see him. But all I could hear was the thumping inside me.

When Mike drew away, to look at Ally, to stroke her hair, I finally saw her face. Ally looked unconcerned, one eye rolled back into her head like she was bored. The other was staring at me, a brightly coloured marble full of blood. Her lips were painted blue. Ally had been strangled. That was the first thing that had been done to her. The first thing. The hands that Mike tried to place around his neck were clenched into tiny fists, the two thumbnails blue also. As he held his wife's body, Ally's fists banged onto Mike's back, looking to me like she was desperately trying to get him off her.

I saw all these things, but not in the way I've just described them. I was too far gone, the booze and the drugs like a gauze, filtering everything. I tried to leap into the moment but something in me, not just the alcohol, kept me drunk, hobbled. A chemical reaction more than a man. I tried to fight it, claw my way into the present, but when I got near I found that I couldn't. I couldn't push right through. I couldn't let it into my life. I tried harder, I tried to see. I still couldn't move. Not my feet, my hands, my lungs or anything.

Ally's one eye was still fixed on me. Her hair was stuck to one side of her face. She was red. Everything around her was spattered with red. The table Ally was lying on, the floor beneath it. Mike's hands were red, his face, his shirt where he was holding her. My hands were stained, and my shirt too, because I'd moved, I'd

74

tried to get hold of Mike, to get him away. Blood spots had found the chairs, even the walls somehow, and they all revolved round Ally. They all came from her. Moving back from Mike I stood still again, blows raining down on me like a fat fighter who can't respond. Mike was kneeling on a chair, still lifting Ally, speaking her name, shaking her shoulders, kissing her blank face.

Something told me that I had to do something. I had a flash: this was a crime scene. Mike was trashing a crime scene. I tried again to pull him away, ignoring his elbows, his kicks, his screams, which I could hear now. Finally I stopped. What was the point of it? What good would it do? Instead I fumbled for the phone and hit three nines but nothing happened. Of course. The world had stopped. It couldn't go on any more. Not past this. My eyes found the socket and saw that the cord had been torn out. I used my mobile instead.

I heard screams from the corridor. Annoying, irrelevant sounds. Mike's words were also unreal. He kept speaking Ally's name as he kissed her face, as he pressed his lips against hers. Ally still looked unwilling, slipping out of her husband's arms like a virgin pawed at by a fat prince. What was he shouting for? Didn't he know she couldn't hear him? The noise he was making was unbearable, bursting out of a mine of pain so deep he didn't sound human. I couldn't bear it. Again I thought about getting him into the corridor but I couldn't. My hands would no longer reach out to him. He was somewhere else. Another dimension. Instead I found myself backing away, right out of the room, and I wanted to keep going, so far back that the room was just a dot, the doorway far too small to see inside.

Nicky stepped aside for me. He was standing in the

corridor, unable to do anything but stare into the cafe at Mike, practically wrestling with the body of his wife. I stood beside him. Once again I knew that I should act, grab Mike, comfort him, anything. But instead I saw my hand. I saw my hand reaching forward. I saw it push until the door clicked shut, leaving Mike and Ally in the cafe alone. Instantly I felt better, until I heard the girls again. They were huddled together, still screaming. I wanted to shut them up, to bind their mouths or else shove them in there with Mike. And then go home. Instead I leaned back against the wall and slumped slowly down it to the floor as Nicky did the same. We stared at the back of the door. At the handprint I had put there. It was thick and clear, the pressure of Mike's embrace having restarted the flow of blood from Ally's body. Two lines began to detach themselves from the print, like a cut wrist. They started to speed up and then were racing, overtaking each other as they ran down to the floor.

Chapter Ten

I don't believe in fate. Most of the time when people use the word fate they really mean chance. We met in Hawaii and we were both drinking pina colada, and his mother's name is Betty too. It was fate! No, it was chance. As far as fate goes I'm a sceptic, but when the first police officer to arrive at the Lindauer Building that night turned out to be Andy Gold it seemed like fate had sent him.

Andy had been in the station all night taking confessions on his gang rape and was on his way home again when he heard the call go out on his radio. Andy might well have ignored it if he hadn't recognized the name of my building. He was alone when he ran up the stairs to the third floor and found us huddled in the corridor, the girls screaming louder at the sound of his footsteps. Andy pushed the door open gingerly and looked inside. Within ten minutes he'd been joined by thirty of his colleagues, flooding into the place like a drug injected into the veins of a patient when it's far too late.

Ally is dead. Ally is dead. The knowledge kept scrolling round in my mind. Nothing else got in. For the next hour everything else was a blur. Every possible light was on, questions were being asked, people were being calmed down. Mike was being brought out into the corridor. He was lost, he didn't know where to turn. He made a bolt to get back to Ally but the uniforms who had brought him out managed to get hold of him. When he realized that they weren't just taking him out of the room, but out of the building, he struggled harder, kicking and punching until a medic stuck a needle in his leg. When they eventually took him along the corridor towards the lift he was still conscious, just, looking like it was him who had been stabbed. Ruth and Heather scurried away from Mike as if he had the plague.

Ally is dead.

I don't know how long I stayed in the building. I was a mess. This new world I lived in was horrible, terrifying. I wanted the old one. I found myself taking only short, small breaths, shaking my head every time I saw Ally's face, trying to keep the image out. Her eye still looked at me. I was cold, shivering. Andy took me into my office, keeping Nicky and the two girls outside. He asked me what happened. He was patient, but insistent. Somehow I managed to get past the three words that were pounding into me to tell him where we'd been that night, what we'd been doing. He wasn't taking notes, just wanting to get a picture. When I told him about the absinthe and the champagne it all surged up inside me and I nearly puked over the desk. I just held it together. Andy asked me if champagne and absinthe were all and I said no, telling him how good the coke was. He smiled and said that when all this had died down I'd have to get him some.

'Coppers' rates, of course,' he said.

We were in there what? fifteen, twenty minutes. I

78

knew it wasn't over, though. I wanted my bed, I wanted to sleep and to wake up and for this not to have happened. But I knew I wouldn't see my bed for a long time. Andy led me out of the office. The brightness backed me up, making me shiver again. Nicky, Heather and Ruth were all gone. In their place, in front of us, four officers were crawling along the corridor on their hands and knees towards the lift. I couldn't help thinking they looked quite funny. You won't catch him going that slow, you'd better get a move on. The officers had white coverall suits on with hoods up, paper slippers over their shoes. Andy started to walk me along the hall.

'Come on, Billy.'

I couldn't move. Andy took my arm but I pushed back against him. The door was open. The door to the cafe. Up ahead. Andy glanced at me and then signalled to the two plain-clothed detectives standing just inside the opening. When they didn't get it instantly Andy made it obvious and they stepped inside and shut the door behind them. Andy helped me on. He wanted me to keep to the left side of the corridor and I tried to help him. But the absinthe had risen again, it didn't care what the hell else was going on. I had to hold onto Andy. Andy's arms felt strong around me. I wanted them to take me, to lift me, to fall asleep in them as they got me out of there.

But when we got level with the door I stopped again. I looked at it. My print was already drying, like a child's picture. Behind the door I could hear muffled sounds, movements.

Andy shifted his weight under my armpit to move me along. The last, deepest level of drunkenness was calling to me. It was high tide for sure now but something was keeping me back, struggling against it. Something in me knew that I had to fight the booze, just for one minute, no more. I pulled myself up, a hand thrust out of the swell. I turned to the door. I heard more sounds. I knew what would be happening in there. I could see it all as though there was no door in the way. The plastic envelopes, the thermometer, the masks. A flash of light lit up the bottom of the door, followed by another. The photographer. The video would be later. I heard movements, low voices, another click and another flash of light.

'Tell me,' I said to Andy.

'Billy?'

'*Tell me,*' I said again.

Andy shook his head. He was confused. 'But you were there, Billy. You were in there. You know.'

I saw it all again. I saw Ally, saw her face, her hands. Saw her body. The blood.

'Just tell me. Say it. You say it. I . . . I don't know. I thought but . . . I don't know. I couldn't . . . Tell me. Then I have to know.'

He did. He told me what I'd seen the moment I'd stepped into the room.

He told me what I'd turned my eyes, my mind, my whole self away from.

My body began to tremble. Andy took my arm again and led me along the corridor. In the lift my legs went and Andy had to get another officer to help me out and into car. In the car I shook and cried and I threw up and cried and threw up more, all over the seats and me and Andy and then finally I just curled up into a ball. The absinthe was still fighting for me and I wished to God that I'd let it win an hour or so earlier. That it had left me in some alley on my back for the muggers or the cops or just the morning to find me. Because however close it would come it would never win now, it would never beat the picture, never beat what I'd seen.

Chapter Eleven

The station they took me to that night was the one I'd worked in for most of my career. Calshot Street, a step away from King's Cross, is one of the few remaining genuine Victorian nicks, complete with painted brick walls and interview rooms so dingy and cold you'd confess to anything just to get out of them. I know this because I'd not only harangued people in them for some sort of truth, I'd also been on the other side of the desk. Most stations now are more like leisure centres than lock-ups, with the Coke machines in the foyer and the rounded, blond-wood furniture. In contrast Calshot Street still retains that oppressive, flat feel, the aura of a building most people spend their entire lives hoping never to enter. The feeling of a building nobody wants to be in.

I say nobody, but one man I knew relished his role as grand inquisitor so much that he positively rubbed his hands together whenever he walked through the door of the nick he was in charge of. Chief Superintendent Kenneth Clay is a huge mound of a man with a sharp, quick mind and tiny eyes so keen you think they can see into your pockets. When they took me out of the car and into the station, I saw Ken Clay going in before me. Clay is a hands-on copper, not likely to let something like this fall through one of his junior officers' grasp. He won't have been pissed off to get the call in the night – his heart rate would have gone up like mine had in the toilets of the Soho House. Strangely, I was buoyed by the sight of Clay, both in the Lindauer Buiding and here, hurrying through the door, briefing a breathless DC on the hoof. He'd be nasty, sly, he'd make Andy Gold seem pleasant as Cliff Richard on E. But he'd sort this. Whatever else Clay was he was too much of a copper not to absolutely have to sort this.

It was still dark, no sign of the sun. I was taken through the main door of the building, coppers and the general public alike drawing back at the sight of a man whose impeccably cut suit was liberally decorated with tears, blood and vomit. In a dank, featureless interview room I gladly surrendered the suit, my shirt and my shoes and was given a faded T-shirt and a pair of old jeans in return. Once inside them I sat, my elbows on the desk in front of me, my mind crammed full of static, unable or unwilling to fix on anything, like a TV that can't find a station. The only thing I was aware of was the uncomfortable glances of a PC, sitting in a chair by the door, his face blank, his palms on his thighs. Neither of us said anything until we heard footsteps outside the door. The PC stood and unlocked it. I looked up to see Ken Clay bustling in, Andy Gold on his heels.

When Clay sat down, all signs of the chair beneath him disappeared so that if you'd come in right then you might have thought he was levitating. I sat up a bit, my stomach rolling at the sight of my former governor. I remembered again how we used to call him Condor. Condor Clay. Not because of the graceful flight of the bird but because of the way a condor goes about eating a dead animal. The condor wants to get at the guts. The guts are, of course, hidden inside the animal but the condor doesn't make itself a hole in the corpse to get at them with its beak. It uses the one that's already there.

I didn't for a moment think that Clay was going to pussyfoot around so his first question surprised me.

'So, Billy, Christ. Are you OK?'

It was what I'd asked Jemma. It was only then that I realized what a pointless question it was.

'I don't know what I am,' I said. 'Where's Mike?'

'He's not here. They've taken him off to UCH.'

'UCH?'

'He's OK, don't worry, but he's freaked out. He's in shock, or so they say. They've sedated him and they won't let us near him.'

I nodded. 'That's all right. You don't need to hassle him. Speak to him when he's ready. I can give you it all. There's nothing I can't tell you.'

'OK. Good.' Clay nodded to the PC, who slid a tape into a desk-top recorder. 'So tell us. Take your time, and if you need to stop it's OK, Billy. We're in no hurry.'

'I won't need to stop.'

'OK then.'

The PC hit the record button and then activated a camcorder fixed high up on a wall behind the two detectives. It was angled high but I figured it would just get the bald spot that sat towards the back of Andy's head like a shallow bunker in the rough. I took a breath. I tried to find a voice, a character who could tell all this, go through all the stuff I'd already blurted out to Andy. I settled on the voice I used to use in court: the polite copper, unemotional, rigorous. It felt odd that way, already making the events I was telling seem like history. Things that had actually *happened*. As I went on it became more disconcerting, largely due to the expressions on the faces of the two men right in front of me. It was pity, but not the right sort. Not pity because of what had happened to my friends but a different kind. As if I was telling them how great my wife was when they already knew she was sleeping with someone else. I was confused, their smug patience needling me towards anger. When I got to the end a soft, wistful smile settled on Clay's face and Andy smiled too. Andy thanked me for my candour concerning the coke. He assured me that no action would be taken on that score. But then he shook his head.

'Very touching, Billy.'

'I'm sorry?'

'Earlier, in the pub. I asked you how long it had been. You remember?'

It seemed like a lifetime ago. 'Yes. But . . .'

'I meant since we'd seen each other but it's been even longer since you were a cop, hasn't it?'

'I suppose.'

'So I shouldn't really be surprised at what you just told us. Not really. But I didn't think you'd ever stop thinking like a copper, Billy. It seems odd that you have.'

'What are you talking about?'

'You said you'd tell us what happened.'

'I did tell you. What did I just do? You think I don't want to help you here? She was my friend. Of course I do. We went out, we ate, then Mike came. We did coke, we drank. We met the girls. We went back to my office. Heather wanted mixers so Mike opened up the cafe.'

'OK, OK. We got that. But do me a favour. Try

85

answering like a copper. Think back. Who suggested going back to the Lindauer?'

I frowned. 'Ruth. Yes Ruth. I don't know why, some romantic notion of—'

'Anyone else keen to go?'

I frowned more, thinking about it. I did want to help them. Maybe I had skipped stuff. But how could it be important? 'Nicky,' I said. 'He was. Then we were going to go to his bar after.'

'And what about Heather?'

'She was keen enough, didn't seem to care either way. She'd have done whatever Nicky wanted. Why?'

'And you?'

'Me? I didn't mind. It was a laugh, we were all just getting blown along. Wherever we went it didn't matter.'

'And what were you intending doing up there? In your office.'

'Drink, mess about, finish the stash, I guess. Andy, I'm trying to help, but I really don't know what you're getting at.'

'Got a bed up there, haven't you?' he went on. 'You and Nicky were in, weren't you? You'd have probably stayed there while they went on to his. You and Ruth, the tall one?'

'No. You're wrong. By what does it matter? I can't see why it's relevant what I was going to do . . .'

Andy didn't seem to be paying any attention to me. 'Five of you there. Odd number, no? With you four in pairs Mike was a bit of a gooseberry, wasn't he?'

'Not really, we were all having a great time. As I say I wasn't intending . . .'

'Did he seem happy about going up to your office? Like you all were?'

I thought about it. 'No. Actually he wanted to go home, to take the cab on.'

'Did he now? So why did he come up?'

I shrugged. 'I persuaded him to.'

'And why did you do that?'

'I don't know. Oh, all right, maybe so that he *could* be a gooseberry.' I tried to laugh. 'Protection, you know, so I wouldn't do anything. I wasn't intending to but it couldn't hurt, could it, having Mike there to make sure?'

'Because you're seeing that girl again. Sharon, isn't it?'

'Yes, but I don't see—'

'Answer me this. Like a copper. OK? Mike was reluctant to go upstairs. Why?'

I shook my head. 'I don't know.'

'He knows you're seeing Sharon, right?'

'Yes.'

'I'd have thought he'd be keen to go up, keep you out of trouble. As a mate. But he wanted to go home. I wonder why. I wonder why he was so keen, *desperately* keen, not to go up to the third floor of the Lindauer Building this morning. Can you think of a reason, Billy?'

There was silence in the room. I hadn't seen it coming. Without any warning Andy's words had smashed straight into me like a lump of concrete thrown off a motorway bridge. I couldn't speak. My eyes opened and my throat closed. All I could hear was the tape machine whirring. I began to feel sick again. I couldn't believe I'd let Andy lead me where he had.

'There's no way,' I managed to say. 'Don't waste

87

your time on that.' I tried to laugh again. It sounded like an animal being strangled.

'No? You said that Mike phoned you, asked if he could join you and Nicky on your girls' night out. Right?'

'That's right.'

'Well, tell me what he said on the phone.'

'I told you. We'd just had dinner when he called. He wanted a blow out. A big one. Ally told him to go. His last chance.'

'His last chance?'

'Before the baby, the baby.'

'What time did he call?'

I shook my head. 'Ten, ten-thirty.'

'And what was he like?'

'Fine. He was normal.'

'And when he met you?'

'The same. No different.'

'The girls said he was behaving strangely.'

'We all were. We were mashed. Fucked. Wine, beer, coke, absinthe, champagne.'

'Yes, but they said *he* was all over the place. Something in his eyes. They also said you practically had to force him to go upstairs.'

'He wanted to go home, to Ally.'

'He didn't want to go back there, more like! Knowing what was waiting for him. What he'd already done.'

'No!'

'Calm down, Billy. And tell me this. When he found her, when he opened up the cafe tonight, what did Mike do?'

'He was distraught. He held her, put his arms round her.'

'Which means we can't pick up any latent blood on him. He covered himself, so to speak.'

'That's insane. Crazy. OK, as a copper, tell me why. He's going to have a baby, he's got a lovely wife. Go on, why?'

Andy smiled that smile again. I wanted to ram it down his throat. 'When did you see him last?'

I hesitated. Andy would check. Someone from the Tate would have seen us.

'The day before yesterday. At Tate Modern. We met for a drink.'

'What did you talk about?'

'I don't remember. Nothing much. It was just a casual thing.'

'Nothing personal?'

'No.'

'Was Mike a jealous kind of man, Billy?'

'How the hell do I know? You only know that about your partners, not your friends.'

'A good point. A copper's point. But, I wonder, did he ever find out?'

I knew what Andy meant but I looked confused. 'About what?'

'About Ally. Ally and me. I've filled Chief Superintendent Clay in on our little affair. Was Mike ever filled in?'

'I don't know. He never told me if he was.'

'What if he suddenly found out, huh? That wasn't what you talked about at the Tate, was it? Or, since our fling was years ago, did he think she was seeing someone else? Did he have reason to believe that kid was someone else's?'

'No. No. She wasn't seeing anyone and he didn't think she was. We didn't talk about that.'

'Then what did you talk about?'

I thought again. I shook my head. They were wrong.

'Nothing. Listen, you were a mistake. They were just having problems then. Ally loved Mike. And he loved her.'

'Think like a *copper*, Billy. You do so well and then you blow it. How many times did you hear people sticking up for their friends, their husbands, their brothers, just like you're doing now? Think. You asked me to tell you and I'll tell you again. The baby: it's gone. *Gone*. There was nothing inside her. You saw, remember?'

Andy looked at me, making me acknowledge what he'd said. I wanted to turn away from it but I couldn't. I felt Andy's breath as he leaned forward.

'You know it's got to be someone close to her to do that. Someone seriously screwed in the head. Not just some killer. You know, Billy. Statistics alone say it was him but we've got more than that.'

Everything inside me stopped. Andy's eyes were wide open, gauging my reaction. More. What more? No. Whatever it was, no way. I knew Mike. I knew how he was with Ally. Only the other day, his arms round her, joking about Chelsea. I saw him on the Tate balcony but pushed that aside. Finally I summoned the courage.

'What more do you have?'

'You don't know? About your friend? Three years in a young offenders' institute? Called them borstals back then. Well? Never told you? Just flipped, the records say. And he never mentioned it, well, well. Nearly killed a boy, some stupid fight over nothing, when he was fifteen. Kid teased him in a shopping centre. Never leaves you that kind of thing. Found out Ally'd been shagging someone else and he lost it again.'

'No. He didn't think she was being unfaithful.'

'You know what?' Andy smiled. 'I always thought you must have given it to her at some point or another. That bun in her oven, you the baker were you?'

'Go fuck yourself.'

'Be more fun than doing it to her was, I can tell you. I thought Italians were supposed to be hot but she was insane, cut my back up so bad . . .'

I tried to get over the desk but the PC got to me. When I was back in my chair again Andy carried on. Beneath it all, beneath the horror I felt at what had happened and the disgust I felt for Andy, I couldn't help thinking he was good, damn good. He was the bad cop all right and he didn't need the good cop.

'Your problem is that you think women are saints, Billy. I could tell at the time you thought she was too good for the likes of me.'

'Her and any woman not on death row. And most of them.'

'Good one. But women do sleep with inappropriate people sometimes. That Sharon. Your brother Luke's fiancée, isn't she?'

'Was. She's not now.'

'But if medical science ever comes up with a way of bringing him round he won't be too happy about it, will he? No. Face it, Billy, Ally was seeing someone else and Mike found out. In some spacked-out rage he attacked her, did that thing that you saw. I saw.'

I turned to one side, then the other. Andy was trying to bind me with string. 'Josephine Thomas. Two women from the same building—'

'Sorreee. DI Carpenter's put that one to bed. Just today, I was going to call you. Good piece of police work. Picked up loads of junkies on possession charges and fingerprinted them. One matched with the wallet that was found. Young lad, lives on the next estate. Bloodstains on a T-shirt in his drawer, you believe? And what's a simple mugging victim like Josephine Thomas got to do with this? A baby stolen from a pregnant woman?'

'Ok, it hasn't, but it was someone else, someone—'

'It was Mike! Jealousy, it's the biggy. A woman gets killed, look at the partner. And it happened close to home. In their bloody cafe! So what I want to know is did he say anything to you, about Ally, about any fears he might have? At the Tate, or the days before? Did he ever confide in you?'

'I was there, in the cafe. I saw how he was. He didn't know. And he was crushed. It *wasn't* him.'

'Not answering, huh? Well, I was there too. And my take on him's different, probably because I'm not his mate. I even spoke to him. Whispered in his ear, with Ally lying there. She was a nice girl, Ally, I liked her. Great tits: those ones that point upwards if you really never did get to see them. I was there and I thought husband straight away. I probably shouldn't have but I told poor Mike straight off I knew it was him.'

I closed my eyes and opened them again. I knew that my world was different but I suddenly thought about Mike's. His world was gone.

'Bit cruel, I'll admit, but honestly it just seemed

right. Why should I be gentle with someone who could do that. *That*. "Pleased with yourself?" I said. I even asked him where the baby was.'

The question hadn't even occurred to me. Pictures came before I could shut them out.

'Not going to ask me what he said? Well, he told me as a matter of fact. He told me straight away.'

The silence in the room was so sudden and cold it stopped my heart. No. He couldn't. Andy's eyes were boring into mine, his face hard, the mocking levity nowhere.

'In heaven,' Andy said, answering his own question as he sat back in his chair. 'You believe that? He told me it was in heaven. Been listening to too much Eric fucking Clapton if you ask me.'

Chapter Twelve

A nervous young PC ran me back up to Exmouth Market. It only took five minutes. I hadn't expected it to be light, like when you come out of a matinee. A yawn shot through me as though it had been waiting for that moment to escape. I gazed out at the streets as they passed, staring at them like a tourist coming in from the airport. A young, exhausted-looking lad was pulling his sleeping bag from the doorway of a chemist's, two uniforms standing over him. A lone artic pulled up at the lights and hissed like some huge animal. The PC didn't say anything to me, pretending to concentrate on his driving. On Rosebery Avenue I told him where to pull over and then mumbled a thank you as I pushed myself out onto the street.

I watched the car move off and then walked the few yards to Exmouth Market. Andy's words were ringing in my ears. It was Mike. I remembered the feeling inside me when he'd told me Mike knew where the child was. The shock. The fear that Mike might really have done it. It was similar to the shock I'd felt when Mike had called me at the gym. His words, so unexpected. But no. Mike hadn't left his wife in the end. He'd just been scared. And, whatever Andy said, he hadn't killed Ally.

None of which changed the fact still seared across the front of my mind. Ally was dead.

Even though it was cold, I stood gazing down the empty street towards Moro. I had an image of myself from what seemed like a horror film: walking down to the restaurant. Then I saw myself and Nicky, joking as we came out. My phone ringing. The images continued into town, to the Sixty-Two club. All the way to the Lindauer Building. They continued into the lift, but that's where they stopped. The doors wouldn't open. I thought of Nicky, and of Heather and Ruth. I wondered how were they dealing with this. I allowed a wave of self-pity to run through me at the thought that this wouldn't be so bad for them. Nicky knew Mike and Ally but not like I did, and the girls didn't know them at all. I wanted to crumble, to fall to the floor right there. But I didn't. I knew that if I did I'd be finished. Instead I took a deep breath and tried to focus.

I remembered something I'd seen once. I'd stopped my car on the motorway, fascinated to watch a bridge being built. Enormous cranes were being used to pour liquid concrete into huge, cast-iron moulds. In spite of the way I was feeling, that's what I had to do. Seeing Ally had emptied everything out of me. Clay and Andy had finished the job, leaving just a shell. I wanted to fold in on myself but I couldn't. I had to fill myself with concrete. Mike could do the pain. He could do it for both of us. His grief would be big enough. What would mine be compared to his, anyway? No, I had to harden myself. Let the concrete make me strong, let it help me do the only thing that was left, the only thing that would make the future anywhere near worth living.

Identify him.

Find him.

Not just that.

Find him before anyone else could find him.

I stood on the Market a little while longer, wondering why it was so quiet, before realizing that it was Sunday. The only sign of life came from the Catholic church to my right, a red-stone edifice with a bell tower that on a sunny day makes you think you're in San Gimignano, if you squint just right. The doors were ajar and there was movement inside. A young priest came out to sweep the steps, clenching his jaw against a yawn, his eyes watery. He looked up when he saw me and smiled. He said good morning but then straightened, the look on his face changing. He held his broom by his side.

'Do you need to talk to someone?' he asked.

Yes, I thought, the bastard who did that to my friend. I turned away from the priest and walked towards my flat.

I spent most of the morning sitting at my desk, pointing my eyes out of the window, across the junction at the end of Exmouth Market to the Mount Pleasant sorting office. I was paralysed. I thought with scorn of the naive, fired hope that had been my sole emotion for the past few weeks. I watched people walking past, some with their arms full of the Sundays, and self-pity came back as I wondered how they could have escaped so lightly. Why my life had been blown apart like it had. I felt vindictive towards them. I saw a man answering his mobile and hoped that it was news, news that would crumple his face, send a huge shard of grief into his guts like the one sticking into me. The wish only made me feel worse, ashamed. I thought again about Ally. How drunk I'd been, how I'd defiled the fact of her death by being too pissed to really take it in. The shame grew, paralysing me even more.

I wanted to break free from it but I didn't know how. Clay had told me not to go anywhere near my office. He was heading the investigation, with Andy as his number two. He said that he was keeping my name, as well as the other witnesses, out of the papers. He said he'd get Andy to fill me in on what the tech boys came up with, what the CCTV showed, knowing I'd only get someone else to tell me anyway. And he said that he wasn't going to waste his breath telling me not to go after whoever I thought was responsible. He knew me too well. He just told me not to get in his way. He also wanted to know what I came up with. Whether it pointed away from Mike, or right to him.

Even though it was Sunday, red postal vans still shot in and out of the depot. A shift changed. Sunday city silence bellowed round my flat. I saw Max opening up Fred's, hands on hips as he inspected another daubing of graffiti. At some point I heard the bells of the Catholic church, backed by a distant peal from St Paul's, like a memory that sits beneath a repeated moment. I thought of Mike, whether he was still at the hospital. Just as he had been in the cafe he was still in a different space from me, far, far away. Andy would come back to me with the forensics report but until he did I tried to think of something, anything, that would be worth doing. I couldn't. There was no space for me, no roads to walk down that weren't full already. The machine I'd once been part of would be rolling. Police officers would be swamping the Lindauer, grilling the few people who showed up on a Sunday to work. Others would be fingertipping through gardens, nearby school grounds, scrabbling through the bushes in Highbury Fields, praying that they wouldn't be the one to put their hand behind a dustbin and find it.

I found it strange to think of so much activity only a few miles away. I pictured the residents of the streets surrounding the Lindauer waking to find police officers at their doors, asking if they had seen or heard anything out of the ordinary. Gathering their dressing gowns around them when they were told what had happened. I saw the reporters who would be hassling detectives for comment, saw them perk up as Ally's body was removed. I saw people, with nothing better to do, stopping to watch before getting bored, looking back in case they missed something. I was very aware of myself, doing nothing, listening to each breath go in and out of my body, aware that somewhere, maybe somewhere not too far away, someone else would be going over the events of the previous night. Would be seeing it all again. Somewhere someone's mind would be as full of it as mine was.

Frustrated by my inactivity, I eventually stood up. I moved the table I was sitting at further into my living space, back beneath the other window. That left the entire west-facing wall blank, but for a framed Salgado print Sharon had given me for Christmas once. I took that down, slid it behind my sofa and fetched a ream of white A4. Using Blu-Tack I covered the now empty wall with it, from the floor to the ceiling. When I was done I did what I'd done so many times in the incident room at Calshot Street. I fetched a magic marker and uncapped it. In the centre of the blank space I wrote a single word. The victim's name.

Ally

I capped the pen and stepped back, thinking of what to write next. Other words, words that were connected to Ally, could perhaps be connected to her death. Words that might lead my thoughts somewhere, begin to open them up. I stood for ten minutes. I couldn't think of anything. Not one word. I couldn't see anything reasonable, rational, work-outable, that could lead back to what had happened. So I wrote nothing, Ally's name sitting there on the wall alone, surrounded by emptiness.

But I had to do something. Turning from the wall, I picked up the phone and dialled Nicky's number. The phone just rang. I looked around the flat and was aware, for some reason, of the state of it. Old newspapers littered the floorboards and I could see fluff balls where the table had been, clinging on to the phone cable. A line had been crossed without my having noticed it. I threw out the newspapers before dusting the table and the window sills. After that I Hoovered, hoping that I wasn't waking my downstairs neighbour, currently a film maker whose career seemed to consist of sitting in Fred's drinking cappuccinos.

With the living room spick and span, I had a go at the kitchen, washing the sides down and cleaning the hob. I tipped out a year's worth of crumbs from the toaster and pulled from my message board countless fliers and cards for concerts and private views that had happened months ago.

When I was done I sat by the window again, looking out onto the street. It was pre-dark, that empty, graphite stillness that always used to frighten me as a child. I felt like I should get some air, but I found that I couldn't. Nor did I have any desire to eat. What I knew I needed was sleep but that was the worst idea of all. Awake, I was in control. I didn't know what sleep would bring.

Instead I tried to call Sharon. Even the thought of her voice was like a salve spread on my heart. I dialled her number. Her last message had said that she was away, in the north of the country, but she might have come back. I looked at my watch, trying to remember the time difference, wondering if it was fair to tell her about Ally on the phone. I didn't get a chance to find out: the phone just rang, that long, international purr, repeated. I knew it was no good but I didn't hang up. The sound was comforting. I couldn't speak to Sharon but somewhere, halfway round the world, I'd made a phone ring, ring in a room that held her things. I tried to picture her clothes, her bed not made, some of the books I'd sent her. I lay on my sofa listening as Sharon's phone called to her like a hatchling, looking at the sky.

I closed my eyes and imagined that Sharon wasn't away at all. That she was in the other room. Not just that but we were living together. She'd moved in with me. I'd never had that thought, not even two years ago when we were a lot closer than we were now. But as soon as I had it, it seemed so right. We lived here, or somewhere else, it didn't matter. Sharon was in the other room. She was working on a brief for the morning, her glasses on, shrouded by orange lamplight. She'd come through in a minute and settle next to me, in time for some documentary she wanted to watch. She'd try to concentrate but I'd be bored. I'd put my hand inside her top and then I'd push it up and she'd say, oh, Billy, stop it! but I wouldn't stop it because I'd know what she really meant. And then I'd be kissing her stomach and her thighs and pulling her pants down as she tried to set the video and we'd be laughing and joking and wrestling with each other and then we'd stop the joking and be kissing and she'd be calling out my name.

Chapter Thirteen

I came to suddenly but without drama, the way you sometimes do when you didn't know you'd fallen asleep. My eyes were closed and I kept them that way, staring into a hot red. I tried to remain still, not wanting to do anything to break the spell, the amber stillness encasing me like a prehistoric fly. But already I could feel it fading. I opened my eyes, surprised by the amount of light flooding into my flat. Then my eyes locked onto the word, sitting on its own in the middle of the wall in front of me.

I let the knowledge rush in, not trying to stop it, to fight it with disbelief. My mouth felt dry and the back of my throat was burning. The presence of the hangover felt rude, disrespectful. I blinked into the light and then sorted the sounds I could hear into pieces. Traffic, like a BBC tape. A car horn. People laughing on the street, their laughter moving past. Something else? I reached around for the phone and found it on the floor by the side of the sofa. It was still ringing. They can't have had the cut-off we do. The wall clock told me that it had been ringing for twelve hours straight. I hit 'end' and then pushed myself up onto an elbow, feeling so heavy I was barely able to make it.

I hadn't dreamed but my mind can't have been idle

while I was out of it. I knew this because, sitting in the centre of my mind, there was a realization which I'd had no hand in coming to. It was as if someone else had snuck inside my head and left it there for me to find. I looked at it, turning it round and round, amazed that it was there, but more amazed at its simplicity. It stunned me. I tried to turn away from it but I couldn't. It was too obvious. However much I wanted to, I was unable to deny it. I'd been a policeman long enough to know that people are capable of acting way out of character. Or within characters they've kept perfectly hidden for years. What other feeling could have driven someone to such a double murder other than the belief that both parties had done wrong? Not, as Andy had thought, by committing adultery, or being the product of it. But by being pregnant and being the product of that. Think like a copper, Billy, think like a copper. I saw Clay and Andy looking at me with that expression on their faces. I didn't know if they were right, but I did know how I must have sounded to them. I thought what I'd have been like ten years ago. I wouldn't have done it the way Andy had, but I would have thought what he thought. I knew I would. And even if I hadn't been certain, I'd have had to accept the likelihood of it, the possibility. What had changed? I suddenly remembered something Andy Gold had just said to me. He'd called Mike my best mate. But Mike wasn't that. He was a good friend, yes, but without Ally what was he?

I got up shakily. I walked towards the wall with Ally's name written on it and I stood for a minute, thinking about it. Again I tried to turn from it, deny it, but I couldn't. I just couldn't. I picked up the magic marker and next to Ally's name I added Mike's. As soon as I began to write a heavy plumb line of disappointment began to sink right down to the bottom of me. When I was done I looked at the two words, together as usual. Horrified to my core that they were together in this way.

Stumbling into the kitchen I pulled the blind and set the kettle on the stove. I felt sick, leaden, as though I'd woken up on a different, far bigger planet. While the kettle creaked up to the boil I thought once again of the Lindauer Building. Monday morning. All those people showing up to work. I thought about pretty, sunny Jemma, a confused look on her face as she approached the cordon. What now? Then thoughts of Mike deepened the sickness inside me. What was I going to do? When I'd been sure that Mike was innocent I'd known exactly what I intended doing to Ally's killer if I found myself in a position to do it. The certain knowledge that I wouldn't flinch had been comforting. But what would I do to Mike? If it was him. I didn't know. I didn't even know if he'd been interviewed yet. For all I knew, forensics could already have proved he'd done it. I suddenly realized that he'd never actually denied it. What I'd seen as grief could easily have been remorse. Had he already confessed? I walked back into the living room and picked up the phone.

Andy had just got into the station. He asked me what I had and I told him that I hadn't even left my flat since I'd seen him. He told me there was no trace of Ally's baby. So far. CCTV was still being gone through. Mike was still at UCH and forensics were ongoing but Ron, on the gate, had been able to establish Mike's presence at the Lindauer at about the time Ally had been killed. I nodded. Then Andy asked me again if I was sure that Mike had never expressed any concern about Ally to me, any sort of jealousy or problems with his wife. I held the phone in my hand for a long time, taking deep breaths in and out, until Andy asked if I was still there.

'He didn't want it,' I said eventually. 'The baby. It made him feel trapped, he said he wasn't ready. It was supposed to be a mistake but he suspected Ally had done it on purpose in some way. He was freaked out. He was on the point of leaving her.'

'Thanks, Billy. Thanks. You could have told us that yesterday but thanks anyway.'

I hung up and then searched myself for traces of guilt for having helped Andy's case against my friend. I found quite a few but ignored them straight away. Mike wasn't my friend, not if he'd done that. A last flash of certainty rose up, outshining the logic, telling me it wasn't him. I turned from it. The clock on my kitchen wall told me it was nine forty-five. I drank two cups of coffee and showered. I dressed quickly and then packed my bag before walking down the stairs to the street. It was ten-thirty by the time I'd tricked my car into starting. By eleven I was standing outside the estate that Josephine Thomas lived on and where she had died, a quarter of a mile south of Dalston Junction.

Thirty-six hours ago I'd let shock, horror and friendship blind me to what was standing right in front of my eyes, while Andy Gold and Ken Clay had behaved like policemen. They'd used judgement and experience to assess what was most likely and then looked for motive, opportunity, proof. Simple police work. But there was another side to investigating something thoroughly. It was never allowing the obvious to make you lose sight of the hidden, the maybe, even the seemingly impossible. Two women from the same building had been killed in the space of ten days. The killer of one had been found, and the crimes seemed totally different from one another, but the fact remained. Two women from the Lindauer Building had been murdered.

I didn't have any illusions as to why I was chasing it down, though. I didn't think they were wrong to go full steam for Mike, not now. But even if they were wrong, the idea that someone was stalking women from the Lindauer Building was a hell of a long shot. It might have been plausible if both women had been attacked in the same way. Or if they had anything else to link them. But, as Andy had just confirmed to me, Josephine Thomas had been stabbed only once and then left to bleed to death. Her purse had been taken. There were no obvious links with Ally, and the kid the police had looked perfect for Jo's death anyway. The kid had been pinched in the morning of the day Ally was killed, which meant that there was no way he could have killed Jo before going on to her. I just couldn't sit in my flat any longer. I needed something to do while I waited for forensics. Even though Josephine Thomas was a near-certain dead end, her murder was an alley I could walk down. Somewhere for my mind to visit instead of the nightmare it kept returning to.

I drove along Upper Street and then through elegant, Georgian Canonbury, until the delis and the gastro pubs and the four-by-fours began to give way to Chinese takeaways and minicab offices. Structurally, Islington and Hackney are very similar, but I've always felt that to move between the two is like spending time with two middle-aged sisters, one of whom married an enthusiastic plastic surgeon while the other hit the gin bottle. Neither seems to look the way it was intended.

After twenty-five minutes I locked up the Mazda and stood, looking at the red-brick estate in front of me. The Kirkland is bang in the middle of Dalston. Josephine Thomas lived there because it was afford-able, subletting a small council flat on the ground floor of the estate. Unlike the surrounding area the estate itself looked well maintained, a Peabody project built at the turn of the century, only four storeys high in attractive, ageing brick. The kind of place that now brings top whack if it's located a mile or so west, the way I'd come. I turned from the building and walked in the direction of Dalston Lane, noticing that the hat and scarf count had gone down a little. It was another beautiful day, herds of huge white cloud migrating slowly overheard.

Andy had told me that Josephine had taken the 277 home. When I got to the nearest bus stop, where Josephine would have got off, I turned round and retraced my steps, following the route she must have taken home from there. I passed a tyre refit place and an empty greasy spoon, trying all the time to imagine the place at night. Dalston is different when the sun isn't shining. In the daytime it looks scruffy, tatty, neg-lected, but it doesn't make your pulse beat faster. At night the threat rises up through the pavements like dew. There should be a sign: Dalston Junction – twinned with Compton.

After fifty yards I turned right and once again the Kirkland Estate loomed up on my left. I was about to cross over towards it but I stopped. Josephine hadn't walked through the estate, preferring to circumvent it and come in from the southern end, nearer to her flat. A safety precaution that hadn't done any good. I walked on, took a left and came upon an alley, a concrete walkway with small rectangular lights fixed to the right-hand side about head height, twenty feet apart. On the night Josephine had died only one of them had been working. I'd have liked to bet someone that the rest of them had been fixed since then.

I couldn't see to the end of the alley because of a kink halfway. I took a look behind me at a row of Victorian houses on the other side of the road facing the estate. Most of them were pretty shabby, twenty-year-old paintwork peeling off in huge flakes, but a couple looked bright and cared for. Outside one of them a middle-aged woman was standing, waiting for a lift. I wondered if someone had stood in a similar place, out of sight maybe, until Josephine Thomas had walked by. I turned back to the cut-through, hesitated for a second, and then sent my feet down it.

The pile of flowers was propped up against the left-hand wall, just after the kink in the alley, which is why I hadn't been able to see it from the street. It wasn't a big pile, seven bunches in all, most of which had wilted. Rain in the night hadn't been too kind to the paper they were wrapped in, leaving the flowers looking bedraggled, the bunches practically merging into each other. Only a cluster of white roses was in pristine condition, the paper dry. They were set on the top of the pile and I bent down to them but there was no card. I looked through some of the other flowers and some did have messages included but I could only make two of them out. One said 'To a dear friend, we'll always miss you', and the other read 'Goodbye, lovely Josephine, from Brian and Sarah'. I pulled Andy's notes back out of my jeans and wrote both messages down.

I stuffed the notes back into my pocket as an arrow of guilt slammed into me. Had any flowers been laid for Ally? I bet they had. I hadn't even thought. Where would they be? I told myself that I had to go and lay some, but then asked myself what the point was. Would it help her in some spiritual way? Or did people lay them in the hope that flowers would somehow clean the site of what had happened? If that was the hope it hadn't worked here; in fact the opposite was true. The sad bedraggled pile just told me that something meaningless and miserable had taken place there.

I turned from the pile and looked up at the tops of the walls, thinking about the possibility of someone climbing them. They were lined with criss-crosses of twisted metal like sharp, oversized jacks. No. Instead I wondered whether the killer had followed Josephine into the walkway or had been waiting for her halfway down. I figured the latter. If I was planning to jump someone there I'd have wanted to see both ways, to make sure no one else was coming. If the kid had followed her down he wouldn't have been able to tell that, especially with both Josephine's footsteps and his own confusing things. He'd waited for her, I was pretty sure. Which meant that Josephine was just unlucky, was just the first suitable victim to come along that night.

Or maybe she wasn't. Her attacker *could* have been waiting for her and her alone. If he knew where she lived, if he knew she'd be coming past that way. If he'd scoped the route and picked the most convenient spot to attack her. If he either knew when she'd be finished, or else had tagged her from the Lindauer Building or the bus stop and got ahead of her, knowing she'd walk home the way she did. It was possible. Josephine wouldn't have been suspicious of a man striding ahead of her into the alley, looking like he was going all the way through, especially if he was wearing trainers and she couldn't hear his footsteps dying away.

I thought about it. It was far more likely that whoever had killed her had simply waited in the alley for whatever the night brought by. To test my theory I stood very still. Soon I heard footsteps. I could tell there was only one person, even though the kink in the alley hid them from me. There was no way they could know I was there. I looked away as the person passed, a guy in his forties carrying a tennis racket. He jumped a little at the sight of me and then hurried by.

So. A smackhead with the yips, three days since his last bag. My eyes moved from the flowers to the street end of the alley. I saw Josephine crawling along, stopping, crawling along, her life slipping quietly out of her like a party leaking people until suddenly it's over. Had she called out, like Jemma had said? Had someone on the street heard her, but hurried past? I didn't know. And I didn't care. I was wasting time on a case that was already closed, wondering about Josephine Thomas's last moments because I couldn't face thinking about Ally's. What it must have been like for her. Whether she had called out. I bent down to the white roses and I took them in my hands and I squeezed until the heads were crushed. Then I stood and walked back the way I'd come.

I was going to sit in Fred's with a coffee and my phone, waiting for Andy to ring. I wasn't going to hide from any more images, wasn't going to try to keep out any of the feelings that were trying to break into me. I dug my hands into my coat pockets and made it to the mouth of the alley, where I turned right, back up to my car. Across the road from me the woman I'd seen before was still standing outside one of the Georgian houses. She was looking at me. I carried on walking but stopped. I shook my head and made to walk off but stopped again.

The woman across the road was middle-aged, round, and just above short. She was wearing a cotton headscarf and both her hands were rammed into a mac, the bottom of which was being turned over by the wind like a page corner. I was puzzled. It was chilly: why didn't she wait inside? I tried to shrug the woman off but couldn't ignore the look she was giving me. Her face was fixed and expressionless, red from the cold. I lowered my eyes for a second. I pursed my lips and headed across the road towards her.

'Mrs Thomas?'

'Police? Newspapers?' Her mother's Welsh accent was far stronger than Jo's had been, from the times I'd heard it. Mrs Thomas's eyes stared straight past me.

'No,' I said. 'I just work in the building Josephine worked in, that's all.'

'Didn't bring any flowers.'

'No,' I said. 'No. I should have done. I just wanted . . . I just wanted to come. I'd like to say how . . .'

'You could have brought some flowers.'

'Yes. Yes. I could.'

'Lots of others have. Her friends. Just people. They keep clearing them away so folks can get past. What's your name?'

'William,' I said. 'Billy. Billy Rucker.'

'No, she never mentioned that.'

'I didn't know her well. As I say I just came . . .'

'Rucker. I'll remember. I'll tell the police that. All sorts of funny people come here. When I saw you I knew you didn't live on the estate. I knew you came to look. Lots of *lookers*. I bet he's come, or else he will.'

'He?'

'The one who did it.'

The woman stopped, her face tightening, her eyes almost closing. She must have known about the arrest, surely? She'd have been the first person they told.

'When you didn't bring any flowers, and you came out again, I thought it might be you.'

'Me?'

'What done it. It wasn't you, was it?'

'No.'

For the first time the woman looked at me, her eyes dark and direct.

'It wasn't you.' She turned back to the alley. 'And it wasn't that boy the police have got neither.'

'Oh? No? What makes you think that? I understand the evidence is pretty clear.'

'It doesn't matter. Evidence. They're good at that, the police.'

'Yes,' I said. 'Sometimes. But why do you think so in this case? Why do you think it was someone else?'

Mrs Thomas's smile was full of scorn. 'I asked them if I could see him and they let me,' she explained. 'Through this mirror thing. He was crying, he was. Only a baby, really. It wasn't him. I'll know when I see him. He won't be able to hide it from me.'

'And you've been here. Coming here? Waiting?'

There was no answer. 'Can I buy you a cup of tea? There's a cafe just round the corner . . .'

'No. Thank you all the same. So you knew Josephine, then?'

'I'd met her. She was a friend of another girl in the building.'

'She was a good girl, Josephine. I didn't want her to stay in London but she said she had to, being an actress and all. We argued about it.'

'I'm sorry.'

'It wasn't much. We made up. I said I'd come to see her in the West End, in *Cats* or something. When she'd made it, like. You ever see her, Josephine, on the stage?'

'No, I'm afraid not.'

'Me neither,' Mrs Thomas said. 'And now I never will, will I?'

Mrs Thomas's mouth moved up towards her nose and stayed there. The wind picked up the back of her headscarf and set it down again quickly, like a car thief checking a handle. She didn't say anything else, preferring to focus her energy on the alleyway in front of us.

I left Mrs Thomas and walked back up the street to my car, parked on the other side of the estate. The look on the bereaved woman's face stayed with me. Righteousness oozed out of Mrs Thomas, but she couldn't have been *right*, could she? The kid, innocent? It didn't look like it, not with the prints Carpenter had. I wondered if Mrs Thomas really could tell, just by looking. It made me think about Mike. Would I be able to tell, looking through the two-way at the nick? Or staring up at him in the dock? As a police officer I'd often got it wrong, both ways, but this was someone I was close to, who I'd shared confidences with. And so was the victim. I decided that yes, actually, I would. Mike wouldn't be able to keep it from me. I'd be able to tell and thinking about it, however it would make me feel, I wanted the chance.

I was going to call Andy but I'd left my phone in the Mazda. When I got to the car I did call but only got a message. I put the phone on the passenger seat and pulled out into traffic. I wouldn't go to Fred's, I'd go to the station. Mike had to be there by now and I was pretty sure I could get Andy to let me into him. I wondered what I'd feel. If I *knew*. Or what if looking at Mike had the same effect on me as looking at the kid had on the woman I'd just been speaking to? I heard her voice again, the scorn: he didn't do it. What if I knew it wasn't Mike? How would I find out who'd really done it? Would I carry on looking into what happened to Josephine? I shook my head. With everything else so completely different the Lindauer had to be coincidence. If there was anything else to link the murders, anything at all, then maybe, but as it was . . .

The traffic had moved me on twenty yards and left me at the top of Beechwood Road, the road I'd just walked up. Halfway down it I could see Mrs Thomas, still standing there. I found the idea of her vigil moving, dreadful even, but it wasn't that that had caught me. I frowned. Mrs Thomas was a large woman. Not tall but big, especially wrapped up like she was. When I'd seen her I'd realized who she was because of her demeanour, but also because of her resemblance to her daughter. Josephine was big too. She was seen as such. I remembered the one conversation I'd had with her, in the lift, how she'd made me laugh telling me about a casting she'd just been to. It was for a lucrative TV commercial, thousands of pounds involved, and they'd wanted a really big girl.

'It was probably the only room in the entire world where a bunch of women were sat around praying they were fatter than they were,' Josephine had said.

I didn't bother pulling over. I just got out and walked around to the other side of the car and stared down the road. From where I was standing I couldn't tell much about Mrs Thomas. Not her age, her colour even. But there was something else. I couldn't tell if being big was her natural state. My mind flashed to a party, years ago, a police party. I was talking to a woman I'd trained with, a woman who'd put on a lot of weight. Andy Gold turned, saw the woman and smiled. Then he asked when she was due.

'Due to punch your bleeding lights out?' the woman had asked. 'You're not so skinny yourself you know, Gold.'

There were car horns behind me, a voice asking what the hell I thought I was doing. My eyes were glued to the distant figure opposite the alleyway. Out of my back pocket I once again pulled the notes I'd made. Josephine had been stabbed through her winter coat. Once. But the coat had been found open. Oh, Jesus. They'd thought the mugger had been looking for money but everyone knows that women keep their purses in their bags. How could they have missed that? How had I? Sweet Jesus. It wasn't money they'd been searching for, not money at all.

There was more shouting behind me. I turned from Mrs Thomas to the car and walked round it in a daze. I pulled over, up onto the pavement, unable to drive further. I reached for the phone and saw that my hand was shaking.

'Billy. Where are you?'

Andy was outside. He was at a scene, by the sound of things. A siren, shouting.

'I'm in Dalston,' I said. 'I need to speak to you.'

'OK, right. You know the Rotherhithe?'

'The tunnel? Yes but, Andy, listen.'

'I don't have time. Billy, come over here. The north side of the tunnel? It won't take long from Dalston. We can talk here.'

'No. Just listen, Andy. For a second.' Thoughts were swarming round my mind like flies trapped in a bait box. 'Please?'

'OK, but make it quick.'

'Mike didn't do it.'

'Billy . . .'

'He did not do it. He didn't. I've just been to where Josephine Thomas was killed. She was big Andy, *big*. Like she looked pregnant. Especially in her winter coat. She was killed because of that but then left there, when they realized. Two women from the Lindauer. One pregnant, one who could have been. Mike didn't do it.'

There was a pause. Live static until eventually Andy spoke.

'I know.'

'What?'

'DI Gold? The fire officer wants you, sir.'

'Billy. North side of the tunnel, OK?'

'Andy? What the hell do you mean you *know*?'

'The north side of the tunnel.'

'Andy!'

'There's been another one,' Andy said. 'We just found another one.'

Chapter Fourteen

It took me forty minutes to get to the Rotherhithe, forty minutes that seemed like forty days. The traffic got worse the nearer I got. As I cut down bus lanes and leaned on my horn, Andy's words rang round my head. Another one. So it wasn't a one-off, a jealous husband. Josephine Thomas and Ally – the Lindauer was the link. It had to be. Christ – were there any other pregnant women there? I didn't know. The place was too big. I had the urge to forget about Andy and just head straight there. I pictured the building, saw the flow of people leaving later on. Or maybe for lunch, to take a stroll in the park. Someone could have been watching it, right now. Should I go? No, I needed to speak to Andy. I wondered if he'd had the same thought about Josephine. No, if he had the Bill would have been down there, at the alleyway. Another one? I couldn't believe he'd cut me off like that.

The Rotherhithe Tunnel forms a direct link with east and south London near Limehouse. If you're going down to New Cross or Greenwich it's the quickest route from anywhere east of the City, meaning that you avoid the snarl at the Elephant and along the Old Kent Road. It's an old two-way tunnel and it seems very narrow when you drive through it for the first time, the lanes barely wide enough for your car, let alone the vans thundering towards you or the occasional lorry, not allowed to use the tunnel but sometimes doing so anyway. A small mistake can lead to a major pile-up if the circumstances are right, something which happens once or twice a year, or used to when I knew anything about it.

I found out soon enough why the traffic on Tunnel Approach was so bad. The tunnel was closed. It was a crash scene that I was looking at when I finally got down to the Rotherhithe. A flatbed truck was pushing its way out of a police cordon, a mashed pile of metal on the back that must have once been a car but didn't look anything like one now. I swore as I was forced to back up to let it through. When it had passed I pulled up as close to the cordon as I could and got out. Beyond the cordon I could see shocked-looking uniforms coming out of the tunnel mouth, holding their helmets like miners after a pit fall. Traffic duty, it could give you as many nightmares as homicide. I hurried up to the tape towards a stout copper, who didn't wait for me to say anything before telling me that there was no way I could leave my car there.

'I need to speak to Andy Gold,' I said to him. 'DI Gold. My name's Rucker, he told me to come down.'

'First name?'

'Billy. Billy Rucker.'

'OK, sir, he's in the tunnel.'

'Thank you.'

'But you might not want to go down. I can get someone to let DI Gold know that you're here if you like.'

'That's OK,' I said. 'Don't worry. I'll find him.'

'If you're sure,' the copper said.

Inside the tunnel it was fairly bright, portable emergency lights glaring in addition to the strip that snaked along the tunnel ceiling. I jogged down into it, towards the sound of heavy machinery. I could see an arc of sparks streaming over the heads of perhaps ten men, standing in front of another pile of twisted metal, bigger this time, completely filling the tunnel. What was it – a container lorry and a car? Or two cars moulded into one? I didn't know and I didn't care. In an instant all of the strength went out of my legs. I couldn't move. I wasn't able to take another step, as though I was running into an intense wall of flame. People had died in this tunnel. That was immediately clear. But that wasn't why my legs had suddenly refused to work. Or why my heart was hammering inside my chest like it wanted to leap out. It was because I'd been here before. I'd come upon another sight like this, another burnt tangle of steel and tarmac like a mad sculptor's vision of pain. Eight years ago. I stared ahead of me. The way they were working, there was obviously someone in there. I didn't know who, or how many, I had no idea what this wreck held within it. The one eight years ago had held my brother. My brother had been trapped inside. In many ways he still is.

I was still stuck, physically unable to force my legs to move forward no matter what I told myself. Thinking maybe I should get the copper on the tape to fetch Andy after all. But no. I had to push through this. I had to. Time could be crucial; I had to get to Andy, and fast. Maybe it would save someone's life if I did. The thought fired me, and I forced my feet forward, casting my eyes around, unable to see through the small crowd in front of me. Memories dive-bombed into my brain but I deflected them with a question. Andy was on a murder case: what the *hell* was he doing here at a smash? Even one as big as this. It made no sense. My eyes scanned every figure in front of me but I still couldn't see him. The noise was getting louder. Finally I picked Andy out, standing to the side five yards from the wreck with his arms folded. I moved towards him, wanting to pull him aside, but my attention was drawn to the sight beyond him in spite of myself.

The violence and speed involved in the pile-up were perfectly preserved in the twisted display of charred metal and body parts. No sculptor could convey horror like this. It stopped me yet again, picked me up violently and hurled me backwards into the past. My eyes were glued to it.

'Fuck,' I said.

Andy swung his head round quickly before turning back towards the pile-up, nodding. Then he turned again and I could feel his eyes on me.

'Billy,' I heard him say. 'Jesus. I'm sorry. Shit. If I'd thought. Are you OK?'

My throat turned over. I swallowed what little saliva there was in there and shook my head to dismiss his question. 'What happened?' I said.

'Joy rider,' Andy replied. He turned his head back quickly to the crash. 'Joy rider, car full of mates. Happened four o'clock this morning.' He pointed a finger. 'That little cunt. See him? He's the only one survived. Lorry driver dead as well. These guys have been trying to get him out for the last six hours and they won't let me speak to him until they do. Another car went into the back of him but that's been shifted. Can't get any

120

lifting gear in, obviously, so they've got to cut through the truck, then the car. Slowly. They're scared the weight of the truck'll shift onto him, though why they care, the little shit.'

Andy touched one of his colleagues, who moved aside for me. Through the space I got a clearer picture. The truck was on its side. The car had slammed into the mashed-in cab like a cruise missile. The lorry driver must have tried to turn when he saw the car coming, sending his vehicle over onto its side moments before the car impacted. The car had tried to turn too but must have spun, going in backwards, which must have been what had saved the driver. The car was now the size of a small table. I tried to force my mind to stay straight as I looked at the feet twisted up in it, and limbs, none of them connected. The car was stuck beneath the cab, but also rammed up against the tunnel wall. Suddenly I saw what Andy was pointing to. A face on the driver's side. Two eyes, scared as a monkey's, darting up towards the welders working above them.

I took Andy's arm. I didn't want to look at this. And not just because of Luke. Again I couldn't believe that Andy had bothered with it. I shook my head.

'Listen. Listen to me. I meant what I said. On the phone. Josephine Thomas was killed by the same person who killed Ally. You need to seal the alley she was found in, and start thinking about the women at the Lindauer Building. Warn them.'

'It's being done.'

I stopped for a second. 'Right. Good. But I don't understand. Another one? So what are you doing here? Andy?'

I was relieved and surprised at what Andy had said

121

but still confused. And exasperated. Andy had turned his back on me. He was walking away, round towards the rear of the truck, closer to the welders trying to cut through to the trapped boy. I followed him, angry. Wanting to know what he was doing. He walked on and I sped up to keep pace, unable to stop my eyes darting to the car that was the focus of everyone's attention. It had once been blue but I had no idea what make it was. I couldn't tell. Luke had been driving a Cavalier, a silver one. My car. Just like then I found it almost beyond belief that anyone was alive inside. Luke hadn't been conscious but the boy was, trapped in a space barely big enough for his head, terror making his eyes shiver as he watched me go by. I thought that he was holding his arm out to me but I was wrong: the arm was pale, almost blue. I pulled my eyes away and followed Andy as he skirted the tails of sparks leaping out towards him and made his way towards the front of the truck.

I was pissed off with Andy but maybe he was just going to give someone instructions, leave his mobile number, and then talk to me properly. Get the hell out of there. I watched him walk to the back of the car, which had been crushed against the wheel arch of the lorry when it had gone over. I'd expected to see firemen working from that end too, but I didn't. The three men at the back of the car were dressed in civvies. All three were focused on the crushed boot. The man in the middle nodded at Andy's approach, confirming something they'd clearly already spoken about. Seeing me, he looked a little confused, but a shake of Andy's head told him that I wasn't really there. Andy stopped now. He pointed towards a whorl of red, staining the dirty white tiling of the tunnel wall.

'That's what made the fireman curious,' Andy said, for my benefit. 'He managed to get most of the lid up with a crowbar and then he called us. I didn't realize what we had until just before you phoned.'

Andy nodded towards the back of the car. I hesitated. Suddenly I knew why he was there. Why he'd come to a crash. Why he'd got me to go too. Andy nodded to me again and before I could think about it I stepped forward. To the boot. The three men stepped back, watching me. Taking a breath I looked inside.

The body was naked. It was the body of a woman, lying on its side. In the foetal position. The woman was white, had been white, her age uncertain, although I'd have guessed that she was youngish if someone had made me guess. Her height was difficult to distinguish too because her legs were pulled up under her.

And that's it. I don't have much else to say about the woman. But if this sounds like a scant description I didn't have much else to go on. It wasn't because of the blood, though there was plenty of that. The woman had had her head stove in so absolutely by the impact that there was nothing left of it. I couldn't see teeth, eyes, nose, anything, just sunken shards of skull. Slowly I moved my eyes away from it. Down to the rest of the body. I didn't want to but I did. I saw that the body was relatively untouched by the impact. But it was harder to look at than the remains of the woman's skull had been. Much harder.

'Must have stashed her in there before taking off,' I heard Andy say behind me. 'I thought she'd been stuffed in alive, that they were taking her somewhere to rape her or something. But she can't have been. Right?'

One of the three men beside me nodded. I kept my eyes on the torso and a wave of revulsion surged inside me. All I had to push it back with was the sure knowledge that this huge wreck had meant nothing to this woman. She hadn't felt any fear at the speed, hadn't screamed at the sound of a skid or felt anything as her skull disintegrated. The revulsion kicked up stronger as I realized that what she had gone through must have been far, far worse than that.

The woman had been opened. Like a tent flap. There was nothing inside her.

Chapter Fifteen

I stared at the emptiness, the lack in front of my eyes. The shock had climbed up through my stomach and grabbed hold of my throat. After it had spread out into the rest of my body, I felt cold. I ran my hands up my arms but didn't move away, trying to fix everything in my mind. My eyes stayed bound to the sight before them, transfixed almost, until a crawling sense of dirtiness started to move into me. I knew then that I was no longer learning anything. Just looking. So that I'd have to believe it. I felt small and scared, like I used to as a child, listening to the silence from downstairs that told me my father had finished arguing with my mother. That he was on his way up.

I raised my head from the woman but the sight of her stayed with me. Just as it had in the cafe, another image had burst into my mind, burst into the most private quarters there like storm troopers before I could bar the door. Andy was pulling me away and I let him, shivering, waiting for the image to fade. I wanted to ask Andy what he knew. I took three steps and stopped. The disgust and the shock were vast, but they were already being pushed out by something else. Relief. Relief was flooding in. The strange, awful relief that certainty brings. Even as I'd shouted at Andy over the phone I knew that my theory about Josephine Thomas was no more than a guess. I knew how I'd have sounded: Mike didn't do it! There's a maniac out there! I wouldn't sound like that now.

The relief deepened even as I tried not to feel it. Mike wasn't involved in this. He had not killed his wife. Anybody. I wanted to see him. Not to look at him, to try and read him. I wanted to take him home. Two days had past since he'd lost Ally and he'd been alone during that time. I was his friend, I hadn't been there for him. The fact amazed me. I looked round for Andy, wanting to say: let's find out who's doing this. But once again Andy was striding away from me, back around to the other side of the lorry. I wanted us both to look at the woman, to compare notes, force each other to see things. I was frustrated, but again I followed him.

"Ello 'ello 'ello.'

Ignoring the sparks showering down towards him, Andy strode right up to the front of the wrecked car and bent down to the pale, terrified face peering out from inside it. I watched as the sparks died. Above Andy one of the firemen lowered his torch and flicked his visor. He didn't look happy.

'How many times do I have to tell you?' he spat. 'You can speak to that boy when we get him out of there!'

'You all right, sonny?' Andy said. He didn't even glance at the fireman or acknowledge that he'd spoken. He reached in through the narrow gap and stroked the kid's face. It stopped the fireman, who was beginning to make his way down to us. 'You OK?' Andy went on. The fireman relaxed further. 'You happy there with all your mates, are you? Nice and comfy all squashed in like that?'

'Get away from the vehicle. This second.'

'Now then.' I could see Andy smiling. 'These brave fire fighters above you are trying to get you out of here. They have, however, confidentially informed me that the odds are less than good. The actions they're taking might, instead of releasing you, just cause the truck you ploughed into to shift. If, or rather when, that happens, you're pretty certain to end up looking a lot like your mates here. Or the lorry driver. He's dead as well, or didn't you know? Were they trying to keep that from you? Oops. Somebody's dad, he was. All of which should make you feel very, very sorry, you naughty little boy. Speeding. Tut, tut. You were speeding, weren't you?'

The kid's face was only inches from Andy's. He used what space he had to nod. Andy shook his head.

'Oh dear. That's three points, that is. And in a stolen car. Yes?' Another nod. 'Where did you nick it from?'

The kid hesitated for a second but Andy didn't need to ask him again. 'Lewisham,' he managed to say. 'The High Road. Wasn't even locked, keys in it.'

'I see. Thank you. Now, under normal circumstances I'd be very happy to arrest you for this. But what I'm more concerned about is the lady in the boot.' Andy gripped hold of the boy's cheeks, his voice getting louder. 'The naked, formerly pregnant lady someone took a butcher's knife to. Now what have you got to tell me about her, eh? Come on, now. I don't want to wait until you're a piece of minced topside like your mates in there, so what have you got to say? What?! I asked you a fucking question . . .'

Andy screamed at the shaking face peering out of the debris as two firemen pulled him backwards. Andy asked him why he'd done it, what he'd done with the baby. The kid didn't understand, he had no idea what Andy was talking about. It wasn't him, I could see that. He'd just nicked the wrong car. It had been left with the keys in for someone like him to come along. The kid's eyes were wide. Here was more information he couldn't deal with. I kept my eyes on the kid while one of the firemen got in front of Andy and butted him back with huge, gloved hands.

Andy dodged the guy and made a break for the car but I caught his arm and spun him round, signalling to the fireman that I had him. I pushed Andy back ten, fifteen feet, succeeding in calming him down, and then I turned back to the fireman. His face was setting into anger. He took a step towards us, about to give Andy more grief but instead he stopped. We all did. We turned towards the car. Towards the deep, metallic lurch that was beginning to fill the tunnel. That was getting louder. A voice behind me said, 'Oh, shit.' I searched for the kid's eyes among the wreckage. They were shaking. The huge, bellyache of a creak increased in volume, again and again, seeming to go on for ever. I gave up trying to hold onto Andy and we both stared at the car. The kid's eyes and face were shaking and then his body began to shake too. He was screaming, in a frenzy, bucking his body again and again, trying to break out of the tiny space he was trapped inside. Whether or not he caused it I don't know but the door arch above him began to buckle. The crowd let out a grunt like a rugby scrum. Next to me the fireman had begun to run. As he sprinted forward he called out, 'Stay still. Don't move.

Do not move!' but the boy only intensified his struggling.

I managed to close my eyes in time, but I couldn't
shut out the sound that ended the boy's screams.

Chapter Sixteen

At the mouth of the tunnel I stood, letting the city static fill my head, waiting for Andy to finish talking to Burg, the pathologist. The tunnel mouth was relatively calm. Few people knew what was really going on in there. I watched the traffic being directed away, saw a man with a shoulder-mounted camera at his feet warming his hands round a polystyrene cup. Next to him stood a petulant-looking woman in her mid-twenties, obviously wondering how long she'd have to spend on traffic stories before she got anything juicy. She didn't know it but it wouldn't be long. I couldn't see anyone else covering what appeared to be just another pile-up. She didn't know she would be the first to report that a serial killer's third victim had just been found. That someone living amongst the people of London was stalking pregnant women. Stalking them not like a lovesick, nuisance fan, but like an animal. I saw that a strand of hair had escaped from the reporter's Alice band and was blowing against her cheek. She'd be pissed off to see that on the news later, if she didn't fix it.

I kept my eyes on Andy as the cogs inside me clicked and turned. A serial killer. I nodded to myself. It was shocking, appalling, so much grief had been caused to so many people. But I wasn't bothered by that. I wasn't bothered by Josephine Thomas or this girl here. In fact I felt cheated by them. Ally had only been dead two days and there was so much other stuff crowding in. I wanted to give myself to Ally, if not yet in sorrow then in action. I wanted to find the person who had killed her. That Ally's killer had clearly murdered two other women also seemed irrelevant. Any other murders were just clues, serving initially to prove that Ally's killer wasn't my friend. Again I felt that certainty. Mike, he hadn't murdered his wife. Once again I felt the relief. It was bigger by far than the shock. Bigger even than that, though, was the shame I felt. I could hardly believe it. I'd let Clay and Andy get inside my head. I'd let them pull me back eight years. Made me think like them: a copper, a professional cynic. Not a friend, with faith to beat down any arguments put forward. I felt dirty and cheap. I told myself that I had to get to Mike, to stand up with him now.

I looked across at Andy, his tie snapping in the wind like a rattlesnake. When Burg turned to his car I walked over, wanting to get out of there, but before I got to Andy he hit some keys on his phone. Andy told Clay that the pathologist had confirmed that another heavily pregnant woman had been murdered, possibly strangled, and then mutilated. Just as in the previous case the baby she'd been carrying had been removed. It was his opinion that the victim was fairly young. He also thought that the perpetrator probably had some medical knowledge, from the incisions made, and that there was no doubt that the person responsible had done the same thing to the victim found at the Lindauer Building. More than that, he needed to get the corpse on his table, and wouldn't even guess at time of death until then. What he did say, when Andy pushed him, was the same as he had apparently said in the first case. It was something I hadn't entertained for a second. Burg had told Andy that, depending on the stage of pregnancy, depending on the medical knowledge of the perpetrator, on their intentions and on many, many other variables, there was one possibility that could not be categorically ruled out. In both cases it was just conceivable that the foetus had survived.

Andy held the tape for me and we walked through the melee to the Mazda. Andy was leaving the car he'd come in for the officer he was posting there and had asked for a lift. I backed away from the tape into all-but stationary traffic, clogged with vehicles that would have taken the tunnel. I drummed the wheel, frustrated, wanting to get to Mike. Andy, in contrast, looked thoughtful, his eyes straight ahead, happy to watch the world not going by. His eyes looked a little weak for a second and I thought he was going to say something, but he didn't. What was there to say? Shaking his head, he reached into his jacket pocket and then lit up a fag before chucking the rest of the pack onto the dash. I leaned across and cracked his window, which made him bark out a laugh. He took a deep drag then blew a cherub of smoke towards the gap, most of it curling back on the inside of the windscreen.

'Just like old times,' Andy smiled. 'And earlier. You getting in the way, as per.'

'In the way?'

'I'd have chinned that Fireman Sam.'

It was my turn to laugh. 'And now be in intensive care.'

'*What?* Those nancy boys? Gay as the vicar, every

132

one of them. Couldn't keep their hands off me, didn't you see? They only join up for the hose.'

'You'd still be in intensive care.'

'Yeah, well, maybe. But it was a good job I did get to that kid, wasn't it? Lewisham. How long would it have taken to find that out? Couldn't they see that I had to speak to him? Square-jawed, sanctimonious cunts.'

Andy rubbed the tops of his hands and then shut his window absentmindedly.

'Didn't want to be in Blue Watch then? Or weren't you tall enough?'

'Fuck off. This "Coppers are racists and firemen are saints" shit just winds me up, that's all. You know how many of them are in on insurance scams? People think they're brave but they're just stupid, otherwise they wouldn't run into burning buildings, would they? You know why they have poles?'

'Tell me.'

'They can't work out stairs. Stairs are too complicated for the fuckers.'

'They just wanted to get that boy out.'

'Cunts. Fucking cunts. Fucking bum-bandit cunts. You get that guy's phone number did you?'

I shook my head and gave up speaking to Andy, while he lit up another fag, turned on the radio and changed the station. Just like old times. The sun was behind a cloud but the bright grey light still showed me the sandbags beneath his eyes, the creases crossing his forehead like the mark of Zorro. Andy looked old. His neck was beginning to spill over his collar like water from a paddling pool. The belly sitting in his lap seemed separate, not part of him. I wondered how he'd allowed it to happen. Why so many guys in their thirties seemed happy to let it all slip away like that. And why the toned, gym-obsessed women they went out with or married put up with it. Mike would have gone like that. He was already beginning to. He'd feel old now all right. Jesus. Andy asked me what I was thinking but I shook my head.

'Come on.'

'All right.' I shrugged. 'I was thinking what a fat fuck you are. That you should slim down before it's too late.'

'No need to, mate, I rely on natural magnetism. Lauren from the pub the other night certainly responded to that.'

'No way.'

'Way. And a different way in the morning actually.'

The traffic freed up a bit until we were caught at a light near the Angel that seemed to stay red longer than Russia had. I shifted in my seat and willed it to turn. It felt all too easy, being with Andy, heading back from a scene, chucking it back and forth. I remembered how much I used to like it, and how it had begun to turn and get to me. I thought about some of the cases we'd worked together and tried to identify the moment it had started to sour. It had been a gradual, incremental thing but one collar stood out.

Andy and I had been trying to break the grip that the dealer pimps had on the young girls who decorated and still decorate the streets of King's Cross like bright, cheap buttons on an old, stained mac. A grass had fingered one guy for us, a Turk who went by the name of Jolly for some reason. The marks we often saw on the girls he ran told us he was anything but. We knew what Jolly was doing but he was careful and we didn't have anything on him. It seemed like a lost cause until

Andy and I worked out a way to get to him. We got background on a couple of his girls and we chose one, and went to see her mother and younger sister in Southampton. We found out what kind of girl Vanessa was and the reason she had left home, why she was vulnerable to a guy like Jolly. Finally, we managed to get a tape of the two women, telling Vanessa how much they wanted her to go back home. The plea her sister made might even have moved Jolly himself.

One night I posed as a John and, in the moth-eaten hotel room Vanessa took me to, I told her who I was and I played the tape to her. It didn't take long for her to break down. I told Vanessa that she could start again, that we'd help her kick her habit, that she wouldn't have to suck any more cocks or take any more punches. Her sister had a nice home where she could stay. I played the tape to her one more time, paid her and left.

Vanessa had told me she would think not only about testifying against Jolly but also giving us enough to catch him red-handed. I went back to the station and waited. I didn't know how much hope to hold out – the station bookie was giving long odds – but two weeks later Andy told me he'd got a call from her. When, six months after that, Vanessa sent Jolly away for eight years, Andy and I got a lot of brownie points. They felt good, almost as good as seeing the disbelief on the guy's face as they took him down.

After the trial we went out to the Rising Sun to celebrate with some of the rest of the squad. When the others had left Andy and I carried on, knowing that, being a coppers' pub, last orders wasn't going to come at eleven. We were both pissed, but Andy was pissed off. It was because I had got most of the credit, something I didn't actually mind because it had, really, been my idea. We ended up arguing. Soon we were on to the usual ends and means rubbish and Andy ended up laughing at the very plan we'd just been celebrating, which had sent down an evil fuck and made us local celebrities to boot.

'But it worked didn't it?' I thought that pretty much ended the argument.

'Like fuck!' Andy's laughter was dirty, loud.

'No? Then why is that evil bastard beginning eight then?'

'You don't want to know, St William.'

'Bollocks. You just don't have any answers.'

'No? Try this question. What do junkies want?'

'Er, smack. They want smack.'

'Wrong. They want good smack. Better smack than they have.'

'So?'

'You didn't make Vanessa see the error of her ways. I made her see the error of Jolly's smack.'

'What?'

'I got her some good stuff. Real good stuff. Told her she didn't have to swallow any jiz for it either. She'd get it for nothing. All she had to do was sing.'

'This is bullshit.'

'Is it? I've been seeing her three, four nights a week. Keeping her steady. Promised to keep her going after the trial too, though she might find her free supply has suddenly dried up, poor bitch.'

'I don't believe you.'

'No? Ask Clay. He's the one got it for me. And before you go on about morals any more, Billy, just ask yourself this. Where is lovely Mr Jolly now? And where he would have been if I hadn't sorted it?'

I stood up from Andy as my hands curled into fists. I was stunned. I felt hollow. But as quickly as the anger rose, it wavered. I tried to hold onto it but I couldn't. It had already changed into depression. Andy and I apologized for yelling at each other and I thought about it. He was right. I was glad Jolly was behind bars. The girl hadn't lied in court, we hadn't planted any evidence. I just couldn't help feeling flat and beaten.

'What about Vanessa, though?' I said, suddenly a lot more drunk than I had been. 'Where does that leave her?'

'In the car park on the Pancras Road. On her knees.'

'Christ.'

'But we didn't put her there.'

'We just left her there.'

'Which is why we're coppers, Billy, and not social workers. Or did you not realize that? Fill in the wrong form, did you?'

The lights changed but we didn't manage to make it through. My eyes wandered to the old pawn shop, now a brightly lit estate agent's full of men in shiny, cheap suits, as if a worm hole had opened up into the 1980s. I looked away, across the junction, and saw a woman standing at a bus stop, reaching down to hold the hand of a small child. The woman looked tired and the round ball of her belly told me why. After a few seconds she looked around, a little scared, scanning the traffic for the eyes that were touching her. When she spotted me she glared, and I felt her discomfort, but I couldn't turn away. She just looked so precious. The most valuable thing in the entire world. And someone wanted to hurt

137

her. She didn't know it yet, but they did. For the first time I wondered why. The shock that Ally had been murdered by some kind of serial killer, and the relief that her husband had nothing to do with it, had both subsided, leaving that simple question. Why? What in God's name could motivate a person to do something like that?

I was also aware of the everyday frenzy surrounding this woman, the normal action of the city. The cars rushing by, mere feet from her. The people jostling, pushing past her on the pavement. The street was full of potential danger but the woman seemed blithely indifferent. That cyclist, mounting the pavement, he hits her and that's it. Christ. I wanted to shout out, to warn her. Instead I blinked, suddenly amazed that we could leave the entire propagation of our species to the uncertain, shifting, delicate process the woman across the junction was going through.

Chapter Seventeen

'You just tipped him out onto the street? After what happened to him? How could you do that?'

'He was innocent,' Clay said. 'That's what we're supposed to do, unfortunately. I'd like a change in the law, of course, but as it stands now innocent people *are* allowed to walk the streets. We're not a babysitting service, Billy.'

It wasn't Clay I was angry with, it was myself. I was playing catch up with Mike and every second that passed took me further away from him. I had a visceral desire to be near Mike, to grip hold of him. I tried him at home and then dialled his mobile. I left messages on both, kicking myself for not getting Andy to ask Clay to keep Mike there until I arrived. I wanted to get straight out and find him but Clay insisted I go over my theory concerning Josephine Thomas. As quickly as I could, I told them how I'd gone there to scope the route, how I'd seen her mother standing opposite the alley. Clay didn't look too impressed but then he never had: until the guilty came back.

'It doesn't change a whole lot one way or another, though,' he said. 'Two women or three, we've still got a Champions League sicko on our hands.'

We were standing in the incident room. The office

behind Clay was busy. Additional desk units were being assembled down the side and more computer equipment was being installed. This wasn't a murder case any more. The police weren't looking for someone who had killed someone else, full stop. The verb was present tense, not killed but killing, an ongoing process. The additional urgency was almost palpable. Every second mattered, every minute that passed without the perp being collared put another woman in danger, brought the guy closer to her. It was a race now and while the police had resources, manpower and technical equipment at their disposal there were two things they didn't have. They didn't know who the killer was. They didn't know when he'd strike again.

The fact that Calshot Street was being used as base HQ surprised me, but Clay told me that the commissioner had been persuaded to use the station rather than Scotland Yard, way over in Victoria. Clay looked psyched as a general the night before a big scrap. He told me that forty plain clothes had been signed over to him, as well as his usual team.

'They're also sending me a profiler,' he said. 'Some university don who's going to charge us a grand a day to tell me the fucker doesn't like women very much.'

After pulling the plastic off a new office chair Clay told me that, as yet, the investigation into Ally's death hadn't yielded much. Unlike me, he wasn't pleased to eliminate Mike. Without him the team had precious little to go on. The problem was the CCTV from the courtyard at the Lindauer. Ally had been murdered on a Saturday, so there hadn't been many people in the building. The CCTV covers the forecourt and there's no back entrance to the complex, which backs onto private gardens. Clay told me that everyone on the tape had checked out. All the people who were in the building when Ally was killed. There were only eighteen of them, including Mike and Ally, and they all had at least one other person to verify their movements. All but Mike. The police had been over their studios and their homes but hadn't found anything. Clay told me that he had sent a team back to the Lindauer that morning to talk to people again. To tell everyone to be careful. To find out if any pregnant women with connections to the building had gone missing recently.

The last thing Clay told me was that no trace of Ally's child had been found yet. Burg's words came back to me but I didn't say anything. It was just possible. I nodded to Clay and walked outside to the car park, passing a line of detectives coming the other way, all carrying cardboard boxes. The machine, the pistons starting to pump. I wondered whether it would be so thorough and extensive that a result would be guaranteed. Or whether it would be too big, too sluggish. Whether more women would have to die. Outside, in the Mazda, I breathed the remnants of Andy's smoke and thought about the woman at the bus stop. Statistically she'd be very unlucky to be the next victim but if there was to be one it had to be somebody. She would probably be home by now. She'd be making her daughter some lunch, keeping half an eye on the TV news. Did they have it yet, the woman in the tunnel? What it meant? I didn't know, but they would soon. I tried to imagine what it would be like to learn that someone was plucking pregnant women from the city like nuts from a tree. Discarding the shells. To know that the parcel of life growing inside you could very

141

well be drawing someone to you, someone like that. I pictured the woman, feeding her little girl, the spoon stopping in midair as Anna Ford broke the news. Would she go and make sure the front door was locked? Would she call her husband at work, just to hear his voice? Would she tell him about me, the man staring at her through the traffic?

I tried Mike's mobile again but didn't get anything. I started the car and backed up, thinking where he might have gone. If it was me I wouldn't have cared, I'd have just walked around, collapsed on a park bench somewhere. I figured that Mike would be completely thrown, to be suddenly out in the world that used to contain Ally and didn't any more. I drove round for half an hour, stopping to peer into Coram's Fields, where you can only go if you have a child with you. I drove round Mecklenburg Square, past the American college, and then along Lamb's Conduit Street and the cafe Mike went to, the one with the Portugese pudim cakes that Ally liked. I couldn't see him. It was a useless task, really. I thought about going home, waiting for him to call back, but I wanted to find him. I wanted him to know I'd tried to find him and that I hadn't stopped until I had.

I considered trying the Lindauer but the Sanctuary would be sealed and surely it was the last place he'd want to go anyway. I tried him at home again but just got his machine. After asking myself if I'd pick the phone up if I was in his place, I drove down there, to Borough, just the other side of London Bridge. Mike and Ally's flat is on an estate much like Josephine Thomas's: red-brick public housing turned private. Theirs was built in the Thirties, however, and so sports curved art deco balconies and glass bricks around the entrance door. When I first went to visit them the area hummed with old south London villainy. Today I was met by a plummy estate agent showing a young couple out, using the words 'sought' and 'after' as though he'd only that second thought of putting them in a sentence together.

I leaned on the bell for five minutes and then walked up the stairs and peered through the letter box. Mike wasn't there. Back in the Mazda I sat, wondering where to try next. Several places suggested themselves but I knocked them all down until I was left with only one. I nodded. I'd been kidding myself before. The Lindauer Building was the most obvious place to look. I'd just wanted to avoid it, that was all. The Lindauer had been at the centre of my mind ever since I'd seen Ally's body. I'd tried to turn away from it, telling myself there was nothing I could do there. I'd gone round and round it, tied to the place with a piece of string that had got shorter and shorter until it had run right out.

When I pulled in towards the barrier I was glad that it wasn't Ron I saw in the booth, setting aside a copy of the *Sun* to reach for the lever. It was someone I didn't recognize, a younger man. I didn't want to see Ron. I didn't blame him for what had happened: anyone is allowed in the Lindauer Building and CCTV seemed to show that Ron hadn't missed anyone anyway. But the image of him, fast asleep, was still strong. He'd probably been asleep when Ally was being murdered. Had the cafe window been open? I couldn't remember. Had she screamed, and if she had, would Ron have heard her if he'd been awake? Would he have been able to get to her in time? I didn't know. I just didn't want to look at him and I was glad I didn't have to.

I parked in my usual spot and locked up. The building in front of me looked impassive, taciturn, as if it knew the reason two or perhaps three women with connections to it had died. As if the answer was written in the bricks, the mortar, under the roof tiles. I walked across the car park. In the lift it all came back and then down the corridor. All the time I stared straight ahead, walking through the pictures and images that were jumping out on me with every step I took. I walked past the cafe, hardly even looking at the closed door crossed with tape, and then stopped outside my office.

I stood for a second, listening. I couldn't hear anything. I'd half expected Mike to have let himself into my office with the spare key he keeps but the place was empty except for another small hill of mail. I picked it up but there was nothing in it apart from a Visa bill and two application forms from newly opened fitness centres. It seemed to me that I was getting one of these a week now, at least. How many fitness centres did London need? Surely there had to be a limit to the world's already depleted supply of Lycra. I dumped them in the bin on top of the last pile and shut the door. I was disappointed not to see Mike but relieved too. I walked round my desk. Sunlight was gushing through the wooden slats of my blinds. I thought I'd left them closed but I couldn't have. Before I could get to the window to turn them the light dimmed on its own, as though someone had killed a switch. I pulled the blind up to see that the sun had made its last appearance that day, ranks of grey-bottomed cloud were marching in from the east.

The last time I'd looked out of the window I'd then gone down to the cafe and joked about football with Ally and Mike. I would never do that again. I saw the smile Ally had given Mike, her hand curling under her belly. The irony not quite strong enough to hide the genuine love. I blinked it away. Instead I stared through the stark branches of the oak tree at a bird scurrying off through the bare branches. I hadn't pulled the blinds carefully, not like I usually did. The bird was about as big as a thrush, but the wrong colour. The shrike, the rare bird that had visited me last year? I didn't know. I thought so but it was too far away, gliding down to sit on the fence of one of the gardens backing onto the building.

Out of habit I kept my eye on the bird and reached into my desk drawer for my binoculars. I lifted them to my face but as soon as I'd got them to my eyes I stopped. I discarded the bird. I moved the glasses instead to a man, standing in the garden beyond the fence the bird had perched on. I rolled my finger over the focus wheel until he was clear. Yes. As I thought, the man had something in his hand. He was standing at the side of his house, looking at the door that led out of the garden to the front, to the street. The man dropped whatever it was that he'd found before walking towards his back door and disappearing inside. I frowned. I refocused and studied the fence, a good five feet lower than the ones bordering the gardens on either side of it.

Ten seconds later I was running back down the hall.
'You were quick.'
'Sorry?'
'Quick. I only just called. Five minutes ago. Just

passing, were you? Anyway, come round this way. You can see the damage. Nothing taken as far as I can tell, they probably got frightened off. You fancy a cup of tea? I'll get the wife to put the kettle on.'

He was in his fifties, small, with a deep, winter tan. He'd opened the front door of his house on Aberdeen Park, the road the Lindauer Building backs onto. His name was Stephen Sprake and he'd just got back from Tenerife, barely an hour ago he said, to find a note from the police asking him to give them a call. He'd assumed it was about the door to his back garden, which had been forced in his absence.

'Though how you lot knew about it I don't know,' he said. 'Only noticed myself when I tried to open it. The door was still shut but there was no lock in it. They just unscrewed the whole thing, you can see. Found the lock on the other side of the door.'

'You touched it, right?'

'Yes, how do you know that? Police instinct, I suppose. Anyway, why shouldn't I have? You're not going to fingerprint it, are you? I didn't think you'd bother for just a break-in, especially when they didn't even get into the house. Thought you'd just give me a note for the insurance. I'm impressed, I have to say.'

When I told Mr Sprake the reason the police would be fingerprinting the lock that had been removed from his garden door, as well as everything else on the outside of his house, his two-week tan faded in less than a second. He told me that he'd seen the story in the *Standard*, on his way back from Gatwick, but hadn't thought that it had happened next door to him. His mention of the paper pulled me up. I hadn't seen one since Saturday, even though I knew they'd all have run something. I hadn't been able to face it. I didn't want to think about what they might have written. Mr Sprake asked me if what the paper was saying was true. I said I didn't know. I used my phone to call the station and then followed Mr Sprake into his garden, looking up at the Lindauer over his shoulder.

At the bottom of the thin green swathe my eyes rested on a compost heap piled up against a brown slatted fence. The fence was topped by three rows of barbed wire, not enough to cause much of a problem to anyone who was determined. Especially going that way: the wire was slanted backwards, Mr Sprake had been far more worried about people trying to get into his garden than out of it.

'You haven't touched anything else, anything down here?'

'Only been back an hour. Grass needs raking but I guess it'll have to wait, won't it?' I nodded. 'You reckon they got over here then? And killed the woman in the building?'

'Got in the back door, to avoid the cameras.' I was talking to myself as much as to Mr Sprake. 'Must have come back this way too. Might even have used that, pulled it over with them.' I pointed at an old wooden ladder lying against the bottom of the fence. 'That must be why they didn't just jemmy your garden door open, why they took the lock out. Someone might have noticed if they'd just busted it, called the police while they were still in the building. They'd have been caught coming out.'

'Sounds well planned. So who was she, this girl? The victim?'

'She worked in the building.'

'Tragic,' Mr Sprake said, 'just awful. I hope they catch the bugger. What's the motive? Why would someone do something like that? To a pregnant lady?'

'I have no idea,' I said. 'No idea at all.'

'How are you involved then? If you're not a policeman?'

'I used to be one. Some old colleagues are on the case. I work in the building there.'

'So you must have known her.'

'Yes.'

'Well, I'm sorry. Knew her well, did you?'

'That tea, Mr Sprake. If you really were offering.'

'Yes, of course. Shall I get Norma to make a pot, with the police coming?'

'I'm sure they'd appreciate that,' I said.

As Mr Sprake made his way inside, I looked up towards my office window. I could see the outline of a bird sitting on a branch right outside, and thought I caught a flash of white. The bird wasn't round enough to be a pigeon. A little small for a magpie or a jay. Had the shrike flown back up there? I strained to hear its song above the traffic but almost immediately it was lost among the sirens cutting through the streets towards me.

Chapter Eighteen

While the police were combing the garden I waited in the kitchen, drinking tea, watching them through the window. The *Standard* lay folded in front of me and it didn't take long for curiosity to win. I picked it up, opened it out and saw that the front page was split in two. The left side showed a brightly coloured picture of Ally, from two or three years ago, her smile leaping right off the page. Next to her was Mike, but he wasn't smiling. His head was bowed, his hands cuffed. If you've ever wondered why photographers chase after prison vans on the news, jumping up at the seemingly impenetrable black windows with their boosted flashes, this is why. One in ten gets lucky. Mike was a grey thing, turning away from the flash a fraction too late. As is the case with all these pictures, his face had stone-cold guilty written all over it. In case you didn't get it, though, the banner made it perfectly clear.

DID THIS MAN MURDER HIS PREGNANT WIFE?

When Clay had got everything going outside to his satisfaction, he came in and thanked me. I took his thanks but I knew the police would have found out about the lock soon enough. They had in fact already checked the garden for clues, going in from next door after being told the owner was away. They'd found nothing, no footprints or torn remnants of clothing, and didn't expect to now. The mystery was explained, though. The killer had come in the back to avoid both Ron and the cameras. The last thing tying Mike to the murder was brushed away.

Clay told me what he thought it all meant, and I nodded. The killer must have deliberately entered the building for the commission of the crime. He hadn't seen Ally and just decided to kill her on the spur of the moment, waiting until he was alone in the cafe with her. He'd been watching her, watching her and the building too. He'd known that the building was quiet on a Saturday. He'd staked it out, first latching on to Josephine Thomas. Then Ally's pregnancy drew her to him. That time, he'd been right.

Clay insisted that the killer must have been inside the Lindauer Building prior to the murder, and I agreed. He can't have just watched Ally going in or coming out. That would have been enough for Josephine, who he had followed home, but not Ally. How would he have known where to find her once he was inside if he hadn't been inside himself? It was a break. He must have been caught on film. He must have gone in during the day, during working hours. How long ago? I didn't have a clue, I just hoped they didn't wipe their tapes. While Clay told an officer to get round to the security booth straight away I had a thought that sickened me. He'd been in the cafe. He must have been. Ally had probably made him a coffee. A sandwich even, passing the plate to him, her eyes smiling at him. And he'd killed her.

She'd smiled and called out goodbye and he'd come back and killed her.

Clay saw the look on my face. As he walked me through to the back door, he took my arm.

'Thanks again, Billy,' he said. As usual, his tiny eyes seemed to say something different from the words coming out of his mouth. 'You know what, it's a shame we lost you. I've always said that. And I've always said, if you ever reconsider. Maybe even put you back with Andy.'

'I'd rather be a fireman.'

'What?'

'It doesn't matter.'

'Well, the offer's there. But what I want to say is, I need this guy.'

'Of course.'

'In court,' Clay said. 'For the families. You've helped and I'm grateful. We need to find out what link this one in the tunnel had to the Lindauer and I know you're going to try find out. I won't tell you not to. I know this is close to you. But you understand me, what I mean about court?'

'You'd better find him then.'

'Before you do? Is that what you mean?'

'You'd just better find him.'

'I'll go after you for it, Billy. I will, you'd better understand that. Evil fuck or not, I'll put you away. I want him. Do you hear me? Do you hear me, Billy?'

I brushed past Clay. His voice jumped after me like a tethered Dobermann as I walked up Aberdeen Park and back round to the Lindauer Building.

*

I cranked up the Mazda and drove back to Exmouth Market. I'd done everything I could think of to find Mike and now I was going home. Clay had told me that Mike's mobile had been taken from him and hadn't been returned. That meant that he hadn't got my messages but also that he wouldn't have had my mobile number, which was in his phone. So, obviously, he wouldn't have been able to call me except at home. He could have left ten messages on my home machine without my knowing it. I cursed myself. It was almost as if something in my mind was trying to trip me up, as if I didn't really want to find Mike at all.

Knowing that I would never get a space outside my flat at that time of day, I parked in a delivery bay at the other end of the Market. I walked down the street quickly. If there was a message from Mike, I'd call him. If not, I'd go down to his apartment again and just wait for him to show up. I saw Max talking to the manager of Cafe Kick. He waved at me but I pretended not to see him. I wasn't going to get sidetracked again. I was determined to get to my answerphone, determined not to let anything else keep me from my flat. I saw Mike when I was three-quarters of the way down the street. He was sitting on one of the tree-covered benches outside Fred's, next to a bank of payphones. He was staring in the general direction of my street door, but his gaze wasn't taking anything in. I stopped, then carried on towards him.

Like blind people can, Mike didn't look present. The cold and the traffic and the people meant nothing to him. Christ knew what present hell or gone paradise he was visiting. I felt stupid, like a man who tips his flat upside down, only to find his glasses in the case he put

152

them in. Of course. Mike had had two days for reality to hit him. He wouldn't have been wandering around in shock. Nor would he have instantly hunted down comfort from a friend or his family. What comfort could he get? I knew what he'd want. Who else would he come to but his friend the investigator? Who else could offer him anything? I swore at myself, wondering how long Mike had been sitting there while I was fucking around.

Mike looked dishevelled, worse off than the old tramp sitting next to him, the one who screams abuse at you only after you've given him a quid. As I walked up, the tramp pushed himself to his feet and stalked off up the Market, the way I'd come. I stood in front of Mike, waiting for him to look at me, not knowing what I was going to say. When he did look at me I didn't say anything. I just began to cry. I couldn't help it. Mike had changed. There were no marks on him but he looked grotesque, worse than a fighter announcing his retirement. It was all there, on the skin hanging from his cheekbones, in his eyes, on his lips most of all for some reason. His face was dried up, it was dead. It killed me to look at him and I suddenly realized where I'd seen the look he wore. Too late, too late. Where the hell were you?

My legs buckled and I couldn't stand. I reached out and I held Mike, clinging on to him, burying my head in his neck. I desperately wanted him to but he didn't respond. I couldn't keep myself from sobbing, my chest almost exploding, trying to connect with him. But Mike was still. Then I felt his hands, gripping the tops of my arms, pushing me away. I gulped for air, hardly able to breathe. I had to get myself together, tell Mike what had happened and what I was going to do for him. He didn't realize it but I had access to a lot of money and to a lot of people, the kind of people who heard things. I also needed to ask him to think: who had he seen in the cafe in the last weeks? Anyone different or unusual? I wanted to tell him that I was going to sort this for him, the way he'd want it sorted. We'd get to him before Clay did.

Mike's hand went to a copy of the *Standard* sitting on the bench beside him. He held it out to me, so that I could see the front page. He asked me if I'd seen it and I nodded.

'They kept at me, Billy,' he said. His voice was quiet, amazed. 'They drugged me and then they kept at me, in the hospital, at some police station. They said things about Ally. That friend of yours, the copper. They pushed me down even further than I was.'

'Mike . . .'

'Then they showed me a tape. It was of myself, outside the Lindauer Building. Gold. He made me look at a tape of myself. I'd just left Ally in the cafe, I was on my way to meet you, and Nicky. The cameras picked me up walking out onto the forecourt. To the van. They stopped it and then they pointed to the bag I was carrying. In my hand. The bag. Do you know what they asked me?'

I shook my head.

'They asked me if my little baby was inside it. In the bag. If I was carrying my own baby. They asked me that.'

'Mike.'

'And then they let me go. This morning. Hoped I'd understand, they had to ask me certain things . . .

154

bollocks. I didn't listen. I was beyond them. I just wanted to see you. I called you but you weren't at home and I didn't have your mobile number. It was on my phone and they wouldn't give it me back. So I came here to find you. When you weren't in I went home, but I couldn't stay there, not for ten seconds. It smells of her, Billy. I just grabbed your keys, your spare keys. You still weren't home when I got back here so I decided to let myself in. I knew you wouldn't mind because you were my friend. It was the only place I could stand to be because I knew you'd help me. It was what had been getting me through. For two days, with what I was feeling, while they were on at me hour after hour, asking me, I focused on that, I grabbed hold of it, knowing that whatever those stupid, useless bastards were saying you'd be strong. I knew that Billy Rucker would be out there looking for the person who killed my wife. You, at least, would be out there.'

'I was. And I will . . .'

'I was going to wait for you. I knew you'd be back eventually. I figured you were after them, you know. Like a cowboy, riding around. And then I saw what you'd written on your wall. Her name. And my name. And nothing else. And when I realized what that meant I was sick. I was physically sick, Billy, on your floor. And I ran out of there and I've been waiting for you.'

'Mike.'

'Because I wanted to tell you what I think of you. That this is the last time I'll ever see you. Because you're weak, Billy. And you're just like them. Because you thought it was me, you thought I'd done that to Ally. You saw what someone had done to her and you thought it could have been me. You saw. You thought it could have been me.'

Mike stood up from me. I tried to speak but I couldn't. My stomach and my chest were contracting. The way he stood I thought he was going to hit me and I wanted him to. Without speaking I begged him to. But he didn't. I tried to reach out to him but I couldn't move and I couldn't see anything through the sheets of tears. I tried to force the word sorry out of my mouth but I was paralysed. I looked round for Mike but I couldn't see him. The world was a blur, it was one swirling mess. The only thing I was aware of was footsteps disappearing into traffic.

Chapter Nineteen

Upstairs I cleaned up my flat and ripped all the paper from my wall. I wished I had a fire to burn it in but I didn't. I thought about how I'd woken up, almost certain that Mike had killed and mutilated Ally. I knew that, whatever happened, even if somehow one day Mike got to forgive me, that fact would never change.

Once I'd filled my kitchen bin with the screwed-up pieces of A4 I told myself that there was only one thing I could do for Mike now. Find out who had killed Ally, as well as one and perhaps two other women. I phoned Andy but only got his voicemail. I wondered if he'd seen my number come up and decided not to take the call. Clay would have spoken to him, told him to keep me out of it. I suddenly felt isolated. On my own. I was frustrated at the thought that there could be information that I wouldn't have access to. Once again I had that feeling of there being nothing I could do that wasn't being done. I had to wait for Andy to get back to me, tell me if the car had been traced, whether the woman in the boot had been identified. Whether he'd got his hands on the CCTV tape from the Lindauer. I just had to trust that he would call me. While Andy would want to do what Clay told him he'd also want the collar. That would be it for him, he'd go sky high. I

157

banked on the hope that Andy wouldn't want to pass up the chance of me helping him get it.

I dialled Mike's number but didn't leave a message. I thought about going down to his flat again but he didn't want to see me. What good would my explanations be to him? I took the ten-minute walk down St John Street instead. A hundred years ago there were fifty pubs on St John Street because it was a major thoroughfare. There aren't fifty now but the bars and restaurants have been steadily increasing in number over the last ten years as the City workers have moved into the lofts that artists can no longer afford. The Old Ludensian, at the bottom of St John Street near Smithfield, is still the best. I walked in and saw Toby, Nicky's head barman, pulling a pint.

Toby jerked his head to a corner table, where I saw Nicky looking into an ashtray, a bottle of Middletons beside him, the foolishly expensive Irish whiskey we'd drunk on the day we'd met. He looked up when he saw me, using his leg to push out the chair opposite him. I was about to turn round to the bar, to get another glass, when I noticed that there was a spare one in front of Nicky.

'I had a feeling you'd come down,' he said. 'Have you eaten?'

'No.'

'Neither have I. And we're not going to, are we?'

'I don't think I am.'

'Me neither. You want a beer, anything?'

'This is fine,' I told him.

Nicky and I spent the next six hours together, going through the rest of the bottle in front of us before moving on to another. It could have been meths for all we tasted of it. We talked about what had happened, what we felt about it, while the bar churned around us. I told Nicky about Dalston, then the tunnel. And Mike. Nicky told me that I wasn't to blame, in fact I was right to think what I had. What Mike had said had nothing to do with reality, it was just what he was going through. I told him that Mike's reality was something I should have thought about.

'Imagine, Christ, if Sharon had been killed. Would you ever have thought it was me?'

'No,' Nicky said. 'Not even if I saw you do it.'

'So how must he feel? Did you think it was Mike? In the office that night?'

'I didn't even wonder.' Nicky shook his head. 'I just didn't want to be anywhere near him, whether he did it or not. And you know what? This is terrible, but I still don't. It's like he's contagious. I'd hide if I saw him in the street, I really would. Why the hell is that?'

The bar emptied and Toby closed it down and at some point closed the door behind him and left Nicky and me alone. The bar was dark but for the bands of orange street light pushing in through the huge slats of the blinds. We talked some more and sat some more and drank some more too. I had that feeling again, the solid numbness inside, as the events of the day sorted themselves out within me. I knew I needed the time just to sit, not to rush round trying to do things, and I also knew that I needed to do it in the Old Ludensian. Spending time with Nicky had always helped me, allowed things to settle. Maybe one day I'll understand why.

When we'd finally gone through everything we could think to say about what had happened, another deep silence sat in the air between us, coaxing us back into our own thoughts. Eventually Nicky managed to find the distant cousin of a smile.

'Would you have slept with her?' he asked, stretching back in his chair. I looked at him. 'The TV exec, the funny one. You know, Ruth?'

I shook my head instantly but then thought about it properly. I saw the long, slender body and felt Ruth's hand on the top of my knee in the cab. I remembered how much I'd enjoyed her company but for some reason I knew that, if it had come to it, in spite of any paranoia I was feeling about Sharon, I'd have resisted any advances she might have made.

'No,' I said finally. 'I was tempted but we'd have just crashed on the sofabed in my office, then woken up to monumental hangovers. And relief. Both of us. She was married, you know?'

Nicky nodded, accepting my answer. 'Why not, though? Because you felt guilty, or you were too mashed?'

'Neither.'

'No?'

'No.'

'Why not then?'

'I'm past it.' I laughed. 'Meaningless shags when you're pissed. Why do something when you've done it so many times before? When you know it isn't going to do anything for you. I'd had a great time, I'd got everything I wanted out of that evening. What about you with the other one?'

Nicky laughed too.

'I already did.'

'What?!'

'In the khazi. Nice and spacious at the Sixty-Two, I'll say that for the place. She was bending over the sink to do a line. I just couldn't help myself. If it's any consolation . . .'

Nicky let his words tail off. He frowned to himself and the expression on his face caught me. He looked old, but not like Andy Gold had done. It wasn't in his body, it was in his eyes. As if what he was telling me had happened in the distant past and his memories put a nasty taste in his mouth.

'That was the last time,' Nicky said. 'I'm finished with all that. I want what you have. What Mike had. I want the thing I've been running from all my life.'

My friend looked so earnest, so intense, I almost believed him.

Nicky offered me the sofa in the flat upstairs but I said no. I walked back up to the Market, glad of the cold night air. I reached into my pocket for my keys but stood for a second before going upstairs. Again I had the intense wish that Sharon was up there. I wondered what it would really be like to share my life with her, my space, everything. I wondered what she'd say if I asked her. I thought about the foreign correspondent again, the one I'd imagined that night, this time edging closer to Sharon as he told her about the poverty he'd witnessed up in the mountain regions. The image was ludicrous, stupid and clichéd. But it really got to me. I shook my head and laughed at myself, but wasn't able to shake the pang. I pushed up past my bike, chained to the banister halfway up my stairs, struck by the fact that everything, everything in my life had changed. For ever. The world was different and when Sharon came back it would be more so again, one way or another.

The little red light on my machine was winking and I took a breath. Sometimes you just know who has called you, you know with a certainty that doesn't even strike you as odd. I felt tense, my arms light and my stomach suddenly cold. I looked down at the machine as Sharon's voice filled my apartment.

'Oh,' Sharon said. 'You're not there. I really hoped you'd be there.' Sharon's voice sounded small and a long way away. 'You're not at your office, though you know that! Listen, Billy, it's all turned a bit dodgy over here. The camp got surrounded by people trying to get in and the people who are inside were getting angry because there's not enough food reaching us. Some shots were fired at our buildings. The Marines came and took us out and flew us to Islamabad, where I am now. And I'm coming home. The UN said they wouldn't make us go back to Afghanistan, and though most of the team are going I've decided not to. I'm about to get on a flight. I only have two weeks left anyway and well, well, I just thought why risk it? Shit.'

I heard a flight announcement but I couldn't make out what it said.

'I've got to go. My plane gets into Heathrow to-morrow morning. Ten-fifteen your time, allegedly. BA 97. If you could be there I'd love it, Billy, but I know it's last minute and you're probably working, so don't worry. If I see you there I see you. I've got to go now but, oh, I'll say it, you can freak if you want. I love you. And I can't *wait* to see you. Get a sausage casserole on or else. Bye.'

I let the tape rewind and then I played the message over. Those two, last, impossible weeks. They'd been removed, cut out of my life like a cancer. I couldn't believe it. I looked at my watch. Eight hours, that was all I had to wait. Then I'd be with her. I smiled as I waved goodbye to the foreign correspondent, hopefully for the last time.

But then I realized; she didn't know. I thought she might have seen something, in the international *Guardian* or a report on the World Service. But I could tell, by her voice, that she hadn't. I'd have to tell her. I knew it. Yet I also knew that I wouldn't be able to, not straight away, not for a minute at least. I'd leave it. I'd hold her first and kiss her. I'd wait until I'd seen the smile that always cut a canyon straight through my heart.

It would be like going back in time.

Chapter Twenty

The terminal was like a moving maze, with trolleys instead of hedges. The place was rammed. I was early, especially as the arrivals board told me that flight BA 97 was slated to come in twenty minutes late. I made my way to a coffee bar near arrivals and managed to find a seat at a small round table. I took out a notebook and pen and looked at the notes I'd made on the Heathrow Express. I'd taken the train instead of my car so that I could do that. And take less than three hours to get there.

There was no way I was going to miss Sharon. I know she would have understood if I hadn't gone but I wanted to see her, to spend every second I could with her. The gesture too was important but there was something else as well. I didn't want her to see a newspaper. I didn't want her doing that on her own.

I did feel guilty, though. What would Mike have thought: instead of finding out what had happened to Ally I'd gone to meet Sharon, my girlfriend? The girl I still had. For this reason I took my daybook and my phone, calling Andy from the train just after nine. This time he did pick up, saying, 'Just a minute,' before walking into a different room. I was relieved. Andy told me that the car from the tunnel had been traced. It was a Mondeo, four years old. Though the kid had found it in Lewisham it had originally been taken from a street in Bethnal Green last week. I asked him about the girl in the boot and he said they'd found a possible print match but were waiting for it to come back with an ID. She'd been about six months pregnant but no one with any link to the Lindauer seemed to be missing. Andy told me that he wanted to speak to Mike again, to go through CCTV stills, which were being pulled off the tape, and he asked me if I'd seen him. I told him that I hadn't.

I thought about what Andy had said about the car, but I couldn't really focus on it. All I could think about was Sharon. As Andy had reminded me at the station the other night, Sharon was my brother Luke's girl-friend when I first met her. Luke had served her in the bar where he was working and fell in love with her right there. They were planning to marry when Luke had the accident that left, and leaves, him in a PVS. A coma. Sharon and I had been almost inseparable after that, the only people who seemed to have any relevance to each other. We'd been friends for nearly four years before it had gone any further and we'd fallen in love ourselves. It was an amazing, wrenching time, but I thought we'd managed to deal with all the guilt and the weirdness of it. I thought we'd last for ever. Sharon had thought that too, but after a year and a half she realized that she couldn't do it any more, she couldn't stand to be reminded daily about what had happened. I saw her again, sitting on my futon, and felt my stomach plummeting down through me at the words she'd said.

'I'm seeing someone else, Billy.'

I hadn't seen it coming and the pain, and betrayal,

took me months to come to terms with. I had a brief relationship and some meaningless encounters and managed to function, though I couldn't stop my mind turning towards Sharon. I heard she'd dumped the guy she'd got together with and I thought about calling her on several occasions but I never quite did. More than a year later, out of the blue, she called me. I was instantly defensive and I asked her what she wanted. She told me that she was going away to work and wanted to know if I fancied dinner before she left. That was all. Actually, she laughed, she wanted to know if I fancied cooking it for her.

'Those lamb shanks,' she said, 'in white wine. I can never get them the same as you do them.'

I must have spent three hours cooking that night but I needn't have bothered. We'd been so nervous we'd hardly been able to eat. Eventually we gave up and without saying much just walked into the bedroom. We made love in a kind of sickened, terrified daze, just wanting to get it done. To get past it. In the morning I couldn't believe she was there. Sharon and I spent every night together after that until she left for Afghanistan. Only nine days, but I knew. I'd imagined the nerves I'd feel seeing her again, but they were nothing compared to what I was feeling now.

I sipped an espresso but instantly regretted it, the caffeine soon playing chase with the adrenalin in my veins. I was weak, my throat dry at the thought of seeing Sharon. There was a different fear in my head now. Not that she'd met someone else, but that it might go wrong again. If, like last time, she couldn't handle seeing her ex-lover in the face of his brother every day. I wasn't sure I could deal with losing her again. I told myself to calm down and not crowd her. I'd put off asking Sharon to move in. I'd be a little cool, let her drive it forward if she wanted to. The news I had to give her would blow it all away anyway.

BA 97 – Landed.

It was ten forty-five. The airport was even busier now if that was possible, waves of bodies moving out of the arrivals' hall, riptides of single people cutting against them. I tapped my feet and turned to my note-book, knowing that Landed could mean another thirty minutes. I tried to concentrate on the list I'd made. The bus driver, the one who'd driven Josephine. The police would have spoken to him at least twice but it wouldn't hurt if I gave it a shot. I wrote a list of questions for him but my eyes kept flicking from the page to the screen up above me.

BA 97 – Baggage in Hall.

My table was on a platform and I looked down over the heads of the people at the barrier, all facing one way. A pickpocket's wet dream. An endless shoal of weary faces streamed through them, the odd individual fished out with shrieks and hugs. I pictured Sharon at passport control, then at the baggage carousel. She was only yards away now but she'd still be another ten minutes at least. I couldn't stay seated, though. I walked down to the gate, making sure I didn't miss anyone coming through. I stood to the side where I'd see her first, before she could see me. I wouldn't shout out straight away. I'd just watch her. I was trying to peer into the baggage hall when my phone rang. The display said private number and I answered, thinking it might be Sharon, calling from a payphone on the other side. Instead it was Andy and he sounded urgent.

Andy told me that the girl had been identified. I told him that was great. I asked him if I could call him back but he pushed on. He said there was something else.

'The pathologist found a note,' Andy said.

'A note? Where?'

'It was in the girl's mouth. Well, I say her mouth, that was where Burg thinks it was most likely stuffed before her head hit the wall of the Rotherhithe. Either that or it was just left with her. Anyway, the note was a mess, a real mess, but Burg's good. He's the best. He put it under a lamp and he *thinks* he can just about make out what it says.'

'And? What was on it?'

'Just three words,' Andy said. 'But what I was thinking. You went down to the alley the Thomas girl died in, didn't you?'

'Yes.' I turned my head. Was that her? No. Not blonde enough. 'I looked through the cards that came with the flowers.'

'Good man. We didn't find anything but figured that might have been where he left it, if he did. Do you remember any of the messages?'

'No, but I wrote them down, the ones I could read. It had been raining. I'll check later.' Her? Another guy was kissing her so I hoped to hell it wasn't. 'What am I looking for?'

' "It Was You",' Andy said. 'Nothing else. They're pretty sure. It didn't mean anything but then I remembered I'd seen the phrase before. In Ally and Mike's cafe, written on the bottom of a shopping list. I read it at the time but took no notice. But we have to remember, the perp didn't know the girl in the Mondeo's head would get mashed. He expected us to find the note. When Burg told me about it I remembered the shopping list. You seeing the same thing in Dalston would prove Josephine Thomas was the first victim. Billy? Billy?'

I nearly laughed.

' "It Was You." '

'What about it?'

'Are you sure that's what it said?'

'It. Was. You. Well, did any of the cards say that?'

'No.' I shook my head.

'Damn.'

'But . . .'

'But what?'

'But I've seen them.'

'What?'

'I've seen them as well. "It Was You". Written.'

'What the hell do you mean? Written? Written where?'

'Outside. They . . . they were outside my house. All over Fred's.'

'The cafe? On the corner? All over it? I don't understand.'

Neither did I. I was there, talking to Max again.

'In graffiti,' I said. 'Sprayed on the windows. The owner was trying to get it off.'

'When was this?'

'Last week.'

'Bloody hell. But Exmouth Market is still Islington, right? Same as the Lindauer. Maybe it's wider than we thought. Why don't you meet me there, tell me what you saw?'

'The girl,' I said. 'Andy, tell me about the girl.'

'No connection,' he said. 'None. This isn't the

169

Lindauer, Billy. The girl in the car wasn't even from London, though we'll check on any Islington connection. She was from Birmingham.'

'What was her name?'

'It's here somewhere. She had a few minor priors, that's how we ID'd her. Prints on the central database. Here. Husband reported her missing about a month ago. Came to the Smoke to seek her fortune by the looks of her. Type of girl you waste your time looking for . . .'

'What was her *fucking* name?'

'Hey, calm down. We haven't found her husband to tell him yet so keep shtum. This makes today's *Standard* you're in shit.'

'Andy . . .'

'It was Denton. Denise Denton. Why?' Andy laughed. 'Know her, do you?'

'No.'

'Good. For a minute there I thought . . .'

'But I know her husband.'

'What?'

'His name's Jared.'

'Yes. Yes. It fucking is. How the hell do you know that?'

'He hired me to find her,' I said.

My voice was no more than a whisper.

'He came to my office. He gave me a picture of her. I went down to Brixton. I've been looking for Denise Denton for the last two weeks.'

'Well, you found her, Billy. In the boot of that car. You found her.'

Chapter Twenty-One

'It was you. Billy, it was you. It's not the Lindauer, Islington even. Josephine Thomas, Ally, this Denton girl. It was *you.*'

Even though it was Andy who was speaking the words seemed to be coming from my own brain. They ricocheted round my head. I moved the phone away from my face as if it was radioactive. I stared at it. The airport was rushing round me in a swirl of noise.

'Billy? Are you still there? Where the hell are you, anyway? Billy! You need to get here, get here right *now.*'

The phone was calling out to me like a sick bird. I turned away from it. I couldn't take it in. Me? This had all happened because of me. At the same time as knowing that it couldn't possibly be true, I knew that it was true. The words, outside my flat. Ally. Josephine Thomas. Now this girl. Another voice was coming at me. Not out of my phone, out of the clamour.

'You came,' it said. 'Oh, thank you. You know I said I didn't mind? I was lying. I've just spent the last eleven hours hoping you'd be here, imagining you being here, and here you are. Oh, honey.'

Sharon was standing right in front of me. A trolley of luggage was by her side. I just stared at her. I couldn't speak. Me. It was me. It was all about me. I couldn't, I refused to believe it. And Sharon. I couldn't take her in either. I knew it was her but my mind had crashed. I was supposed to see her walking through the gate, her eyes searching the barrier. I thought she'd be in her leather jacket, the one I'd seen her off in, the fitted rust-coloured jacket that hugged her like a second skin. She was in Pakistani dress, a salwar kameez. Her green eyes flickered from the recesses of her headscarf. She was smiling, a little confused. Scared even. A canyon was cut right into my heart.

'What do you think?' Sharon did a quick turn to the side, trying to keep the puzzlement off her face. 'Classy, huh? Practical too. Thought I'd surprise you and I obviously have! You look, I don't know what you look. Well?'

I couldn't move. Sharon didn't know whether to kiss me, shake my hand, anything.

'Rucker? Are you still there? Rucker?'

I hit 'end' on the phone, as if by doing so I could not only shut it off but snuff out what Andy had told me. I shoved the phone into my pocket. I tried to draw myself together from the fragments I'd just been blown into. Sharon's eyes drew back, hardening as she prepared herself.

'What's wrong?'

'Nothing.' I swallowed. 'You look lovely. Really lovely. That suits you.'

'Thank you. Thanks. It's handy too.' I'd done enough to push back the doubt on Sharon's face and though she still seemed a little wary she also seemed relieved. She was studying me, weighing me up, taking deep breaths.

'Are you sure you're all right?' I nodded again. 'OK then. So, did you miss me?'

'If you knew how much. I've just been telling myself not to crowd you, to be cool. But I don't want to be.'

'Then don't.'

Sharon put her arms round me and I held her, melting into her, not melting enough, wanting to dissolve into her body.

'Listen.' Sharon took a deep breath as she moved back, staring into me. 'I have to ask you something. And you have to be honest with me.'

'OK.'

'Really honest.' She closed her eyes and paused. Her face grew serious, determined. 'I was going to wait, play it easy for a while too, but I can't either. I can't even wait till we're home. I messed you around once and I'm not going to do it again. I need to know what it was all about for you. Us getting back together. I'm going to tell you now that I love you. And I always have. But was it just nostalgia for you? Or do you want to carry on?'

'Sharon . . .'

'Not just carry on, actually. What, what I really need to know is if you love *me*. God, that sounds stupid. You told me that you did but you've had time to think, really think. I need to know. So please tell me and don't worry if you're not sure. I can manage on my own.'

'I love you,' I said. 'I want you to move in with me. Or me with you, I don't care. I've been thinking about that.'

'Good. For a second, when I saw you, I was worried. I want you to know that I'll never hurt you again. I know I did and . . .'

'That's in the past. We've done that. I believe you.'

'Good, because it's true.' A smile was born on

Sharon's face, one that just kept growing. Tears balanced in her eyes. 'So. You don't mind, then?'

'Mind?'

'Oh, some detective you are.' Sharon moved forward again and took my hand. 'I didn't want to tell you on the phone. I wanted to see you, and to decide what I'd do if you didn't want to be with me. It's why I came back, why I didn't go back for the last two weeks. If it was just me, you know?'

Sharon moved my hand so that it was sitting on top of her belly. There was a little belly. Or was there – when do women get bellies? Sharon was leaving a gap for me but I didn't know what to say. She nodded.

'Don't worry, it was a bit of a surprise to me too! We only slipped one night. That first night. Remember? How about that, Mr Super Sperm?'

I still couldn't speak. Sharon's eyes were reaching out to mine like a toddler's arms.

From my pocket my phone began to ring again.

Part Three

Chapter Twenty-Two

'Billy, you have to say something.'

Sharon's bright green eyes seemed to be speeding towards me, opening more and more like a flower in a nature film. In contrast, the airport and everything surrounding us had pulled back at the speed of light, leaving us alone in our own private bubble of space and time.

When the airport crashed back in I nearly stumbled, suddenly realizing that I needed to breathe. Sharon's eyes had opened as far as they could, and though she was trying hard to hold it, she couldn't. Fear began to tinge her pupils, making them shiver, making them lose their hold on mine. Almost imperceptibly her eyes moved away, to my brow, my mouth, to the expression that must have been taking shape on my face. I watched a similar one take shape on hers. Then the noise came back in, the crowd of passengers, the hiss and clang of a bank of fruit machines in the arcade behind me.

In front of me Sharon let go of my hand and bit her lip. She didn't look scared so much as resigned, her face etched with regret. Annoyance at herself. I wanted to say to her: no, you don't understand. But I couldn't speak. Still stunned I took hold of Sharon's hand again and held it tightly as I pushed her trolley through the crowd, heading back to the coffee bar I'd been sitting at.

My mind was as full as the terminal. A scalding wind burned through my chest. The bubble returned, following us as we walked along. I saw the people going past me but I couldn't believe that this was the world I lived in. Sharon was fending off her fear with words. She said that that she wasn't trying to trap me, that it was her decision to keep the baby. The baby. I steered her trolley through the crowd that appeared like a gas, each person an atom in random motion. I was choking, I wanted to ram the trolley forward, scatter the people out of the way, but then I stopped. I felt my throat contract. Oh no. Panicking, I looked all around.

My eyes jumped from one face to the next in a millisecond. I was looking for the person who was watching us. For the person who could have followed me out to the airport just as they must have followed me down to Brixton. Seen me handing out photos of Denise. Seen me with Josephine. With Ally. I ignored the confusion coming from Sharon. Him? Him? I didn't make anyone out but then how could I? I didn't know who I was looking for and even if I did they could have been anywhere: up in the gallery, off to the side, in front of my face for godsake. I pushed the trolley forward again, hard, but then told myself to calm down. It was too late. They would have seen me meet Sharon by now. They would have seen her. The hollowness spread to my stomach, my arms. I wanted to throw up. The only hope I had was the headscarf Sharon wore, that and her loose robes. I'd had to look twice at her myself.

We made it through to the coffee bar but Sharon wasn't keen on staying there.

'I can see you're surprised, but can't we just get out of here?' Sharon tried to make herself laugh but she didn't really manage it.

'Listen . . .'

'I should have waited.'

Sharon nodded to herself, like someone who knew the correct answer but only after giving Chris Tarrant the wrong one.

'I should have told you in a day or so. I just saw you and I wanted to tell you so much. I've fucked it up, I know. But did you really have those thoughts, about us living together?'

'Yes.'

'And you really missed me?'

'Yes.'

'God. I kept imagining you out on the town.' Sharon shook her head. 'Billy, I didn't sleep at all on the plane worrying about this. Can't we just leave? Can't we just pretend I never said anything? I don't want you making rash promises after I've just dumped this on you.'

'Just give me five minutes, please.'

'I could have got rid of it and it was my decision not to, so if you don't want to be a part of it . . .'

'Please,' I said again.

We were on the tube. I'd sat Sharon down in the coffee bar and told her what had happened, beginning with Josephine Thomas. She was concerned, but no more than I had been when I'd heard about it. A murder on the news, a little closer to home than normal. I could tell Sharon thought that was it and I tried to prepare her for the fact that it wasn't, but I didn't know how. I felt like a fighter pilot, locked in on Sharon's matrix, my thumb poised over the red button. Eventually I let it go and I watched from ten miles up as the news of Ally's death blew Sharon apart. I explained how I'd found her. I told her about the girl in the tunnel and then I told her how Andy had just called me. I told her that somehow, in some way I couldn't fathom, I was the cause of all this.

Sharon's first question was about Mike, how he was, and my stomach filled with ice to think of him. I couldn't think of him. I said we should go and I pushed Sharon's trolley down to the train station, where I bought two tickets for the Heathrow Express. When it came we climbed aboard but when the doors beeped I put my foot in the way and stepped out onto the platform again, dragging Sharon's cases after me. Sharon stepped out of the carriage too. No one else got off the train. The train left and the only person on the platform was a conductor. If we'd been followed, the person doing it was on that train. I found another trolley and pushed it in the direction of the Underground. Sharon didn't say anything, accepting what I'd done, just gripping my arm for reassurance. I wasn't sure whose.

When the tube came we found some seats and sat down next to each other. Sharon's headscarf was annoying her and she went to push it back over her head.

'Don't,' I said. 'It suits you. Leave it.'

Sharon looked at me but left the scarf there. She took hold of my hand and we were silent for a long time as the tube clattered in towards central London.

I'd pictured this moment in my mind for weeks. Months. But it had never been like this. Instead of enjoying the fact that Sharon was back, or thinking about what she'd told me, my mind bucked forwards, sideways, all over, searching for some kind of answer to the news I'd been given. I hadn't called Andy back. I wanted to think first, try to pull something out of the tangle of events that I seemed to be at the centre of. I thought of all the cases I'd handled, the people I'd put away. It had to be one of them but I had no idea which. None stood out, no pregnant women I'd sent to prison or anything like that. No doubt Andy was already pulling the files. I suddenly realized that he'd probably be worried too. We'd worked so many cases together. Would it be his turn next? I remembered that he had a sister. Did she have any kids? Sitting beneath all of these thoughts, like the foundations to a house, was the news that Sharon had given me.

I was holding Sharon's hand, not realizing how tight my grip was. She smiled at me.

'Whatever is happening, it's not your fault,' she said. 'It might be to do with you but you're not to blame. How could you be?'

'I don't have any kind of idea.'

'Because you're not. You just have to be patient, you'll see. As for Mike, you couldn't help suspecting him. He probably knows that by now. He should understand why you thought it. OK?'

I smiled but didn't say anything. I didn't think Mike would see it like that. Three women had died because of something in my past and I'd thought he had killed Ally. I remembered the woman at the bus stop, how she'd looked at me, looked at me as if I was a danger to her. She'd been right. Hoping she wouldn't notice I drew my hand out of Sharon's. Again, I saw it, all over the cafe: It Was You. I looked around the carriage for the fifth time, my eyes resting on each of the faces there. I counted six people reading the free paper, *Metro*. The front page carried a picture of the blocked-off tunnel mouth, opening like a grave. 'Carnage' was the headline, beneath which were the words, 'Tunnel Crash Holds Chilling Secret'. The faces of those reading the paper were all the same. Stilled by horror. And hooked by it. This was how it was playing out there, amongst people not connected. A chilling story, unfolding, until they turned the page. I looked at them with a distaste I couldn't justify and a huge spike of envy. I couldn't turn the page.

I told Sharon that I wasn't going to be able to come back to her flat with her, that I had to go straight to Calshot Street. She nodded, said she understood. Sharon still looked shell-shocked but I wasn't surprised by how calmly she was taking this. She was thinking about me, about Mike, not wanting her own feelings to confuse things, to get in our way. As a barrister, working in the most challenging field, she'd made a living out of keeping her feelings to one side. I told myself not to be fooled, though, not to ignore her just because she looked like she was coping. Right then I saw a flicker of doubt rather than fear in her eyes, and it was directed towards me. I tried to reassure her.

'I'm sorry but it's best,' I said. 'Go home. I'll call you from the station, OK?'

'And you'll come round, though, after?'

'I'll try. I will, but I don't know how late I'll be.'

'It doesn't matter. Just come.'

'Sharon, you have to understand what's happening here. All these women are dead because they were pregnant and connected to me, or at least someone thought they were. And so . . .'

'I know,' she said, 'but I need to be with you. Can't you see that? No one knows about this except me, you and the doctor at the British embassy in Islamabad. And he won't tell. I don't *look* pregnant either except in my pants and then only a bit and I'm not going to walk round in my pants, am I? So, you'll come round? I need you at the moment.'

'And I need you. But you understand? The graffiti outside my house. They know where I live.'

'Just come round,' Sharon said again.

I took Sharon's hand again and said that I would come. Once again I thought about how this could have played itself out. I'd hoped we'd just fling ourselves into each other's arms and live happily ever after but I'd been prepared for a strangeness, a need to adjust. Nothing like any of this. And I had so many questions to ask her, about Afghanistan, Pakistan, her work, none of which seemed even slightly relevant now. Instead I returned to my own thoughts, trying to keep a lid on the waves of panic that rose and fell within me. Jo's mother flashed into my mind, asking me if I'd killed her daughter. Then Denise came in. I'd never even met her. Her husband had asked me to find her. I'd looked for her and for some reason that was why she was dead. What could I possibly say to him?

We were in that long gap between Turnham Green and Hammersmith, the carriage swaying from side to side like a battleship. A gang of fifteen-year-old lads had piled on, hormones spilling out of them like drool from a bulldog's mouth. They were gangly, loud, intimidating, stripping away the muted calm of the carriage like

183

a swarm of locusts. The other passengers shrank back in their seats, an old lady visibly afraid, wincing at the vocab. The only white kid was trying to pick up a pair of girls opposite. Another lad, wearing a yellow bandanna, was swinging on the straps, flipping himself over backwards.

'Hey,' he said, after he'd righted himself one more time. 'What did the pregnant bird say to the man who was strangling her?'

The white kid turned. 'Dunno.'

'Cut it out!'

They all howled.

'My sister's knocked up,' another one said. 'I keep telling her the cutty man's going to get her. She won't even go out the house. I say he's watching, that she's like a loaf of bread and when she's baked enough he's going to get the knife to her. She cries and everything, you should see her.'

'You wouldn't like it if he did get her, though, man.'

'Yeah! Thing's only like gonna cry all night innit, keep me awake? Serve her right for being a slag.'

'Your sister's a slag?'

'Yeah, man.'

'When we coming round?'

'She pregnant, man, that's sick.'

'That's best, means I won't have to worry. Tell you one thing, though. Cutty man should come round my estate, plenty of pregnant birds for him there. You think it's the fellas, they payin' him? Cheaper than child support innit?'

They all laughed again.

'We better shut up guys,' the gymnast said. 'That man don't look happy. Think we offended him. Tell you what, though, it's a free country and I'll say what I like. Less he's got a problem with that, which case he knows what to do.'

All five kids were looking at me. I hadn't been aware that there was any sort of expression on my face. It made me feel old. Sharon's hand pressed down on my arm.

'They're just kids. Please, Billy.'

The kid in the bandanna was looking at me with lazy, insolent eyes, his long legs stretching out across the carriage. I saw him in class, dealing out that look, knowing the teacher couldn't touch him.

'Billy. Stay with me. OK?'

'Looks like his bitch has saved him a kicking. Lucky fella. Hey, darling, what you doing with that loser for, hey? Pretty girl like you might stand a chance with me.'

Sharon's grip on my arm grew tighter. It stayed there until the kids got off at Piccadilly Circus, the gymnast flipping me a lazy finger as he stepped down onto the platform, another tossing a half-empty can of Dr Pepper back into the carriage, the contents glugging out over the floor.

'The cutty man,' Sharon said, when the doors had closed. 'Nice.'

We rode the rest of the way in silence.

Chapter Twenty-Three

The incident room was flat out when I got there. It was jamming with the sound of phones ringing, printers running and detectives shouting to be heard above the racket. The new equipment had been installed and the room was full, junior detectives sharing phones and desks. Andy led me through to his workspace, which was right in the middle of the mayhem, partitioned on three sides.

It was two hours since Andy had called me at the airport and he was apoplectic at the delay, that I'd left him hanging. He himself had just got back from Exmouth Market, where he'd been talking to Max about the graffiti his cafe had been daubed with. Forensics were still there. I tried to stay calm. I tried not to give way to the cold sickness sitting inside me that still made me want to vomit. Andy pushed a seat towards me and I sat next to him, a rash of Post-its saluting from his desktop, fag burns already lining the edges like dead fingernails. Andy was brisk, decisive, his eyes alive, the sluggish aura that usually surrounded him gone. This was a break. Someone had been linked to all three killings. The random element that made catching serial killers such a problem was removed. Andy made no reference to what I might be feeling about it, but though

I was pissed off at that I tried to match him. To stay cool, to realize that he was right, that having something to go on meant that we had a greater chance of preventing any more deaths. But when I thought of Sharon it all dissolved.

Andy pointed out a few of the key people to me, told me what they were doing, and then turned me towards the board. A picture of Ally smiled out at me and I looked away. Next to it was a shot of Josephine Thomas. I handed Andy a copy of the shot of Denise Denton that her husband had given me and he stuck it up there too. I looked at the girl with the spiky black hair and shook my head. Jared hadn't told me she was pregnant. Maybe he hadn't known. That was probably why she'd left him.

I felt helpless, confused, my mind churning with all that had been shoved into it. I kept reaching out in every direction for some kind of meaning. Raising his voice against the racket surrounding us, Andy immediately told me to think back.

'Some old case, someone with a reason to come back at you like this. You must have some ideas.'

'Me?' I said. 'You think. In case you've forgotten, you were on most of my cases. So which of the fucks we sent down would want to do this? None of them? All of them? I don't know. Practically nine out of ten promised to come back at us but you used to laugh, you used to say it was bollocks, something to impress the missus. None of them ever did anything.'

'Until now.'

'OK. But how am I supposed to know who it is any more than you are? What do you think?'

'I don't know. I've been racking my brains and I'm

nowhere. I could understand either of us getting a bullet in the kneecap one dark night, but this? This is specific, particular, and I can't think of anything.'

I took a few deep breaths and relaxed my arms. I wasn't proud of my eagerness to pull Andy into it. Maybe it was about him too, but if it was, why had the killer only gone after women I knew? Not even knew, had some sort of connection with. I still couldn't believe someone had done what they had to Denise just because I'd passed her picture round. I asked if Denise's identity was a hundred per cent and Andy told me that it was. I nodded but then shook my head and then I had another thought. When Andy and I had worked together he'd pushed the envelope far further than I ever had. If this was about something he'd done without telling me, I'd kill him for it. I would. Andy flipped a page of his daybook.

'Listen. If you haven't got any definite ideas, we'll leave it, we'll go over who the bastard might be in a minute. In the meantime, I need to ask you. Do you know any other pregnant women?'

I hesitated. I had to decide. Instinctively, I knew. I couldn't trust Andy. Sharon was right: it was still a secret. The fewer people who knew the better.

'No.'

'Because, if you do, they are in serious danger.'

I shook my head.

'Good. But what about women you might have just spoken to, not friends as such but in your local pub? The bookie you use, stuff like that. Bumped into. Anyone.'

'I don't know. You'd better send a squad out to check. Places near my flat, near the Lindauer.'

'OK. Let's start with them. Whoever's doing this needs only the slightest connection. That Denise girl, you weren't shtuping her or anything?'

'I told you. I never even met her.'

'Right,' Andy said. 'Let's concentrate, OK? Women you might have any sort of link with.'

'And women you know, too.'

'Of course,' Andy said. 'Them as well.'

When I'd run out of places where I hung out, where I'd been in the last few months, Andy wrote his own list. He handed both to a DC and told him to get some uniforms out. I then gave Andy a detailed rundown of my hour spent in Brixton, finishing with the skeletal hooker I'd tussled with. We agreed that the killer must have followed me, must have picked up Denise there. I hadn't handed out pictures of her anywhere else. I gave a description of the girl who'd tried to knife me and he took it down, nodding like what I was telling him was his favourite tune. I could see the connections knitting together inside Andy and I felt them too, but it didn't stop me feeling that my whole life had fallen apart.

After I'd told Andy what I could about the apparition I'd seen on the street corner that afternoon, he made me go through it again with a police artist, sitting next to him at his Mac. I rejoined Andy and told him that, as well as the hooker, a woman in the traffic had seen me too. She'd given me the evil eye. She might have noticed something. Andy asked me if I'd pegged anyone following me but I said I hadn't. I'd been in my own little world, preoccupied with thoughts of Sharon and how wonderful my life was going to be.

Andy and I hit it back and forth for another exhausting, frustrating hour. It was more French Open than Wimbledon, each point taking a hell of a long time to get made. Apart from finding the girl, the other route in was CCTV from the Lindauer. I needed to go through it for the last six months. See if anyone stood out. I wanted to get to that straight away but Andy said that all the clear facial images from it were being isolated by a team of officers. It would be far quicker for me to go through the stills than sit through hours of tape, my finger on the pause button. It was frustrating but he was right, six months was a hell of a long time. Andy said he'd have most of them for me by tomorrow lunchtime at the latest.

When we came to a natural pause Andy asked a DC to get us some coffee and we didn't speak for a while, letting our thoughts sink to the bottom of our minds to see what we were left with. The rest of the room still hummed. This was what you prayed for on the Met. This was what got you through the interviews with teenage car thieves, helped you take the abuse as you led single mothers out of Tesco for slipping jars of baby food into their bags. I breathed in the activity, the concentration, also noticing how I was being eyed up furtively, a room full of detectives all wondering what the hell I'd done to bring this on. Rucker. One of us, wasn't he? Left when his brother got put in a coma. Couldn't hack it after that. Tell you what, I'm glad I'm not him. Someone slicing up women he knows, some twat those two put away on a plant, something dodgy? I bet he hopes we catch the fucker pretty quick. He won't get laid again until we do, will he? Birds'll run a bleeding mile from him.

When the coffee came Andy took a sip and then ran his fingernails hard across his scalp. He told me that he'd ordered copies of the files on every case we'd ever worked. Some had already come up and we started to go through them, looking for any sign of someone whose grudge against me might have taken this particular form. It took us another two and a half hours and we couldn't find anything, though Andy did order a couple of cross references, wanting to know release dates, things like that. He said that he was going to give the rest of the files to his team to look at.

'What about the profiler?' I asked. 'Where's he?'

'On the M4 by now, I should think.'

'Huh?'

'Heading back to Oxford. He wanted his own office and secretary, and five detectives to chase up his leads. Watches too much Channel 5, I think. Condor sent him packing.'

'Psychiatrists?'

'We're putting the word out, hoping that any quack treating a nutcase who's expressed a desire to cut up pregnant women will call us on the QT. I think it's a dead end, though. If our boy was going to seek help, I just don't see him doing this, do you?'

Flipping the last file closed, Andy put a foot up on his desk and I sat back in my chair. We were finished. We couldn't do any more. Andy folded his arms and yawned.

'New bird then?' he said.

I hesitated. 'Sorry?'

'You. New bird? Well? Have you got a new girl-friend?'

'What makes you say that?'

'You were at the airport when I called. I could tell.

You weren't going anywhere so I assume you were meeting someone.'

I could have thought of any number of reasons to be there but Andy had thrown me. When he saw me hesitate he smiled and went on.

'You don't meet people at the airport unless you're shafting them. And then only if it's a recent acquisition you want to hang on to. So, Watson, I surmise there's a woman involved.'

'You should be a detective.'

'I know. Instead of someone who sits at a desk filling forms in.'

'That hasn't changed then?'

'It's got worse.'

'I wouldn't have believed that was possible.'

'Believe it.' Andy yawned again, wider this time. Then he laughed. 'So?'

'What?'

'The airport. Who were you meeting?'

'Just an old friend.'

'Why didn't you get back to me then? Old friend would have understood, something as big as this.'

'I needed to think. I was freaked out. Anyway, am I done?'

'It's OK, Billy, you don't have to tell me. Scared I'll steal her away, I know. But, yes, you're done for now. Just don't go far. And keep your eyes open. You're at the centre of this. This nutter has killed women only so far but that's not to say he won't want to get to you. We've put a van outside your flat but Clay says you can have a safe house if you want one. How about it?'

'No thanks.'

'Good. It wouldn't be a bad thing if the perp decided

to knock on your door, would it? Just be very careful, as I say.'

'They armed? In the van?'

'Tooled like Tarantino. He comes, they'll get him.'

'And you've given them a photo, right? So they don't just open up on me when I get home?'

'No need,' Andy laughed. 'Carpenter said he remembered you well enough. He's on the first shift with three others, poor bastards. Imagine being cooped up twelve hours straight with that smelly twat.'

Chapter Twenty-Four

I left Andy in the incident room and walked through the station to the main entrance. Outside the sun was holding on by its fingertips to the rooftops of King's Cross, as if a giant beast was trying to drag it down into the bowels of the capital. I took a deep breath, squinting into the sinking orange slice, and tried to focus. When the sun was gone I waited, listening, almost expecting to hear it scream.

One thing at a time. It was the only way through this. Sharon came first. She'd be at home, in her flat in Hackney. She'd bought it last year and had thought about letting it while she was abroad. I was glad she hadn't. She'd be safe there. We hadn't been followed. No way. Also, no one knew she was coming home because it had all been last minute, not her friends or anyone, so how could the person doing this know? A small measure of calm spread through me. I called her but only got a message, so I figured she was asleep. At least, I hoped she was. After the elation of seeing me had gone she'd looked tired. I shook my head, thinking how hard it must have been for her. Her job was demanding enough, but then finding out she was pregnant. Thinking about it, wondering what to do. As much as I'd been scared that she wouldn't want me, how much worse would it have been for her? And then she'd come back to this.

I pictured Sharon curled up on her bed, and I prayed that she'd sleep long. I wondered if the creature inside her would be sleeping too. It stunned me to think of it. I pushed everything aside and thought about it there, inside Sharon, inside my girlfriend. I tried to picture it, what it was doing. Did it wake and sleep yet, did it know the difference? I didn't know. I thought about the time we'd made love and made it. That first time. To be able to pin the moment down like that felt bizarre, the beginning of a life traced back to one, isolated, definite event, which hadn't seemed like an act of creation. We'd fumbled at each other's clothes like fifteen-year-olds and then we'd hardly moved. We'd just held on to each other, inside each other, barely able to believe it.

Pregnant. She was pregnant. I suddenly wondered. If none of this other stuff was happening. If I'd gone to the airport and she'd told me. What would I have felt? There was no way I could know. It was far beyond that.

After calling Sharon, I called Sally and asked her if she could come down to the gym an hour early that night. She said she could but when she asked why I said I'd tell her when I saw her. It left half an hour to kill. I thought about heading down to Loughborough Junction to find the girl I'd seen, but I didn't have time. I remembered what she'd said to me. 'What are you? Daddy?' I'd thought she'd meant Denise's father but she hadn't. She'd meant the father of Denise's child. So she must have known Denise. Denise had probably shown up after I'd left. She must have been picked up by the person who'd followed me, and probably picked

195

up soon after I'd gone. The girl I'd fought with would almost certainly have seen Denise. And if she had, she must have seen the person who took Denise away.

Half an hour wasn't enough time to go down there, though, and I really did want to see Sally.

Instead I walked towards the gym, stopping to lean on some railings across the junction from the station, breathing in the peculiar ambience of King's Cross. The area that used to be my beat hasn't changed, in spite of the renovation programmes, the companies who have escaped the hiked rents in the City or the West End to set up there. It still oozes its peculiar mixture of shabbiness and weary danger, something that must puzzle the city planners and developers every time they come down. Clerkenwell was the same when I moved in but it has changed beyond recognition with its coffee bars and bookshops, restaurants and trendy tailors. In contrast, King's Cross, surrounded though it is by Clerkenwell, Islington, Bloomsbury and Camden, continues to resist gentrification like Asterix fighting the Romans.

The word 'Shit' had been sprayed on the window of the McDonald's opposite, accompanied by an anarchist sign, and my mind skipped back to the graffiti on Fred's. I remembered talking to Max about it. Assuming it was just kids. Just as I had for the last four hours I tried to dredge something up, anything, that might give me a clue as to what I'd done to prompt this. It Was You. *What* was? Had some crim's wife lost her baby while he was inside, something like that? I just didn't know. I sighed and shook my head, looking across the junction, where I saw Lucas, a rent boy I spoke to now and then, his back against a lamp post. He was chatting to another boy. The other boy was two or three years younger than Lucas, fifteen maybe, and when a man in a long blue overcoat came to speak to them it was the other boy he left with. Lucas folded his arms and stared after them, the question spinning round his head easy to read on his startled, horrified face. How did life wash me up here? The same question spun round my head too.

I was also wondering: is he watching me? Right now? King's Cross was swarming with people. Some, like Lucas, were static, had their business there, but most were moving through: to the train, the tube, the buses or the cabs. Could he see me leaning against this railing? I also wondered about the women around me and I searched the crowds for one who might be pregnant. Now I felt that everyone was looking at me. That all of these people must surely be able to see what I had brought into their papers, their TV news programmes, into their city. I shrank in on myself and bowed my head. A young kid in the back of a car caught my eye but I turned away.

Sal must have left right after I'd called her because the gym was open when I got there. Open but quiet. I walked down the steps, past the recumbent machines, and found Sal in her office. She was frowning over some accounts, her dark curly hair piled on top of her head like a nest. A gas fire burned in the far corner. Sal looked up with a bright smile when she saw me, but her face changed in a second. She said she was pleased to see me, but guessed that it wasn't a social call. I said it wasn't. I took a seat and told her what was going on. I told her everything from Jemma's visit, to the graffiti,

to the phone call I'd got from Andy. How I'd realized that I was at the centre of this. When I'd told Sharon about it I'd been stunned, had stumbled through it. Telling it to Sally, clearly, so she'd get it all, felt like walking on ice. I was testing it out, amazed that it really was true. The ice held. I could see Sal's mind working. I could see that she knew why I was telling her what I was, why it was her that I'd gone to.

How big a part of the fabric of London's underworld Sal is I've never really known. It's not something we talk about unless we have to, just as Sal seldom mentions my previous career. But I do know that she's deep in the mix. That Sal's gym is just a sideline for the business she took over when her husband was killed, ten years or so ago. I know that she has dealings with serious men, with serious faces, who do serious things. I also know that she is privy to the undercurrents of rumour and counter-rumour that move largely unnoticed around London like the dark, unseen rivers that flow constantly beneath all our feet into the Thames. I hadn't gone there because I expected Sal to know anything, though. I just wanted her to ask around, to see what was being said. I also wanted Sal to get something for me, something you couldn't buy on the High Street.

As I went through it, Sal listened, her face impassive to begin with before tightening with concern. It then became impassive again, while she thought about it. I was glad Sal didn't gush, tell me how terribly sorry she felt for me. She knew I hadn't gone there for that. When I got to the end, Sal told me that she'd read about the murders, of course, but hadn't given them a lot of thought. It was different, though, me being involved. I nodded. Then, without me asking, Sal told me that she'd put the word out: if anyone knew anything, any- thing at all, she should hear it. I nodded again and thanked her. I told her to let it be known that there was cash available for anyone with anything worth hearing. A lot of cash. I'd come into some money by accident earlier in the year, something I suspected Sal already knew about. At the mention of the cash Sal sucked in her cheeks.

'It'll help,' she said. 'It nearly always does, though I'm not sure how much good it'll be in this case. I don't want you to expect too much, Billy.'

It was what I'd told Jemma. 'I won't.'

'Good. You see, this just isn't the sort of thing pro- fessional villains do.'

'I know.'

'No profit in killing pregnant women and getting half of London's Bill on your case. And where there's no profit, there tends to be no firm.' Sal shrugged. 'There's also the fact, and you don't have to believe this if you don't want, but as far away from normal morality as your regular crims operate, this is as far away from them again. I can't see anyone I know being involved. The thing that is on your side, though, is that they will all want it sorting. It's likely to bring a lot of unwanted attention to people who make very good livings because they don't normally get any. They won't want that. So you never know.'

'Thanks,' I said. 'In advance. Even if you don't hear anything.'

'It's nothing. But Billy.' Sal paused a second, weighing me up. She looked at me with the dark brown eyes that I knew could convey soft, intense emotion, but right then were hard and steady. Then she said the exact opposite of what Clay had.

'If we do find out who's doing this, I know people who'll sort it for you, given the right price. Going to the police? I know I wouldn't want that. Not if it was my friend. Not if it was me it was all aimed at.'

'I don't want that either. Unless it's the only way.'

'Then I'll have a quiet word with Mountain Pete in case you need him.'

'Have a word with Pete,' I said.

Sal pushed out a long breath, nodded, and gave me a frank look that said: I'm glad I'm not you. Her face then, finally, flooded with sympathy, and she looked relieved at having been able to let it out. She smiled the smile that didn't belong to the person she was now, that had somehow survived from the time she was just a normal young girl who'd fallen in love with the wrong type of man. She shook her head, the hair tied up on top wobbling. She drew her chair in.

'In the meantime,' she said, 'you told me about the hooker at Loughborough Junction. Don't go down there again.'

I frowned. 'Why not? I've got to find that girl.'

'I know. You do. But, as you know, the 22 Crew are the gaffers down there. They're a pretty tight unit and they don't like gatecrashers at their party. The Bill'll be all over the place anyway and most likely the girls'll be laying low. You won't find her, for a start. Listen, I don't like what the 22 do, and I don't like dealing with them. But they'll know it's for the best to put an end to this. They'll be losing revenue, losing it right now. I'm pretty sure the girl works for them if she was where you say, but let *them* speak to her. Let them get a description of the guy you're looking for. They might even let you talk to her yourself but only if you ask first. Don't go down there sticking your beak in again. It really won't get you anywhere and you might just get it bitten off.'

I thought about it. I didn't really care about upsetting people but it made sense that the streets would be empty. 'But you'll speak to them?'

'I promise. And I'll tell them what you want. They'll probably come back through me but I'll give them your mobile number. They might phone you direct.'

'OK. And thanks again, Sal.'

'Save it. The 22 – you might not thank me if you get tangled up with that lot.'

'I'll try not to.'

'Good. Most of them are just in it for the money and you shouldn't have a problem if you're straight with them. But if they do contact you, to say it's all right to speak to the girl, for instance, be careful. Especially of a guy they call Charlie Baby.'

'Charlie Baby?'

'One of their captains. He likes getting his hooks in, seeing how far he can stretch people.'

'Stretch them?'

'Ask Pete sometime. His cousin got into trouble with Charlie and Pete had to sort it. No, don't ask, wait till he tells you. If he ever does. What Charlie Baby made Pete do isn't something he likes to brag about.'

'And if I can't stay away from him?'

'Then you'd better ask yourself how much you want to sort this. Because, even though he'll most likely help, he'll take something from you and it'll be more than just the money. It'll hurt.'

'I don't care.'

'You'll care,' Sal said. 'Believe me. Or you'd better pretend you do. And pretend good. Because if he can't hurt you Charlie won't help you. And then he'll find a way to hurt you anyway.'

Chapter Twenty-Five

The gym was filling up now. I could hear voices behind me and the deep drill of a Miss Dynamite tune. I felt a little better than I had done an hour ago. I'd done something, set a plan in motion. It gave me a small feeling of control, though it didn't stem the terror. I knew that I was still a blind man, waving his stick at the attacker he knows is there but can't see. Waiting for the next blow. Sal looked at her watch. I told her goodbye but she shook her head. As she stood up from her desk she tried to persuade me to put some work in.

'You've already piked out of two training sessions, Billy Rucker, and you're not going to miss a third.'

I said no on reflex but let Sal change my mind. As much as I wanted to get to Sharon, I thought it might do me good, give my brain time to regroup. I changed into some shorts from my locker and joined the circuit training that puts Sally one place behind Torquemada in the Torture Hall of Fame. Finding myself still breathing when Sal called a halt I used the bike and the rower and then the heavy bag, stopping short of getting into the ring itself, even though Jeff did his best to persuade me into a rematch.

All the while I was thinking that I didn't know whether or not to feel guilty, guilty about the deaths of three women. Until I'd found out who was doing it, and why, how would I know? My frustration was added to by the fact that whatever the police were doing, and they were doing a lot, the answer was inside me. It had to be. And I couldn't get to it. The workout hadn't helped. As I was leaving the gym, I remembered the massage girl and wished she was there now. Maybe her ministrations might have had a greater effect.

Back on Exmouth Market I made the van easily enough but only because I was looking for it. It was an unmarked blue Transit, perfectly anonymous but for the smoked plastic window on the side. It was parked at the top of the street, at the end of the market, with a good view of the door to my flat and all the approaches to it. It felt strange, knowing I was being watched as I unlocked the street door. Carpenter would be pointing me out to the other officers, getting them to remember my face. He'd probably be telling them all about me. How the drug cartel I'd been after as a DS had tried to finish me, but got my brother instead. I thought of Luke, lying motionless in his hospital bed as the world drifted past him, unnoticed. For the first time in nearly seven and a half years I was almost jealous of him.

Upstairs I picked up the phone but put it right down again. I couldn't see the point of calling Sharon again, maybe waking her, just to tell her I was coming over. I ran through the way we'd left the airport, every single face we'd seen, and told myself she was safe. She was. Instead of calling her, I made myself eat a bowl of filled pasta and then tried Andy again, without any success. I guessed he'd be one of the officers down in Brixton, trying to shake out the girl. I wanted to go down there too but I'd trust Sally, for a day at least. If the 22 didn't come through, I'd go and find the girl. I wouldn't care whose party I was crashing. The girl was the key, I was sure of it. If she gave me a description, it might shake something loose, might make me think of the person she'd seen. It was difficult to wait but I had to do it. Unless the police found her, in which case I'd get to her sooner. I couldn't decide whether I wanted the police to find her or not.

Andy had said the CCTV stills would be ready the next day, so that was something else I had to wait for. He'd told me midday but I'd go there first thing, look at the ones they'd already pulled. No point waiting for them all when the first picture I looked at might be the one. But what now? I wanted to do something, something that would keep me from trying to wring the answer out of my mind, which only seemed to send it hiding even deeper. I knew something I could do and the thought was so good it was painful. The clock in my kitchen told me it was nine-thirty. I grabbed my coat and walked down to the street again. It was ten-thirty by the time I was standing on the north side of the bridge that crosses Regent's Canal, at Broadway Market in Hackney.

I'd driven down to Hackney but parked half a mile away from my destination on the other side of London Fields. I'd locked up and then walked away from Broadway Market, all the way to the busy, unfashion-able end of Kingsland Road. Once there I'd jogged down some steps onto the canal towpath. It was a ten-minute walk along it to Broadway Market and as I took it I listened out for footsteps behind me. I couldn't hear any. I ducked behind a bridge to see if anyone came by, but they didn't. Eventually I emerged onto Broadway

Market and stood with my back to the still water. I tied my shoes and took a furtive look across to Sharon's flat. Sharon's flat is on the other side of the canal, looking straight down onto the water, part of a converted machine-tools factory.

I stayed where I was for ten minutes, pretending to smoke a cigarette, making sure that no one had followed me. I didn't think they had, and I couldn't see anyone else watching the buildings opposite. Sharon was home, I did know that. Orange light pushed through her curtains. I stood, trying to act casual, and whether I did a good job of it or not no one seemed to notice me. I pictured the inside of Sharon's flat and remembered the last time I'd been there. It was the night before Sharon had gone away and we hadn't fumbled around then or been very still either. I smiled. I'd been impressed by Sharon's flat. It was light, with high ceilings and a good kitchen, ducks to feed right outside the window. There was also a boxroom and I wondered now: was it big enough for a nursery? Probably. I had to admit that the place was a lot more practical than my flat. Without even thinking about it I knew that we'd live at Sharon's. It would be weird to move out of my place but it made sense, though if we had another kid then we'd have to move out of Sharon's too and find a house somewhere. Another kid? What the hell was I talking about, another kid?

I was still standing on the other side of the canal. I still hadn't crossed the bridge and rung Sharon's bell. I scanned the towpath, where a bow-legged Arsenal fan wearing a thick gold chain was walking his bull terrier. He passed the looming gas tower and was gone. An old couple followed in the same direction, not speaking. I took another step forward but I couldn't do it. I couldn't go there. The thought was terrifying. I wanted to run across the bridge, to be there with my pregnant girl-friend, to press my face against her belly and listen for the sounds within. But my feet wouldn't take me. Instead I stood for another ten minutes before turning round. I walked off quickly, down Broadway Market, to my car. I thought about calling Sharon but I couldn't do that either. She'd only persuade me. I just had to go, but when I got to the brooding space that is London Fields I remembered that there was a pub on the far side that did lock-ins. I'd been there with Andy, years ago, a fleapit of a place called the Prince or something. It was just before eleven and the doors were closing when I got there. I ordered a pint and drank it quickly and then ordered another and a double shot of Jameson's in case there was no lock-in.

There was a lock-in but I put both drinks down quickly enough anyway, ordering more, emptying my head as I filled my mouth. The pub was half full, as decrepit as I remembered. Foam fought its way out of twenty-year-old upholstery and the thin, green-paisley carpet was matted with fag ash and beer. A drunk by the jukebox was playing the same Tom Jones song again and again. I was sitting at the bar next to three builders. I don't know how long I stayed there, the noise around me was just noise. The Guinness was thin and ferrous and so I emptied the whiskey right into it. Then a man's voice stood out from it, one of the buil-ders. He was telling the joke, the same joke that I'd heard on the tube that morning. But he never got to the end of it. He was heading backwards by then, his nose closer to the back of his head than was usual. His colleagues objected and I laid one of them out too before someone managed to get me in a bear hug. It was the landlord and when the first guy was up, and then the second, the four of them managed to get me outside. I thought that might be it but instead they got me back behind some wheely bins, the landlord being the most enthusiastic. I covered up as best as I could but I didn't try to stop them. I laughed through most of it.

The phone woke me, which meant that I was at home. The digits on my alarm clock told me it was just after nine. When I reached out to silence the ringing a sharp, barbed spike jabbed into my ribs. It was followed by a sticky pulling, as if all the muscles in the side of my chest had been Velcro'd to my ribcage. I winced, instantly remembering everything that had happened. The canal, the soft, comforting glow behind Sharon's window. Everything up until I was dragged out of the pub. After that it was a blank. I couldn't remember how I'd got back, or got undressed, how I'd got into bed. I was just glad I had. The phone was still ploughing a furrow through my skull. I pulled my cheek from the pillow it was stuck to and shuffled closer to it, so that I wouldn't have to hold my hand out very far. I hesitated before picking it up, knowing that as soon as I did my life would begin again.

I thought it might be Sharon and I was braced for what she'd say to me. But it was Andy. He asked me if I was awake and I said I was, just. In a hurried voice, he told me that the girl in Loughborough Junction hadn't been found yet and I nodded to myself. She must have been in hiding and me looking for her would probably have been fruitless too. Sal was right. Andy did say, however, that he had located the flat Denise Denton had been using before her death. It was a squat, in a derelict block near to the corner she'd been working. I asked him about the CCTV stills. They'd be ready by ten. I said I'd be down there, which meant I'd have forty minutes in the bath.

'One more thing,' Andy said.

'Go on.'

'The husband. In Birmingham.'

'Jared?'

'We picked him up.'

'Good.'

'But not in Birmingham. Here, wandering around Euston station. Trains to Birmingham leave from there.'

'I know. Did you tell him?'

'Someone else did. I'm about to grill him. Tell me, what was he like?'

I shrugged. It hurt. 'I don't know. He missed his wife, seemed pretty cut up.'

'Not as bad as she was.'

'For fucksake. Anyway, you don't think he's got anything to do with it?'

'Why not? He's connected to his wife obviously but he was in the Lindauer. He came to see you. So he's connected to Ally and the Thomas girl too. All three. Left his job, apparently without saying a word.'

'Come on! Why? Why do this? I'd never met him before he walked into my office, I've got no link to him at all!'

'Not that you know of. We'll be checking that but think about it, OK?'

'I'll think about it. Ten then?'

'Ten,' Andy said.

I put the phone down and looked at it. I picked it up again and dialled Sharon's number, swearing when her voicemail picked up. I left it a long time, trying to think what to say, some way of explaining my feelings as I'd stood on the bridge last night. I couldn't do it, not to a machine. I'd have to speak to her in person, call her later. I tried to imagine what she'd felt last night, waiting for me, realizing finally that I wasn't going to show. Had she looked out of the window and seen me there? I doubted it but I didn't really know. I hung up.

In the bathroom I yawned and stretched gingerly, seeing how far my body would move. I'd hoped to be at the station before now but I needed to get myself together. I thought about Andy's suspicions. I couldn't imagine there was anything in them, though. The machine, just going through all the possibilities, leaving nothing out. I spun the hot tap and then looked in the mirror. I wasn't feeling as bad as I should have. My left cheek was grazed, embedded with grit, but that was all. I cleaned it with cotton wool and Dettol, ending up looking like a Duran Duran fan who'd forgotten half of his blusher. Then I headed downstairs to get a pint of milk while the bath ran. That's when I saw it. It was sitting on the doormat, at the foot of the stairs. A plain, white, letter-sized envelope with a handwritten address.

I saw the letter but I didn't pick it up until I came back in with the milk. I don't get much mail at home other than utility bills. The rest goes to my office, gives me an incentive to get out of bed and go there in the morning. I grabbed it and hopped back up the stairs and saw that it had a London postmark. I tossed it onto the side, intending to ignore it, but when I reached for the kettle I stopped and picked it up again. The entire address was written in very deliberate block capitals. Who writes a whole address in capitals? Not just the town or the postcode? I turned the envelope over. There was nothing on the back. I stuck a finger beneath the flap and jagged it all the way along. Inside was a folded rectangle of shiny, coloured paper. A page clipped out of a London A–Z.

I held the page in my hand and frowned. I searched for some kind of note but there was nothing else in the envelope. Tossing the envelope aside, I opened the page out and saw an area of London stretching east to west from Queensway to Shepherd's Bush. I frowned again. I looked at it for a few seconds but it didn't tell me anything, other than the fact that the Round Pond in Kensington Gardens was more of an oval. I turned over, expecting another page of London streets, but my eye went straight to the arrow. There was an arrow stretching from the very edge of the map to the centre, an arrow, ruler-drawn, in blue biro. It looked like a party invite but there was no indication as to whose party it was. And wouldn't they have photocopied it anyway? I was irritated, about to shrug whatever it was aside, when my ribcage suddenly seemed to contract. The breath I was taking stopped in my throat as though a vice had tightened round my windpipe.

The arrow was pointing to the Westway. No, not the Westway, not the flyover itself. It was pointing just beneath it. To the exact spot where my career had ended seven-and-a-half years ago. Where everything in my life had flipped, been turned on its head, come crashing straight down.

Chapter Twenty-Six

When I'd jogged down into the Rotherhithe Tunnel to find Andy Gold two days ago images of a different wreck had come to me and I had pushed them aside. I couldn't do that now. I drove fast towards the Westway but my mind was already there.

A wet night, a low ceiling of cloud, the streets almost flooded after a whole day of rain. More of a mist now but still coming down. A car driving east towards the Marylebone Road and then King's Cross, and Exmouth Market. A car that didn't get there. My car. But not me driving. The car is speeding, the driver desperate to get where he's going, but that's not why it spins. A car transporter veers across in front of it, on purpose, and the car takes off from the kerb of the raised road, mashes the barrier, leaps into space. The car seems to stop in midair, looks like it can fly for a second, but of course it can't. It flips like a salmon and lands on its roof. Lands on my brother, on his life. The Westway. It was in the papers seven and a half years ago. There were photographs and everything.

Anyone could have seen it.

I've driven over the Westway many times since then but never been back to the place beneath, where Luke finished up, where I saw him being cut out of my car, thinking he was dead, sometimes wishing in the years since that he had been. The place where I'd turned to see a girl, his fiancée, Sharon Dean, screaming to be let through the barrier to get to him. No, I've never been able to drive up there and look at the place where it happened. What would be the point? I see it in my dreams enough as it is.

But now I was going there.

I pulled on some clothes and then spent ten minutes looking for my car keys. They were in the pocket of the jeans I'd worn yesterday. I wondered if I'd have to spend even longer looking for my car but once I was outside I saw it, twenty yards down on the left, one wheel on the pavement. The boys in the van must have seen me put it there. I wondered if they'd thought about boosting me, getting a drink-driving under their belts. They must have thought, he's lost it, it's got to him. And they'd have been right. I wondered who was in the van now, whether it was anyone else who knew me.

I took the same route that I'd taken when I got a call on my car radio that told me what had happened to Luke. The feeling was the same too; fear at what I'd find shaken up with intense impatience to get there. Last time I'd known what to expect, though not what the result would be. This time I was in the dark, had no idea what the hell I was heading to. It intensified the frustration, made me curse the traffic even more.

Like last time I tried to avoid the snarl at King's Cross and I hit the Marylebone Road near Euston. I drove past UCL, where Sharon had gone, past Harley Street, and Baker Street, burning with impatience in a slow Nile of vehicles. As soon as I could I broke off left and then swung back, finally cruising beneath the broad concrete supports that hold up the Westway. I made my way back in the direction I'd come until I'd reached Alfred Road. I stopped. Alfred Road. The sign was in the same place. Exactly. It struck me as amazing, but why should it? What reason would they have had to move it? I hesitated, suddenly wanting to forget this, to ignore the page I'd been sent. Wanting to phone Andy. Or just go home. I did neither. I pushed the car on a little, then parked on a meter at the top of the street. I looked around but I couldn't see anything. I stepped out.

I shut the door and cast my eyes around some more, ahead and behind me. I could see nothing. The street was just a street. It was quiet. Again, though, this seemed odd. That night it had been manic, like the tunnel had been. Firemen, flashing lights, shouting. My memories hovered above the street as it was now, playing themselves over. I looked through them at the two lines of parked cars, at the Fifties terraced houses that were probably worth a mint now in spite of the endless maw of traffic passing almost directly over-head. I had another memory from that night. It almost made me smile. A thinner, younger Andy Gold pulling me away from the buckled, flattened vehicle Luke was trapped in, telling me to let the firemen do their job.

I was still standing by my car. I turned one more time, again trying to pull my thoughts from that time to this. I looked at the car in front of mine, at others ahead. But still I had no idea what I was looking for, what I was supposed to be doing there. Was this some kind of joke? Or would someone be waiting for me? I didn't know. I moved my feet forward and walked slowly up the street, keeping my eyes open. I was tense, vigilant.

Soon passing the spot where Luke had come down. I didn't feel anything. Nothing happened, either inside me or out on the road. I let out a breath. In spite of the circumstances I was glad I'd finally come back there. There was no trace, nothing in the air, no vibes left to tell you what had happened. I realized that most of the people living on the street probably didn't even know, though some would remember. I walked on, putting it out of my mind, asking myself again why the hell I'd been sent there.

I walked right up to the end of the road and then back again, not knowing what to expect. Someone to meet me, contact me in some way? I checked to make sure I had my phone in case they called. But nothing happened. I began to walk up the street again. A postman passed me and I looked at him, obvious expectation on my face. He seemed confused. I turned away.

I looked inside cars and into houses through any windows that weren't curtained or covered by blinds. I braced whenever a car drove up or down the street, only to see them all go by. I stood in the middle of the road, making it obvious that I was there for anyone who wanted to speak to me. Was this stupid? Was I opening myself up to something? I didn't know, but I did begin to feel it: that I was missing something. That the reason I'd been sent to the street was right there. In front of me? Behind? Again I scoured the street. The houses were all set three yards back from the road, looking onto small front gardens, most concreted over, a couple with scooters parked. Most neat but a couple overgrown with weeds that the neighbours probably tutted about as they left in the morning. Still nothing. Again: was this some kind of joke? I watched as the postman

216

finished his round and walked off round the corner towards the Edgware Road.

I walked from one end of the street to the other until I'd been there about forty minutes. I was loath to leave but I couldn't think of anything else to do. And I was late for Andy as it was. What I did was stay visible, leaning against a meter, looking at the lumpy, mottled grey patchwork that subsequent cable-laying companies had made of the road surface. I counted the satellite dishes, averaging them out at about one for every three houses. That particular battle was over. I looked at my watch and tapped my feet, deciding to give it another ten minutes. No more. I wanted to get to the camera stills. I thought about them, what they might show me, and then my mind began to wander in a different direction. I began to slip back again to that other time, the lights of the fire engines hazy through the rain, the rain on Luke's face, his pale face, how heavy the car looked, such weight to fall down so far on top of him. Once again I heard Sharon's screaming, which had ripped open my heart, made me love her in a second. I thought about the baby inside her right now, which would have been Luke's baby. They would have had kids by now, I'm sure they would. If he hadn't gone off that bridge, that flyover. The flyover was above me. I could feel its weight. Hear the weight it carried. Finally, I looked up. For the first time I looked up at the road my brother had plummeted down from. I hadn't been able to before. I just couldn't. I wasn't there, of course, but many times I've seen him, seen Luke swerve, seen the car reach up into space and then turn. I saw it again, the wheels spinning with nothing to grip but the air.

217

And then the car vanished. My eyes were wide open. I pushed myself forward off the parking meter.

The letters were huge. On the concrete sides of the raised road. Someone must have climbed down over the railing sides to spray them there.

IT WAS YOU.

And then beneath, in case I didn't get it.

RUCKER.

My gaze stayed bolted upwards. The letters were red, the same colour as on Max's bar. The addition of my name was like a thunderbolt. It was huge. For all the world to see. I'd spent most of yesterday coming to terms with the fact that the messages had been directed at me but to see my name underneath those three words stopped me cold. My eyes were stuck to them for what seemed like an age, drips beneath where the paint had run.

But then I turned away. Quickly. If anyone followed my eyes they would see the words. And they would know, they would know the words referred to me. I felt ashamed, that the whole city would say You! You! It was you who caused this! The shame spread and then died in an instant, snuffed out by fear. Fear close to panic. I spun around again, crouching behind the meter next to me.

This wasn't it. Not just this. I could tell. There was something else. I could feel it. Something. He was close. Was that it? He was watching me. Laughing. Waiting for me to see it, his little note. This person I had no idea about, no idea how I'd hurt so he'd want to do this to me. And now I'd seen it what would he do? I swivelled round the bottom of the meter, ducking behind the bonnet of an old Beetle. I felt vulnerable, alone, the street closing in on me. The blank windows of the houses all seemed to be looking down at me. I was terrified but a surge of anger, overriding the fear, carried me upwards. To my feet. I wanted someone to grab hold of. To face. Or if he was going to shoot me I wanted him to, to do it now, to stop sneaking round my life. I told him to come on. I told him to get on with it. I readied myself for a shot, a knife, a speeding car. Something. But nothing happened.

And then it struck me. And I thought: no. No, please. One of these houses. Was there a woman in there? Someone I knew, had forgotten to tell Andy about? Or was . . . ? No, it can't have been. Not her. How could it? She was at home. We hadn't been followed. I told myself that again and again but my heart leapt into my throat, elbowing the logic aside. I began to jog down the street and then run, looking at each doorway. What could I do? Knock on every one? Ask if there was a dead woman inside. Are you sure? Can you check? No: I had to speak to Andy. He needed to get down here. With numbers. Bang the whole street up. I reached for my phone but my hand never found my pocket.

Because there was a scream.

Towards the far end of the street, near my car. A man had screamed. On the left-hand side. He was still screaming. I looked towards the sound and saw him. He was in his late thirties, balding with a straggly pony-tail. He was wearing a black heavy-metal T-shirt straining over a taut belly. For a second I couldn't

219

understand why he was only wearing a T-shirt but then I saw the bin bag by his side. The door behind him was open. The man had stopped screaming but now he was making another noise, not exactly a scream, more guttural, as if he'd taken a body punch. He stepped back. His feet tangled with the bag and he went over sideways. I began to move, crossing the space between us quickly, the pain in my side pulling like I was running through tangled string. When I got to him the man was trying to scurry backwards to his door.

'There,' he managed to say. 'There. Oh God, there.'

He was still on the floor. He was trying to speak but he couldn't do it, not properly. Frustrated, he held out a shaking hand in front of him, pointing towards the bins he'd gone out to. They were heavy plastic, surrounded by tall grass and weeds. Behind them a badly kept wall just higher than they were separated them from the pavement behind. I stepped forward slowly. The bins weren't flush with the wall. I could see that. There was a gap of eight or nine inches between. Not much of a gap. But it was enough. Using the toe of my left boot I inched the bins apart.

And saw a face. A very small face. More than a face. A child. A small child. A baby lying there.

Chapter Twenty-Seven

My throat went through a swallowing motion, and then another. My hand came up to my face and I bit down on my knuckles. The baby was wrapped in clingfilm. Through the plastic I could see that it was covered in blood. My eyes were stuck to it, my mind needing to be absolutely sure. There was no doubt about it. It was a white baby. Denise had been white but Jared wasn't, his skin was a deep black. So. So this was Ally's baby I was looking at. This was Sophia. The beautiful little girl with the curly black hair, running through my office door, who had just learned to call me Uncle Billy.

I tilted my head back. I was taking breaths, trying to hold on. My eyes fell again on the words, my name, writ large on the overpass above.

It wasn't long before Alfred Road was looking pretty much the same as it had seven and a half years ago. Police, photographers, forensics, medics, a cordon set way back, a huddle of press behind it. This time, however, they'd got up a huge scene tarp that covered most of the middle section of the street. I was under it, with Andy, shielding my eyes against the glare of the halogen lamps they'd set up. Clay was part of a group standing ten yards away around the bins, watching while a cameraman videoed the scene. The man in the heavy-metal T-shirt was inside his house. He wouldn't come out, not until the nightmare image he'd seen had been removed.

I stood watching the group of men, my arms folded. My face felt like it was made of stone. Andy was talking to me but I couldn't hear what he was saying. Then I realized he was asking me for the A–Z page I'd told him about when I'd called him. It was in my back pocket. I handed it to him and he bagged it. I told him that the envelope was at home. It had a London postmark. Central London. He was keen to get his hands on it but I couldn't see the point. It would be covered in prints but I didn't think any of them would be significant.

The tent was a big one with perhaps twenty people beneath it. I could hear cars pulling up to it, sirens sounding and then cutting out. I felt like a lone cyclist in the Tour being overwhelmed by the peloton. I pictured the press at the far end, could almost feel their interest pushing in. They'd be looking this way, not back up at the flyover. They wouldn't see what was written there. Clay hadn't released the little messages we'd been getting to the press anyway so, even if they did see it, it would probably pass them by. If it didn't, if one of them remembered my name, I'd be in every paper in the country by the morning.

There was movement at the door to the tent and I saw two men walk in. I'd seen them before, at the Rotherhithe Tunnel. One of them carried a small bag in his hands. It was a body bag, but tiny. The fact that they even made them that size hit me like a kick in the stomach. I watched as they approached the house, the bins, as the more senior of the men bent down. Ten minutes later he had the child in his arms. With his long white coat and breathing mask, it looked like he had just delivered it. Gently he lowered the child into the bag, held open by his colleague, who then held it himself while the bag was zipped up. Everybody beneath the tarp stopped what they were doing and watched as the two men walked slowly to the door flap and out of it.

Andy told me that he'd been about to go in to Jared Denton when he'd been called down here. He asked me what had happened to my face. I told him that I'd got into a fight, told him how the joke I'd heard had set me off. He nodded, accepting my explanation. He'd probably already been informed about the state I arrived home in. He told me that I had to hold on, to keep it together. He was being very sympathetic towards me, something that always made me wary where Andy was concerned. I wondered for a second but then I knew what it was. Andy was relieved and he didn't want to show it. Relieved because this had nothing to do with him. The writing above our heads told us both that. Andy could relax. He could look at me with the same measure of curiosity and disgust most of his colleagues were showing.

Andy radioed for a car to be brought right up to the door of the tent and we got into it. We drove through the cordon, past the press, and then up to my flat to get the envelope. I felt dull and heavy. When we pulled off Rosebery Avenue towards the Market Andy stopped the car dead, but then sped up. The street door to my flat was open. The doors to the blue Transit were open too and there were detectives climbing out of the back of it. I saw them as if in a dream. Andy gunned the car forward and then skidded to a halt and we both jumped out. I could see my neighbour, the film maker, standing on the street. He was rubbing his wrists, talking to a sandy-haired DC I'd seen in the station the day before. I ran up to them, Andy at my side. The DC stood with his hands on his hips.

'You left your bath on,' he said. 'This guy came running out onto the street as if the place was on fire. Scared the shit out of us. When we bagged him he said it was coming through his ceiling. Didn't know what he was on about. Had to kick your door in, I'm afraid.'

'My sofa's bloody soaked, mate. Woke up, couldn't understand what the noise was, banged on your door for ages, then thought you might be in the cafe. Came out, nearly had a heart attack. What are these coppers doing here? Six of them just bloody well grabbed me and those handcuffs really hurt, actually.'

The DC turned to him. 'Sorry about that, sir, no offence meant. You can go now. But, oh, who is your father, by the way? You asked me several times if I knew, and I must confess that I haven't the faintest idea.'

Before the police had arrived at Alfred Road I'd called Sharon again and once more got her voicemail. This time I did leave a message, figuring she'd listen to it even if she didn't want to take my calls. I apologized profusely for not going round, more for not phoning. I told her that I'd been freaked, terrified for her, afraid she'd talk me into something dangerous if I did call. But I said that events had justified my fears. This person knew everything about me. I wondered out loud whether we should tell the police about Sharon after all and I urged her to call me to talk about it. In the meantime stay at home, I said. And don't call anyone except for me.

I spent the next three hours in the incident room sitting next to Andy, going through CCTV stills from the Lindauer Building, looking at the grainy indistinct faces of delivery men, visitors, people attending classes in the building and numerous others, all no doubt with perfectly legitimate reasons for visiting the place. Andy had told me to keep it together but it was hard, difficult to keep my mind from the bins on Alfred Road. Without even knowing it, I'd been hoping that somewhere, in a bedsit or a flat, a house maybe, Ally's baby was living on throughout all this. It was a stupid, vain hope, which was why I'd never consciously thought about it, but nonetheless I'd entertained it somewhere inside me ever since the night I'd seen what had happened to Ally. I wondered if Mike had entertained it too, whether he still did. I wondered if he knew that he could feel even worse than he was feeling now. Andy said that a DNA test on the child would take three or four days but I didn't see what it could tell us. Ally's baby was dead and so must Denise Denton's have been. Ally had been close to term but Denise had only been pregnant six months. Enough time to give her child a chance of survival if it had been delivered in a hospital, but not if it was torn out of her in a flat somewhere. Both the children were dead.

My mind also drifted to Sharon. Would she agree to go into a safe house? I didn't know. I didn't even know if Clay would offer her one or whether he'd see her as some kind of chance, bait to catch the killer with. I felt hemmed in, not knowing what was right, not knowing how I could decide. And as I continued to go through the stills I felt further trapped. This thing, bearing down upon me, which I had no control over, which I just seemed to have to wait for. The powerlessness was almost physical, sitting in the centre of my muscles, paralysing me. I wanted to do something, to get out there. Not sit at a screen. But I knew this might be the most fruitful thing of all and so I made myself concentrate, forced myself to stare at the images in front of me.

Stills had been taken from tapes dating back six months. I looked intently at each and every one, but out of the clear shots none stood out, no face I recognized from past cases or from the public gallery of courtrooms where I'd been testifying. I always used to check out the gallery for future reference. I was frustrated but not surprised and moved on to the rest of the images. There were a number of indistinct ones, men in baseball caps, a woman wrapped in a huge scarf, her head hidden beneath a giant fur hat. It seemed logical to conclude that the killer was one of them. If that was the case then the killer had been just as careful as I thought he'd been. There was no way you could get an ID from them. The problem was that the cameras at the Lindauer were set too high. They looked down on people not at them. You couldn't blame the security firm, though, because it was standard practice. Set them any lower and they're far too easy to tamper with.

I went through all the images again, every one. It was depressing, tiring work but I stuck at it. Apart from the hooker in Loughborough Junction, this was the main lead, the mistake we'd thought the killer had made. Getting caught on film. Except he hadn't. Andy was as depressed as I was. Beneath his who cares slouch he was beginning to look strained. I could see the panic beginning to build, the nervousness in his eyes. The papers had already begun to ask when the police were going to do something to protect London's women and this morning's find would only add to the noise. He told me that the girl would be picked up soon, trying to convince himself as much as me. He asked me to go through the stills a third time and I nodded. Nothing. Andy sat back and his whole body seemed to deflate as he let a breath out. I knew what he was thinking. Someone else had to die before he could get moving again.

Andy continued to look defeated. It was only when I was about to leave that he snapped out of it. An earnest young DC called Chamberlain interrupted to tell us that forensics had identified some prints from the flat Denise Denton had been using in Brixton. Given Denise's profession there had been scores of different ones and Andy hadn't held out hope of tracing any. But the latest, and most numerous, were easy to pick out.

'Well, whose were they?' Andy sat up.

'They were Denton's, sir,' the kid said.

'Great. The clowns found the victim's own prints in her pad. What a bunch of geniuses.'

'No, sir. Not the girl's. The husband's.'

'The husband's?'

'Yes, sir. Jared Denton's prints were all over the place.'

Andy hadn't interviewed Jared yet, preferring to

wait and see if he showed up anywhere on the CCTV stills, anywhere other than the one time he'd visited me. He hadn't but that didn't mean anything. He could have scoped it in one go, when he'd come to see me. As Andy had said, he was connected to his wife, obviously, and to me, but his presence in the building connected him to Ally and Josephine Thomas too. Andy was jubilant. His prints. He'd obviously found his wife before I had, something that didn't surprise me. Because she was sixteen I wasn't really looking for her, and if Joe 19 hadn't called me I probably would never have gone down to Brixton. For Jared it was a full-time thing, though I didn't know whether or not it meant he'd killed his wife and two other women. It was something for Andy to give the press, though, something to get the commissioner off Clay's back, and Clay off his.

I left Andy as he was gathering up papers, telling the young DC to put a fresh tape in the room four's video. He was so preoccupied he didn't even ask me where I was going and I was glad. I walked out and saw that as well as Andy the whole room had changed, the whole nick even. The place was buzzing with the news, from the detectives on the case to the desk sergeant, who was being told about the find by a constable just leaving to go out on the beat. Everyone was waiting to hear about the outcome of Andy's chat with Jared Denton and I thought about just sticking around to find out the result myself. But I had to see Sal again. If it was Denton, fine. If he broke down and confessed I'd be more than happy. I could understand why Andy was excited. It just looked way, way too easy. I was sure the answer still lay with the girl. The police still hadn't found her and I had the feeling that Sal was right: I wouldn't be able to either, not now. Not without help from the 22 Crew.

I stopped at the bank on the way down to the Pancras Road and then made my way to the gym. Sal was in her office, and she was expecting me. I put the money I'd withdrawn on the table; eight fifty-pound notes, bound with an elastic band. Sal ignored it. She told me that the 22 had heard her out and were going to get back to her, maybe as soon as today. She didn't know if they'd spoken to the girl yet or if the girl had seen anything. She said she'd let me know as soon as, and then she reached over and rested her hand on the bundle of notes. Instead of picking it up, she looked at me.

'You know I won't be making anything on this, don't you?'

I nodded.

'I'd assumed that, and thank you, but I wouldn't have minded if you were.'

'I would have. But, Billy, are you sure about this?'

I nodded again.

'*Really?* With the Bill all over you? Outside your drum? They've probably got a tail on you as well.'

'I know. I haven't made it yet, but they might well have.'

'Then how'd you expect to keep it without them knowing?'

'I don't,' I said. 'I'm not going to keep it.'

'No?'

'It's not for me.'

Sal leant back a little and then nodded herself. 'I see. Which is why you wanted something fairly light. Easy to use.'

'Uh huh.'

'Well, we can get you that all right. But you think she'll actually agree?'

'I don't know. She won't at first, I know that. I hope I can persuade her.'

'And you're sure you want to? Really? This isn't going to buy you a toy, Billy.'

'I know.'

'But do you know what the consequences to her would be, to her career, etcetera, if she was caught with it?'

'I do,' I said. 'Yes. But I know what the consequences would be if she was caught without it. I've seen them. I've seen them on Ally and I've seen them on Denise Denton and I've seen them on a little thing behind some bins, tossed out like rubbish. And I'm not going to see them on Sharon. Get me the gun.'

'Give me a day,' Sal said.

Chapter Twenty-Eight

It was outside, back in the gym, that we ran into the girl. She was sitting astride the lats bench, pulling the handlebar down behind her shoulders, lean and muscular in a Lycra bra top and shorts. Her hair was scraped back and her plain, square face was taut with determination. The counterweight was moving upwards slowly and I was impressed: it was as much as I ever lifted. When she saw us her face relaxed and she let the bar up slowly until it clicked back into place.

I was surprised to see the girl, not having heard anyone come in. She was the only person there. Surprised also because she seemed to come from a different time, from before any of this had happened. It reminded me of the way my life had been.

'This is Cherie,' Sal said to me. 'Our resident trainee masseur. She's been making us all feel wonderful for a week and I've been letting her use the facilities in return.'

Cherie stood from the bench and smiled. She had the powerful, frank aura of someone completely at ease with her body. She wasn't as nervous as last time and seemed at home in the gym.

'We've met,' I said.

Cherie squinted. 'Have we?'

'Last week. My name's Billy.'

'Oh yes. You couldn't make it but you were going to come back in on Sunday. I wrote your name down. But you didn't show up.'

I wasn't surprised I'd had to jog her memory. I felt like I was a completely different person from the one who'd cancelled on her.

'I know, I'm sorry. Something . . .'

'No, I wasn't telling you off! There have been plenty of people to work on. But anyway, I've got exams next week. What about now?'

She'd asked that last time and again it backed me up.

'Now?'

'Unless you have something you need to do? Or we could make another time, but you look like you're a busy person. I don't want to seem pushy.'

'Don't worry,' I said. 'Just let me think for a second.'

I thought about the one thing I wanted to do. But I had to trust Sally. I didn't like being at the whim of a bunch of hustlers like the 22 but there wasn't anything I could do about it. Loughborough Junction would be quiet as a morgue. There was nothing I could do about Sharon either until she got in touch. I felt the frustration again, sitting with Andy, trying to wring the answer out of my brain, knowing it was never going to come that way.

'OK. OK.'

'Well, all right then,' Cherie said.

She was working my left shoulder, lifting it from the bench and manipulating the joint. If Cherie's shoulders

232

were powerful her fingers were even more so, pushing their way between my muscles, bringing heat out
from within them. At first I thought I'd made a mistake
agreeing to go with her. I was bruised from yesterday,
but Cherie was careful enough for her actions really
to help the soreness I felt. Soon I found the insistent
motion hard to resist, waves of stress pulsing out from
within me. My mind began to spread out, like a horizon,
unbidden thoughts drifting across it. It was what I had
wanted to happen. Jared Denton came but moved
straight through. No connection presented itself. I saw
images from the CCTV, tried to let something click, a
posture perhaps. All the time Cherie chatted away,
asking me what I did, how long I'd been going to the
gym. I gave distracted, noncommittal answers, and
when Cherie started chattering on about those horrible
murders in the paper I didn't say anything at all.

'You don't have to talk. It's OK. I'm just trying to get
you to relax. You are so tense. I can tell I'm going to
have to try extra hard on you.'

I was lying under a short white towel on her
massage bench, in the small, bare bedsit Cherie rented.
It was only five minutes from the George, up towards
Camden, a cheerless place with smoke-stained walls,
the only warmth coming from a small, rusting radiator,
stupidly positioned beneath the one window. I could
smell a cheap aftershave, one I'd noticed in the gym
a few times. Once again I thought it odd that Cherie
invited men up to her flat, alone. She had all the right
massage equipment, a new-looking bench, the oils and
the towels, but I felt she was a little naive; it still might
have given people the wrong idea. Or maybe it was the
right idea. Maybe she had other services in mind, ones

that she would want paying for. I began to get this impression after five to ten minutes. Cherie's hands were moving in long pushes down my lower back but soon they weren't stopping there. Instead they moved beneath the towel, onto my buttocks. I couldn't help but tense, and Cherie stopped.

'Sorry,' I said.

'It's OK. I don't have to do your gluts. It's just muscle, though, and it needs work by the feel of it.'

'I know. I didn't mean to. It's just, well, you know. But go ahead.'

'With pleasure. Just say if it's too hard, though.'

'I will.'

Cherie worked on my gluteus maximus for a few minutes. Her use of the correct phrase made me relax but I was relieved when she moved down to my calves. She asked me to turn over and she lifted each of my feet in turn, moving them round in slow circles in the joint. She did the same with my arms and then my head and all my concerns melted beneath her touch, as my head got slowly heavier. My mind seemed to float free, leaving my body where it was, until I was barely aware of the bench I was lying on.

By the time Cherie set my head down I was no longer in King's Cross, no longer trying to find a serial killer. Images of palm-fringed beaches had come to me and I was lying on one, a warm, turquoise sea washing up over my calves. I was dissolving into the sand. Cherie's hands were on my ribcage now, though I could barely feel them. They pushed down to my stomach, moving in broad circles around my navel. The tips of her fingers found the muscles at the tops of my legs, her touch lighter, less insistent. I couldn't help it. I found myself responding. The part of me that was in the Caribbean just wanted to let it happen but part of me had surfaced, and that part was embarrassed. I was pulled between two worlds, not knowing which way to turn. Cherie didn't stop what she was doing.

'Don't worry. You men can't help having one of those. My father, he couldn't control his either.'

The comment was so unexpected and so wrong that it didn't register for a second, it didn't quite penetrate the spun-out world I was inhabiting. Had she really said that? Just as I was telling myself she couldn't have, something broke the ambient quiet I was encased in. My phone. I'd left it on a small table next to the bench, where I could reach it. Its ring was high-pitched, impossible to ignore. I came back into the room, feeling foolish at the notions I'd succumbed to and I tensed my muscles, preparing to sit up.

'Leave it,' Cherie told me. 'Don't answer it.'

I ignored Cherie and sat up. The tone of her voice was oddly harsh. I decided that after the call I'd thank her politely and leave. I'd had enough. I picked up the phone and saw the caller's ID displayed. Sharon. The word was like a dam, bursting. I'd wanted the massage to release my mind, but it hadn't helped any answers come to me. Instead it had released the need I felt for Sharon, the one I'd bottled out of fear for her. But now I just wanted to lie with her, to look at her stomach, the beginning of her bump. Only in my pants, she'd said. But that wouldn't be for long. I lassooed the feeling and tried to rope it back. I'd be careful, really careful. Maybe we could get a hotel even. Then I'd give her the gun, once Sally got it for me. I'd make her take it. I'd tell her about the child I'd found. Ally's child. If anything could convince her, that could.

Sharon's voice was brittle. She'd got it wrong, thought I didn't want her. I told her again that I knew I should have called her yesterday. She said well, OK, but she was still annoyed.

'Are you coming *today*, though?' she asked.

'I am,' I said. 'I promise. Yesterday I was scared. Please understand. I don't want you to think . . .'

'What, Billy?'

'Oh, nothing. Listen.' I glanced to my side where Cherie was standing. Too close to me. 'I can't talk to you now.'

'Why not? Where are you?'

Sitting naked in a towel being massaged by a talented but seemingly mixed-up young woman.

'Listen, is there somewhere we could meet, a cafe on Broadway Market or somewhere? That might be better than . . . hey. Hey!'

'I said, *don't answer it.*'

Cherie had taken the phone right out of my hand. I was amazed. All I could do was watch as she hit 'end', before letting it fall with a clatter to the floor beside her. I could hardly believe it. After a second of simply looking at her I made to slide off the bench to get it. I was thinking right, that's it, but before I could move more than an inch Cherie put a hand on my stomach. Her other hand pushed against my collarbone and she tried to move me back. I resisted, but she pushed harder. I could hardly process what was happening. I would have laughed but it wasn't funny. And I didn't get the chance. Cherie brought her knee up onto the bench. Using all of her weight to press me down.

'Hey, what the hell?'

'I was *telling* you about my father,' Cherie hissed.

'Your father? What the hell?'

'What you have in common. Oh, not any more I see, how sad. Daddy's would do that too but not so quickly. He'd use it a few times first.'

'Listen,' I said. 'I have to go. I'm sorry if I offended you in some way . . .'

'You were keen enough before,' Cherie said. 'Let's see if we can reawaken your interest.'

'Please.' I shook my head. 'I have to go. Thanks for this, but . . .'

'Shut the fuck up, Billy Rucker. Just shut the fuck up.'

An ice-cold pain speared me. Cherie's right hand had moved down to my thigh. In a flash she'd found a place on the inside of my right leg, some kind of pressure point or something. She'd gripped it between her index finger and thumb. How tightly she was holding me I didn't know because the exact spot beneath her fingers went completely numb. In contrast, the area around it seemed to burst into flame. The pain was so intense that the rest of my body had shorted, the power was cut. I couldn't move.

'Daddy liked the rough stuff too,' I heard Cherie say. 'I was too young to do anything about it then but I know what to do now. You want to try and hit me again?'

I thought: oh shit. Just what I need in my life right now. Some psycho girl with father problems. I told myself to play along.

'I wasn't trying to hit you. I . . . I'm sorry, only that call was important.'

'Important?'

Cherie released her grip and I thought I'd calmed her. But it was only for a second. Her hand flashed to my testicles this time. Before I could even move she had hold of them and the pain, localized and spiked before, was different. It was total, pain like a sickness inside. It was bigger even than the shock.

'You men,' Cherie said, her voice strangely light. 'This thing, you use it to cause so much pain, and yet it makes you so vulnerable too. Strange that. I first got hurt by one when I was ten. That's when he started doing it to me. He was very, very big, bigger than you.'

'Please,' I managed to say. 'I'm sorry, but . . .'

'This hurting you? I bet it is. I should have done this to Daddy but I was too young then wasn't I? If only I'd known.'

Cherie's other hand had taken hold of my penis. As she began to force her thumbnail into the end of it the pain rose to such a level that the effect was similar to her earlier massage. I was sent into a different world. I couldn't move my hands, not even my mouth now, to plead with her. All I could do was wonder what was happening. Cherie was speaking, talking to me, but I couldn't make out what she was saying. I forced myself to focus through the agony and the sounds did form into words. She was still speaking.

' . . . my mother never stopped him and then she died anyway,' Cherie was saying. 'After that it was every night. Every night without fail. I never got used to it, ever, but you know what was almost worse? He never gave me anything. Ever. I never had any toys. Dolls. Anything. I just had an empty room, where he'd lock me. Until he wanted me. Can you, even for a second, imagine that?'

'No,' I said. 'No . . .'

'But *then*, one morning, I realized that I did have something.' Cherie let out an amazed laugh. 'I had something of my own. It was unbelievable. I was four-teen. When I realized, when I was sure, it was like magic. My own thing, given by him but mine, *mine*. And he hadn't meant to give it to me, I knew that. It made me laugh. I was so happy. I'd never been happy and didn't know what it felt like but I knew it was happiness. It couldn't have been anything else. It was like a piece of the sun, glowing inside me. I knew I had to keep it, that it was my chance of something warm, something good. A real blessing. So you know what I did?'

'No. No I don't. Please.'

'Don't you? Don't you, Billy? Come on. Catch up. I ran away, didn't I? I ran away to London.'

Without any break in her story Cherie lifted me up again, towards a shivering whiteness, the borders of unconsciousness. Her eyes were burning but they weren't looking at me. Her free hand moved casually to my ribcage, where the bruises from the night before had begun to flower. I don't know what she did but I heard a scream. It took me a second to realize the sound was coming from me.

'When I got here, I thought I was free,' Cherie said. Her voice was a whisper. 'I hadn't only escaped to a place where no one knew me. I'd found something to love. To *love me*. The joy, it made up for everything. And all I had to do was wait. It was simple. Wait. Patiently. And hide. I was happy, happy for the only

239

time ever, and I just kept getting happier. You see, every day brought me closer. I had names ready for it and everything. I'd bought it things, from Oxfam, you know. I imagined the things I'd say to it. I got off the street and I found somewhere, not nice, far from that, but safe. At least I *thought* it was safe. But it wasn't, was it? Because he found me.'

'Please.'

'Because you found me. *You!* Cherie was laughing but there were tears forming in her eyes. I still could not move. I couldn't speak either. I heard every word Cherie said but I couldn't connect it to the present. She was moving her head from side to side. Her voice getting harder with every word.

'You didn't recognize me. As soon as I saw you in the gym, I knew. Because I'm strong now. Changed. Then I was weak. When you brought him to me I was a stick. Do you remember? I was a terrified little girl with greasy hair who pissed herself. I wet his car seat. I knew what I'd get for that later, when he got me home, but I didn't know the worst. That he knew. Somehow, he *knew*. I'd never told him but he did, like he could just look inside me and see it there. When I realized, I was sick. I didn't know what he was doing at first, tying me up, an old sheet underneath me on the hall floor. It was as soon as we got home. He hadn't spoken to me all the way and now he didn't say a word. He just got on with it. First my feet, then my hands till I couldn't move. It was like he was doing DIY. It was then that I realized. He knew. And I knew what he was going to do. I tried to get away but how could I? He was kneeling on my chest. He started punching me. In my stomach. Just like he was hammering nails in. He just carried on punching me and punching me. I woke up in hospital and they said I was lucky, lucky the muggers hadn't killed me. They said I should be thankful, and not to worry that I'd never have babies. Ever. When I closed my eyes, they thought I was crying. But do you know what I was really doing?'

She was crying now, the drops falling down onto my chest and stomach. I was stuck. The pain was total, so all-consuming that when she released me I didn't know it at first. It carried on. When I did realize I was free I tried to stand, but I couldn't. All I could do was roll off the bench, onto the cold lino. My body was still closed. Cherie was standing over me. I saw her hands reach behind her and then her hair fall in front of her face, like a curtain. Like it had been before. She bent down to me, her fingers in front of her.

'I was thinking what to do to you. I knew what I'd do to Daddy. He'd be first. But you? I thought I'd just kill you, it's what I planned. I waited a long time, got myself in shape. Didn't realize it would be this easy. But then I saw you outside your building. With that woman. That's when I knew what to do. It just came to me, just arrived in my mind, and it felt so right. Got the first one wrong but not the second. We had a lovely chat in her cafe. She told me she was stock-taking later, so I knew to come back.'

'No.'

'Oh yes. It was a pity because she was nice – but just killing you? You would never have known then what it was like. For me. You have to know what it's *like*. It's bad, isn't it?'

I nodded.

241

'But you haven't got there yet. I'm going to make it worse, I'm afraid.'

'You can't make it worse.'

'I think I can. I've got an appointment to keep. With another one of your girls. I didn't think there were any more but, hey presto, there she was.'

I shook my head. 'What are you talking about? There are no more.'

'Oh, Billy. Good effort. But it won't work. You showed her to me! Anyway, can I give her a message? One last message from you?'

I managed to push myself up onto my knees. With everything I had I tried to tackle her, bring her down. She laughed as she kicked my arms aside. Then she bent down to me.

Pain rose like wind from the mountains.

It was too strong.

It snuffed me out.

Chapter Twenty-Nine

I don't know how long I was gone. It could have been hours or just a few minutes. My watch was on the table, across the other side of the room, and I couldn't reach it. I wasn't by the massage table any more, though I was still on the floor. I was lying on my side beneath the window. My hands were bound behind my back with what felt like washing-line cord. I couldn't move them. I thought of my wish, the day before, to have the answer massaged out from inside me.

It had happened.

Deep, booming detonations crumped inside my head. The pain there played tag with the pain in my ribs, where her thumbs had gouged into me. My groin hurt constantly, a sickly sweet nausea rising every time I tried to move. Unconsciousness rose too, calling me back, but I managed to squeeze my eyes against it and stay in the room. I could see my jacket on the back of a chair near the massage bench.

Pulling at my hands, I realized that the line my hands were tied with had been attached to something behind me. The foot of the radiator. I was bound tight. I scrabbled madly at the knots at my wrists, trying to get free, swearing at myself for not seeing this. I tried some more before realizing that I wouldn't have a chance, not without seeing what I was doing. Instead I called out. I screamed for help. I could hear a stereo somewhere, giving out drum and bass. When I screamed again the music just got louder.

The pain in my head was matched only by the panic inside me. I thrashed again and called out again but neither was any use. Nor was trying to untangle the tightened twists of cord behind me. Instead I shuffled and pushed until I'd managed to get myself into a squatting position. Then I moved myself up, like a weightlifter. There was a little give in the radiator but it was nowhere near enough. My hands felt like they were being sliced off at the wrists. I had to try again. The radiator creaked once more and it might have worked, but slow pressure like that would take ages. Instead I closed my eyes. In a frenzy I piled myself forward and upward, rocking hard, screaming against the pain, until I could feel the radiator beginning to rise out of the floor, out of the pipes leading into it. I didn't stop until I found myself careening forwards into the massage table, my head connecting with one of its corners, sending it sideways. I was on the floor, my hands still tied to the radiator that I'd pulled from the wall. A flood of brackish, stinking hot water gushed out of the pipes behind me.

I managed to get my hands free of the radiator and I stood. Too quickly. I had to kneel again to stop myself blacking out, swallow to keep back the rise of vomit from my guts.

I still didn't know how long I'd been lying there. I had to wait for my eyes to clear and then I crawled over to my phone, lying on the floor near my jacket. Without waiting to get my hands free I found Sharon's number in the phone book and hit 'call'. Holding both hands up to my face I listened to the ring tone. As weakened as I was physically, the fear I felt made the phone in my hands practically impossible to hold. How long did the phone ring? Longer than anything, longer than the rest of my life had taken to live up to that moment.

'Hello.'

'Sharon?' I closed my eyes. 'Thank God. Sharon, is that you?'

'Billy, what the hell's going on? First you don't phone me or come round, then, after I've swallowed my pride and called you, you just hang up on me. Now you phone me back.'

'Sharon, listen.'

'No. You listen. I'm bloody sorry about what's going on and I'm sorry I added to your worries but I haven't put any pressure on you. We had a great time before I went away but if you don't want to base the rest of your life on that, I'm not going to make you. No pressure.'

'Sharon, please. You have to hear me out.'

'I will, but it really pissed me off yesterday. I cooked for you and waited. You said you'd come. You said some really lovely things to me too. And then you just vanished. Listen, I'm overreacting, I know I am. I just want you here. You were probably with Andy Gold all night. I'm all over the place – my hormones, I guess. Hey, I've got that excuse now. I know you're stressed at the moment and God, what happened to Ally. But it's not my fault. So *call me*, in future.'

'I will. Just listen to me a second. Sharon—'

Hold on, Billy.'

'What is it? Sharon?'

'Calm down. It's just someone at the door.'

245

'Sharon. Listen. Sharon? Sharon?!'

I heard a heavy clunk as Sharon set the phone down on the table. Then I heard footsteps moving away. I screamed Sharon's name but I knew she wouldn't hear me. Even if she did it wouldn't register as important, not from the hall in her flat. I didn't know what to do. Should I hang up and call her again? It wouldn't work, she hadn't set the phone back on the cradle. I screamed again.

'*Don't open it. Don't open the door.*'

But I couldn't hear anything on the other end. Making the decision, I hung up. I dialled Andy's mobile. When he didn't answer I dialled his desk phone, hoping he'd detailed someone to monitor it.

'DI Gold's phone.'

It was the kid, the kid who'd told Andy about forensics' findings in Brixton. I fumbled for his name.

'Chamberlain?'

'DC Chamberlain speaking.'

'Chamberlain, it's Rucker. Billy Rucker. I was just with you.'

'Yes, I remember. Of course.'

'Chamberlain, listen to me. Carefully.'

'OK. What is it, sir?'

'My girlfriend is in danger. Serious danger. You have to get as many feet round to 62A Wharf Place as you can, understand? Right now. It's Hackney, opposite Broadway Market. The killer's there, there right now.'

'I don't think so, sir. DI Gold's pretty confident we have him right here.'

'Well, you haven't. You have to believe me. Please do it. 62A Wharf Place. Make a priority, all units call and get the nearest three units there. Please. Please, please trust me and do this.'

I'd put everything into it. There was silence for a second.

'As soon as I'm off the phone to you, sir.'

I hit 'end' as quickly as I could and took three deep breaths. I don't know how I got my hands free. I just pulled them out of the cord, tearing with my teeth then pushing down with my feet. When I was clear I called Sharon again but I only got an engaged tone. I pulled on my clothes and made it outside to my car. My car. Where the hell was my car? I felt for my keys but they were gone. She'd taken it. As I ran down the Pancras Road to King's Cross I dialled Andy's number again and once again Chamberlain picked up.

'A Mazda,' I said. 'An old brown Mazda. DTL 108M. She took it, the perp. Tell all units to look for it.'

'She?'

'She.'

'OK, sir. I will. I've put the call out. Try not to panic. I've informed DI Gold and he's heading there too. There should be a patrol car at the address any time now.'

Any time now. The words clanged through my head as I burst to the front of the queue at the cab rank. The driver was old, practically moulded into his vehicle. I told him where to go and he responded to my urgency at once, ignoring the outraged protestations of the people behind me. We shot up the Pentonville Road and down towards Old Street. The driver swapped lanes and cut people up, he made it through amber lights and put his foot down whenever there was space in front of us. The streets flashed by and in my mind images of Sharon flashed too. Sharon in her flat, just like Ally had been. A scream made flesh. The helplessness I felt made me want to tear the cab driver out of his seat and drive myself, on pavements, the wrong side of the street, anything. I couldn't do anything, anything but wonder: was I going to be like Mike? A ghost walking the streets, everything taken away from me before I'd even had a chance to touch it?

The driver swung the cab round past Shoreditch Town Hall. He couldn't have gone any faster but I couldn't stop myself urging him too. The binding connection I felt to Sharon was almost physical, a bungee cord picking up speed as it pulled me back towards her. And not just to her. Our child. In a flash, from nowhere, an immense bond of love had materialized between us. Even though it was barely formed. Even though I'd only known about its existence for forty-eight hours. I'd always wondered how fathers could love babies, how they could feel that they had anything to do with them. But now I knew. I'd never envied Mike for his upcoming fatherhood. I didn't want to be that old. Now I would have given anything to still be on course for that. It was a part of myself that I was hurtling towards and it was the best part. It was my own life I was trying to save.

'Here. Pull over here.'

I had the money ready, everything in my wallet. I was on the bridge, the place I'd stopped at the night before. I sprinted across and then round the back of the building, towards the door of Sharon's flat. But as soon as I turned the corner my legs began to slow down. There were two patrol cars parked outside the entrance door. Next to them were three unmarked vehicles. My arms clenched into my sides as the speed went out of my limbs. The wind out of my stomach. The blood out of my veins.

It had happened. One way or another. It had happened. There was nothing I could do.

Two uniformed officers were standing guard at the door to Sharon's apartment block. I walked towards them, each step like a marathon. I'd rushed there so fast and now I didn't want to ever cross the next twenty yards. The two policeman saw me walking towards them. They turned in my direction and straightened. Their faces were closed. I couldn't tell if they knew who I was. Or what they'd have to tell me if they did know. My feet continued to take me towards them. As they did so I began to feel oddly calm. Even though the whole world was using my heart to beat through. I was walking to the guillotine, oblivious to the roar of the crowd. I passed two women, onlookers, pointing towards the door and talking. At my approach they stopped talking and just looked at me. One of them put a hand up to her mouth.

Before I could reach the two uniforms, Andy Gold emerged from the doorway, stopping when he saw me. Andy's face was pale. Somehow I pushed my feet on. Shallow breaths ducked in and out of me like children playing a parlour game, none of them wanting to be found there when the music ended. When I was two yards away from Andy I stopped. I wanted to ask him. But I was too afraid. I just couldn't speak.

'You should have told me,' Andy said. His voice was quiet, and measured. 'You should have told me about Sharon. That she was pregnant.'

249

I nodded. Again I tried to force myself to speak, but I couldn't.

'I could have put some men on the door. Looked after her.'

'I know.'

'What were you thinking?'

I shook my head. 'That if no one knew, then she'd be all right.'

Andy pursed his lips, 'I see. But it was stupid. Really stupid. Now, you have to tell me what's been going on. What just happened to you?'

'I know who it is,' I said. 'A girl I found, years ago. Her father was abusing her, only I didn't know. He seemed genuine. I took him down to the squat I'd found her in and he beat her. When he got her home. She was pregnant and he beat the baby out of her. She couldn't have any more. She's been doing all this because she hates me. And the sight of pregnant women, I guess. Andy. What has happened? Please tell me.'

'They found your car. They just found it.'

'Where?'

'In Clapham,' Andy said. 'It was found outside a house in Clapham.'

'So . . .?'

'So Sharon's OK. She's upstairs. She's all right.'

'Oh. Oh, God.'

'It's OK. You can go up. But first I need to ask you something.'

'All right.'

'Who's Jenny Tyler?'

'Who?'

'Mrs Jennifer Tyler? Who is she?'

'I don't know. Why? Why? Why are you asking me?'

Chapter Thirty

'*Tyler*? I've never heard the name before in my life.'

'Think, Billy.'

'I am thinking. I don't know her. I don't know the name, I don't know anyone in Clapham. I haven't been there for, Christ, I don't know how long.'

'Then why is she dead, Billy? And her baby? Why did someone break into her house this afternoon and kill them both? In Clapham? Her husband found them twenty minutes ago.'

'I don't know. I *don't*. Maybe she's just started killing any pregnant women. She's crazy enough.'

'But you said she told you it was to be "another one of your girls".'

'Then she made a mistake. I don't know a Jenny Tyler. I don't know any other pregnant women. Just Sharon. This one, there's no connection to me.'

'Sir?' It was Chamberlain. 'CID in Clapham have given a description of the victim. Will that help?'

'Go on.'

'She was a redhead, thirty-five years old. Five-seven, blue eyes. Wore glasses. She was an optician, actually, had two kids already.'

'Billy?'

'No. And she's not my optician because I don't have one.'

'Married to a solicitor. David Roger Tyler.'

'I don't know him either.'

'Jenny Tyler, née Ballard sir. Maiden name was Ballard.'

'*Ballard?*'

'Billy?'

Andy turned to me. Everyone in the room turned to me.

'Jen,' I said. 'Jen Ballard.'

We were upstairs in Sharon's flat. Andy Gold was there with three other detectives. Sharon was sitting in the corner, by the window. She was very quiet, sipping a mug of tea. Halfway through our phone conversation she'd answered the door to a man from a disabled charity who wanted to sell her some kitchen products. She'd been happy to buy some from him and had gone outside to do so. The man suffered from a mild form of cerebral palsy and it took him a while to get the products ready for her and to take her payment. So Sharon had witnessed the first of the patrol cars arriving. She'd seen the way the police had dealt with the man they thought might be a serial killer. He was terrified, Sharon had told me. He couldn't understand what he was doing wrong.

It was almost seven p.m. Through the window behind Sharon the dying autumn sun had thrown a can of oil across the canal, setting it alight. I'd been unconscious in the bedsit on the Camden Road for an hour, at least. It had given the girl time to get out of there and to do what she had.

I stole glances at Sharon while Andy spoke to me, trying to gauge her feelings, but I couldn't really tell what she was thinking. Andy and the other four detectives in the room talked about her as if she were a commodity not a person. Just someone with a baby inside them, someone to be managed, sorted. Or used. I could see them thinking it even if no one was saying it. Sharon had her legs crossed and her arms folded, her mug in front of her face while she listened to us.

I told Andy what had happened that afternoon. I even remembered the girl's name. How could I forget it? She'd changed my life once, and now she'd done it again. It wasn't Cherie. It was Carolyn. Carolyn Oliver. Her father's name was Brian. They were from Chester, in the north-west. I still had their file at my office. I kept all my files. Even as we spoke the police in Chester were hunting stuff out about the family, trying to find the father. I saw him again, sitting at my desk. Then I saw a thin, terrified young girl walking out to the car her father had come to fetch her in. I couldn't match her up to the person I'd just been attacked by, to the killer of Ally and now three other women. But it was her. Life had twisted her, changed her, made her into something she was never meant to be. And while going back into the girl's past and putting that right would have been my preferred option, it wasn't one that was available to me.

When Chamberlain said the word Ballard, however, it was just as if I had gone back in time. Shy, quiet Jennifer Ballard. Clever Jen, prettier than she thought she was, scarlet as a stop sign whenever you went near her at a party. Awkward, good, normal. Someone I hadn't seen for so long I might well have lived the rest of my life without thinking of her again. Someone I hadn't spoken to for, what, seventeen years? And yet she was dead because she'd known me. And what was even more unbelievable was how the girl had got to her. I wouldn't have known where to start looking for her myself.

Everyone in the room was still staring at me.

'I was at school with her,' I said finally.

Andy sat up. 'With Jenny Tyler?'

'Ballard,' I said. 'And we called her Jen. Everybody did. Jen Ballard.'

'You sure it's the same one?'

'Ginger hair? Glasses?'

'That's right,' the kid said.

'Then yes. She was in my form. At King Edward's. From the fourth form to the upper sixth, when we left.'

'And this was in Lincolnshire, Billy, where you grew up?'

'That's right.'

'Chamberlain, make sure this woman was from Louth, Lincolnshire, OK? If she was, then it's a definite.'

'Sir.'

'But I think we can assume it's the same woman. It has to be. Right, when did you last see her, Billy?'

'I haven't,' I said.

'You haven't recently?'

'No. I mean I haven't, not ever.'

'What?'

'Not since school. Not once. I don't go back to Louth much and when I have gone I've never seen Jen.'

'Are you sure?'

'Absolutely.'

'You haven't been to a reunion, anything like that?'

'No.'

'Then what about down here? You run into her on Oxford Street? In the supermarket?'

'I didn't even know she lived in London. Or that she was married, had kids, was pregnant. Anything.'

'Than how the hell has this happened?' Andy turned his palm upside down. 'How did she find her?'

'I don't know,' I said. 'I have no idea.'

There was silence in the room for a long minute while we all thought about it. I asked Sharon if the name meant anything to her but she just shook her head. Andy said he'd check the Lindauer listings, see if she showed up. It wasn't likely that she attended any antenatal classes there, though, not if she was from south London. I couldn't figure it. It had to be some sort of mistake.

'Sharon? Ms Dean?'

It was Chamberlain again. He'd come off the telephone and was now looking serious, his face pinched through lack of sleep. He looked to be about twenty-three, only six months or so out of uniform. A permanent furrow had already cut a path, though, down from his hairline to the bridge of his nose. I had an image of myself at his age, that quiet, unbreakable focus powered by the belief that the world might actually become a better place if only I could break the case I was working.

Chamberlain asked Sharon if she had a PC he could use and she fetched him her laptop. I'd noticed Chamberlain before, at the station, spending all his time looking at his screen. Andy told me that he was the resident computer whiz, but I didn't know what he was doing now. While Chamberlain tapped away at the keyboard Andy told the other two detectives to head back to the station. Then he turned to me, asking if there was any way in which the girl, Cherie, or Carolyn, could have followed me there that afternoon.

'Not if she was in Clapham,' I said. 'She won't have had time to come back afterwards. So no.'

'In that case it looks like you're OK. Now then.' Andy nodded and turned to Sharon. 'If it's all right by you, I'm going to set up twenty-four-hour protection. But it's going to be covert. People will be watching your flat but you won't necessarily know that they're there.'

'Wait a minute.'

'What is it, Billy?'

I looked at Andy. He knew what it was.

'You're not going to let her stay here?' I said. 'In London? You can't mean you're going to let her stay here.'

'As you said, Billy, no one knows she's here.'

'Only four detectives and the same number of uniforms. And soon their wives and boyfriends and then some guy down the pub and . . .'

'Which is why I want to put the protection on Ms Dean. It's probably not necessary but . . .'

'Not necessary!? After the girl somehow found some woman I was at school with, who I myself had forgotten even existed.'

'Billy, calm down. No harm will come to Sharon as long as she's being observed. How could it?'

'No,' I said. 'No way. She has to get out of here. Go away. I know what you're doing and I'm not having her staying here.'

'Oh, you're not? You're not, are you?' It was Sharon. She hadn't said a word since all of this had happened but now she'd cracked. She was looking at me, her hands on her hips. 'What about me? Do I get a say? Or do you just get to push me out of the way, to make life easier for you?'

'Sharon,' I said, 'relax. Please. He just wants to use you. As bait. I know him.'

'Does he?'

'Yes.'

'What if I agree with him? What if I think that's a good idea?'

'What?'

'Well, if I can help, why not? Women are being killed. Our friend was killed. If that girl comes here, the killer, and they catch her, surely that would be great, wouldn't it?'

'If they catch her. *If*. They've done fuck all so far, haven't they? No, I'm simply not going to take a risk like that.'

'*You're* not?'

'Oh, shit, *we're* not then. However you want me to say it. But you're leaving.'

'I am? And where shall I go?'

'Anywhere.'

'As long as it's away from you! You don't need to tell me why you're doing this.'

'Sir. Sir! Ms Dean. Mr Rucker! Please. Hey! Everybody!'

He'd shouted loudly enough to get us all to shut up and take notice of him. Chamberlain was looking up from Sharon's laptop, his eyes open wide. When he had our attention, he stared down again at the screen in front of him.

'What is it?'

'I think I've got something. I think I know how the killer found her. Jen Ballard.'

'You do?'

'Yes. And how the girl found out she was pregnant.'

'How? How the hell do you know that?'

'Because I've just found her myself,' Chamberlain said.

Chapter Thirty-One

Chamberlain told me to pull up a chair and sit next to him. Sharon and Andy stood behind us, looking over our shoulders. We were hunched in tight so that we could see the screen properly.

The list of names was a long one, running right down the screen out of sight. Jen Ballard was second from the top, just below Peter Addington. I remembered Peter Addington. He played right wing for the first eleven. He was only a little kid but he was quick and skilful. I remembered a goal I'd scored, a header, from a free kick he'd taken.

Further down I saw more names that stood out from the list. Damien Gregory. Nigel Hampton. They were in the team too. Who else? Karen Jenson. I'd gone out with her for two weeks. She was the first girl who'd ever let me put my hand inside her bra. I hadn't wanted to move ever, ever again.

'You can leave messages about yourself. To say what you're doing with your life. If I click on a name it shows the message.'

Chamberlain moved the cursor at random and highlighted a name. It was James Waits, someone I didn't remember. I thought that was odd. It was a small school, how could I not remember?

'Still living in Louth,' the message read. 'Two kids. In the Wheatsheaf most Friday nights if anyone else is around.'

'What a thrilling guy,' Andy said. 'Your best mate was he?'

Chamberlain hit the back button and we were looking at the list of names again. He scrolled up until the tiny arrow hovered over Jen Ballard's name and then he looked at me.

'Open it,' I said.

The site was a meeting place, a forum for old schoolmates to get in touch. I'd heard of it, but never visited it before. You could tell your peers what you had been doing with your life. All you did was find your school and type in the year that you left and then everyone who had registered was listed, along with their biographies. I found the idea depressing, and seeing it now, the reality was more so. Nigel Hampton for instance: he was the first eleven's captain. It was largely due to his left foot that we won the county trophy, beating Gainsborough in the final. He'd been a real star that night, driving us on when we were two–one down with ten minutes to go. Did I want to read that he was now a supermarket manager living in Hull, with four kids and a hatchback?

Maybe it was just that I didn't have any particularly great memories of school, apart from that golden half-hour with Karen Jenson in the sports hall. I'd been happy enough at King Edward's but made no lasting friends, largely due to the fact that I had to keep my home life pretty private. Friends weren't welcome at the Rucker house. At King Edward's I put on a front mostly, one I got off pretty well but never felt comfortable with. Leaving was a release from all that and there wasn't anyone I even remotely missed. I'd certainly never felt the need to tell the kids I grew up alongside what was happening in my life. And nor did I have any desire to get into any sort of dialogue with them.

Jen Ballard, however, hadn't felt the same.

'Went to Manchester Uni after school where being a specky four eyes anyway I studied optometry. Had a wild time (it's true, honest) before moving to London in 1994. I'm now an optician living in London with two lovely kids and an even lovelier husband. Though, if you ever meet him, don't tell him I said that.'

Chamberlain moved the cursor down to see if there was any more text but there wasn't. I read the entry through, then frowned.

'She doesn't say she's pregnant. Or living in Clapham. OK, so Cherie, Carolyn Oliver, she found her through this, but how did she know about those things? Why choose her and not one of the other women on the list?'

'There's something else. You can leave individual messages for people, have an individual dialogue with them. Maybe Jen Ballard did that, with her killer.'

'But why would she, with someone she didn't know?'

'She wouldn't,' Chamberlain said. 'She'd only do it with someone she remembered. Someone who'd got in touch with her first.'

'Well then.'

'But someone *could* have left a message for her.'

'Like who?'

'Like you.'

'But I've never seen this before. I've never signed up.'

'Then how come your name's listed?'

'What?'

'Your name. It's there. See. I found it just now.' Chamberlain moved back to the list of names and scrolled down to mine. It really was there. 'Billy Rucker. Left 1985.'

'How the hell did that get there?'

'Click on it,' Andy said.

Chamberlain did so. The screen went blank and an hourglass appeared. I was nervous, waiting to see what would happen. The page became clear. Then, there it was, everything I'd apparently been doing for the last seventeen years, encapsulated in two short lines.

'I've been messing people's lives up and getting away with it,' the message read.

'So far.'

'Shit,' I said. 'Shit. So. So she went on here. Carolyn Oliver. She wrote that about me. But it still doesn't tell us how she found out Jen was pregnant.'

'She must have signed up as you,' Chamberlain said. 'I logged on as myself so I'll have to go out and then back in. Then we can see if she left Jen a personal message. Or if Jen left her one. You one. OK. It'll only take a second.'

Chamberlain hit the backwards key several times until the home page appeared. 'FriendsFound, helping you get connected.' In more ways than one, I thought. I watched as Chamberlain typed in my name. He moved the cursor down to the next field but then he stopped.

'Bugger.'

'What is it?' Andy asked.

'You need a password to log on. Otherwise you can get in, as I just did, but you can't leave or access any messages. Mr Rucker, what would your password be?'

'How would he know?' Andy snapped. 'He never registered, did he? The girl registered pretending to be him. She could have used anything.'

'We only get three tries.'

'Fuck. Oh well, good work anyway. We'll have to get a warrant and then get in touch with them. But it could take days.'

'Wait,' I said. I leaned forward and hit some keys. Eight asterisks appeared in the box. When I hit 'enter' the screen changed to a dialogue box, asking me to enter the name of my school.

'It's worked. How did you know what the password was?'

'It Was You,' I said. 'I typed in It Was You.'

'Bingo,' Andy said.

It was all there. You could access your own messages, the ones you'd sent, as well as the ones coming back to you. Every woman whose name was listed had received a note purporting to be from me. Billy Rucker. The message I'd sent to each and every girl in my year was simple and easy but it was clever, too. The note was individually named and addressed but the body was the same.

'Hi,' the message said, 'remember me? I was really pleased to see your name when I signed up for this. Thought I'd drop you a line. What's going on? Still in Louth or did you move? You a career girl or done the mum thing? If you have, let's hope your kids are as cute as you were! Let me know.'

No wonder I'd got some replies. Fifteen in all out of

the twenty-six I'd sent. Over half expressed some sort of surprise at hearing from me. Some said that yes, they'd had children, some said no, they hadn't. One said no way and two said no, not yet. Most were brief notes but one reply was quite a bit longer.

'Hi, Billy,' it read. 'Course I remember you. I read your entry last week, as a matter of fact. I should update mine. What's all this about ruining people's lives? You broke a few hearts I remember (blush, you probably never even knew) but I can't imagine you being horrid to anyone. Anyway, I've done both the career thing *and* the mum thing, which should impress you immensely. And I'm going to do it again! In about four months. What about you? Where do you live, anyway, you didn't say?'

Chamberlain moved on to the reply I'd sent and we all read that I'd told Jen I was living in London. The same day she'd got back to me and asked where, telling me that she was in Clapham. After four more back and forth we'd tentatively arranged to meet. In her last message Jen had sent me her address, telling me to pop in if ever I was in the area, her tone not quite believing that I would. It was dated 2 November. Three days ago. Jen had said that she had a few days off work and would be home in the afternoons. I'd replied to assure her that, yes, I really would stop by.

We all read the last message over a few times, none of us saying anything. It had been so easy. I remembered what Cherie had said to me. She'd thanked me for finding her latest victim for her. I let out a breath. Chamberlain shook himself together and took us out of the site. He hit 'start' and then 'shut down' and the screen hissed as it went to black. I stared until it became a blackboard, the pluperfect chalked up in an elegant, sloping copperplate. I was moving all of my stuff from the back row to the front, changing places with Julie Smith for staring out of the window. I was red-faced but Jen looked horrificd, like she wanted to hang onto Julie and never let her go. When I sat down next to her Jen seemed to cringe, shrinking away from me, as far away in her seat as she could get.

'Did you go out with her?' Andy asked, as Chamberlain passed the laptop back to Sharon. 'Was she your girlfriend?'

'No,' I said, 'I hardly knew she existed. I barely took any notice of her at all.'

I sat on a chair in the corner while Andy and the rest of the officers left, leaving two in the hallway downstairs. Another on a roof opposite Sharon's door. While Sharon went down to talk to them, give them keys to the street door, I gazed out of the window over the darkened water. Across the canal I watched as Andy's car drove over the bridge and disappeared up Broadway Market. He had to drive slowly because there were a lot of people about. It was Bonfire Night and crowds were beginning to head towards London Fields for the display. Through the window I could see mums and dads holding on to toddlers, bigger kids with luminous sticks of plastic in their hands. A man was selling bug ears with flashing lights inside and I could see some teenage girls down on the towpath wearing them. They were waving sparklers, orange name trails chasing the silver flashes through the black night air. I stood up and above the heads of the growing throng I could see the top of the pyre, soon to be ablaze. The figure balancing there had his arms outstretched, as if he was pleading. As if he was saying abuse me, humiliate me, *burn* me, whatever you want to do to me, do it.

Just do it now.

I felt flat and defeated. Humiliated. This person, this girl, she could do whatever she liked with me. I was a puppet and she was moving around from place to place as she chose. The helplessness I'd felt in the taxi stayed with me, it wasn't changed by the fact that Sharon was alive. Someone else wasn't. This girl, Cherie, she could do these things, to people near to me or far. And I couldn't stop her.

When Sharon came back in she sat on the side of the table and held my hand. She smiled softly but didn't say anything. I thought about the drive I'd just taken, across London, to get to her. I thought about how prepared I'd been for what I might find and then I thought about Jen's husband. David Tyler. Coming home, with no idea. He hadn't been prepared for what he'd see. His wife, his unborn child, lying on the kitchen table. He would have heard about it all on the news, maybe would have warned his wife to be careful when she was out, but there was no way he'd have thought it could happen to her. To him. To his family. I shook my head and thought about Jen, seeing her at Manchester, coming out of herself, thought how bright and funny her emails were. What would her family do without her? Her lovely kids, her even lovelier husband? And what would they say on the website? Would Karen Jenson ask Nigel Hampton: did you *hear* what happened to Jen Ballard?

Sharon was looking out across the canal. The fire

had been lit and flames were shimmying towards us along the windows of the shops and flats on the market, leading up to the Fields. After five minutes Sharon stood up.

'Let's go,' she said.

'What?'

'I love Bonfire Night. Let's go. Now. Just you and me. I mean it. We'll be in a big crowd, all dark. Come on. I want candyfloss, I bet they have some.'

I looked up at her. 'OK.'

'And I don't want to talk about anything. Just you and me. There's still you and me and through all this tangled mess we need to get to each other. To reach each other. Even just to see each other. It's like I'm still in Afghanistan.'

'OK,' I said again.

Russian cannons split the sky into fragments of blue and gold and indigo. The music was loud, perfectly timed with what was happening overhead. Sharon and I edged through the crowd and I wasn't worried, not at all. We were invisible, pressing our way through swathes of people all rooted to the spot and looking upwards, barely even noticing us. Sharon found a tree and we leaned back against it, watching the show through the branches above us like a scared child with its fingers in front of its face. As jags of light slashed the sky my mind went to Cherie, and I saw her in the act of her crimes. Cutting. Slicing. Trying to get to the thing she'd been denied. I went over her words and then I wondered: what if she'd found me dead? What if I'd been hit by a car last year? What would she have done?

Or what would she do when there were none of my women left to hurt? She'd carry on, that's what. I knew it. And she'd have started with no prompting from me. It had just come to her, that's what she'd said. And it felt so right. As much as she thought this was about me, her desire for revenge, an equalizing of pain, it was about her. Her needs. I was her focus for now because she needed one. But she'd find another excuse. The agony of seeing women about to be granted what was taken from her for ever would be too strong. I doubted, actually, if she'd really blamed me from the start. Her father would have taken it all, in spite of what she said. Only if he was removed would her need drive her to the next person in line. Me. Once again I thought of him, Brian Oliver, and I tried to imagine the trauma he had caused his daughter, how great his abuse must have been to have turned her so far. Chester police were looking for him, Andy said. I was pretty sure they were never going to find him.

I also knew that, though she'd let me go this time, she'd come for me. I suddenly realized. For the last fifteen years of my life I'd looked for people, hunted them down in one way or another. Now it was my turn. The research the girl had done, the time spent at the Lindauer, on the Internet. It was all directed at me. She'd caught me then let me go, like a cat with a mouse in its paws. I wondered when she'd decide to finish me off. I wanted her to try. Again I felt powerless, knowing that she had everything on me while I was nowhere, even though I knew her name. I didn't know how she'd strike, or when, but I knew that she would. Waiting for it would be the worst.

I felt a nudge in the ribs and I turned from the

burning rivers in the sky. Sharon was shaking her head. I asked her what was wrong and she asked me how I could look at boring fireworks when there were her lips to be kissed. Lips about as unkissed as lips could be. I kissed them and we stayed kissing and there wasn't anything else. When we paused, Sharon brought a hand up to my face. It was Strauss now, via Stanley Kubrick, the sound seeming to rumble out of the earth beneath us.

'I love you.'

'I love you too.'

'What?' Sharon said.

'I said, "I love you too." '

'Oh.' Sharon laughed.

'What?'

'Well . . .?' she giggled some more. 'I actually said, "Hello, you." Not I love you. It's the noise.'

'Hello, you. Oh, great.'

'And you said, I love you too!'

'Yes, I did. But I didn't mean to, not if you just said hello! I'm taking it back. It wasn't fair.'

'You can't. You said it. Ha ha. But I do love you and I wish I'd said it. Oh, Billy.'

'What is it? Hey, come on. It should be me who's crying, lulled into a confession like that. What is it?'

'It's just. Well, we're not understanding each other at the moment are we?'

'It's hard. It is. With . . .'

'No. We're not talking about that.'

'No, but it is.'

'Just me and you. I'm going to try to understand you, Billy.'

'I don't know what you mean. There's nothing to understand . . .'

'Shhh now, enough. You didn't finish what you were doing. I've been away a long time, you know.'

I bent down and Sharon lifted her mouth to me. I moved past it and pretended to find some dirt in her ear.

'What, you thought I was going to kiss you did you? Oops.'

Later, when I was in bed, waiting for Sharon to use the bathroom, I tried to imagine what she'd look like. If there really would be anything to see. I was curious but nervous about it too. But when Sharon emerged she was wearing a pair of silk pyjamas and as she got in next to me she turned the light out. The pyjamas didn't stay on long but in the dark it was difficult to tell. I thought about putting the light on but Sharon didn't want me to. Just you and me, she said, nothing else. No complications. But there was something else. I felt it, living, between our moving bodies, in the very centre of us. Afterwards, in the dark, I couldn't help but continue to feel its presence, lying there, waiting, waiting. Turning everything on its head without knowing it. I remembered the bond that I'd formed with it in the taxi over there. With this rapacious little thing that would grow and demand and suck and cry and take over my life. Sharon stroked my face. She turned onto her front. Should she do that?

'You're a sweet man, Billy Rucker. And you don't deserve any of this to have happened. The girl you found, Carolyn Oliver. What happened to her was terrible but she's crazy. You don't have to say anything, but it's true. It's not your fault. Anyway, thanks for the fireworks.'

'No problem, babe.'

'I don't mean that. Though I do as well. Thanks for giving me a little time. Us a little time. We don't have much time left now do we, just you and me? Are you scared?'

'I'm excited.'

'Well, I'm scared. This feels like an end just as much as it feels like a beginning. The end for the us that was before. Each of us, and us together.'

'You can't have a beginning without an end.'

'You're right. I love you, Billy.'

I smiled and kissed the side of her face and Sharon turned back over. She took my hand and pressed it against her belly.

'Hello you, too.'

Soon Sharon's breathing begin to level out. I closed my eyes and was back in London Fields. My back was cold but my face was burning, as I stared at the darkened, tethered figure up above me. He was completely surrounded now, the pack of unleashed flames, tongues out, leaping up at him. I watched until the pyre shifted decisively and he disappeared, quickly and without protest, into the blaze.

271

Chapter Thirty-Two

It Was You. It Was You. All of London's buildings, the churches and the skyscrapers, the museums and the townhouses, all of them arranged to form the words. It Was You. In my dreams a whole city telling me what I'd done. And in the buildings people pointing from the windows, pointing their fingers at me. All of them saying it, over and over and over.

It Was You.

Sharon woke me up just before seven. Or rather the sound of her vomiting did. She thought she'd gotten over that but the morning sickness had returned since she'd come back. She put it down to change of diet. She asked me to make her some very strong, sweet coffee and I said I would. I was heading out of the door for croissants from the local bakery but the policeman I met out in the hall offered to go for me. Andy had put plainclothes officers in there and it would have looked as if the guy just lived in the building. I made coffee for him as well, and for his colleague, and Sharon put a small table outside on the landing for them.

I hadn't slept very well. After making love with Sharon I'd drifted off but had come back after a couple of hours. One reason was my mind, it just couldn't turn away from this. The other thing was the pain. My ribs were still sticky and my balls ached, but it was the inside of my thigh that was the worst. There was a patch of skin there about the size of a fifty-pence piece that was dark brown with an edge of scarlet, like a bite mark. It was so tender I could barely touch it. I don't know what the girl had done to me, what she'd found there, but she'd known what she was doing. The pain at the time was almost matched by the after-effects.

Thinking of Cherie, the scars she'd left on me, I tried once again to match her up with the little girl I'd seen seven and a half years ago. Carolyn. I'd managed to convince myself that I was just an excuse, someone to take the run-off of hate that had spilled over from her father. Now the guilt came back, fast and accurate, right into my stomach. There were two images side by side: a little girl I'd wronged and a crazy woman, cold and deadly. Could I have prevented one from turning into the other? Could I have stopped her father taking her, once I'd realized? No. She was only fourteen. I had actually phoned the police, in Chester, and told them what had happened, what I thought was going on at the Olivers' home. They'd put me on to social services, who'd promised to investigate. When I called back a week later, the woman I spoke to didn't even remember my name. When I asked if anything had been done about Carolyn Oliver she said that individual cases were strictly confidential.

And after that? I'd let it go. And if I hadn't? If I'd gone up there, tried to help her? If I'd apologized for my part in her pain? If I'd made someone see what was happening to her, something I could tell in a second?

If, if, if.

I also thought about him, the father, and wondered

why I'd been so ready to believe his story. He'd been convincing but was there more to it? He was well spoken. He was a teacher. He wore horn-rimmed glasses, looked like a man desperately trying to hold his family together after his wife had died. He'd told me she'd had MS. It was probably a lie; everything else was. Once again I couldn't believe how he'd suckered me.

I called Sal, knowing she'd still be sleeping, and left a long message, telling her about Cherie. How we'd both been conned. I didn't for a second think that Cherie would go down to the gym again but I told Sal to call me right away if she saw her. Not to do anything, but call me. I also called the station. Andy Gold had already been at his desk an hour.

'He's dead,' Andy said as soon as he picked up the phone.

I nodded to myself. 'The father? When?'

'Nearly six years ago. A year and a half after you found his daughter.'

'How?'

'House fire. The report says he'd been smoking in bed. The daughter wasn't there, she was staying with her uncle apparently. But you think she did it?'

'She practically told me she did.'

'I don't know how, though.'

'She's resourceful. Anyway, did you get anything from the bedsit, where she went for me?'

'Not much. She cleaned it out. No sign of any bloody clothing, no blood traces on the walls or the floor.'

'None?'

'Not a speck. She must have taken the Denton girl somewhere else. I think she's using another place, or at least if she wasn't she must be now. There were lots of her prints in the bedsit but we know who she is anyway. A couple of other sets too.'

'Guys from the gym,' I said, remembering the smell of aftershave there. 'She was pretending to be a masseur.'

'Thanks, we'll check them out. She might have said something to one of them, you never know. In the meantime, we don't have a photo of her.'

'There's one in my office but she doesn't look anything like that now.'

'I still want it, but I also want you to come in and do another Mac-Fit. ASAP. You think that's why she left you so long? So it would be harder for us to find her?'

'Maybe, but it could be more than that. She's strong, Andy, and she knows stuff about the body. How to hurt it. She's had training. Her father would have been easy if she knew his habits but she might have thought she needed to train up for me. Tell your officers to be careful, if they find her.'

'They've had training too, Billy, you needn't worry about them.'

'Just tell them to be careful,' I said.

I left Sharon at eight. I wanted once again to run through the list of precautions I'd made for her but I bit my lip. She knew. I took a cab to my office and it took me just twenty minutes to find the photograph. The answer had been there all along. I hadn't needed a massage to get it out, just a bit of filing. I tipped the photo out onto my desktop, pushing aside an invoice marked paid. No, this wouldn't be of any use. A girl in school uniform smiling for the camera. Smiling not because she was happy, I could see that now. Smiling to please. Smiling for the mantelpiece. I put everything back into the folder and tucked it beneath my arm.

Out in the corridor I stopped. Something was different. The smell of fresh coffee; it was gone. I stood for a second. Next door I could hear the stutter of light machinery and I bit my lip. I'd completely forgotten about Jemma. Jemma had started me in on this. She'd wanted to know what had happened to her friend. I hesitated, then knocked on the door, holding the file tight against my side as the machine stopped. I'd tell her. I'd tell her why Josephine was dead, and Ally too, and Denise Denton. And Jennifer Tyler. Jemma had wanted to have more information at the very least, and I'd certainly be able to give her that.

'No,' Cass said, folding her arms. 'She's not here. She hasn't been in for days.' Cass looked right at me. 'Jemma's not going to work here any more actually. She told me yesterday. I'll have to find someone else. It's a pain in the arse, if you really want to know. She really should have given me a bit more notice.'

'Oh. Will you tell her that I stopped in to see her, though? When you speak to her?'

'*If* I speak to her,' Cass said.

Cass shut the door and I walked towards the lift. The Lindauer Building seemed quiet and it wasn't just the time of day. I wondered if other tenants had decided to leave, scared or spooked or both. I passed the cafe and wondered if someone else would open it up and, if they did, would I get along with them? Would they save me cakes to take home at the end of the day and give me stupid presents when they came back from holiday? Would I even be able to step through the door? In an instant I knew that I'd never find out. I'd never meet the new owners of the cafe. Whatever else happened, I had to leave. Like Jemma. I knew that. The place was dead. It was over. I pressed my palm against the smooth, cold paintwork of the cafe door and walked off down the hall.

The lift took me down to the car park and another cab took me to the station, where I handed Andy the file. The incident room was only a third full, detectives either yet to come on shift or else out on the street chasing up leads, running down possible eyewitnesses in the various locations where bodies had been found. The Mac artist was there, though, waiting for me. I sat next to him again and it didn't take long for us to fit together a decent likeness of Carolyn Oliver, the girl who'd called herself Cherie. I put her in her tracksuit, the postman's bag slung over her shoulder. Every policeman in London would receive a copy within twenty-four hours, from traffic cops and beat bobbies to the organized crime team and the fraud squad.

But would it help? I hoped so, yet I couldn't help wondering what the girl was up to. I knew why she hadn't killed me. I hadn't suffered enough. But why had she revealed herself to me? She was bright enough to realize that as soon as she did the police would be onto her. I suppose she needed me to know who it was that was hurting me like this. She couldn't see the point of revenge if the person she was aiming it at didn't know who was firing. Still, I couldn't shift a nagging feeling that while Andy was happy, full of the belief that the girl would be picked up within hours, she knew exactly what she was doing.

When I was done I went back over to Andy and asked him if there was any news on the hooker from Loughborough Junction. He said no, and he didn't seem too bothered.

'We're doing everything we can to locate her but we know what she's going to tell us, don't we? We know who picked the Denton girl up.'

I said we did and I was a little relieved; I didn't have to go begging favours from the 22 Crew any more. Andy needed the girl to tie up loose ends, but I didn't. I asked Andy about my car and he told me that it had been brought over from Clapham that morning to the Calshot Street pound. Forensics were done and I was free to take it. I asked him if they'd found anything.

'Something strange,' he said.

'Strange?'

'Kind of. There were no prints in it. Except some latents of yours in the engine.'

'No others?'

'None. The car was wiped. It's obvious.'

'So? Oh, I see what you mean. Why should she wipe the prints in my car when she's already told me who she is? When I've *seen* her.'

'Exactly. It's weird but it's probably just habit, she was being extra cautious. She wiped all the crime scenes down including the kitchen in Clapham. She just got into the habit, after she didn't need to any more.'

'Shit,' I said.

'What?'

'She still needed to.'

Andy frowned. 'Why?'

'Why? Because it means that you don't have any

evidence. Doesn't it? You don't have anything to place her with the victims. All you have is what I've told you. You can charge her with assault, but murder, what have you really got?'

'We'll worry about that when we find her,' Andy insisted. 'The girl from Loughborough Junction can finger her for a start.'

'Evidence from a smack whore?'

'OK, but it won't be everything. We'll blitz everywhere with her picture, see if anyone remembers seeing her in Clapham, under the Westway, in Dalston. That or we'll find blood on some clothes, or some hair samples. She's been in contact with a lot of the stuff, don't forget. No, this is too big, she's been to too many places. Once we've got her, we've got her. Trust me. And with the amount of people we've got on this, we'll get her.'

'But what if she walks, Andy? What if that's her plan? The final insult; to laugh at me from the witness box? Or afterwards, going free, my testimony not enough to nail her, thanking her lawyer, telling the press she's innocent? I can't bear to think of Mike watching her do that. Or David Tyler, Mrs Thomas. Jared Denton. All of them.'

'They won't have to, Billy.'

No, I promised myself. They won't. I'm going to make damn sure of that.

In the pound round the back I discovered that Cherie had thoughtfully left the keys in the ignition and that's where they were now. I got in the car and looked around to see if anyone walked out of the building after me. No one did but that didn't mean I wasn't being tailed. They'd do it well if they were doing it. Andy had told me they weren't but that didn't mean anything. Now that it was likely that the girl had killed her father and was probably not going to stick with women, he'd actually offered me protection, the same that Sharon had. I'd turned him down and we both knew why. I needed room. He hadn't pushed it, and that's what made me sure he had someone on me anyway, some-one far better than I would have imagined. Andy did, however, ask me what I planned to do for the rest of the day and I told him.

I pushed my seat back, started the engine and looked in the mirror. And stopped. There it was. On the roof of my car.

It Was You.

I hadn't even bothered to think about the message. I turned round and the letters were all backwards. It only worked if you looked in the mirror. I reached into the ignition and pulled out my keys. I jammed them into the fabric covering the inside of the roof until I'd made a hole. I got a finger in and ripped the yellowing plastic off in a long strip. I threw the strip out of the window and pulled out onto Calshot Street.

I parked at home and then walked quickly down to Euston, trying to ignore the newspaper boards I passed. When I got there I didn't hand out any photos, or ask any questions of the people who spend their time in or around the station, for whatever purpose. I wasn't there to look for a missing kid. I was there to do something that, strangely, I very rarely did at any of London's mainline stations. Get on a train. I walked up to the ticket office and waited until the woman behind the glass looked up at me.

'Chester,' I said.

Chapter Thirty-Three

The 10.40 left in six minutes. The queue was long and I was at the back of it and by the time I got aboard the train I could hardly move. Needing a seat and somewhere relatively quiet, I pushed my way through to first class and took one of twenty seats that were available. When the conductor came by I paid him an excess that would have got me to Barcelona and back.

I didn't care, though. I had to get to know her. To find out what had really happened to Cherie, to Carolyn Oliver as she was. I had to go back to go forward.

I'd remembered to charge my phone at Sharon's the night before and I was glad. I spent a long time on it, finding the numbers I needed, getting through to the people I wanted to speak to. I told them all that I was investigating a string of murders in the capital and was coming up to check out a Chester connection. I may have used a more official tone of voice than I usually do. I may have mentioned that I was working alongside Chief Inspector Ken Clay and Detective Inspector Andrew Gold. People may have assumed that I was a police officer myself.

The journey took two and a half hours with a change at Crewe. When I walked into the station hall at

Chester I put down my case and pulled out my phone again.

'John Hammond.'

'Mr Hammond, it's William Rucker. I'm at Chester station.'

'On time? A bloody miracle. I'd assumed you'd be late. Can you wait twenty minutes?'

'I can, but if you give me directions I'll happily walk and meet you there. I'd like to walk, in fact.'

'Oh, well then. Thanks, it'll save me ten minutes actually. It's Woodvale Road. Right out of the station, over the footbridge and right again. Walk about half a mile and Woodvale's on your right once more, just after a Barclay's bank. Number 214, you'll find it just after the road starts to bend. If I'm late, there's a pub practically opposite.'

'Thanks,' I said. 'I'll see you there.'

It was a raw, windy day, the temperature a good three degrees lower than it had been in London. I was wearing an inexpensive, not-very-well-fitting suit that had been sitting in a bag in the boot of my car for some time, as had the brown knitted tie that was around my neck. I'd bought the suit ten years ago when I'd wanted something to wear for work, something that I wouldn't mind getting torn or sweat-stained. I wore it when I was in court, or interviewing relatives or when I didn't need to blend in. It was the kind of suit a copper would wear.

I did as John Hammond told me, crossing a footbridge and walking up a slight incline opposite a big green space. Cars and lorries thundered by me on the road to my left but I still got a feeling of relaxation from the streets and shops that I passed. It just wasn't London. It was different, even though it looked quite similar to parts of the capital, any of the roads leading out of the centre of Hammersmith for instance. Tree-lined but urban. Maybe it was the people. They weren't bound up so tight. An old lady passed and rather than looking to be in constant fear for her life, she said hello. A teenager pulling on a roll-up nodded to me as he slouched by. I smiled back, a little too late, then turned to see a taxi stopping to let a cyclist turn right against the traffic. I blinked and looked again. No, the cyclist was waving thanks; it really had happened.

I turned onto Woodvale Road and saw that it was a pleasant enclave complete with a deli and a butcher and a cafe up ahead filled with curled wickerwork chairs. I had a thought. Surely, as an expectant father, I should come and live somewhere like this. Where people didn't seem to actively loathe members of their own species and I could afford a house and a new car and a garden for the kid to play in. Quality of life, it was far greater here, wasn't it? I saw myself saying hi to my neighbour, asking him if he wanted anything from B&Q. My arms filled with a cold terror. I could never do it. I passed the cafe and saw that the wickerwork chairs – *wickerwork* for godsake – had pink padded seats. And the deli, it was one of those poncey ones with nice jam, not an Italian with Parma ham and Vin Santo. Where would I buy my roasted artichoke hearts? I couldn't help wondering: why did all these people, who had one life each, live *here*? Not in Barcelona or New York, Berlin or Paris? What did they do if they wanted to go to the new, must-see contemporary dance group from Uzbekistan? Or eat in some TV chef's new restaurant? Wasn't life hurtling past them like an express train when you're on the local service? I shook my head. Life did that in London too. You just had the tube to annoy you, the congestion charge to bitch about, house prices to laugh at, and just enough burglaries and muggings to read about or endure that you didn't notice.

Number 214 Woodvale Road was a semi-detached house of red brick in a row of identical properties. It was two-storey, Thirties, and looked to have three bedrooms. It was a normal house, or rather would be when the builders had finished with it: planks were laid along the drive leading in through the front door, one of which was being used by a builder pushing a barrow load of cement. I could see more men inside. I turned from them to the windows of the top floor, noticing the blackened brickwork around the edges of the sills, like mascara that's run. The windows themselves were newly installed, a simple design made of UPVC.

'It was completely gutted,' a deep, powerful voice behind me said. 'The upstairs at least. The poor bugger never stood a chance. We tell people about those things, you know? Electric blankets. Cross that with smoking in bed when you've had a few like he did and you may as well jump in front of a train. The result's the same. DC Rucker? Hammond, John Hammond.'

I turned and shook hands with Chester's assistant chief fire officer and then followed him as he negotiated the planking and general debris to get to the front door of Number 214. John Hammond was a tall man in his late forties, carrying a lot of weight around the middle. He was an ex-fireman I guessed, who didn't get as much exercise as he used to, though he was still a powerful presence. His face was long and heavy, the skin thick as a Wellington boot, a broken nose flattened onto it like a wad of Plasticine. Ex-rugby man too, I said to myself, as we stood in the hallway of the house.

The walls around us had yet to be plastered and the floor we were standing on was concrete.

'Don't need to ask what it's about.' Hammond's voice was loud enough to address a conference. 'Chester CID got in touch yesterday and I showed them round last night. Connected to the women being killed down in the smoke?'

'We're pretty certain.'

'That's what they told me. You London fellas needed to come and look for yourselves, then? Didn't trust our lot?'

'I just thought it was worth checking out.'

'Don't blame you, it's your job not theirs. I never let anyone else investigate anything for me. Anyway, you got any questions before we start or do you just want to go up?'

'One,' I said. 'Why's it been so long? Six years before the place was done up?'

'The daughter,' Hammond said. 'She only just sold it. The house wasn't written off after the blaze, it didn't need demolishing. I wrote the report. The girl's uncle was in charge of it until she came of age and he said to just leave it. We made sure it wasn't going to fall down and then got it boarded up. Neighbours weren't happy but there was nothing they could do. Shrewd move as it turns out with property prices shooting up the way they have. Not like in your neck of the woods but they're still rising. She'd have made a killing on it.'

I trailed after the fire officer through the downstairs rooms, a plumber at work connecting water pipes in the stripped kitchen. There was no sense of atmosphere in the place, nothing to give away what it had looked like when the Olivers had lived there. Upstairs was the same. Apart from the scorched brickwork round the windows there was nothing to show what had happened there. Nothing to show what had gone on in the days, months and years before the blaze. As we stood in the empty, echoing master bedroom, Hammond showed me where the bed had been and told me what had happened. What he thought had happened.

'The guy was on his own,' he boomed. 'His wife was dead, you know that?'

I nodded.

'Colleagues said he was pretty down, had been for a while. Anyway, his body was too charred for the forensic bods to tell much but we found a bottle of whisky by the bed, the remains of one. There were beer cans downstairs, eight if I remember right. Empty. It was a Saturday night, January, and we think he just had a binge and fell asleep, the blanket on high and a fag in his hand. Neighbours called three nines but by the time the engines got here it was all over.'

'And you're certain about the electric blanket and the cigarette?'

Hammond shrugged. 'The fire definitely started from the bed. We found the remains of the blanket, and while we can't say if it was faulty because of the condition it was in, it was an old one. You've got to go with what you've got when you're trying to figure these things out.'

'Of course. But was he conscious at all during the fire? Where was the body found?'

'In the bed, what was left of it.'

'Isn't that a little odd? Wouldn't he have at least tried to get out, once he realized his bed was on fire?'

'If he realized. In answer to your question I don't think he regained consciousness. He was out cold from drink don't forget but, anyway, there's the smoke. Mattresses, blankets, they can smoulder for a long time before they go up.'

'I see. So, no suggestion of foul play then?'

'None that we could find, though I can't rule it out. You very seldom can with fire, it's a weapon anyone can come by. Someone could have put something in his whisky to help him sleep, could have left the cigarette burning when he was sparked out. It's possible. No one saw anyone leaving the house, though, so what can you do?'

I nodded. 'Suicide?'

The fire officer smiled. 'That's what buying an electric blanket is.' I smiled back. 'It could have been but I doubt it. It's not exactly a foolproof method. The possibility of severe pain puts most people off it. There's easier ways.'

'And the daughter, where was she?'

'At her uncle's, thank God. He was taking her off walking or something early next day so she'd stayed over with him. She was lucky.'

'Or she was clever,' I said. 'Clever enough to set this up so that no one ever found out.'

'The daughter?' John Hammond stood tall and put his hands on his hips. He was amazed. Chester CID had obviously kept him in the dark. 'But she was only, what, fifteen at the time? Why on God's earth would his daughter have wanted to do something like that?'

*

287

The fire officer and I chatted away a little while longer. When he asked if I had any more questions I said just one: how do I get to Stevenson Fisher High School? John Hammond told me and I thanked him for his time. I walked up Woodvale Road until I came to a crossroads, where I took the left fork. After five minutes I came to the edge of a small park. The modern, box-shaped mass that was Stevenson Fisher loomed up on the other side of it.

I was early for my meeting, having expected the tour of the Olivers' house to take longer than it had. I spent the time sitting on a bench in the park, chatting to another old lady, who offered me some of her bread so that I could feed the pigeons too. As I did so I thought about what John Hammond had told me and wondered – could it really have been an accident? If it had been, then maybe that explained the force of the girl's venom, directed now towards me. She'd been denied revenge once, she wanted to make it count this time. It was possible but I doubted it. She'd either tampered with the electric blanket and got lucky or set the blaze herself. On a dark night in January she'd probably have been able to get out the back way without anyone seeing her. What hit me was the timescale. The fire had happened a long time after I'd found her for her father. Carolyn Oliver had had to endure another year and a half's abuse before she'd managed to pluck up enough courage to end it. I couldn't help being hit by sympathy for her. Sympathy. For this person who had done what she had to Ally.

It was exactly five minutes to three when I pushed open a pair of heavy double doors and was assailed by a smell which, while made up of many different elements, from canteen food to floor polish, said only one thing to me: school. It brought Jen Ballard to me and I remembered another time I'd sat next to her. At the Charter Day Dinner. She'd looked suddenly beautiful and I'd wanted to ask her to dance later but was too embarrassed: she wasn't one of the cool girls the cool guys danced with. I shook my head and let the doors swing closed. Before I'd taken more than two steps I was stopped by a blonde fifteen-year-old wearing a grey skirt and a burgundy sweatshirt with a Stevenson Fisher badge over her left breast. What's the other one called? I might have asked her, twenty years ago. Even though the sweatshirt was quite shapeless the girl still managed to make it look slutty, a fresh coating of lipgloss sealing the effect.

'Can I help you?' she asked, her hands behind her back.

'Maybe,' I said. 'But shouldn't you be in a lesson?'

The rest of the hall was deathly quiet.

'Got thrown out,' the girl said, 'for being a naughty girl. This is what we get, have to mind the doors. Who are you? New teacher?'

It was better than being thought one of the parents. 'No,' I laughed.

'It's just the suit. It looks like a teacher's. But you're not?'

'I'm here to see the deputy head. Mr Fanshawe.'

'What a shame. I wouldn't have minded having you. You could have smacked me any time.'

'And no doubt you'd have deserved it. But Mr Fanshawe's office – fancy showing me the way?'

'If you like. What you seeing Fanny for? You been a naughty boy too?'

289

'No,' I said, 'though I'm thinking about it. This way is it?'

I followed the girl down a corridor to the left, trying not to smile every time she looked back over her shoulder and grinned at me. We turned a few corners, the lemon yellow walls lined with the results of a painting competition. The girl stopped at a door and knocked and we were greeted by a harassed, bobbing man in a crumpled beige jacket and green trousers. He motioned me into the room.

'Thank you, Natasha. You've been very helpful.'

'My pleasure.'

'I'm sure. Next time try to be as attentive to Mr Cruikshank, then you won't have to stand in the hall all afternoon.'

'If Mr Cruikshank looked like him I would be.'

'*Thank you*, Natasha,' the deputy head said again. He shut the door of his small office and turned to me. 'Sorry about that.'

'No problem. Being flirted with by attractive school-girls doesn't hurt the ego any.'

'I remember. It's when they stop that it hurts, some-thing all male teachers have to come to terms with sooner or later. Some years ago for me. Now the likes of Natasha Girton just get on my nerves. Me on hers too, no doubt. But anyway, sit down. Tea?'

'Would be great. Thank you, Mr Fanshawe.'

'Sam,' the teacher said. 'Call me Sam.'

Unlike John Hammond, Sam Fanshawe wasn't a big man. He was a little over five-seven, with wavy unkempt hair that was receding and should probably have been cut a lot shorter by now. Sam had a disparate, jabbing energy that seemed to move in six directions at

290

once as he looked for the kettle, turned for the teapot, then fumbled with a milk carton. He seemed like a nice guy, though, something I could tell before I'd even met him. The girl in the hall had called him Fanny but she'd sounded like she tolerated the deputy head. From Natasha it probably meant a lot. Sam Fanshawe's next question, however, was not one I wanted to be asked.

'You don't mind if I take down your warrant number, do you? I wouldn't ask but the head insisted. She's a bit of a fussbudget I'm afraid, though I would say that, wouldn't I? She got the job, not me.'

Sam Fanshawe was laughing, embarrassed by his request, but he stopped when he saw the expression on my face. I told him that I wasn't a policeman and before he could get me out of the door I told him who I actually was. Not going into too many details I told him what connection I had to Carolyn Oliver, a former pupil at Stevenson Fisher, and to her father who had been a teacher there. Sam Fanshawe was silent as I went through it, blanching when I told him of the discoveries I'd made. He remained silent for a minute or so after I'd finished.

'He was a friend of mine,' he said eventually, his eyes hazy.

'Brian Oliver?'

Fanshawe nodded, closing his eyes for a second. 'Hannah was too. His wife. She taught English here. He was economics. They were both friends. Such a damn shame. And now their daughter, she's doing this? Carolyn? Are you absolutely sure?'

'Positive. She told me for one thing.'

'And it's because you found her for Brian? She blames you?'

'Yes,' I said. 'She was pregnant.' I hesitated. I hadn't told Sam Fanshawe about his friend's abuse of his daughter. 'She lost the baby on her return and was told she couldn't conceive again. She blamed her father and me, as well as developing a hatred of pregnant women. Pathological, I guess you could say. It's possible that her first murder occurred while she was actually right here in Chester. That of her father. She might well have been responsible for the fire that killed him. I doubt we'll ever know for sure.'

'Wouldn't the police have discovered that at the time?'

'Perhaps, but perhaps not. There wasn't much evidence and I believe that Carolyn is a very resourceful woman. Did you teach her?'

'Yes,' Fanshawe admitted. His eyes were cast upwards, his head moving slightly from side to side. Trying to remember if there had been any signs. I thought he was going to say something more but the words tailed off before he could utter them.

'What was she like?' I prompted him.

Again Fanshawe shook his head and then he shrugged. 'She was a quiet girl,' he said eventually. 'Quiet, withdrawn. She might have been resourceful like you say but if she was I never saw any sign of it. Sorry, but that's the best I can come up with. I wish I could say more. It's background on her that you want, isn't it? So that you can find her?'

'That's right. Anything you tell me might be useful. And about her parents.'

'Of course. Well, as I say, Carolyn was quiet. Diligent, got her work in on time. I teach science when I can find the time. Carolyn was one of those invisible students. The sort teachers pray for and then get bored with. The bright ones and the bad ones make the hours go more quickly, you see. We tend to let girls like Carolyn drift along, I'm afraid. We shouldn't but we do. They get Cs and Bs and then you find yourself sitting in front of their mums and dads at parents' evening, trying to remember who the hell you're talking about. If it weren't for the fact that she was the daughter of friends, I'd probably be sitting here now telling you I've no recollection of the girl. Although, no, I probably would have remembered after what happened.'

'You mean the fire? That killed her father?'

'The fire, yes. But not just that. Before. The fire didn't surprise me, though you telling me it could have been the girl's doing is a shock. No. Before then. I mean Carolyn had always been a shy thing but then, well, she just disappeared into her shell.'

Sam Fanshawe stopped speaking, suddenly realizing that he had a cup of tea in his hand. He put it down with an irritated jerk to his left and then looked away from me. His eyes were damp and his breath was coming in short bursts. I thought he must have known about the abuse Carolyn suffered, or at least suspected, and that he was being assailed by waves of backdated guilt. I wanted to ask him but I knew I was on dodgy ground; he could tell me to leave in a second. He looked at me, and smiled and I realized that, no, he hadn't been thinking about his friend's treatment of his daughter. He waited while footsteps disappeared down the corridor outside.

'They were a wonderful couple,' Fanshawe said. 'I have to admit it. The school's golden pair. Brian and Hannah. Brian came in – when was it? – eighty-one.

Before then, well, I had my sights set on Hannah. It wasn't that she was the most beautiful girl but there was something about her, she was just such a lovely woman. Sunny, lit this place up like a torch. I can't have been the only chap who had a crush on her. It was probably unrealistic anyway but it soon became a no-go when Brian turned up. You could tell what would happen straight away and it wasn't long before it did. And you couldn't be jealous, they were just so perfect for each other. They had a kind of aura you couldn't get inside. Brian absolutely adored her, you could tell that a mile off. Sometimes you'd be embarrassed to be with them. Not because they'd be smooching or anything. You just knew that, as soon as you left, they would be. They seemed to be waiting to be alone. Then they had Carolyn and they seemed even closer. She was the spit of her mother. When Hannah died, well, you didn't need to be a psychologist to guess what would happen to Brian.'

We were interrupted by more footsteps, which turned into a knock at the door. The school secretary with some forms for the deputy head to sign. I was disorientated by what Fanshawe had told me. The picture of Brian Oliver didn't fit. Not with the picture I had now. I thought of how he'd conned me. It was obvious that I wasn't the only one. I felt the need to enlighten my host, but I didn't know if I had the right.

'How did she die?' I asked, when the door was shut. Was it MS, like Brian Oliver had told me, weeping at my desk?

'Hannah?' Fanshawe reached for his tea. Almost diffidently he said, 'Oh, she drowned.'

'Drowned? Where?'

'North Wales, somewhere. It's very accessible from here. One of the rivers up there. They'd gone up there for the day, to a beauty spot I believe.'

'What happened? Did she fall in?'

'No,' Fanshawe said. 'No. She went into the river on purpose.'

'How come?'

'Well, it's been a long time and I'm not sure of the details. Oh, what am I saying? I know exactly what happened. It's as if it happened last week. They were walking along a path when Hannah said she was cold.'

'They?'

'Brian and Hannah.' Fanshawe sighed. 'And Carolyn. They hadn't gone far so Brian offered to go back to the car, to fetch a coat.'

'And?'

'And he went. He went to get it. But before he did, he told Carolyn not to go near the water. She was what? Five or six. I remember him insisting to me. The river was in spate and he told her quite clearly not to go *anywhere near* the water.'

'But she did?'

Fanshawe nodded. 'Apparently. No one knows how, of course, but she must have got too close and she fell in. Into the river.'

'And Hannah tried to save her?'

'That's right.'

'And she drowned?'

'She got Carolyn to the side, onto a rock. It must have taken a mighty bloody effort because the river was high. That's where Brian found the little girl, clinging on. But Hannah, she couldn't hold on herself. She was swept away. Brian was only gone ten minutes. When he came back, it was over.'

I looked at the deputy head. I was confused. 'I don't understand. If Hannah was a grown woman, how could she save her daughter but not make it herself? A rock you say? If the girl could hold on to it, why couldn't she hold on too?'

Fanshawe was startled, shocked. As if the answer were obvious. Then his face changed as he realized what he hadn't told me.

'She was pregnant,' he said. 'Eight months pregnant. With their second child. She can't have been able to hold on, though she must have tried.'

'And Carolyn saw this?'

Fanshawe didn't answer. 'There was a weir a little way downstream and more rocks. Hannah was swept down onto them. That's where Brian found her. She was . . . she was . . . I'm sorry. She was in quite a state, the baby and everything. It must have been a terrible sight.'

'Yes.'

'I wasn't there, of course, but I could almost see it in Brian's eyes, reflected there. I went round to see him that night, as soon as I heard. And quite frankly it was one of the worst nights of my life. The look on his face. I can't describe it to you. All I can say is that from that moment on it never, ever, left him.'

'Did you see Carolyn?'

'That night? No,' Fanshawe said. 'She was up in her room. I asked Brian if she was all right but he didn't seem to hear me. He just kept saying, "I told her. I told her." I could tell that he blamed her. I wanted to tell him that he shouldn't, that she was only a child, but he was in such a state. I think he found it very difficult to be with her after that. I mean, with her every day. As I say, Carolyn looked a lot like her mother. I think Brian kept getting reminded.'

'Yes,' I said. 'And so did she. He reminded her almost every night. He reminded her over and over again.'

When I left Sam Fanshawe, after thanking him for his time, I told him to write down my warrant number. My old warrant number. Your head will never check, I told him. Fanshawe agreed that I was probably right and he did what I said. He fussed around for the right book to put it in and I bit my lip. I still hadn't told him about the abuse his friend had inflicted on his daughter. I didn't much want to – the episode seemed to have affected him a lot as it was – but I didn't like to think of him reading it in the paper in a month from now, and realizing that I'd kept it from him. As he shook my hand at the door I filled him in, told him how Oliver had dealt with his wife's death. The breath went out of Fanshawe and he looked nauseous.

'I didn't know,' he just managed to say.

'I'm not saying you did.'

'I knew he wasn't a perfect father after what happened. That she wasn't loved, Carolyn, not at all.' He shook his head. 'And you know what? And this is terrible: I'm not surprised. You're telling me what my friend did to his daughter and I'm not surprised. I wouldn't have been then, not really. What does that say about me? Christ.'

'What is it?'

'I've only just realized. All these years. I got images of Hannah being swept away every time I saw Carolyn, every time I saw her empty, expressionless face. She

297

wasn't just a quiet girl, Mr Rucker. There was something about her. As if she were empty inside, a machine almost. I never liked her and I thought it was just who she was. But it wasn't. Every time I marked her neat, acceptable, average bloody homework I remembered what Brian had told me. He told her not to go near the water. He *told* her. I blamed her for what happened just like he did. She was six years old and I blamed her too.'

Back on the train I sat in first class again. I was the only person in the entire carriage and I was glad. As the inky silhouette of the countryside ran past my eyes, taking me back to the city, I let everything I'd heard run through my mind. I was left with a shivering, traumatized, terrified little girl sitting alone in her room, needing someone to soothe the images out of her brain. Those first hours were probably the most important, the most damaging of all. I remembered something Cherie had told me while she had my balls in her hand and was trying to make me share her pain. She had no toys, no dolls, nothing. I called John Hammond and he confirmed it. Nothing was found in the girl's bedroom after the fire but a bed. Not even a poster on the wall. Hammond had assumed her father had taken them down to decorate or something. But he hadn't. Brian Oliver, in his anger, in his bitterness, had taken everything away from his daughter. Everything, no doubt, but the pictures in her head.

I called Sharon and told her I'd be staying at mine tonight. She said she understood and asked me how I was. I said fine and hung up but what I really felt was flat and tired. Worst of all, helpless. Helpless because there was nothing I could do for the little girl in the room on her own, dreading the sound of footsteps on the stair. It was over for her. She was dead. I had to push her from my mind. I had to do everything I could to try to stop the thing that she'd turned into, stop it before it found out about Sharon, or else invented a reason to kill another woman. I'd always intended to find Cherie before the police did. Now I knew that I had to. It wasn't just that she might get off in court. I knew Andy would be working on Sharon, trying to get her to act as some kind of bait. I had to find Cherie before that happened. How I did it was another matter.

I thought about it for three hours, staring out into the rushing darkness. I didn't have a clue. I had no idea at all. It was a race, between Clay and myself. He had an F1 team behind him. I had a knackered old Mazda. I couldn't think of any way to beat him. I carried on racking my brains, though, and didn't stop once I was back at my flat, staring out onto the street at Fred's.

And that's when the answer came to me.

I picked up my phone on the second ring.

Chapter Thirty-Four

'Mr Rucker?' It was an unfamiliar baritone.

'Speaking.'

'A mutual friend gave me your number.'

'Oh?'

'The lovely Sally Sullivan.'

I nodded to myself. 'I see.'

'She asked me to call you. She told me that you might be willing to pay for some information. Would she be right?'

I sat back in my chair and thought about it. It was depressing. What could the 22 give me now? As Andy said, we knew who had picked Denise Denton up. I was annoyed at myself for not getting Sally to phone the 22 back, to tell them not to bother speaking to the hooker I'd tussled with. I didn't want them giving her grief.

'I'm sorry,' I said. 'It's too late. I wanted a description of someone but I don't need it now. The person I was looking for, I know who it is.'

'How *clever* of you,' the voice said. 'I'll tell Penny to skip the description part. It's a good thing, actually, she's not what you'd call articulate. You'll find that out when you meet her.'

I frowned. 'Meet her? Why would I want to meet her? As I say, I've got an ID, so I don't need to know what the person looked like, the person she must have seen.'

'I understand that. As *I* say, she can forget the description. But, my friend, Penny has more than that.'

'More? What more?'

'She has an address,' the voice said with mock patience.

'An address? How did she get it?'

'She'll tell you that herself. When, I repeat, you meet her. After you've handed over the money. A lot of money. Well, are you interested?'

I'd sat up but I felt my shoulders beginning to slump again. 'Not if the address is on the Camden Road near King's Cross,' I said. 'I've got that too. I've been there.'

'King's Cross? No. It's nowhere near there. This is way across town. Mr Rucker, I was told you were serious.'

'I am. Yes. It's *not* the Camden Road?'

'For heaven's sake. The police have put up a reward, you know?'

'OK, OK. She has an address. I want it. But how do I know it's legit? What if it's rubbish?'

'It isn't. You have my word. You see, Penny would never lie to me. About anything. She, like everyone else who knows me, is fully apprised of what would happen if she did.'

'OK then. Yes.' I tried not to sound too excited. But I was excited. The phone creaked and I realized I was gripping hold of it as tightly as I could. 'I want it, definitely. There's no need for the police. Just tell me where and when?'

'Where? Number 74 Poland Street. Top buzzer. When? Tomorrow afternoon.'

'What's wrong with now? Or later tonight?'

'The boys in blue, that's what. The ones you, I believe, have caused to swarm all over us. Penny has to be careful not to be spotted, and they're still everywhere. I think she can move tomorrow.'

'What time?'

'Between four and six. She'll be here if you come then. No later. I've heard a lot about you, William, and not just from Mrs Sullivan. I'm looking forward to our meeting.'

'Who am I speaking to?'

'Me?' The voice sounded outraged. 'Didn't Sally tell you? I was pretty sure she would have. Oh well. Listen carefully and remember. You're having the *pleasure* of speaking to Charlie Baby.'

I took three Percodans before getting into bed. I wouldn't have slept otherwise. I called Sharon when I woke and we chatted, not about anything. The police were still there. Nothing had happened. She was bored. I didn't know when I'd be round but she understood. I said I loved her. She made a joke but agreed that she loved me too before telling me please to be careful. Whatever I was doing.

'You have to think about your own safety more now. You know that, don't you?'

I told her that I did.

Mid-morning I made myself eat brunch at Fred's, sitting under one of those heat lamps that are supposed to give London a more European feel. Which they will do. When the seas rise because of the heat they kick out it'll be just like Venice. I spent a little while gazing down the Market, watching Grace, the huge bag lady who comes down the street most days to see what the bins have to offer. I saw her empty one out onto the pavement, then walk off with two smeared magazines for some reason. She left the pavement the way it was, covered with filth, and it made me think of Cherie. No matter what terrible things led you to the place you found yourself, you still had responsibilities, you could still decide what was the best way to behave. You can only blame other people for what they did, not for what you do in their name. The crap Grace had left began to blow down the Market but I didn't do anything about it. I had my own clearing up to do. Soon it had nearly all dispersed and the people walking up and down the street didn't seem to notice. It had blended right in.

I spent the rest of the day upstairs in my flat until it was time to leave.

The ground floor of 74 Poland Street housed a digital processing company dealing mainly with animation. Their window featured several cut-outs of cartoon characters from films and computer games. The latest fantasy female was running straight towards me, brandishing an Uzi as well as two oversized nipples. She looked like she could do more damage with them than the machine gun.

Number 74B advertised itself as a model agency. The top buzzer had no name on it at all. I waited while two guys in their forties wearing the same clothes as the kids on Exmouth Market walked past before hitting it.

'Yes.'

'It's Rucker. Billy Rucker.'

'To see?'

'Charlie Baby.'

'On the recommendation of whom?'

'Sally Sullivan.'

'And what is the name of the other party, the person you want to talk to?'

'Penny.'

'Good,' the voice replied as a buzzer sounded. 'That's not what it is but it's what you were told. Walk right up the stairs.'

I pushed the door and entered a narrow passageway. At the top of the stairs I was met by a door that looked like it belonged on the inside of a nuclear submarine. It was aluminium grey, studded with rivets that had been painted over. There were three locks to it, two at the usual height and one about eye level. Doubtless there would be inside bolts as well. I imagined that without the correct equipment it would be almost impossible to breach the door and get inside. Or, once you were inside, to get out again.

I could also see a peephole but it remained covered. A security camera pointed down at me from the top left-hand corner.

'Wait a second,' a muffled voice told me. 'You came alone?'

'Yes.'

'Sally said you wouldn't be stupid enough to invite the police. She was right, wasn't she?'

'Of course.'

I'd been concerned about being tailed in the last few days but not overly so because I hadn't been going anywhere I minded the police knowing about. Today I minded. I'd driven an incredibly circuitous route to get to Poland Street and if Andy had got a car on me I was sure I'd lost it. I began to think that actually he was telling the truth. He hadn't. In the last few days I'd had no sign of anyone on me, either behind a wheel or on foot. The only presence was the van outside my flat, which had still been there when I'd got home at midnight and was there when I left for Soho. I found it very strange. There was my safety to consider but what about any leads I might dig up? They must have thought that I couldn't help, that they were way ahead of me. If they did they were wrong.

'OK. I saw you park that excuse for a motor and no one else followed you. You didn't use your phone to call anyone. Take a step back. That's unless you want six inches of galvanized steel in your face.'

The door swung open without a sound and I stepped forward into a room, the size of which astounded me. It was at least a hundred feet in each direction, as wide, I realized, as the production facility downstairs. The floor was a dark hardwood block tile, patched by rectangles of light. The light could have come from four huge windows on the far wall but these were completely covered by heavy drop blinds in a light coffee colour. Instead it came from a series of roof lights, thick glass panels that could also be covered but were not at present. The man who had opened the door to me was by no means small but he was dwarfed by the space behind him. As my eyes took in the room he grinned.

'What do you think?'

I shrugged. 'That someone would have to run a lot

305

of girls who gave a lot of head to afford this kind of place.'

'You'd be right. Not just the cock bags either. Gear shifters too. I've got a lot of people helping me on my way. Lucky, aren't I?'

'So far.'

'So far, indeed. I know this all too well. Which is why I'm renowned for taking such extreme measures to protect my good fortune. Won't you come in?'

'Thanks,' I said. I recognized the voice but I thought I'd ask anyway. 'Are you Charlie or do you work for him?'

'Oh, I'm Charlie. I thought we'd keep this intimate. I wanted to see what kind of man you are.'

Charlie Baby himself was the kind of man who liked to work out. I could tell that because an extensive array of gym kit gleamed in the distant far corner and also because nobody gets to look the way he did without effort. Why he wanted to was another matter. Charlie wasn't that tall but he was wide. His shoulders and biceps were in the grip of a tight, beige-coloured long-sleeve in a thin, synthetic fabric. The beige went well with his deep black skin, a lumpy, rock-hard slice of which was visible beneath the shirt and above the waistband of some loose, expensive denims. I took this in before looking hard at Charlie's face. Or faces. There seemed to be more than one. The skin was Charlie's but the nose didn't come from his mother. Unless she worked on Harley Street. It was a button turned up between two over-sharp cheekbones, which stretched his face up and backwards. He looked like he'd been caught in a wind tunnel and I guessed that quite a lot of blow jobs had gone to paying for that effect too.

I walked into the room and my host walked behind me, drawing two bolts over the door as well as turning one of the locks with a key chained to his waist. I was in, and I wasn't leaving until he either said I could or I took the key off him. It made me really hope we'd get along.

'She's not here?' I scanned the room.

'She's here. I'll call her through in a second. Why don't you sit down? Don't worry, it won't bite you.'

Charlie was talking about the sofa he was pointing me to. It was bright red in the shape of a pair of huge lips and was the centre of a boxed space in the very middle of the room. In front of it was a glass coffee table and on either side were deep armchairs, one in leopard print, the other zebra. Charlie used the leopard, though I don't know if he was trying to demonstrate anything by it. He intrigued me. The poise and Home Counties tones were celluloid gangster cliché but the surgery wasn't. I couldn't decide whether he was the real thing or just playing. He crossed his legs and looked at me. He nodded in front of him.

'Put the money on the table. Then we can talk. If it's not all there we'd only be wasting time.'

'It's there. It was a bastard to get hold of and there isn't any more.'

'Yes there is. We know who you are. We know what you did to that Maltese fucker last year. But don't worry, we won't come after you for the rest. We're losing a lot of wedge at the moment and you'll be doing us quite a favour if you sort this nasty business.'

Doing the 22 Crew a favour was an unfortunate side effect I was just going to have to live with. I was impatient, wanting to get on with it. I was pleased that my host didn't seem to be messing around either, in spite of his obvious desire to impress me with his poise and control, with his measured, educated tones. I opened the postman's bag by my side and pulled out a jiffy bag. It was stapled shut and I had to yank it open. I tossed ten bound bundles of notes onto the table, bundles I'd taken from the floorboards of my apartment that morning. It felt strange to do that, with a van of coppers outside, but I didn't have any choice. The money had been there for ten months now, ever since I'd done my best to help Nicky, whose life was being threatened over it. Not just the ten actually, quite a bit more. Fortunately, events had played themselves out well. Nicky had got out of the mess and I'd been left holding the stash. He'd lost nothing and I'd gained the ability to get past the steel door behind me.

'Right,' Charlie said, leaving the notes where they were. 'You'll be wanting to get to the girl.'

'Yes.'

'Well, you're the first guy who has wanted to for quite some time, I can tell you.'

Charlie must have pressed a button somewhere or else he had a telepathic connection with his employee because one of only two doors in the room opened and the girl I'd seen down at Loughborough Junction appeared. She shut the door behind her and tried to keep steady as she walked towards us, like a trainee waitress with a tray of champagne glasses. She hadn't changed her clothes since I'd seen her. She looked appalling, worse even than last time, and I felt the same revulsion as I had before. It wasn't aimed at her, though. She was ill. It was aimed at the fact that she sold sex, it was aimed at the people who bought it from her.

The girl didn't seem to notice me. She looked at Charlie instead. Her eyes reached out like a beggar's hands to his.

'Soon,' Charlie said. 'First you have to speak to the gentleman.'

'It would be easier if I could just do a little now, Charlie, just a little bit. Then I'll be able to concentrate . . .'

'I said soon. Then you'll get as much as you want. Sit down. On the sofa. Do it or you won't get anything. You hear me?'

'Yeah, Charlie, I'm sorry. I'll do like you say. But after, yeah?'

'Sit down,' Charlie told her again.

The girl perched on the other end of the sofa from me, her hands splaying out to steady herself. She looked nervous, eager to please, wanting to do the right thing. I didn't know whether this meant that she'd tell me the truth, or just tell me anything.

'I'm sorry,' the girl said to me. ''bout last time. I just get a bit freaked, when it's been a while, you know?'

'I doubt he does. He's not a junky bitch is he? Get to the point. Tell him what happened.'

'Right. Right. Where shall I start?'

I smiled at the girl. 'Why don't I ask you some questions? Then you can answer them.'

'OK. Yeah. If you like.'

'Right then. So. You knew the girl, didn't you? Denise, whose picture I showed you?'

'Yeah.' The girl nodded. 'We was mates. She was new and I took her under my wing. Some of the other girls were jealous of her 'cos she was pretty and she got their

309

trade, but I liked her. We looked out for each other, she lent me money if I needed it.'

'Which is why you didn't tell me that you knew her when I asked you?'

'Yeah. You was offering money but she was my friend. I was gonna ask her, tell her we could split it maybe. I was gonna phone you. But I needed money right then and you didn't want to do it with me. That's when we had the fight. I'm sorry, I really am, it's just . . .'

'It's OK, really. No harm done. But what happened after I left?'

'Denise showed up. Only five minutes after. She'd been arguing with her ex. He'd come from Birmingham and found her. She wanted him to get lost, had to get her boyfriend to come and tell him. She looked terrible. I told her to go and lie down again, you know, because she was expecting and everything. But she said she needed money.'

'Then what happened?'

'She came.'

'Who did?'

'The woman. The social worker.'

'Social worker?'

'That's what she said. But I wasn't sure. I thought she was the Bill.'

'What did she look like? Wait a second.' I reached in my jacket pocket and pulled out a copy of the Mac-Fit. 'Is that her?'

'Yeah. Yeah. She said she wanted to protect Denise, that you were a danger to her. She said you was killing all them pregnant women and was coming for her next.

Denise saw the pictures you'd been handing out and she was shitting herself. She went in the woman's car.'

'What make was it?'

'I dunno. It was blue, yeah, blue.'

'A Ford Mondeo?'

'Maybe. I dunno.'

'OK, so. I was told you have an address.'

'I do. You want to know what happened or not?'

'Please. Go on.'

'Well, before Denise got in the car she changed her mind, said she wouldn't go with her. She needed money for her boyfriend. He'd told her not to come back with less than five hundred that night. So the woman gives her money, says she's authorized, and then she even gives me some. Just gives me fifty quid.'

'And Denise left with her?'

'Yeah, but I was suspicious. Social workers with cash?'

'What did you do?'

The girl nodded. 'We had this safety thing. I taught her it. Denise had her phone in her handbag. If she went with a punter she'd phone me, on the sly, and leave the line open, you know? Then she'd say where she was going. Like, "Is this where you live, Herne Hill Road?" or "This is my place, park next to the skips." Stuff like that.'

'And she did that?'

'Yeah. I used our code to remind her when she got in the car. I said: your mum phoned. That was to get her to do it. She did and I listened. The woman kept asking her stuff, whether she knew you at all, and then they got to where the woman lived.'

'Which was where?'

The girl stopped speaking. To my left, Charlie sat back in his chair. The girl, who seemed to be linked to him by invisible wires, turned. I had the feeling then. I was so close. But it wasn't going to be simple, like I'd hoped. I saw Charlie smile and my stomach tensed.

'That's enough,' he said to her.

'Wait a minute. What was the address Denise gave you?'

'I said that's enough. Don't worry, Mr Rucker, I'll tell you the address. In a second. You did well, Helen.'

'Can I have some now?'

'Of course you can. I'll deduct it from your ten grand.'

'What?'

'The ten grand Mr Rucker here is paying for the information you gave him.'

She just stared. 'It's mine?'

I have to say we were both surprised. The girl, Helen, hadn't even dared to look at the cash.

'All but the seven hundred you owe me. And what you want to pay me now. How much do you want? I tell you what, give me a round thousand and I'll sort you out nicely, keep you going for a while. That'll mean you get nine grand now.'

The girl nodded, trying to make out that it was nothing. 'All right Charlie, yeah. OK. I'll do that.'

'Right. I'll get some for you but you can't shoot up here. I'll get Johno to drive you home.'

'Thanks, Charlie, thanks.'

'Wait. The address. She's not leaving with the cash until I get it.'

'I told you. You'll get it when I say. And if you don't like that, take the money now and leave. Well?'

Charlie Baby was glaring at me. The girl at my side looked like she might be sick.

'I just better get it.'

'You will. I told you, we're on the same side. Relax.'

'OK then,' I said. Next to me Helen nearly collapsed with relief. 'But one other thing. You had this safety thing and it worked. You knew where Denise was. So why didn't you tell anyone when she disappeared?'

'I meant to,' the girl insisted. 'I really did. But I had fifty quid. I spent it, you know? And then I couldn't tell anyone anything for two days. I'm sorry. I . . . really am. I liked Denise, we were mates, we were.'

Helen looked down at her hands, gripping one with the other against the vibrations running through them. I turned away from her and watched as Charlie Baby walked quickly over to the door she'd emerged from and pulled it open. Before he closed it behind him I heard him speak and I nodded to myself. It made sense that he had back up. I kept my eyes on the door and let out a breath. I wasn't happy about the girl leaving before I'd got the address but there wasn't really anything I could do about it. I was impatient, though. The address wasn't the Camden Road. In that case I couldn't see any reason for Cherie not to still be using it. She'd still be there. Unless, of course, she'd spotted Denise's little mobile phone ruse as they drove. I prayed to God she hadn't.

Charlie came out of the room with a baggie in his hand, which he tossed to Helen. Helen still hadn't dared touch the cash and her boss had to scoop it into the bag I'd brought it in. He handed her the bag and told her that Johno would be waiting in the cafe for her. I still couldn't believe he was letting her take the money, though I imagined that most if not all of it would make its way back to him. Charlie walked her over to the door and let her out. He came back over but remained standing.

'You must really want to stop all this,' he said with a smile.

'I do.'

'Why?'

I shrugged.

'Someone you know got sliced? That it? Sad, I agree, but is she worth ten grand?'

'She is.'

'Even though she's dead? It won't mean anything to her.'

'It will to me.'

'A man after my own heart. Punishment. It's necessary otherwise everything crumbles. Not revenge but punishment, which equals efficiency. You want the address now?'

'I wanted it before now.'

'Well, it's in the bedroom. I wrote it down. Just go right in and you'll find it.' I didn't move. 'Well? Go ahead. Either go in there and get it or leave. It's up to you.'

Charlie's eyes were boring down into mine now. I moved mine away, to the door, and Sally's warning shot back into me. He'll hurt you, or if he can't he won't help you. There was also the fact that I'd caused the police invasion of his territory. My eyes stayed on the door. I thought about it. There had to be at least one person in the other room. Probably more than one. Were they going to give me a spanking, just to show me what kind of men they were? For snooping around their girls, flooding their manor? A spanking or worse? Who knew I was there? No one. My eyes went back to Charlie and I wondered if I could get his key from him and get out of the front door before whoever was waiting in the room got to me. I didn't think I could and, anyway, I didn't want to. I wanted the address. I had to have it. I could take the kicking if that's what it was to be. Ally had got worse. I told myself: he wants this ending too. I wasn't going to get the address unless I did what he wanted. I stood up. Without saying anything I walked across the huge space towards the door.

When I got there I stopped, just outside. The door was ajar. I strained but I couldn't hear anything. I waited a second then pushed the door and a sound did come to me. A movement. A rattling. I stopped again and my stomach clenched one more time. I realized that my jaw was clamped tight. Whatever surprise Charlie had for me, he was already getting the effect he wanted. The rattling continued, then slowly petered out at my lack of movement. I waited. I left it a bit longer. Then,

'I'm coming in,' I said. There was no response. I took another breath. 'I'm coming in, OK?'

I took a short step forward and put my hand on the door. Again I wondered: maybe Charlie was going to kill me. But if so, why the charade with the girl? I didn't know but if that was what he was planning there was nothing I could do about it. I pushed the door open and walked through. My eyes instantly found the man, the man in front of me. I stopped dead.

The room was about a quarter of the size of the one I'd just left. Which meant it was still bigger than my whole apartment. A huge round bed sat slap in the middle of the space.

The man was next to it. Not sitting. Not standing. He was hanging. Hanging by his wrists from a chain, attached to an iron hook on the ceiling. The man was in his late twenties by the look of him, with limp, blond hair streaked with highlights reaching down almost to his shoulders. He was naked, his hands cuffed above his head, pulling his arms upwards. The chain ran up from his wrists to a pulley on the ceiling. He'd been cut. He was marked by maybe ten incisions, the blood on a couple of them still running down his body, yet to congeal. I swallowed. Charlie must have done them just now, seconds ago, while Helen and I were waiting for him.

I still didn't move. My eyes opened into those of the man in front of me and I realized that he was trying to speak. Or was it scream? He couldn't do either. He was gagged, masking tape wound tight around his mouth and head, turning everything he said into shapeless grunts. More tape bound his feet together. I watched his eyes suddenly leave mine and make a bid to leap out of their sockets, over my shoulder.

'Meet Steven,' the voice behind me said. 'He's my house guest.'

'Just give me the address.'

'Soon. Relax. Can't you appreciate a little beauty first?'

'The address.'

'In a second. First, I'd like you to do something for me.'

Charlie moved over to the man hanging in front of us, small beads of light seeming to dance in his eyes as they ran over his captive's pale, blood-streaked body. Charlie ran a rough hand over the incisions on the man's chest, making the man turn and wince and then cough with pain. He moved the hand down over his stomach until he was gripping the man's shrivelled testicles. Then he turned to me.

'Pretty, isn't he?'

'I gave you the money,' I said. 'It's what we agreed. Give me the address.'

'After.'

Charlie's face split again into the grin I'd seen earlier.

'After you've fucked him.'

'What.'

'After you've fucked him. Then you can have it. Only after. Or don't you care about your dead friend as much as you thought you did, after all?'

'I care.'

'Well then. Come on. Now. I want to see you do it.'

I didn't move. Suddenly the man in front of me began to buck, his body lashing to and fro like pegged washing in a gale. It was pointless, useless, but he didn't stop until Charlie spun round and rammed an elbow into his chest, sending all the air out of his body. Charlie dug the nails of his left hand into the tape that bound the guy's face.

'I told you! Don't sell anyone's coke but mine, Steven. It is my shit only that stimulates the nostrils of your D-list friends. No one else's. This is what I do to people who fuck with me, Mr Rucker.

'I tell them off in my own special way. It's to keep them in line, of course, but why not make your business work for you? If Steven behaves, I get rich; if he

317

doesn't, well, you can see what I get. I didn't mind at all when I heard that Steven had been straying. I was overjoyed, in fact. That's why I wanted to meet you. To show you. I won't be angry if I hear that you've spoken to the police about me. It'll be a pleasure to discipline you, and you'd better believe that I will. But in the meantime you're going to help me with Steven. If you don't I'll tell you nothing, and don't bother looking for the girl, to get the address off her. You won't find her. Come on. Can't you see he's dying for it? That's why you go out with that skinny baby model isn't it, Steven? She looks just like a little boy.'

The man's eyes were pleading with me. I knew I had to act, get him out of there, do whatever I could to free him. But I didn't do anything. I broke his look, turning my head away, and as I did he bucked again, weakly this time, before beginning to cry, his chest shaking. I wanted to leap at Charlie, wrestle the keys that bound the man off him. I didn't do it. If I did, I'd never get the address. I wondered: could I get it out of Charlie? Beat it out of him? I doubted it. Was there anything more important to me than getting it? This man, was he? No, he wasn't. He just didn't matter enough. I told myself that. And if that was so? I couldn't help him. I found myself taking a step forward, and then another, sickness growing in me with every second that passed.

I still couldn't look at the chained figure, instead turning to Charlie, wondering if there was any way, any other way through this. I knew there wasn't. No. Because this man was the real thing all right, in spite of the veneer. He didn't get the look on his face from the movies. It was distilled, clear evil drawn from a well deep inside himself. His eyes had stopped dancing. They were burning like coals. I tried to focus not on them but on Ally, on Denise and Jo and Jen. On the other women, the ones to come. Sharon. Possibly saving her. I knew then. I didn't have any choice.

Charlie turned from me, pushing the guy's head up. He wound himself round his body, pressing against his cut flesh, pushing his tongue into the guy's left ear. I wanted to retch. Charlie stepped back and Sally's words came back again: ask Pete what Charlie made him do. He was laughing.

I thought he was going to tell me to get on with it. He didn't. Instead he pulled hurriedly at his fly.

'Sorry. I'm going to have to punish Steven myself. I've waited too long and he's been too bad. I don't think you'll be rigorous enough. Come back when I'm finished, if you like. That'll be a week or so. Well, you some kind of pervert?'

Charlie pulled a plain white envelope out of his back pocket and tossed it to me along with the key chained to his belt. I should have been relieved. I had it, I had what I came for.

'You can go. Leave that in the lock. And remember what I told you. Don't even think about helping Steven here. You'll never leave this apartment if you do. And if the police arrive here later, in the next month even, I'll know who sent them. You'll end up like this and we'll also plan something for lovely Sally for putting you onto us. You won't do anything rash, anything at all. And in the meantime do you have any condoms? No? Me neither. Oh well, too late for me, anyway. Far too late. Oh, Steven, calm down. My advice would be to relax. You never know, you just might be lucky.'

The eyes above the tape leapt out at mine again, a last plea for help coming from the depths of one human being, trying to find those depths in another. Their owner was trying to kick his taped feet, struggling to shake himself free. Charlie was wrestling with him, trying to get hold of his body, like a line fisher with a live marlin. All the time he was looking at me. Asking. You going to stop me? My blood was iced water, the muscles in my legs coiled tense, trying to make me spring forward, to drag Charlie off his captive.

Charlie knew I wouldn't. And I knew it too.

Chapter Thirty-Five

The air outside was laced with scooter fumes and the
stink of a half-eaten kebab left on the pavement. It
smelled as sweet as any air I'd ever breathed. But I
didn't take long to savour it. Instead I pivoted round in
both directions, chose one and began to run. Not just
because I wanted desperately to be away from there.
But because of Helen. The sentence was carved into
my mind.

Don't bother looking for her.

I sprinted down the street and put my head in the
first cafe I came to. She wasn't there. She wasn't in any
of the other six or seven I tried either. I ran around Soho
for fifteen, twenty minutes, asking waiters, passers-by,
women standing in the doorways of peep shows, if
they'd seen a girl, a junky girl, carrying a postman's
bag, probably with someone else. No one had, or if they
had they weren't saying. I turned around. Where would
she have gone? Not home, not straight away. Her eyes
had been too desperate. I ran down a side street but
stopped. I could hear a siren, close by, and when I
turned I saw an ambulance pushing through the traffic
on Great Marlborough Street.

I caught up with the ambulance and overtook it as it
swung a right. Up ahead, a man was waving outside

some public toilets, the old kind with steps leading down. I beat the ambulance to the man and didn't stop but ran past him. Down into the ladies, where a woman pointed to the last cubicle. She must have thought I was a doctor. The woman's face was ashen, her other hand clenched over her stomach. The door she was pointing to was half open and I pushed it the rest of the way.

Ten grand. That was what her life was worth. Charlie hadn't needed to kill her to get it but he did know that the police would pick her up sooner or later. And they'd ask her all sorts of questions. Maybe, if it had been another girl, he'd have let her live, scared her into keeping quiet. But Helen wasn't worth anything to Charlie any more. She was probably costing him money.

Helen was lying on the floor between the toilet bowl and the partition wall. The needle was dangling from her thigh. Foam and blood covered her mouth and her face, some still spreading down to her sunken chest. There was, of course, no postman's bag. When I heard footsteps behind me I moved back to let the medics rush in. After a second they stopped rushing. I backed away and pulled myself up the stairs before drifting off through the small crowd that had gathered there.

I needed to think but I couldn't sit in my car, not where it was parked. I'd left it on a meter opposite the digital processing company. The girl with the Uzi was still running straight at me. People walked past, some glancing up at her. Above her and them, behind the covered windows, a man was being tortured, possibly murdered if Charlie wasn't bluffing. Charlie had found a way to hurt me, just as Sally had said. He'd let me look into his life. He'd made me look into myself. I wondered which he thought would get to me more, the death of the girl I'd asked him to find or the fact that he'd turned me into someone who could walk out on something like that, who could let it happen. Thinking about it, I didn't know myself. I just told myself again that I'd got what I wanted. Nothing came close to that. I just hoped, with everything I had, that it was worth it.

I pulled away and drove round to Charlotte Street, where I stopped at another meter.

I closed my eyes and sat for maybe ten minutes, until a traffic warden tapped on the window. I got out and fed the meter then got back in the car. The envelope was on my dashboard. I looked at it for a long time before I picked it up and opened it. The address was written on the inside flap. A few words. The key. At last. It had to be the key. I folded the envelope and slid it into my jacket pocket. I sat for another ten minutes, knowing that I needed to be calm. I had to push on. I had to see it through. I saw the man's eyes again and thought, if I called Andy, how long would it be before he could get a team round there? I knew I wasn't going to do it. And it wasn't because I was afraid, for me or for Sally. I'd come too far. I'd made too many compromises to back out now. I was swimming through a nightmare and if I stopped for a second I'd sink. Forget him, I told myself. Just think about what you have to do. This is your chance, probably your only chance. Think.

I read the address again and looked it up in my A–Z, running my finger along the street. I closed the book and decided. I wasn't going to wait around. What would

323

be the point? The only thing I did wonder was whether to drive there or not. Having the car would be useful but what if she spotted it? I'd park a good way away but even so it was possible. I didn't want to lose my advantage. I hadn't been in the game long and I'd had a lot of catching up to do but, finally, I was a step ahead of her, Cherie, this person who had swept into my life from the past. I had her. If the address was right, I knew where she was staying. And she didn't know that I knew. Remembering a place where I could park safely, I drove down past Leicester Square and then along the Strand, hitting the Embankment at Temple.

I drove east beside the river, picking a way through the City as thin streams of suited pedestrians ignored the pelican crossings and flooded through the stationary traffic. I made it up to Whitechapel, edging along Whitechapel Road past the still-crowded market stalls, sari-clad women gathered in circles to chat. A great pulsing throb sounded above me and I looked up to see the red bulk of the Virgin chopper manoeuvring to land on the roof of the Royal London hospital. The traffic was worse here, traders' vans blocking one of the lanes as they began to pack up for the day. It freed a bit once the stalls ended, though, and I moved on past the Blind Beggar, where a group of American tourists was peering in the door, being told what had happened there. I wondered if they'd go inside. I carried on up the Mile End Road until I came to the huge car park of a new, box-built electrical superstore.

There was no barrier or gate. I wouldn't get locked in and it was only about twenty minutes from there down to Limehouse, if I walked quickly. Far enough away, but near enough too. I parked close to the exit. I locked the car and crossed over the busy carriageway, choked with commuters trying to get back to Essex and Kent. People the City sucked in every morning and grudgingly released at night, on the proviso that they return. People who didn't live in London but hadn't managed to get as far away as Chester. With mobiles pressed to pale, drawn faces, they looked as desperate as I was, every single one of them.

Chapter Thirty-Six

I hit the river at Narrow Street. A path ran at the foot of some executive apartments with windows looking out across the broad mass of pewter in front of me. I walked along it. A tourist cruiser out in the centre of the river ran with the tide, back towards Charing Cross. The guide's amplified monotone made its way towards me across the sluggish, shifting expanse.

I stopped for a second to think what to do. The idea of calling Andy came to me again but only to give me something to discard. The part of me who saw the little girl in Chester wanted to, it told me that she needed a second chance. I had to remind myself that she didn't exist any more. Cherie did. And she wasn't getting away with this, she wasn't going to get involved in weeks, months, maybe even years of argument. No matter what had happened in the past, I knew how this had to end. I just had to play it right. I walked on. It was getting dark now, the river seeming to draw the remaining light down into it. I passed a pub called the Barley Mow, busy with crumpled-looking workers from Canary Wharf, sucking at their beer as if it was mother's milk. Another *Standard* front page leapt out at me from one of the pub's wooden A-frame tables. This one told of the death of Jennifer Tyler. I wondered how many people inside the pub were talking about it. It was *the* story. How strange then that I, one man, should be walking towards Cherie, one woman, to end it all. I remembered the people reading the *Metro* on the tube when Sharon and I were coming back from Heathrow, the kids making sick jokes. The difference between them, outside looking in, and me. Those people had been able to move on, to either laugh or read about something else. Was I, finally, going to be able to turn the page? Ahead of me a bank of cloud was sneaking up fast behind Canary Wharf. The light atop the impossible bulk blinked as if it was showing me the way.

Narrow Street carries on along the river at Victoria Wharf. I took a left and came to a square, mostly made up of modern apartment blocks, all blond brick and chrome, already looking a bit dated. Victoria Place was over the other side to my left and the houses there, just one row left, were older: late Georgian, perhaps, or early Victorian. Semi-detached in blocks of two, pathways leading round to the rear. I walked along, noting that most had been turned into office spaces, on the ground floor at least. An architects' practice, a couple of e-businesses, a consulting firm. I felt my heartbeat increase as I approached Number 14. It was the only house. I walked past quickly but could still be sure that no lights burned within. I crossed back over the square to another pub, where I stood near the window until a seat became free. I sat there for an hour before walking back out again.

'Yes, hello? Can I help you?'

The woman had been carrying a shopping bag in each hand, with a leather purse slung over her shoulder. She'd opened the door to Number 14 with a key and closed it behind her. Lights had come on shortly after. It had been hard to tell the woman's exact age from the distance I was at but it definitely wasn't Cherie. The woman was sixty, at least. I left it five minutes, hoping that Cherie wouldn't arrive back too in the meantime. I made my way across the square towards the front door, to Number 14 Victoria Place.

'Listen, if you're another estate agent I can tell you now to forget it. I've got all your leaflets.'

The woman standing in front of me had hair that was a luminous grey, brushed back into something of a pompadour. Her clothes were colourful swathes of flowing silk. She gave off unstudied elegance but it was a Seventies elegance or even earlier. Her face was kindly but troubled, a pair of overlarge glasses magnifying her eyes so that she looked almost constantly startled. I gave her a nervous smile.

'I'm not an estate agent.'

'No? You don't look like one actually. I'm sorry, it's just they keep hassling me. But what can I do for you, love?'

I shifted from one foot to the next, then back again.

'You have a young girl living here,' I said. As if it was nothing.

'Yes. Cherie. What . . .? You're not a policeman, are you?'

'No,' I laughed. 'Why did you say that?'

'I don't know. No reason. It was just the way you said it. "You have a young girl living here." But you're not a friend of Cherie's, are you?'

'Not exactly.'

'No, she doesn't have many friends to visit. But if

you're not a friend or a policeman or, thank goodness, an estate agent, what are you?'

'It's a little hard to explain. Are you related to Cherie?'

'Me? No. She just rents my loft. It's converted, of course. I wouldn't just rent someone a loft.'

'No.'

'But why do you want to know if I'm related to her? I'm sorry but I have to ask you who you are.'

'I think I might be Cherie's brother,' I said.

'Think?'

'Yes. She doesn't know about me. It's a bit complicated, I'm afraid.'

'I see,' the woman said. 'I see.'

We were in her sitting room. It was a pleasant room, though the majority of the furniture was fairly old. It was mostly heavy stuff, mahogany tables, uncomfortable-looking sofas with huge, carved wooden claws for feet. A lot of it could have done with upholstering but nevertheless the room had charm. The frayed silk lampshades were a change from the uplighters everyone seemed to go for these days and the faded William Morris on the walls was more interesting to look at than white paint. Mrs Minter, as she'd introduced herself, had offered me tea, which I'd declined.

'I'm sorry about the estate agent thing but one of them actually did come round the other day, not satisfied with littering my doormat with their fliers. They tell me I could make a killing on this place, enough to buy one of those ghastly oversized shoeboxes I'm surrounded by. But I was born here, you see, and with my job and the rent from upstairs I'm all right. They can go and screw themselves, if you'll pardon my

French. But now then. It seems like you have a bit of a story to tell me.'

Mrs Minter had already told me that she was a local government officer, working for Hackney in the housing department. I told her that my name was Jonathan Howells and that I was a teacher, PE and English, in Islington. I explained that I'd always known I was adopted but had only recently tracked down my biological parents after my adoptive parents had passed away. Mrs Minter asked me what it was like to meet them but I shook my head.

'I haven't,' I said. 'Once I found out who they were I realized that I didn't want any more than that. From them. They had a choice and they gave me away and I have to accept that. But Cherie never had a choice as to whether or not she wanted a brother. Cherie, that's my sister. I'm sure she is. It took me ages to find her. Months more to pluck up enough courage to get in touch. I thought about writing but didn't know what to say and a phone call would have been worse. So I just thought: hell, I'll knock on the door. And she's out!' I laughed. 'Do you know when she'll be back, Mrs Minter?'

The woman sitting opposite had no idea when Cherie would return. Her lodger tended to come back most nights, but not always. She had her own keys, of course, but still had to use the front door. I asked what kind of girl Cherie was, eager to know more about my sister, but Mrs Minter was noncommittal. I got the feeling that she didn't approve of her, but it wasn't because of noise or men or anything like that.

'She's very quiet,' Mrs Minter explained. 'She just comes in and goes straight upstairs. By the time I can get out into the hall to say hello she's already in her flat. My last tenants were art students. We used to have a real laugh. I like young people. But no, Cherie is nice and polite but she plays her cards close to her chest, shall we say. You know what? I have the feeling that you taking an interest in her, it just might be what she needs to draw her out of herself.'

Mrs Minter and I chatted on for another five minutes, my ears straining for the sound of footsteps, or a key turning in the front door. The street was quiet. After a while I gave a pained expression and asked Mrs Minter if I could use her toilet.

'I'm just so nervous,' I explained. 'I can't believe she's not here. I don't know how I'll pluck up the courage to do this again.'

Mrs Minter told me where the toilet was, feeling comfortable enough to stay in the room and let me go out into the hall on my own. The more sympathy that showed on her face the worse I felt about lying to her, but I didn't have time for that. Closing the door behind me, I went back to the front door to see if I could spot any spare keys, on a hook maybe. I couldn't but I did see that there was no alarm system. That was good. As quickly and as quietly as I could, I made my way past the living-room door and down a passageway until I found a door on the right, just before the kitchen. More wallpaper greeted me, gigantic swirling green fronds as though I'd been ambushed by a triffid. The room was small, containing a toilet and nothing else. The seat was down and I stepped on it, then ran my hands round the window frame above.

The window wasn't barred but the frosted panes were secured by four window locks, which in turn were neatly covered by plastic caps. I stepped back down and looked in a small cabinet, where I found the long slim key to the locks sitting next to a bottle of pine-fresh toilet cleaner and a Jessica Helms novel. I unlocked the windows, put the bolts in my jacket pocket and then slid the small plastic covers back into place. They looked the same as before. I turned the swivel catch and stepped back.

No. Mrs Minter would see straight away that the catch was open. She wouldn't necessarily think anything was up but she'd almost certainly close it. I closed it myself before using my Leatherman on the screws that fixed the tiny bracket of the catch to the bottom half of the sliding window. No one would notice that it was no longer attached, unless they were dusting the sills down. I doubted whether Mrs Minter would do that tonight. I put the screws in my pocket.

After I left the toilet I made my way up three flights of stairs until I found myself on a landing, where two green eyes stared at me from on top of an orange ottoman piled with clean washing. I stroked the cat and then hopped up the steep staircase leading to the loft. At the top was a closed door. I turned the handle slowly but the door was locked. I looked through the keyhole but the room was dark.

Back in the living room I put my hand to my stomach in an effort to explain the length of my absence and received a reassuring smile from Mrs Minter. Mrs Minter asked me again if I wanted tea or anything stronger, adding that it could be a long time before Cherie came home. I said no thanks.

'And as it could be hours, I won't take up any more

of your time. But, Mrs Minter, could you do me a favour?'

'I'll try, but you're welcome to stay. I could cook us a meal.'

'No, thank you all the same.'

'Well, never mind. But I think I know what you're going to ask. You don't want me to tell Cherie you came, do you?'

'I don't, Mrs Minter. It's very wise of you to guess that. I think the news would be a big shock and it really should come from me.'

'I understand.'

'Instead, could you call me? When she comes home? Then I can come round again. If it's OK that I come round again?'

'Of course it is. And I will call. On the QT.'

'Let me write my number down.'

'And I'll give you mine too,' Mrs Minter said, reaching into her bag for a pen.

Back in the pub I had to stand, but I had a good view of Number 14. Mrs Minter had, unfortunately, had the good manners to show me out. If she hadn't I'd have gone straight up the stairs and found a way to get past the door at the top. Instead I thanked her and shook her hand and promised to bring my two girls round for lunch once I'd got to know my sister. Once again Mrs Minter promised to call me the moment she heard Cherie come home, whether it was later that evening or the next day.

'You must be so excited at the thought of meeting her,' Mrs Minter said as we parted.

'I am,' I agreed. 'I can hardly wait.'

'And for her – what a surprise!'

'Yes,' I said. 'A very big surprise, indeed.'

I leaned against a pillar and sipped a Coke. I was happy, pleased by the way things had gone. I'd found her. I'd found a way into the house where she lived. Now I had to follow through. My eyes never leaving the door opposite, I tried to picture the next few hours. As far as I could see, there were two ways I could play it. Both had their merits. The first way would be to watch the house until Cherie came home. I could wait until two or three in the morning and she was asleep. She had to sleep. That way I'd know she was definitely there, I'd know exactly where she was. Then, with the house quiet, I could break in through the toilet window. No one would hear me. The only problem would be the door to the loft conversion but I was pretty confident that I could pick the lock without waking the girl inside. If I couldn't I'd just bust it down and by the time Mrs Minter called the police, and they got there, it would all be over one way or another.

The second way would be to break into the house before Cherie came home and wait for her. The only problem with that was that it was still only seven-thirty. Not only might Mrs Minter hear me getting in the toilet window but the street was too busy as well. So, whichever option I took, I had to wait until later, until Mrs Minter was in bed. And if that was the case there was no point wasting time there. I used my phone and reached Sally at the gym.

'Billy,' she said. 'I was expecting you to call. I got your message. Cherie, the massage girl. I can't tell you how sorry I am.'

'Sorry?'

'For giving her a way to get to you. I feel so stupid. She was just so normal, so down to earth. I shiver to think that she had me on the couch in my office, half naked.'

I shivered at that too.

'It wasn't your fault. I fell for her as well. And I'd seen her before. I'm sorry I brought you into it, that you're having to deal with the police. You are, aren't you?'

'They came down here, asking questions. It's OK, Billy, no sweat. There's nothing here I don't want them to see. But tell me, what's going on? Did you meet with the 22?'

'I did.'

'And how did it go? They told me they had an address for you. Did you get it?'

My stomach turned over. 'I got it.'

'And is it kosher?'

'As salt beef.'

'Excellent. But now you want the other thing, and it's for you now, am I right?'

'You are.'

'Well, I'm hoping I can get it for you by tomorrow. The heat that's out there has made it harder to get hold of. South London's dead but I've left a message with a Camden firm.'

'I need it tonight, Sal.'

'I see. OK, I'll call them back. But I'm not promising anything. It's going to be difficult. But if they do have it they can bring it to you. Where will you be for the next few hours? At home?'

'I've got a caravan of coppers camping on my doorstep.' I thought about it. 'I'll be at my office. I've got some cash there, so you can tell the Camden lot that I'll pay them the same again, *if* I get it tonight.'

'OK,' Sal said. 'But, Billy, you've obviously found her. Why don't you bring Pete in on this? As back-up.'

'I think I have to do this on my own, Sal.'

'Why?'

'Because I started it on my own.'

'Isn't that just pride? Let us help. We were stupid enough to fall for the girl too – and how will you feel if she gets away from you? I'm going to call him and tell him to be ready anyway, he could be with you in twenty minutes. So at least think about it, will you?'

'Thanks, Sal,' I said. 'I promise I will. I will think about it.'

And I did. I thought about it as I walked back to the car. I thought about it in the car and then in the lift, as it took me up to the third floor of the Lindauer Building. Sal was right. The personal score thing was vanity, nothing more. I'd call Pete. He wouldn't be able to get through a toilet window but he would be able to watch from the outside. He could warn me that Cherie was coming, he could even nab her on the way out if everything went wrong. It was a good idea. As I stepped out of the lift into the darkened hall I pulled out my keys and my mobile, needing Pete's number from the address book. I unlocked my office door and pushed it open with my shoulder. I flicked the light switch. My eyes were on the phone in my right hand but they went straight from that to the face of the man sitting behind my desk. I let my hands fall to my sides and I stopped dead in my tracks.

The face was heavy. Motionless. The man who

owned it was so still that for a second I thought he was dead. My gaze flicked down to the gun that was sitting on the desk in front of him. The man's right hand was lying next to it, his index finger resting lightly on the butt. His cold, flat eyes stared at me.

The man was Mike.

Part Four

Chapter Thirty-Seven

There is quiet and there is quiet. There is quiet that only seems to be deep until a greater silence descends. Out in the corridor I'd thought the Lindauer Building was quiet. Now it really was. At least, that is, in the intervals between each of the beats of my heart.

'Sit down, Billy.'

I nodded. I let my arms fan out slowly, taking my hands away from my body.

'OK,' I said.

'Leave the phone on the desk and sit down there, on the chair. Don't come any closer than that.'

'All right.'

'Then listen to me.'

'OK. Of course. But, Mike, where have you been?'

Mike's index finger moved up and down on the stippled black grip beneath it. The gun was a Beretta, 9mm. Point and pull.

'Around. Getting this. Making sure I could use it. Both were easier than I thought. I've been moving around, thinking. And today I've also been in the police station, on Calshot Street.'

'I see.'

'Where they told me that a baby's been found. A dead white baby. The DNA test will take a few days but it has to be mine, they said, because the father of the other missing child was black. Then they told me what's been going on. Why . . .' Mike couldn't stop himself glancing over my shoulder in the direction of the cafe. 'Why Ally died. They didn't want to but they did, eventually. It was supposed to reassure me, I think, give me confidence that because they knew who it was now, they'd catch her. And I'd get justice. But I didn't feel reassured. I didn't feel anything but stunned. Like, all the time you've been here, next to us, this could have happened. We've been living next to a time bomb but we never knew it. We never had a chance to get away from you.'

'Mike . . .'

'I know what you're going to say.' Mike's finger moved from the butt of the gun to the trigger guard. 'That it wasn't your fault. You know what? I know that, really. It was her fault, that girl, she did it, not you. I didn't originally buy this for you, you know?'

His finger had curled inside the guard now and was resting on the trigger. The gun, still lying on the desk top, was pointing at my stomach.

'I bought it for her. Or him, as I thought she was. I never thought I'd find him. I thought the police would, or you. But somehow I'd get to him. In court, while he was being led out perhaps. Then I'd kill him. I wouldn't care what happened to me. But now . . .'

Mike winced as though an ulcer had just flared up. He didn't speak for a second but he kept his eyes fixed on mine. They looked burnt out, empty as a village after the soldiers have left. I'd forgotten him. I'd been swept along so fast I'd left him behind.

'Now I can't help it but I just want to point this at

342

you, Billy. And pull the trigger. You, because I can. And I may never get to point it at her. Last time I saw you I loathed you, but you thinking it was me, that was nothing. I realized that. But then to find out that not only were you stupid enough to think that but it was really *you*. I feel this way because of something *you* did, years ago. I can't help wanting to hurt you. I know it doesn't make sense but then neither would jumping in front of a tube train or driving off Beachy Head, two other things I've nearly done in the last week. You started this and yet nothing is lost to you. Just to me, and those other people. And then the pictures come, you know? Of that night. And I'd crack my own head to get them out but I can't and I get so I just want to do something, to really *do* something. I'm sorry, Billy.'

'Mike. Listen to me. Just listen. Then you can do what you want. But not now.'

I lifted my hands very slowly so that Mike wouldn't think I was going to try and jump him. I pushed my palms down, towards him, as though the air was something heavy that I wanted to move. I tried to feel what he was feeling, take it on board, make it part of the equation I was trying to solve. What I really wanted to do was push it aside and deal with it later. But I couldn't. Mike sat up, tensing.

'I know where she lives,' I said quickly. 'The girl, Cherie. I know where she lives. I just found out and I went there to confirm it. I'm going back. I'm either going to break in and wait for her, or else I'm going to get a call to say she's at home. If that comes I'm going to go there. Either way, I'm going to kill her. If I don't go, tonight, she'll end up getting arrested. Then she'll get off in court. I know she will. Can you imagine that?

So I have to go there. I have to. Give me the gun. Afterwards I'll come back here. I promise. I'll give it back to you and you can do whatever. I won't stop you. I understand what you feel, Mike. It was my fault. I was wrong to do what I did, give a vulnerable girl back to her father. But if you let me, I'm going to finish it. Stop any more deaths. I promise. Those pictures you have? I'm going to deal with the person who created them. You think I'm to blame – well I am, but I didn't do that. It was her, Mike, Cherie, Carolyn Oliver.'

'She won't get off. I'll kill her before then.'

'You want to shoot her?' I shook my head. 'You'd never get a chance, you'd never get anywhere near her without going past twenty officers and three metal detectors first. The best you can hope is that she'll live in prison where you can't find her. Or else out there in the world, laughing at you. At me. At everyone. Give me the gun. This is our chance. Your chance. Your only chance.'

Mike's face still carried no expression that I could read. If my words were having any effect, I couldn't see it. When I'd last seen Mike, on Exmouth Market, he'd looked different, changed for ever from the person he was. Now he looked different again. The horror, the knowledge, they were still there, but they weren't raging through him now. They were focused, channelling all of his energy into his hand, his right hand, holding the Beretta, resting it on top of his left palm.

'How do I know that you're not just making this up? That you won't just leave, you won't just set that copper onto me.'

'Because you know me,' I said, looking directly into his eyes, trying to get through. 'Just as I should have known that you didn't kill Ally, you should know I'm not lying to you. And if you can't believe me it doesn't matter. All we have to do is wait. All . . .'

My phone suddenly gave a little hop from the desktop and began to buzz. Mike started and my stomach nearly came out of my mouth. He'd nudged the gun to the side but he reached for it again, holding it steady. I let out a breath and I glanced at the luminous display on my phone. I recognized the number. I'd been given it less than an hour before.

'That's it,' I said. 'That's the woman. Either pull that trigger or give me the gun.'

'Answer it. I want to hear what she says. Whether you're telling the truth.'

I didn't move. 'I'm going to let it go to message. Then she'll think I'm busy, that I won't be going round tonight. I don't want her to know I'm coming. You can listen to the message she leaves. Come on, Mike, decide. Ask yourself what Ally would have wanted you to do.'

Mike took his eyes off me for a second and looked down at the phone. It was turning round and round on the polished wood surface.

Chapter Thirty-Eight

The sky was so densely packed now that it looked like all the clouds in London had huddled together to watch me. Canary Wharf was still blinking, its top only just fitting beneath the static, weighty ceiling, the underside of which was layered with blacks and greys, smeared with a filthy orange from the lights of the city below. The cold night air was breathless as a vacuum, the wind cowering in a corner somewhere, refusing to come out.

I was on Narrow Street again, where I'd parked in a residents' zone. Cherie was in the house so she wouldn't see the Mazda, or if she did it would be the next day before she did so. It wouldn't matter then. Nothing would.

Mike had seen sense eventually. I'd played the message back and we'd both listened to Mrs Winter's soft, excited tones, telling me that Cherie had returned, though it was probably a bit too late now, wasn't it? I hadn't expected her to mention where she lived but nevertheless I was relieved when she didn't. I didn't want Mike to have it. Mike wanted me to give him the address, telling me he was going to finish the girl himself. It was his right, he said, and I suppose it was. But I wouldn't do it. Mike thought that I just didn't want to give him my trump card, that I was afraid he'd shoot me anyway, before going round there. It wasn't that. I didn't think he really would have done it, not after I'd mentioned Ally. The reason was the girl. Mike just might have been able to get through the window but that would have been the easy part. The girl was good. She was smart, strong and she was trained. What's more she'd killed people, she'd have no block against doing that. Mike wouldn't have been able to get to her without her knowing. No way. I wasn't absolutely certain I could do it myself. He'd have had to barge the door down and hope to get lucky, which was no way to do it. The odds were that she'd have taken him out. If he really cared, I told him, he'd let me go up there. If he really wanted to get the person who had murdered his wife. There was a mixture of shame and relief on his face as he handed the gun over.

I stood in the same pub opposite Victoria Place. It was still busy, even though it was close to eleven on a Tuesday night. I leaned on the same pillar, drank another Coke as the crowd around me murmured. If anyone thought it strange that a lone man had come in three times that evening and just stared out of the window into the darkness, no one said anything. Across the street the living-room window was dark, as were all the windows on the floor above. Just one light showed in the entire house, behind the curtains of the dormers on the top floor. The loft. I kept my eyes on it, trying to press them through to see inside. At eleven-fifteen, just as the pub was emptying, the light went out. A switch seemed to click inside me too. Everything that had happened seemed suddenly to be distilled into the dark square I was looking at. It had all been reduced to that room. To what was going to happen inside. I felt calm but fired, empty of confusion, of any doubt. All I had to do was follow the path that was laid out for me.

I didn't leave it long. Just another forty-five minutes standing behind a goods van, using one of its mirrors to make sure no one left the house. No one did. When I was ready, I walked across the square and made my way along Victoria Place.

Casually I turned down the alley at the side of Number 14. I was inside the toilet within five seconds. I pulled the window down and reattached the catch bracket to the top of it. I reinserted the window locks and replaced the small plastic caps. I wiped the sills down for prints with toilet paper, which I screwed up and dropped into the bowl. I put the long slim key back into the cabinet next to the romance novel. I did these things quickly and efficiently. When I was done I stood very still by the toilet door.

I stood for perhaps a minute, my breathing light, listening for any sounds coming from inside the house. An old clock ticked loudly from the kitchen to my right, underlined by the low, monotonous hum of a fridge. There was nothing else, no stereo, no TV. No footsteps. Making as little noise as I could, I pushed the door open and peered out into the hall, where I'd been earlier, and saw that it was dark, darker than it was outside. I walked out into the hall and made my way to the foot of the stairs, where I stopped and listened again. Nothing. Nothing at all. I peered above me, craning my neck into the black, curving stairwell.

Knowing that the stairs creaked from the last time I went up them, I kept to the edges, taking them four at a time, hauling myself up with the sturdy oak banister on my right. I caused a couple of deep wood groans but no louder than the ones the house must have given out itself during the course of the night, once the central heating was off. Though my heart stood still, no doors opened, no one came out to see who was there. I carried on. When I was two-thirds of the way up I looked over the top step, towards the door above me, the loft door. There was no light coming from underneath it. I kept my eyes on it, watching for any movement from the other side.

She was in there. She had to be. I'd seen her light go out. She hadn't left the house. Even if she'd used the back door she would still have had to come out onto the street, unless she'd hopped over the back wall, like she had when she'd got into the Lindaeur Building. I told myself she wouldn't have done that. Why would she? She didn't know I was there.

Without making any more noise, I made it up to the landing I'd rushed up to earlier. I stopped and listened again but could hear nothing from behind any of the four doors surrounding me or the one above. Staying focused on that one, I slipped my feet out of my trainers. Without making a sound I carefully shrugged off the coat I was wearing and set it down on top of the ottoman I'd noticed last time. The folded pile of washing was gone. Slowly I reached into the side pocket of the coat and slid out the Beretta, the 9mm. I held it in my hand, feeling the weight of it. It was light for a handgun but it still felt heavy. Real guns always do. Especially if you're about to use them. I clicked the safety. A movement to the right caused me to duck and swing the weapon round fast, my finger closing on the thin piece of tempered metal, about to squeeze, taking the pressure right up to the edge.

349

The cat had jumped onto the ottoman and was scampering along it towards me. Before I could move, it had rubbed the top of its head on the barrel of the gun, emitting an electric purr as it arched its back. I closed my eyes and opened them again. I picked the cat up with my free hand and set it just inside the open door of a bathroom, pulling the door to.

I made my way back across the landing, then up the final staircase.

The door in front of me was newer than any of the others I'd seen in the house. It was painted white with four rectangular panels and a cheap aluminium handle. It didn't look too strong but I was hoping that that wouldn't be an issue. Rather than the structure, or the chances of getting through it, I was more interested in the lock. There was a keyhole three inches below the handle. In my back pocket I had a set of picklocks, which I'd taken from my office, fifteen turners on a ring like a set of miniature Allen keys. I also had a small plastic bottle of cycle oil. I bent down to the keyhole and squatted on my haunches.

Yes. I was very glad to see that the key wasn't in the lock. If it had been left in on the inside I'd have had to push it through. I was telling myself what a break that was when I froze. Through the keyhole I could see a very short passageway with a louvred door on either side: a bathroom and an airing cupboard by the looks of them. At the end of the passageway was a room, dark but for the dim light from a lamp post outside. Two dormer windows on the far wall were curtained but there was a door between them, obviously leading out onto a roof space or balcony. Halfway between the passageway and the door was an armchair in silhouette.

It was facing away from me. What had stopped me was the fact that the armchair was occupied.

I blinked to make sure. I could see the top of a head over the back of the chair. It couldn't have been anything else. I realized that the shape sticking out to the side was too sharp for a cushion. It was an arm, the edge of an elbow. Cherie was sitting in the dark. She was looking out of the window, her back to me. I listened. I couldn't hear a sound. I stood up from the keyhole and stepped back.

I couldn't use the picklocks, not if she was awake. She might be asleep but I wasn't going to take the chance unless she was in bed. No matter. I could wait on the landing, or in the spare room I'd seen, for an hour or two. Except . . . I closed my fingers round the door handle. There was no key in the lock so maybe she'd left it open. There could have been a bolt on the inside, which she'd engaged, but I could give it a try. Why not? With the Beretta in my right hand I pushed the handle down with my left. It moved silently until it would go no further. I changed the direction of the pressure I was applying and the door moved a millimetre out of its frame. It wasn't locked. Slowly, without a sound, I pushed it open further, away from me.

The gun felt solid and powerful in my hand. The floor in front of me was carpeted and I took a step, branching my legs out so that my Levis wouldn't rustle, my eyes on the shape in the armchair. I took another step. Cherie didn't stir. Maybe she *was* asleep. I could smell something familiar, a perfume of some sort. Ignoring it, I moved the gun until it was pointing at the top of Cherie's head. My fingers itched and a wave of relief flooded down through me. Josephine Thomas.

351

Ally. Denise Denton. Jen. It was over. Whatever happened now I'd done it, she was dead. I thought about just pulling the trigger. But I could only see the top inch or so of her head. I had to get closer. And maybe I could even get her out of there. Maybe I could gag her and get her down the stairs. Then she would have just disappeared, her body found in the Thames in a week or so. No mess. Maybe, but I'd take no chances. She moved and I'd just do it. I took another step. The smell again. Not perfume but aftershave. Something was coming to me. Where had I come across it before? In her bedsit, yes. And? In the gym. The guys, the ones she'd massaged. But what was it doing here?

I stepped into the room itself. The aftershave bothered me but I didn't have time to worry about it. Out of the darkness something hard rammed down on my wrist, sending the Beretta crashing to the floor. I turned towards the blow but before I could bring a hand up I felt a flashing pain beneath my left eye that sent me hurtling backwards. Behind me was a chair, probably put there so I'd stumble and I did, going over backwards, falling into what felt like a dressing table. Bottles and small boxes came down on my head. I heard the hurried shuffle of footsteps and caught a glimpse of a dark shape, moving in front of me. I moved quickly but by the time I'd managed to turn the figure was straightening up from the centre of the room. It moved to the wall. Cherie flicked the light switch and became the second person that night to point the Beretta at me.

'You can move now,' Cherie said. But she didn't say it to me.

She said it to Sharon.

Chapter Thirty-Nine

'Congratulations. You found me. I thought I'd have to give you some help, but I didn't need to, did I? If coming here wasn't the most stupid thing you ever could have done, I'd have said it was very clever of you.'

Cherie was wearing slim-cut khaki trousers and a black jean jacket buttoned all the way up to the throat. She was handling the Beretta casually, in no way afraid of it the way most people would have been. She had cut her hair into a bob, which curled up on both sides to hide a lot of her face. Along with the lipstick and the mascara I guessed that she was pretty much unrecognizable to anyone who hadn't actually seen her. It would certainly have taken a very keen officer who'd only looked at my Mac-Fit to realize who she was. I saw straight through it all because of her expression. It was the same as in her bedsit when she ripped the phone out of my hand. Cold, dead, her thin, wide mouth a perfect straight line as she held the gun on me.

'Well?' she asked. 'Tell me. How did you do it?'

I looked away from Cherie, my eyes moving instead to the armchair. To Sharon. To her pale, frightened face. I'd assumed that she must have been tied to the chair and couldn't understand when I saw that she wasn't. She was just sitting there. I wanted to know what she was doing there, how the hell the police right outside her door had let Cherie get to her. Had she killed them all somehow? How had she even found the flat? Trying to hide the cold terror I was feeling, I turned back slowly to the girl with the gun in her hand. My eyes scanned the room for a paperweight, a wine bottle, something heavy. I couldn't see anything.

'Denise Denton,' I said. 'The hooker you picked up at Loughborough Junction. She kept her mobile line open to the girl she was standing with when you took her. She relayed everything back to her.'

Cherie laughed, and nodded at the same time. 'I thought she was talkative. Well, never mind. I was going to call you anyway and ask you round tonight. Mrs Minter saved me the trouble.'

'She told you about me?'

'Eventually.' Cherie nodded again. 'She took some persuading. I waited until she was in the bath before coming home with Sharon here, you see? The old bat always has her soak at the same time so she can listen to the play on the radio. We got in without the nosy witch jumping out on us but then, to my surprise, she knocked on my door. She hardly ever did that. I asked her what she wanted but she said she just wanted to know if I was staying in that night. I thought that was odd and so I followed her down to the phone and heard her making a call. Mr Howells, she said, but I knew it was you. When she was off the phone I persuaded her to tell me what was up, and she said how you'd come to call. My brother? You? You've no idea how much that thought disgusts me.'

'Where is she?'

'Mrs Minter? Back in the bath. The poor dear had an

accident, a fall. Hit her head and drowned. Lots of old folk go out like that. But now then, get up. Move your pathetic arse. We've got things to do. We've got some very, *very* exciting things to do.'

Cherie took a step backward and jerked the gun up and down. I stood up from the floor, my head spinning from the blow I'd taken. I breathed deeply and put a hand to my face. Cherie had been wearing knuckle-dusters and I was pretty certain my cheekbone was broken. The knowledge of what had happened hurt far more. The knowledge that Sharon was there. I asked myself, if I rushed forward, just went straight in and took a bullet, would I be able to overpower Cherie, or at least give Sharon the chance of getting out of the door. I waited to see what would happen. I pulled more air into my lungs and got the aftershave again. Cherie noticed the look on my face and she smiled.

'It is pretty nasty, isn't it? I've told him about it but he won't listen.'

I took a breath. 'Who?'

'Don't you know? Come on! I saw you recognize it in my bedsit. I was a bit worried until I realized you thought I'd had men up there to massage.'

'Men from the gym.'

'That's right. Well?'

I thought about it. There were a lot of guys there, some of whom I knew pretty well, men like Pete, who I wished to God I'd called that night. But there were others who only showed up now and then, or just came to use the machines, and didn't box. It could have been any of them. Cherie was smirking, waiting for me to get it. All of a sudden I knew who it was. The expression, the grim, flat determination in the jaw, the eyes. It was the same.

'Jeff,' I said. 'Where is he?'

'We'll get to that,' Cherie said. 'Don't worry. But now then, don't you want to say hello to your girlfriend?'

I looked from Cherie to Sharon, relieved to see that she didn't look hurt in any way. But again that confused me. Sharon just looked scared, fighting hard to stay in control. How come she wasn't tied up, gagged at least? Why hadn't she called out? I couldn't see anything that could have been used to compel Sharon to be quiet when she heard me come in. There was no gun other than the one I'd brought in and there was no knife either. Nothing. Now Cherie didn't seem to be worried about her. She wasn't covering Sharon with the Beretta, only me.

'I'm sorry,' Sharon said, reading my thoughts. 'I wanted to warn you, but she told me not to. I had to do what she said, Billy. I'm sorry.'

I thought about how I'd pointed the gun at Sharon's head and I felt sick. I told Sharon that it was OK, I understood. But I was more confused than ever. I glanced round the apartment for some kind of explanation. It was a neat and tidy studio with nothing to indicate what kind of girl Cherie was. It was stripped, anonymous, a full black grip sitting on the bed to my left. Cherie was leaving. But, I imagined, the plan would be for us to remain. Guilt coursed through me, almost as fast as anger did. I'd wanted Sharon away from London. I'd been persuaded that she'd be safe. Again I thought of the guys in the hall, the man on the roof opposite. My fingers itched with rage, at both Cherie and Andy Gold. Once more I looked for something heavy to throw. I thought of the rug, beneath us. If I ducked and pulled it, would it bring her down? Again Sharon read my thoughts.

'Billy,' she said. Her voice was measured, but urgent. As if there was a tarantula on my shoulder. 'You have to stay calm. Don't do anything. Please.'

I nodded slowly but I was still in the dark. 'How did she get you here? Those coppers, they didn't leave you alone?'

'No,' Sharon said quickly. 'Cherie, she got my number out of your phone. I called you when she was massaging you, remember? She knew from how you spoke to me that I was your girlfriend. She called me,' Sharon said. 'She called and told me to meet her. And I did.'

'What?!'

'Billy, please.' Sharon took a breath and then swallowed a sob. 'I had to.'

'Why? What in God's name did she say to you?'

'I said nothing.' Cherie's voice cut through the room. She was smiling now, enjoying my confusion. 'It wasn't me that persuaded you was it?'

'No.'

'Then what the hell . . .?'

'It was the baby crying. That's what made her come. And what I said would happen to it if she didn't. She's a good person your girlfriend, Billy, a much better person than you. She came out straight away so that the baby would be saved. She cares about people's babies. Because she's normal, unlike you. You didn't care about the baby in me, or the ones I should have had after. You let them all die.'

Cherie's expression was fixed and intense, her eyes

wide. She was back in Chester, her father's fist in her stomach. I was just stunned. The baby? Denise's child couldn't have survived, surely, not out of a hospital. It was too young. And Jen's had been left in her kitchen for her husband to find. I closed my eyes.

'You've killed someone else,' I said. 'You're crazy. Who was it this time, someone I sat next to on a bus once? Someone I played with when I was five? Someone I knew in a previous life?'

'No.' Cherie looked at me as if I was stupid. 'There's been no one else. Just the three plus that first mistake.'

I didn't get it. 'Then whose baby have you got?'

'Whose?' again the look. Surely you know? 'The girl in the cafe. The baby Sharon heard was hers.'

The words hit me like a truck, knocking all the air out of my body. Sharon was completely still but was pressing all her energy towards me. A grimace pulled my face apart.

'Uh uh.' I shook my head. 'No way. I saw Ally's baby on Alfred Road.'

'No you didn't. That was the young whore's.'

I shook my head again. 'No,' I insisted. 'The child was white. It wasn't Denise Denton's baby. I met her husband, he's black.'

'But her *boyfriend* isn't,' Cherie said.

'What?'

'She told me all about it: when she thought I was a social worker trying to save her life. Her boyfriend. It's why she ran away from Birmingham. She'd had a fling with a white boy and was pregnant. She really wanted the baby but she loved her husband. She didn't know who the father was. If it was black she was going to go back home to him. If not she'd have got the thing adopted and gone back anyway. So the baby you saw on Alfred Road was hers, Denise's. It didn't survive, unfortunately, after it was removed. The one I have survived. It was the only one that did.'

'And it's Ally's.'

'Not any more.' Cherie's mouth firmed in an instant and she pointed her finger at me. 'That's where you're wrong. It's *mine*. I've been looking after it. Loving it. Making it smile at me. I'm having it in return for the one you took from me. He'd never have found me on his own. I'd have had a lovely little baby. And now I will. I'll have it to love and to love me. For ever. Isn't that what everyone can expect? Isn't that fair? You didn't think you'd escape, did you? You didn't think you could get out of paying me back for what you took?'

'OK,' I said. 'Where is it, the child?'

'Outside,' Cherie said. 'And this is what we're going to do. We're going out onto the balcony. The baby's on the street in her pram. With Jeff. Uncle Jeff. He's been helping me. He used to be in the Marines, taught me all sorts of things. We have an unusual relationship, shall we say. He hated my dad as much as I did. Burnt his house down, in fact, after I told him what he did to me. Jeff would do anything for me. *Anything*. He'd even throw a little baby into the Thames and let it sink to the bottom. Something he's going to do right now, in fact, if you don't do exactly, *exactly*, what I tell you.'

Chapter Forty

The balcony was small, perhaps twenty feet by ten, bordered on three sides by upright iron railings. I looked over, down to the street below, but I couldn't see anyone with a pram. I could, however, make out the river through a gap in the line of buildings opposite. I thought about Jeff, in the gym, always asking questions, always wanting to get into the ring with me. Could he do it, kill a child? I wondered if he already had, whether it was him and not Cherie who had actually committed the murders. It would make it even harder for Clay and Andy to put her away.

I turned to my right, to Cherie. She was at the other end of the balcony, leaning back on the side of the railings. The gun was still in her hand but she wasn't pointing it at me any more. She didn't have to. I had a thought: was Ally's baby really out there? Or was she bluffing? I didn't know. But if she was, then she was going to win the hand because I couldn't afford to call her. I thought of Ally, my heart scoured raw by the idea that her child might have survived, might still be alive. And that it might die now, after all. I told myself I'd do whatever Cherie told me.

'Well,' I said. 'You got me here. It's all panned out

like you hoped. Congratulations. What is it you want me to do?'

Cherie shrugged. Again that look, don't you *know*? 'Nothing,' she said.

'Nothing.'

'That's right, nothing at all. Just stand there while I leave.'

I looked at her. 'That's it?'

'That's it. Nothing else. I'm going to walk out of here in a minute and meet Jeff. Then we're going to walk away with our baby. And you're going to stay here. And do nothing. Not scream or call the police or anything. Then you'll never see or hear from me again. We'll bring up our daughter, I'll have the life you stole from me, and that will be that. I did what I wanted to do. I'm finished with you, Billy. With you.'

Again I looked at the girl in front of me, trying to find my way through what she was saying. 'They'll find you,' I said, as if that too was obvious.

'No, they won't. I've got plenty of money since my dad died and no one will recognize me; especially as you'll never tell them about my haircut. Or Jeff. Or the baby. You'll never tell them anything because, if you do, we'll kill her. Simple. They might get us but they'll never get the baby. I promise you that. So it's your choice. Your friends' little girl can grow up happy, with us, or else she can die. If I ever see you again, I'll kill her. If I see a wanted picture of Jeff, I'll kill her. I don't care what age she is. You're going to do nothing, except wonder. And hurt. You really are going to hurt.' Cherie made an 'O' with her mouth. 'Did you think I was going to kill you?'

'Maybe,' I said.

'That wouldn't be fair, would it? You didn't kill me. So I'm not going to kill you. You just made my life hell. So yours is going to be worse. Much worse. And this is why. Sharon. Come here. We're going to do what we spoke about now. Are you ready? You've had time to think about it. Now it's time to be brave.'

I was still looking at Cherie but I could sense Sharon behind me, in the doorway to the flat. I glanced towards her as she moved forward. What the hell? I grabbed hold of Sharon's wrist.

'Wait,' I said. 'She's got nothing to do with this. Whatever you've planned, do it to me. You're right, I deserve it. But not her. Let her go.'

'No. This is how it has to end. This is the only way you'll ever understand. Sharon, do it. Do it now. Go on. It won't be hard. Just put your foot on the railing there and jump.'

For the second time that night Cherie seemed to have made time come to a complete stop. I didn't feel anything until suddenly it lurched back into motion.

'Wait,' I barked out. My mind was reeling. I'd been so sure, so certain. Walking up here to end it. Now everything was getting away from me again. I didn't know what to do. I wanted to say: no, make me do it. There was no point. Her face told me that. She was going to make Sharon jump over the balcony to the street below. And I knew that Sharon would. To save the child. But there was no way I could let it happen. What could I do? I had to try to buy time. Find a way to slow her.

'You're forgetting something,' I said. 'You said we

could see her. The baby. If you've really got her, which I doubt, where is she?' I pushed Sharon behind me, keeping hold of her wrist. I was hurting her but I didn't care. 'Otherwise she's not doing anything. You'll just have to shoot me. You don't want that. You'd be caught before you get half a mile.'

'And the baby would be floating down to Gravesend. But OK. I don't see why not. I did say you could. But then, I'm afraid, Sharon has to choose.'

Cherie pulled a mobile out of her jean jacket but didn't take her eyes off me. Behind her the City, the rest of London, looked small, as if it had retreated. Cherie hit three keys on the phone and then hung up without saying anything. Instead she turned to the river, her eyes searching. I followed her gaze. I saw a man appear in the gap between the buildings opposite, on the riverside pathway. About a hundred yards away. The man was pushing a pram.

The man stopped the pram where we could see him and he turned towards us. There was no one else on the walkway. No one else in the square. Immediately, I thought about it. No. Even if I got past Cherie, even if I could do it quickly and then get downstairs and across the square, I'd never get to him in time. I tried to fight the panic that was pulling at my breath, shortening each one. Time was running out. Cherie turned to Sharon.

'Right. Do it. Do it now.'

Sharon made to move but I tightened my grip. I tried to look confused. I cast my eyes around the square, looking anywhere but across to the river.

'I can't see him,' I lied. 'Where is he? You said we'd

be able to see the child. What is this shit? Where are they?'

Cherie looked irritated. 'There,' she said.

'Where?'

'On the river bank.' Cherie pointed out across the balcony. 'The pathway. To the left of the pub. Between those flats. With a pram. Surely you can see. There. Now, Sharon, *do* it.'

It was pointless pretending that I couldn't see where she was pointing, but I still didn't let go of Sharon. I pushed her further behind me.

'She's not doing anything.'

'It's her or the baby.'

'You wouldn't do it.'

'No?'

'No. You want a child. Isn't that what you said? You want something to love. You lost one once, you wouldn't lose one again.'

'You're wrong. I've learned. It's easy. There are so many of them out there. I'll get another one. Just take one from the street. But if you don't believe me . . .'

With a shrug of her shoulders Cherie punched her keypad again and this time put the phone to the side of her head. Sharon tried to move forward but I held her back. I turned to the street. After three seconds the figure across the square put his hand to his head too.

'Pick her out of the pram,' Cherie said. 'Pick her up. That's it. Right out. If you don't see the girl jump from this balcony within the next minute, just drop her. Drop her in the river. Then get the car. I'll be down straight away.'

'No!' It was Sharon. 'No, wait. Please don't hurt the baby. It's OK, I'll do it.'

'Sharon . . . '

'No, Billy. Mike's been through enough. Imagine if he found out about this. That we just stood by. I couldn't live and know that. I'll do it. Billy, let go. Please, let go of me.'

Sharon had moved round in front of me, even though I still had hold of her. She pulled at my hand, trying to free her wrist. I turned from her to the man on the walkway. He'd moved closer to the river.

'Let go, Billy. Don't you see? They'll kill the baby.'

'I don't care. Let them.'

'But if they do, she'll just shoot us anyway. Don't you see? How else would she get away? What would be the point of that?'

I shook my head. 'They'll kill the baby whatever we do.'

'They won't,' Sharon insisted. 'I believe her, Billy. Why would she? She's always wanted one. She's sick but I believe her.'

'Sick's the word. She won't bring this child up. She hates babies. She has done ever since her mother died. Haven't you?'

'What do you know about my mother?'

'That you killed her. She killed her mother, Sharon, pushed her in a river.'

'I fell, my mother jumped in after me.'

'You killed her. You know you did. You killed your baby brother too. Everyone knew it.'

'She couldn't hold on.'

'Because of the baby, that's what you think, isn't it? That's why you hate them. You think she died because she was weighted down. But it was because of you. You, do you hear me? You killed that baby and you'll kill this one too.'

'Time's nearly up.'

'It's my choice. Billy, let me *go*!!'

Sharon wrenched her wrist free and I didn't try to stop her. I couldn't. Suddenly there was no strength in my body. Cherie had the phone up against her face again. Her uncle was standing right at the water's edge. I felt helpless. I'd done everything I could. I just had to watch as Sharon stepped towards the railings. Beyond her, Jeff was standing with the bundle against the side of his chest. Behind him the river looked huge. It must have been twenty feet to the water. I looked at Cherie and saw that Sharon was right. The gun was pointing straight at me again. If she didn't jump the child would die and then Cherie would shoot us both. Cherie was smiling, her eyes full of an electric, rushing bliss. She knew she'd won. I searched for something to say to her, anything that might stop this. Her eyes seemed to fuse into mine.

'It's going to hurt, isn't it?' I didn't know whether she was speaking to me or just whispering straight into my brain. 'Can you feel it yet? What it's going to be like? Can you feel the pain yet, Billy?'

Sharon was holding the railing, gripping the top with both hands. She put a foot up. She was crying but her actions were strong and deliberate. I knew then that she really would do it. My stomach bucked with love for her. I saw her look down, fighting against an impulse to vomit. I looked too. Yes, we were high enough. No doubt. Sharon put one leg over and then steadied herself. I seemed to split in two as she looked back at me.

'Please don't.' I could hardly speak. 'Just don't. Don't.'

'You'll be OK,' Sharon said.

'No. Think. Not about me. Or you even. It's not just us. Is it? It's more than that.'

'What?' Cherie had almost screamed.

'Oh, Billy, don't think about that. You weren't really keen on it anyway, were you? I could tell. It's OK. If this hadn't happened I think I'd have had a termination. It wouldn't have been fair on you, on us. We could have had one later.'

'No.' I shook my head. Molten tears burned my cheeks. 'I wanted it, I did. Really. And I still do. I want to be a father, everything. Please. Sharon. Wait.'

'Just a minute.' Cherie took a step forward. 'You? And her? After what you did to me? Shit. This is so right. Go on, now. Do it. Now. Jeff, are you ready? If she doesn't jump in the next ten seconds do it. No more waiting. And, Billy, if you so much as move once she's over, the baby still dies. OK? You don't move. When I walk out onto the square I want to see you at this balcony. OK?'

I was empty.

'OK.'

'Now.'

'No,' I screamed.

Sharon saw me coming and tried to get her left leg over the railings before I could grab her. She managed it but my hand found her sweater and I pulled her back towards me, gripping her back onto the rails. She struggled but I had her. She wasn't doing this. I fought to hold her as she bucked, ignored the pain as she scrabbled at my fingers, scratching, trying to bite them.

I looked down beyond her. The figure sprinting across the square had nearly reached the gap between the apartment buildings now, where Cherie had pointed. The man by the pram couldn't see him because he was angling his run. But I could.

'Let her go or Jeff kills the baby.'

Sharon was doing everything she could to make me release her. But I got her back over the railings. We both fell, going over sideways. I twisted to get my body on top of Sharon, to keep her from getting up, and as I did so I turned. To Cherie. She was looking down at us, her eyes burning.

'Do it!' she screamed into her phone. 'Chuck it in. Just fucking do it now! Jeff? Jeff!? For fucksake, Jeff, what the hell are you doing?'

Mike had reached Jeff by now. Through the gap in the buildings I could see them, two small figures, tussling. They fell and I couldn't tell who was who. Then, out of nowhere, more figures burst into the square. They swarmed up towards the door below us. Police. Cherie turned to me, panicked. The gun in her hand was pointing at me but she didn't know where to look. At me, at the police, or the river bank.

'What's happening? What have you done?'

As Cherie turned back to the river I pushed myself up to my knees. I pulled my phone out of my shirt pocket. I held it out, towards her. 'You fell for it again,' I said. 'I told you about the trick and you went and fell for it all over.' I turned the phone round so that she could see that the display was active. 'The line was open. Mike was downstairs. You told him where Jeff was. Where his baby was. Between the buildings. You told him where to go.'

'Jeff'll kill him.' Cherie was wild eyed, looking for something to cling to. 'He was in the Marines. He'll kill the baby right after. You've killed it.'

'Maybe,' I said. 'You could be right. Jeff's tough but he's old. Mike's bigger and he's got nothing to lose. It could go either way. Why don't you listen? Here.'

I tossed the phone over to Cherie and on instinct, for a split second, her eyes shifted to it. It was all I needed. I lifted myself up, turning my right shoulder forward. Cherie hadn't really intended to catch the phone but the reflex to do so had snagged her. I was nearly on her by the time she'd got it together to fire and even though I felt a streak of heat in my side, my momentum took me into her. My shoulder backed her against the railings and I carried on with my head, getting it into her solar plexus, then her face, once, twice, then my knee into her stomach. I butted her again, her body slamming hard against the bars behind her.

I managed to find Cherie's gun hand and I battered it back against the bars. She might have been able to hold onto the weapon but she didn't even try. I heard it clattering down through the railings to the pavement below. Cherie had gone limp. She was like a rag doll, not even trying to fight me. I stepped back from her, keeping hold of her jacket, and saw that her face was bloody, some teeth missing from her mouth. She was staring at me, intently, her eyes still laughing. Victorious.

'You fool,' she said. 'You've killed it. It could have lived with me, but you've killed it.'

I held onto the girl and turned to the river. I couldn't see anybody. The pram was on its own. There was no one else. I heard a ruckus at the door to my right and turned back towards the flat, looking back inside. I couldn't understand what the police were doing there. I hadn't called them. Andy didn't have a tail on me. No way. Every time I'd gone out I'd been careful but especially that night.

I didn't have time to think about it. They'd found me somehow and were pounding on the door. Mere feet away. It wouldn't hold long. I knew I only had seconds before a pair of size tens smashed through the jamb.

'I'm sorry,' I said, turning quickly back to Cherie. Her face was broken, a mess.

'What for?' she asked.

'For the life you had to live. For the fact that you had to watch your mother drown. That your father flipped out and blamed you. Hurt you. And I'm sorry for what I did eight years ago.'

'Are you?'

'Yes,' I said. 'I am. I'm genuinely sorry. And I always was. I thought about it a lot and wished I'd done it differently.'

Cherie's eyes wavered. 'I don't believe you.'

'I wish you would, because it's true. I really wish you would. But it doesn't matter now because you know what?'

'What?' She spat blood into my face.

'I'm not sorry for this.'

Cherie started to struggle then but it was too late. I'd squatted on my haunches and with every ounce of energy in me I boosted her up. She was heavy. She wasn't a little girl. Not a frail thing any more. As the sound of splintering wood burst out of the room behind me, I launched her out into the night air.

*

It wasn't Andy. It was Ken Clay. We met in the middle of the flat and I screamed at him.

'Mike!' I said. 'Across the square, on the walkway by the river. His baby's there. Someone's trying to kill it. A man from my gym. Get your men over there.'

'Where? Show me where.'

I pulled Clay out onto the balcony and three officers followed. I pointed across the square at the pram and as soon as they saw it the three men turned and ran. Clay moved too and I followed him, but after taking two steps I stopped. Sharon had called my name. I turned. She was still lying on the floor, where I'd dragged her down. Sharon's hands were balled over her stomach.

'Billy,' she said, looking up at me. Her voice was quiet. 'Before you go. Can you help me? Can you call me an ambulance?'

'What is it?'

'It hurts, Billy. It really hurts. Can you do it quickly? Please?'

Sharon's hands shifted as she pressed them tighter into her midriff. We both stared at the blood that was slipping slowly through her fingers.

Part Five

Chapter Forty-One

I passed the next five or six hours in a kind of trance, a dream state. I know that certain things happened but I didn't then and don't now have any sort of connection to them. Eight years before I'd thought that I could forget Carolyn Oliver. I'd thought I could change my way of working, that the fact that I'd never send another child back to a life of horror was enough to compensate for the fact that I'd sent her back to one. I'd learnt from her pain but let her go on feeling it. And she'd come back to make me pay. Now I'd killed the girl, but even after she was dead I was still paying.

I called the ambulance. While we waited I tore off my shirt and pressed it into Sharon's stomach. Before the ambulance came Sharon drifted into unconsciousness. I screamed for a policeman and when one came I told him to wait downstairs to bring the medics right up. Make sure the way is clear, I told him. When the ambulance came, minutes that never ended, it drove us to the Royal London. I spoke to Sharon all the way, calling her name, squeezing her hand. She didn't regain consciousness.

Sharon was rushed through Casualty and I felt help-less, cut off as I waited for news of her. As a gunshot victim myself I was a priority and got checked out quickly. There wasn't much to see, just a long red streak along my ribs like a cigarette burn. Once I'd had it dressed and my cheek was bandaged, I drank some coffee from a machine. I sat, gripping hold of the seat of my moulded plastic chair, not thinking about any-thing. I suppose I was preparing myself. I kept seeing Sharon's brave, determined face, as she tried to get over the railings. Maybe it would have been better. She might have escaped with a pair of broken legs or some-thing. I felt the burn of the bullet and wished that it had taken a firmer hold on me.

A nurse came and told me that Sharon was being operated on. I remember the nurse's face, that's one thing I can see clearly. She was in her thirties, an attrac-tive girl with the beginnings of good, solid lines around her eyes. What I remember about her, though, was that her face was doing its best to keep any sort of hope out of it. She didn't want me to take any false measure of comfort from her, comfort that was probably only going to make me feel worse later on. She said she'd let me know how the operation went, as soon as there was news.

'Is there someone you could call? To come and be with you?'

'Her,' I said. 'Just her.'

At about two a.m. a doctor came out to see me. He was a little older than the nurse, a Sikh with small, tired eyes and a mouth that turned down at the corners. He told me that the operation to remove the bullet from Sharon's side had gone well. The bullet itself had caused damage to Sharon's kidneys and ruptured other internal organs but hadn't hit the foetus she was carrying. That was as far as the good news went. Sharon had lost a lot of blood internally and he had had trouble stemming the flow. Right now she was stable but, he said, I had to prepare myself. It was almost a certainty that Sharon would lose her baby. The odds that Sharon herself would survive were better, but they weren't great. I nodded. I found some spittle with which to speak and I asked if I could see her.

'Yes,' the doctor said. 'I think you should.'

Sharon had been taken from the theatre and wheeled to a room next door to it. I went in and sat on a chair by her bed and obeyed the doctor's injunction about touching Sharon. I did, however, speak to her, though whether she heard me or not I didn't know. She was still unconscious, her face so white and still that it looked saintly, though I didn't want to think of that. I thought instead of her, Sharon, willing to give her life for a baby. I felt again my arms as I caught her and wished that I could catch her again now, stop her from falling to a place I'd never be able to reach down into. I couldn't use my arms, so I used my voice instead. I begged her not to die, not to leave me.

'Come back to me,' I said. 'Please. Please. Both of you. I love you both. Hello, you. Don't die. Just don't die, my loves.'

The same nurse came and smiled, to tell me that I'd better leave. She asked for my phone number so that she could call me but I didn't give it to her because I wasn't going anywhere. She argued with me, asked what medical qualifications I had that could help Sharon, but I didn't listen.

'If she wakes up, fetch me,' I said. 'Please. Even if you think she's not going to make it. Especially if you think that. She's got special eyes and I want to see them again. Our child, she'll have them, if she lives. Please come and get me straight away.'

'There's a room, for relatives, if you need some sleep.'

'I'll be in the waiting room,' I said. 'Where you found me before.'

I drank more coffee and, obeying a slightly sick-making but all-consuming hunger, I ate two bars of chocolate from another machine. An hour or so later I felt the seating I was perched on move. I was sitting with my head in my hands, endlessly going over what had happened. I looked up, to see Mike taking the seat next to me. His face was calm. When I'd climbed into the back of the ambulance I'd looked to the river where the policemen had run, but I hadn't been able to see anything.

'How is she?' Mike asked. I shrugged. 'Do they think she'll be OK?'

'They don't know. They're not being too upbeat.'

'She was amazing, Billy.'

'I know.'

'I'll never forget what I heard her say. About me. What she was willing to do.' I didn't say anything. Mike stood up from the seating. 'Can you spare five minutes?' he asked. 'Just five minutes. It's OK, I've already told the nurse where we're going. She'll fetch you if, if anything happens. Please come with me.'

I stood up from the chair and Mike led me across the hospital foyer. We didn't leave the building, though, instead walking down a corridor. Soon we were faced with a pair of double doors, a keypad mounted on the left-hand side. Mike entered a four-number sequence and pushed the doors open. I was numb. A nurse said hello like she knew Mike and when she walked forward we followed her. After less than a minute we were standing outside a small room with a large glass window to look through. I thought we'd have to wait outside but the nurse led us in. Then she left us together by the incubator.

'There,' Mike said.

I felt his hand on my shoulder as I looked down at the tiny form lying inside the machine, wires and tubes snaking in and out of her.

'You saved her,' Mike said. 'You saved her.'

I don't think I took my eyes off the small creature beneath me while Mike told me about those last seconds on the riverside. I hadn't been able to think about them in the ambulance, or while waiting for Sharon. I knew someone would tell me what happened eventually. As it was, I barely listened. I knew what had happened. I could see.

'He just put her down,' Mike told me. 'I ran round the corner and I was on him before he even knew. But I didn't know what to do. If I jumped on him maybe he'd drop her and that would kill her but if I didn't he could just do what that girl had said, throw her in the river. I couldn't decide.'

'So?'

'He made the decision for me,' Mike said. 'He was screaming into his phone but he wasn't getting a reply. When I came at him I slowed, but he moved. So I just took him out. I went into his legs and we both went over. He got up and tried to run. He still had hold of her, of *her*. He couldn't run fast, though, and I caught up with him, but not before he'd got to the top of some stairs leading down to the water. He had the bundle in his arms and, you know what, I still hadn't seen her. My daughter. I knew it was a she because of what the girl said on the phone, but she was just blankets. She was screaming. It was the most beautiful sound I've ever heard. I felt amazing, but I was terrified too. He was holding her over the water, telling me to get back. There was nothing I could do. I was just thinking: will I be able to save her if I dive in? It was dark, would I even be able to see her? But I didn't have to worry.'

'What happened?'

'I could hear running behind me. Feet, in the square. Then banging. He could hear it too. I think he knew it was over then. His eyes found mine and we looked at each other and I didn't have to say anything. I just kind of relaxed, my whole body sort of slumped in on itself. And then he moved back from the edge. He just put her down on the pavement, so gently that she stopped crying. Then he ran, he ran away. And I picked her up.'

'Did they catch him?'

'I don't know. And I don't care, Billy. You saved her.'

'I think you did that.'

'No. If you'd gone to the police it would have ended differently. They'd have stormed the house and he'd have thrown the baby in the river. She'd have told him to and he would have. She obviously had a real hold on him. When it was broken, when she wasn't speaking to him, he seemed to change. When he put the baby down, he looked scared. Amazed. So, Billy, I want to thank you.'

'It's OK, Mike.'

'And I'll be praying for Sharon. I still can't believe what she did. In the meantime.'

'Yes.'

'Billy, say hello to your goddaughter.'

'I can't.'

'Why? Why not?'

'I don't know her name.'

'It's Sophia,' Mike said. 'It's Sophia Alessandra.'

The night went on and towards dawn another man sat next to me. It was Ken Clay. He too put a hand on my shoulder and after asking me if I was OK he told me what I'd already figured out. He hadn't bothered with a tail the whole way through, figuring that as a former policeman I'd spot it. But he had bugged my office. I asked him when and he told me straight away, as soon as Ally was killed. My flat and my car too. I kicked myself. Whoever had done my office had left the blinds open and I'd noticed, without taking it in. So Clay knew where I was going and had given me ten minutes' start so that I wouldn't see his team. When he saw me breaking into the house he'd decided not to go in mob-handed, that I was the person to deal with whatever it was that was going on inside.

'After all, Billy, don't forget I trained you.'

Clay had seen Mike sprinting across the square, but figured he'd simply spotted the police and was legging it out of there. It was only when he saw Sharon about to go over the balcony that he'd ordered the team in. He also said he hoped Sharon made it and then, as he stood, he smiled.

'The bugging tape from your office.'

'What about it?'

He shrugged. 'It's mysteriously vanished.'

'Oh?'

'Yes.' Clay sighed. 'Don't know how it could have happened. It would perhaps have proved that two civilians were in possession of an illegal handgun. As it is, we're assuming that Carolyn Oliver was the gun's owner, that she brought it to the house. That would be right wouldn't it?'

I nodded.

'And the fall she took, over the balcony. We're pretty sure she jumped in an effort to evade the police. No one helped her over. I'm right there too, aren't I? I thought so. So you've nothing to worry about.'

'No,' I said, 'nothing at all.'

Chapter Forty-Two

It had been a beautiful autumn but it turned into a stark, bitterly cold winter. In spite of the Home Secretary's best efforts, Siberian winds entered the country illegally and made themselves at home in the capital, only to be followed by snowstorms which left the streets looking delightful for days at a time and slush-ridden for weeks. Spring seemed like a myth, a golden faraway land to dream about, one we would never actually arrive in.

I spent all that night in the hospital and most of the next day there too. Sharon needed another operation and didn't regain consciousness. Again, I was told, the operation went well, succeeding in doing whatever was necessary. I'm sure they told me what that was. When it was over I was finally persuaded to leave. Nicky, and Mike, who had been there most of the day, insisted on it. I woke up early and headed straight back in, only to be met with the two words I least wanted to hear from the doctor.

'No change.'

I drank coffee and ate sandwiches and chocolate bars and prayed to all the gods I'd ever heard of and some I made up myself. Hours and then days passed, as did porters and nurses and managers and doctors, who all nodded hello as they went about their business. It wasn't until a really, really miserable morning five days later that they had anything more definite to tell me than no change. I was asked to go to a small room at the side of Sharon's ward. When I saw not just the doctor waiting for me there, but also the nurse I'd spoken to on my first night and who was in charge of caring for Sharon, my heart nearly stopped. The doctor started to speak but caught himself and turned instead to his colleague, and nodded to her.

'She's going to make it,' the nurse said. 'She's going to be all right.'

And I don't know if she'd have got full marks from Florence Nightingale for it but then she took me in her arms and held me while we both cried and shook and cried and shook and just carried on doing that for a long, long time.

'Come on,' the doctor said finally. 'Come and sit with her. I hear you've got a bit of a thing for her eyes.'

'Yes,' I said.

'Well, don't you want to see them?'

'Yes,' I said again.

Spring did come, but before it had arrived I'd been to four funerals. Jennifer Tyler's was the first, where I met her husband and children. He knew what had happened but bore me no grudge, he insisted on saying. He asked me what Jen had been like at school and I told him: pretty and clever, but shy.

'She just needed someone to appreciate her,' I said. 'Someone good enough.' David Tyler smiled and nodded his head.

The second funeral I went to was Carolyn Oliver's. I was the only one there, if you don't count the priest and the unmarked cars and vans full of coppers surrounding the cemetery. They were hoping that Jeff would attend. He still hadn't been picked up and they didn't find him that day either. The service was short, the priest clearly having no idea what to say. He reverted to platitudes from a book and I can't say that I blamed him. I didn't know what to say either. All I could do was try to focus on the terrified little girl walking out to her father's car. Afterwards I went for a greasy-spoon lunch with Andy and he found some words and they were as good as any.

'Kids,' he said. 'You damage them and you damage everything. Because you damage the future. And not just for them. For everybody.'

Andy and I went over the case, and he filled me in on details that had been garnered once it was all over. Inside the pram I'd seen on the river bank were blankets and a small plastic rattle. A Volvo with false plates was discovered nearby, filled with the usual paraphernalia of parenthood, including a car seat, clothing and feeding bottles. In the boot were numerous toys and games, most far too old for a baby. Receipts traced them to various stores both in London and Chester. Though the toys were all unused, still in their packaging, some of them were up to five years old.

Fingerprints assumed to belong to Jeff had been found in the kitchen of the loft Cherie rented from Mrs Minter. Traces of blood had been found there too, in between tiles and kitchen units. More specks were found in the freezer compartment of the fridge. The blood belonged to Denise Denton and her unborn child. Denise Denton must have been killed in the kitchen, strangled first so that there wouldn't have been any arterial flow, making the clean-up much easier, the blood slippage more controllable. It was why Cherie had strangled Ally first, too, and Jenny Tyler. Cherie and Jeff had done a pretty good job of cleaning the loft and if the police hadn't really gone over the place no one would have found any signs of what they'd done there. But if you know what you're looking for you find it much easier than if you don't. No traces of blood-stained clothing relating to the murders of any of the other women was found, however. They must have dumped it all in the river or burnt it.

'She was careful,' Andy said, a hint of admiration in his voice. 'She really was. We won't know until we find the uncle but I suspect that they used fresh overalls for each killing. He was in the Marines so that would have helped but she knew what she was doing too. She could have got away with it, she really could. Anyway, there's something you haven't told me.'

'Which is?'

'How you found her. How did you know she was staying with the Minter woman?'

I thought of Charlie Baby and of his house guest as he called him and I thought of Helen, a needle dangling from her wasted thigh. I wanted to tell Andy, I really did, I wanted him to know where Charlie lived and what he did there. But I couldn't. When I made my pact with that particular devil he'd made sure that there were plenty of penalties for breaking the contract.

'I spotted her near the gym and followed her home.'

'Of course you did, Billy, of course you did. And that

hooker you did a Mac-Fit of, who was found in some toilets the same day, had nothing whatsoever to do with it.'

I told the truth to Sally, over a pint one night not long after. She didn't seem surprised or shocked, simply giving me a nod that said: well, I did warn you. Sally was more interested in talking about the two people who had hoodwinked us both, how Cherie had been sweet and friendly and a terrific masseur. How Jeff had seemed like a run-of-the-mill, bluff kind of guy. Again she apologized for being the route that Carolyn Oliver had used to get into my life, but I shook my head and thanked her for being the route with which I'd got her out of it again.

At Ally's funeral I said a lot more than I had at Carolyn Oliver's, to her family and to Mike's and to people I didn't know and to some I did, from the Lindauer Building especially. Jemma was there, and Cass; they had made up and were back in business together in their studio. I held hands with Mike by the graveside and hugged a lot of people after the committal, and just tried to get through the day like everyone else. It wasn't easy, but we managed it. I offered to stay with Mike that evening but he said he just wanted to be with Ally's family and so I left the place, going back to the hospital, where Sharon still had a week to go. She was upset to have missed the funeral but the doctor had forbidden her to attend, especially with the weather the way it was. I said I'd take her out to the grave when she was fit and she said she'd like that.

It was three months before we managed it. Sharon caught an infection that kept her in the Royal London another six weeks and then, when she did come home, she was told to stay indoors. When we did get there the weather had finally softened and as we stood over Ally's grave there were birds singing and only a slight chill in the air to bother Sharon. I was wearing the scarf Jemma had made me but I didn't really need it. We stayed for half an hour, looking at the snowdrops Mike had planted, as they bickered with their shadows. We spoke about Ally, remembering times we'd spent together and we both agreed that we'd been rarely privileged to know her. Then we stood for a moment in silence, knowing what had to come next. Eventually Sharon squeezed my hand.

'It's time,' she said, with a sad smile. And we walked along a neatly laid-out pathway to the small Victorian chapel, where the vicar was waiting for us.

We'd lost our baby. It had happened when Sharon was asleep, after her second operation. It was, as the doctor had warned me, inevitable really. The news was still crushing, though, to me and to Sharon when she came round. The only way to cope with it, we both believed, was to try again, as soon as Sharon was well enough. I'd never wanted anything so much as to have a baby with this girl I loved. Just looking at little Sophia, her face glowing with all the light in the universe when she saw her father, made me certain of that. Whatever edge I had to lose, I'd lose it. Sophia was a miracle and not really because of the things that had already happened to her in her short life. She was just a miracle because she existed. I wanted a miracle of my own.

After we'd said goodbye to our baby we went straight over to Mike's, both feeling the need to see his and Ally's child that day. Mike smiled when Sharon told him how beautiful the grave looked. Mike was exhausted, so I volunteered to cook for him and Sharon and for Ally's sister Carla, who was staying with Mike. Once I'd got the sauce on I crept into Mike's bedroom and sat next to Sophia's cot, listening to her breath, marvelling at the tiny fingers holding onto the top of her blanket. I closed my eyes and inhaled the warm, musty air.

And was in my office, footsteps scampering down the corridor towards me. Then the door was opening. Over the top of my table I could see a beautiful little girl with curly black hair – Mike behind her – who already knew she could get anything she wanted from her Uncle Billy.

I opened my eyes to see Mike, sitting next to the cot beside me.

'Sharon tells me you're going to try again,' he said.

'Yes,' I nodded. 'The doctor says it's possible.'

'Well, good luck. If it's a girl, I hope they'll be friends. Good friends.'

'I hope that too,' I said, quietly so as not to wake the baby. Not able to speak any louder anyway.

Mike squeezed my arm and smiled. 'But if it's a boy, keep your son away from my daughter. You hear me, mate?'